NO HERO'S
WELCOME

NO HERO'S WELCOME

Book Three of the
Sweet Wine of Youth Trilogy

Jeffrey K. Walker

Ballybur

Also by Jeffrey K. Walker

None of Us the Same
Truly Are the Free

Printed in the United States of America
First Printing, 2019

ISBN 978-1-947108-04-2

Published by Ballybur Publishing

Cover and book design © John H. Matthews
www.johnhmatthews.com

Page divider designed by Kjpargeter / Freepik.com
Text divider designed by Marzolino / VectorStock®

Edited by Kathy A. Walker

Author photograph by Paul Harrison

Epigraph lyric by Brian Warfield
and used with permission of the artist

Cover photographs in public domain

For Kathy

I don't need your hero's welcome.
I don't want your bugle call.
No brass band, no pipes and drums,
No medal, badge, or star.
But give me what you promised me
When first I went to war.
That's freedom for old Ireland
And I'll go to fight no more.

"A Soldier's Return" by Brian Warfield

CHAPTER ONE

Francis

It's sure to be a bollocks—that's near certain.

The lieutenant was bent over a rail. He'd been there since they'd cleared the breakwater, heading north into the dark waters of the Aegean. Daniel smelled the whisky whenever the officer stood upright between bouts of retching. The overmatched young man had started tippling before sundown while they were loading onto a ramshackle minesweeper pressed into duty as their troop transport. He'd said it was to settle his stomach.

"Lieutenant, you've got to gather yourself to get into one of them boats when the time comes. The lads have to see you're with 'em or they'll lose their nerve," Daniel said.

Jaysus, he's shattered. Green as grass. I'll have Francis see him ashore at least.

"Yes… yes, of course, Sergeant-Major Brannigan," the lieutenant said. He drew a sleeve across his cracked lips before doubling over the rail again. His pith helmet sat upside down on the teakwood deck, wobbling like a plaything with each roll of the ship.

The Irish troops in long wooden boats scraped into the shoreline as the Turks commenced their fire.

"You'll die certain sittin' here, lads!" Daniel grabbed a terrified soldier by the arm and pulled the boy down into the surf. "Take your chances on the beach. There's a little cover ten yards up. Out with the lot of ye!"

The men dropped over the side behind Daniel. A few of the sailors who'd rowed them from the ship were slumped over their oars. Blood from their wounds, invisible against their dark blue uniforms, dripped in delicate crimson swirls into the seawater sloshing at their feet.

Soldiers were hit as they hefted heavy field packs over the side. Some jumped off the stern and were killed wading through the surf. The weight of their kit drowned a few that the bullets didn't kill outright.

Daniel shoved his men toward the dry sand. A few clutches shouldered into the low bank across the ribbon of beach and out of the line of fire. Many more lay groaning or motionless in the sand. A few bobbed in the foaming surf like old tea bags.

A bollocks. A royal fuckin' bollocks.

There was no use staying near the boats. The Turks fired at any movement. Daniel could see the second of the four boats twenty yards down the beach.

A gnarled piece of bleached driftwood lay half-buried a few yards ahead. Daniel steeled himself for the short crawl to the only cover within reach. The Turk gunners marked him, but their shaky fire landed a yard or two long.

Then the steady beat of the machine guns was punctuated by deeper sounds. Daniel watched with dawning recognition as a line of small explosions marched along the beach, emanating from a block fort on the rocky rise.

Shite, it's a pom-pom gun. Boers tore us up with those in South Africa.

The big exploding bullets walked from the fourth boat to the third. Some men off the second boat saw the approaching explosions and struggled for the meager cover of the low embankment.

Pom-pom-pom...

One man rose to a crouch and yanked a second man's sleeve. He urged on the others and lost his helmet in the chaos. Daniel recognized his son Francis rallying his mates in a desperate attempt to flee the inexorable pom-pom fire. The Turk gunner—perhaps he was German—overtook Francis as he darted for the embankment.

Pom-pom-pom...

Francis's rifle flew from his grasp as he spun toward the sea. Daniel lost sight of his son in a spray of sand and smoke as the explosions surrounded him.

The pom-pom paused to reload. Daniel ran for his son lying in the sand screaming in anguished pain. He caught a toe as he leapt the twisted driftwood and fell with a hard grunt. He raised his head, spitting away the wet sand. The khaki lump roused a little and Daniel's eyes widened.

"Francis! Stay down! Francis! I'm comin'!" He pushed himself up with his rifle and dug into a full run.

"Da! No! No! Leave me be! No!" The shouting shot pulses of pain down Francis's mangled leg, the knee a gaping slash of purple blood and gore.

Daniel didn't hear his son's warning. The rounds from the left struck across his chest. He stood upright for a few seconds before staggering. The shots from the right shredded his legs and toppled him to the sand.

29th of April, 1915
Aboard HMHS Gascon

My Dear Mrs. Brannigan,

It is with a heavy heart I convey to you my profound condolences upon the loss of your husband, Sergeant-Major Daniel Brannigan.

The regiment was selected to take part in operations in the Dardanelles, your husband's company given the honour of leading one of the first landings on Ottoman territory. Dedicated as he was to the soldiers in his care, your husband was in the first boat to reach the beach. The boats in which the Dublin Fusiliers landed were open wooden craft, providing little protection from the rifle and machine gun fire the defending Turks immediately rained down upon us. Our losses were substantial, but the bravery of our soldiers won a hard-fought foothold on the peninsula, which we continue to exploit.

As soon as your husband's boat approached land, it came under enfilading machine gun fire from Turkish positions uphill from the beach. Sergeant-Major Brannigan leapt without hesitation from his boat, setting an example for the younger men, but was soon hit by machine gun fire. Several of his men dragged him to cover and attended him as best they could. There being no medical assistance available, Sergeant-Major Brannigan died of his wounds. I can only hope it might be some small comfort to know he passed from this life surrounded by his devoted men.

Your son Francis was badly wounded nearby and was unable to reach his father. He is now recovering aboard a hospital ship but will no longer be fit for service. We laid your husband to rest on a hillside above the beach where he fell, alongside others equally brave. I have provided your son with the location of his grave.

I have no words to describe the depth of this loss to the Battalion and to me. Your husband and I knew each other well, having served together as much younger men under most difficult circumstances in the South African War. It was I who pleaded with him to return to the Regiment and I shall bear that burden for the remainder of my days. I shall never forget Daniel Brannigan, as good a man as I have ever known.

> *With my deepest regards and sympathy,*
> *I am your humble servant,*
>
> *Arthur G. Lawless, Lieut.-Col.*
> *Officer Commanding*

CHAPTER TWO

Eda

Eda loved the violet vestments. Such a beautiful color, even on sour-faced Father Shaughnessy. Hard to believe it was Shrovetide of 1916, the first since her Daniel had been taken. Along with others who lingered after Mass for the rosary with sorrows of their own, she and Molly moved to a pew on the right side, closer to Our Lady in her pale blue alcove.

"In the name of the Faaaaather, and of the Son, and of the Hoooooly Ghost…" The familiar nasal drone of the pastor rose and echoed from the high ceiling.

Just a few weeks until Lent. Comes faster each year, Eda pondered.

Molly knelt beside her mother, gazing off at something or nothing at all, her thoughts as far away as befits any girl just turned fourteen.

Where does she wander? She slips away so easy, far and away from us.

"I believe in God, the Faaaaather Almighty…"

Their lips moved, mother's and daughter's, and the requisite sounds sometimes emerged, but neither was paying much attention. It was all so rote, throughout the lingering grief and upheavals the family had endured these last twelve months. Ever since Daniel was laid below the ground in that strange and awful place.

Small comfort from all the Masses and my worryin' the beads. For the repose of his soul. What about the living?

"... and forgive us our trespasses as we forgive thooooose who trespass against us..."

Get on now, with the wallowin' and the feelin' sorry for yourself. You've children to care for, and Francis needin' just as much lookin' after.

Molly sighed and Eda glanced to her youngest daughter. With her eyes closed, the porcelain skin of her lids revealed fine spidery veins beneath. The girl prayed along with the old pastor, her voice such a whisper it seemed little more than a breath escaping her unblemished lips.

"Glooooory be to the Faaaaather, and to the Son..."

The sun broke through the winter clouds, light pouring through the stained glass and illuminating the vaulted interior. Eda's eyes ran over the inside of the church, head tilting up to the familiar ceiling of the Twelve Apostles gazing down with beatific countenances. The light faded again.

I near trembled first time Daniel brought me here. What a fine thing it would've been to bury him from here.

"The first Sorrowful Mystery, the Agony in the Gaaaaarden. Our Faaaaather who art in heaven..." The priest's voice receded to an indistinct hum at the back of her thoughts.

How hard it's been without you. Powerful hard, every day. The will of God, I know, not for me to question. Oh, but I've missed you.

Father Shaughnessy rumbled on with his monotonous rhythm and Molly looked over to Eda with a private smile. The pastor's unshakable cadence had long been a source of suppertime humor in the Brannigan house. The priest never varied his odd elongated pronouncements of the Hail Mary or the Our Father and Daniel had been fond of mimicking him to amuse his children at the table.

"Haaaaaail Mary, full of graaaaace the Loooord is with theeeee," Daniel would intone as Sean or Francis coughed a mouthful of potatoes onto his plate. "Blessed art thooooooou amongst women and blessed is the fruuuuit of thyyyyyy womb, Jeeeeesus." Eda made a show of chastising her husband, thinking it required of a good Irish wife to defend the clergy. None in the family believed her for a moment, hard as she was choking back her own laughter.

The pastor's drone continued, "The second Sorrowful Mystery, the Scoooooourging at the Pillar. Our Faaaather…"

Oh, my poor Deirdre. Punishin' yourself in France over how you left things with your da. He was always too fond of you, but what father isn't with his daughter? Lord knows he couldn't deny you a thing.

With two decades complete, the joints of some of the old ones in the front pews were aching. The creaks of the hard wooden kneelers became more frequent as the devout shifted to find less painful spots on their knees. One old dear in front of them couldn't settle, tilting to the left and then the right. She finally went still after breaking wind loud enough for half the church to hear. Eda pressed her elbow against Molly's as she saw the girl quaking with laughter, hands clapped over her mouth, rosary dangling between her fingers.

"The third Sorrowful Mystery, the Crooooowning with Thorns. Our Faaaaather…"

Sean's taken his father's death so hard. Wanderin' the streets 'til all hours. He couldn't bear the memories in the old house and now can't abide the strangeness of our new place above the pub. He fears neither man nor beast, that one, but it pains me to see how hard he's become. He'll make his way, if he'd just stop mitchin' his lessons at the Christian Brothers'…

Even nearing the third year of the war, life for most Dubliners moved to the rhythms of the Catholic Church. With plenty of brass in everyone's pockets from the pots of money lavished on the war effort, Shrovetide would have some pleasure in it, right up to Ash Wednesday and Lent. Then the forty days of fasting and abstinence and penance.

"Haaaaaail Mary, full of graaaaace the Loooord is with theeeee…"

It was good to have a little self-denial, to think upon the sad and painful things of the past year, but Eda wondered whether the Lenten season might diminish the revenue of her newly acquired public house. It seemed to her unlikely the pubs of Dublin would suffer a lack of custom whatever the season, but she'd know soon enough.

Daniel was taken from me just after last Easter. Maybe we'll find a little joy this Eastertide. This year'll be better, more time since he passed… Holy Mother of God, don't let me be forgettin' my Daniel!

Eda let out a quiet gasp as tears welled. Molly leaned over and gazed into her mother's face, a gentle quizzical look framed by her white-lace chapel veil. Eda shook her head a little and gave Molly a ragged smile. The girl settled back again.

"The fourth Sorrowful Mystery, the Caaaaarrying of the Cross. Our Faaaaather…"

'Tis Danny I fear will forget his father and that's a sorrow to me. Least he'll bear his da's name now. I don't know if it'll be a blessin' or a curse. It rankled Deirdre somethin' fierce, but the boy doesn't mind. Danny's never troubled over anything.

The fidgeting of the congregants was universal now, four decades into the rosary, but the pastor kept his languorous pace, hypnotic as a metronome. Eda glanced to Molly and saw she had her faraway look again, off to wherever she went in her thoughts.

With Deirdre gone, it's up to me alone to watch over Molly. An older sister's better to talk of the things mothers can't. There's so little time in the day for anything but business. Maybe I should keep her in the pub with me. But all those men and their drink, with her coming up such a beauty. Blessed Virgin protect her.

"The final Sorrowful Mystery, the Crucifixion and Death of our Lord. Our Faaaaather…"

Sean was adept at disappearing on Sunday mornings, so his attendance at Mass had become patchy enough that Father Shaughnessy commented on it. The boy had given up altar serving as soon as word of his father's death came and Eda hadn't the strength to notice, let alone protest. He had to attend chapel at the Christian Brothers' school, so Eda forgave his Sunday truancy by assuring herself his soul was tended during the week. Francis hadn't been to Mass since he came home, hardly the first man to lose his religion to the horrors of this war.

Francis was too young to suffer such a devastatin' thing. Not just the leg. Seein' his own da die.

"Hail, Hooooly Queen, Mother of mercy, our life, our sweeeeetness, and our hope."

Eda was startled that her thoughts had wandered so long, the rosary was nearly over. Molly seemed just as surprised, back from her own meanderings.

"To theeeee do we send up our sighs, mouuuuurning and weeeeeping in this valley of tears…"

Every pub in Dublin stewed in a similar smell by early April. After months of damp and chill, the persistence of acrid smoke, stale beer, and soggy wool brought tears to the eyes of the uninitiated. It crept up the stairs that rose from behind the long mahogany bar, blackened by decades of hands and elbows, slopped pints of porter, and exposure to the dense smokiness. The aroma permeated the flat above, although Eda Brannigan and her children had become inured to it after a few weeks living above The Gallant Fusilier.

The heavy entry door swung open, admitting a blast of blessed freshness along with a pair of thirsty men. Eda looked up from polishing glasses.

"Well, Saints preserve us, 'tis John James O'Fallon himself!" She dropped her towel and beamed across the bar top. "We've not seen you about The Gallant for many a day, Lieutenant. How've you been keepin'?"

She watched Johnny O'Fallon leaning on a blackthorn stick that clacked on the floor boards with each stiff-legged step. He clutched the edge of the bar and hooked the curve of his cane in his right elbow, the arm with three missing fingers. With eyebrows tightly knit and lips pressed white, he willed away the pain radiating from his bullet-mangled knee. Eda was certain he wasn't more than twenty-two, although he'd the wizened eyes of an older man. He'd seen too much in his precious few years, of that she was certain.

"I've been making proper use of my time, Mrs. Brannigan," he said, warming under Eda's wide smile. "I've been studying the Gaelic poets at Trinity Library. Seeing how I left my studies to serve King and Empire, I thought it time to take them up again, now that His Majesty has no further use for me."

"Isn't that a fine thing, so?" Eda patted his forearm and gave him a maternal nod of approval.

The man who'd blown in with Johnny O'Fallon was twenty years older, although he didn't have the look of one who'd spent himself in hard labor. He wore round, steel-rimmed spectacles that gave him an owlish air. His suit was cut well enough, but like most clothing hanging on Dubliners in 1916, it was starting to show shiny at the elbows and frayed at the cuffs after two years of austerity.

"And who would your friend be, Lieutenant?"

Johnny motioned his companion to the bar with his good left hand. Eda saw the trembling that might disappear after three or four whiskies, or might not. Francis told her it was from the noise of the shelling and many men suffered the same.

"May I present Mr. Peter Conway. Or more properly, his being a longtime member of the Gaelic League, *Peadar Ó Connmhacháin*, if you please."

The older man crept forward and reached for Eda's proffered hand, not sure how to proceed. Finally, he gave a light squeeze and made a tiny bow before releasing the hand back to its owner. In that brief touch, she felt the softness of his fine-boned long fingers, so unlike the big rough cooper's hands of her Daniel. She noted the deep hazel eyes behind the round glasses, almost golden in the light reflecting off the mirrored wall behind her. He broke away from her inquisitive gaze with a nervous jerk.

"Dia dhuit, a Pheadar," said Eda.

The newcomer startled and raised his head again.

"Agus fáilte roimh an Gallant," Eda continued, welcoming him to her establishment.

Stammering while he found his Irish tongue, Peter replied, *"Dia's Muire dhuit ..."* he hesitated at using her first name, as she had his, *"...a Bhean Branagain."* He wasn't certain he'd heard her first name correctly and was equally unsure of its Irish cognate.

"Eithne," she interjected, her smile unwavering while providing her true first name, given by her parents and godparents standing round the tiny baptismal font in the old fieldstone parish church back in Donegal, the name by which no one knew her in Dublin. No one at all, now that her Daniel had been taken. She had taught it to him.

Her English name would be Edna, but there was already a daughter of that name within the wealthy family that employed her when she'd come to Dublin, so it would never have done to have a downstairs maid share it. The day she arrived at Merrion Square, the housekeeper thought about it only long enough to slice away the one letter.

"Dia's Muire dhuit, a n-Eithne," Peter said.

There were the golden eyes on hers again. Eda's placid smile twitched a little at the corners.

"Well then, now that we've dispensed with the social niceties, I believe we'll have two large whiskies." There was an edge of need in Johnny O'Fallon's forced joviality, a need Eda had seen in her son and too many others. Small comfort, she supposed, for all that had been taken from them.

"If you please... Eda... I'll have a small whisky," said Peter, "... if it's all the same to you, John." He glanced over to Eda again, letting her know he understood more about Johnny than she might suppose. "I've some essays still to mark tonight."

Johnny shifted his weight to his bad leg, winced once, then shifted back to the good one. "Mr. Peter Conway was my tutor at Trinity before the war, Eda, an expert in Gaelic literature who had very little effect on me at the time."

"You were no worse than your colleagues, John."

Johnny barked a laugh. "And surely no better either. Since there are precious few young scholars left to tutor these days, what with the demands of the Army, he likewise operates a bookshop across the Liffey, back behind the Four Courts."

Eda gave a showy look of admiration and said, "A proper businessman-scholar we've before us?" Peter looked embarrassed at the attention and replied with a nervous shrug.

Having already downed his double whisky and slid the glass back for a refill, Johnny warmed to his subject. "Mr. Conway feeds his ascetic belly hawking law books to the gentlemen of the Bar and provides for his soul selling Gaelic literature to the dozen or so people in Dublin who actually read the stuff."

Eda placed the refilled glass before Johnny and noted Peter had only sipped a little, swirling his whisky about in the glass to make an appearance of conviviality.

"There might be a few more than a dozen, I should think," Peter said.

"No matter," said Eda. "I'm pleased to see the tongue I came up speakin' tended so careful by the Gaelic League. So don't you let Johnny take his sport at your expense, Peter." She gave Johnny O'Fallon a mock withering glare. "A fine thing you're doing, for the young ones in particular."

"You are from the *Gaeltacht*, Mrs. Brannigan?"

"I'm a true Donegal *cailín*. I came to Dublin a girl of sixteen and entered service in one of the grand houses. 'Twas not two years later I met my Daniel and we were wed." Eda's face clouded, but she brushed it away with a sweep of a hand across her forehead, pushing back some stray hairs.

The lightness dropped from Johnny's voice when he leaned into Peter and said, "Eda's husband was a sergeant-major with the Dubs. He was lost at Gallipoli."

Eda saw the golden eyes of Peter Conway fill a little as he mumbled, "I am very sorry to hear that."

"A better man never drew breath than Daniel Brannigan, Mr. Conway. And he gave me five fine children and enough to start fresh with my own public house." She reached out and patted the back of each of the men's hands, then put her towel to her spotty glassware again.

It's a precarious thing, the renaming of a pub. Of all the changes an Irishman might tolerate, the one thing he wants constant as the pole star is his local. Eda Brannigan didn't understand this when she bought an established pub on the Coombe, Shanahan's being a revered—if somewhat shopworn—institution in the Liberties. Her motives had been innocent enough when she hired a sign maker to paint over the long placard, stained by years of coal smoke and mossy about the edges, that ran the width of the building. In an effort to interest her desultory eldest son, Eda suggested they find a new name that might honor her dead husband, assuming they'd call the place some variation of *Daniel Brannigan's*. Francis surprised her when he stated with settled assurance that Da would've wanted them to honor all his men, not just him.

Thus was The Gallant Fusilier born. One of the Royal Dublin Fusiliers' lieutenants who'd lost an arm at Gallipoli suggested to Francis they paint the sign in the colors of the new regimental neckties all the officers were ordering for civilian wear. This being a fine idea, the freshly painted sign featured royal blue letters traced in emerald green on a ruby background. The sign maker insisted on outlining each letter with a thin line of gold and Eda thought that made the whole thing quite smart. She wasn't as pleased that he'd placed her name in smaller letters above the door. The sign painter told her it was required by the Dublin Corporation, so there was nothing more to be said on the matter.

The interior of the pub had suffered from the aging Paddy Shanahan's benevolent neglect. Eda decided to spend some of the money that remained after paying the purchase funds at the solicitor's office, freshening the paint and purchasing new chairs and small round tables to place along the faded upholstered bench that ran the length of the wall opposite the bar. She'd enlisted her available children and several women from the old neighborhood in New Row—just up the street and round the corner—to clean and polish every inch of the place before reopening. The age-darkened bar regained some luster and its brass fittings shined like new pennies. The light pouring through the spotless front windows broadened the once-dingy space to a surprising degree. She knew there was no way to banish fifty years of smells.

What Eda never foresaw was the effrontery all this cleaning and renaming would provoke in the long-time regulars of the former Shanahan's Public House. The first few nights brought curious crowds, after which the place was empty as a tomb. Word soon made it back to Eda, as such things always seemed to do in Dublin, regarding the offense she'd given to the old clientele. What's done is done, however, and she remained steadfast in her determination both to honor the memory of her husband and make a fresh start for her family.

After a week of worrying both her nether lip and her rosary beads over the dearth of drinkers, a new crop of regulars began emerging like mushrooms. Drowning his sorrows over a lost father and a missing leg had given Francis one advantage—he'd become acquainted with other men invalided home, the flotsam of His Majesty's Forces washed back to Ireland after Mons and Ypres, Neuve Chapelle and Sedd el Bahr, and a dozen more obscure battles. Always more after a new unknown place appeared in the papers. Each time, a few more young men back on the streets with an empty trouser leg, a ravaged face. One day her own son had been among them. So many with that peculiar distant look that never left them, at least not without a drink or two. Like poor Johnny O'Fallon leaning on the bar before her.

The crippled ex-officer downed his second large whisky and slapped the glass on the bar. Peter took another polite sip and slid his glass behind Johnny's in an attempt to hide the remaining liquor.

"Well, we're off. Still much to be done before the University shutters itself for Easter Week," Johnny said, settling his weight on his cane.

Peter looked up again to Eda and after a few puzzled blinks, stammered, "It was...it was a great pleasure... to make your acquaintance, Mrs..." She raised a cautioning eyebrow above her smile which he noticed before continuing, "... to make your acquaintance... Eda."

"And I yours, Peter," she patted his forearm again. He tensed with her touch, then gave her another jerky nod.

'Tis a wonder no woman has caught this one, him with the golden eyes, Eda pondered, then shushed her silly thoughts.

"And a very Happy Easter to you, Johnny. Give my best wishes to your dear mother." Johnny replaced his hat and touched the brim with a wink in reply.

As Peter Conway settled his own hat, Eda said, "*Beannachtaí na Cásca ort, an tOllamh Ó Connmhacháin.*"

Johnny looked back over his shoulder with a laugh and said, "Fine to wish him a Happy Easter, but don't be calling him professor. He's a humble tutor and we'll not want you giving him a swelled head, Eda."

Peter nodded, a little sheepish at Johnny's jovial protestation.

"Well, professor or mister, sinner or saint, you're always welcome at The Gallant, Peter Conway, so don't be a stranger," Eda replied, a little more voluble than was her habit with new customers.

CHAPTER THREE

Sean

She'd hesitated at remaking herself into a pub keeper, being the respected widow of a respectable foreman in a reputable brewery. But Daniel was never coming home. She could creep through the endless years ahead eking out a pinched life on the tiny pension of a soldier's widow, consoled by weekday Masses, or she could pull herself up by her bootlaces and make a new life for herself and her children. And no one ever lost money betting on the thirst of Irishmen, particularly Dubliners.

So Eda Brannigan had swallowed her trepidations when she heard talk among the neighbor women that old Patrick Shanahan was looking to sell up, the lumbago and the sciatica getting the better of him after more than three decades behind the bar. With his dear wife passed these ten years gone and his children scattered to the mill towns and shipyards of Yorkshire and Clydeside, he wouldn't need much to live out his remaining days in modest comfort. The Shanahans, husband and wife, had labored and scrimped in their early years, building the pub from little more than a bothy into a fixture on the Coombe, the main commercial street winding through what had over the years become the solid working class neighborhood of the once-grand Liberties.

He'd made Eda a fair offer she could afford with the death gratuity from the Crown and the money from the benevolent society into which Daniel had contributed from every pay packet since the day they'd married. When she factored in the rent from letting their house in New Row if they moved above the pub, the whole transaction made such good sense that it overcame her qualms. Besides, since the war began, several Dublin pubs were being kept by wives and sisters of owners who'd listened too much to the bellicose prattling of their patrons and gone off to the fighting, too.

Molly sat next to her mother at the big dining table, her nose in a book where it was most often to be found. Eda had just made a fresh pot of tea, but Molly's mug sat undisturbed. Curling her hands round the hot ceramic to ease the morning stiffness in her fingers, Eda glanced at the sideboard, a near-empty bottle of whisky standing among the photographs.

We'll not see Francis before noon. Don't see why he leaves a swallow or two in the bottle. Fooling no one but himself, she thought.

Young Danny was still abed, exhausted from their big Easter dinner and running with his mates back in the old neighborhood. It was a comfort to her that he was old enough to wander the few blocks himself. She didn't want him always hanging about the pub at the age of six, and she knew the mothers of New Row would look after him well enough.

Lord knows when Sean will rouse himself—no telling what time he slunk home last night. And on Easter Sunday.

Molly sighed, then laid a frayed hair ribbon inside her book before closing it to attend to her tea. She took a tentative sip, then seeing it had cooled, a more generous swallow. She set the mug back down without a sound and glanced over to her mother.

"I looked in on the boys, Mam. I don't think Sean came home at all last night. His bed's empty and looks like it's not been slept in. You know how slapdash he's wont to make it."

Eda's eyebrows knit as she took another long drink. It wasn't the first time Sean had stayed out all night since his father was taken, but it seemed strange he'd do so on Easter Sunday. There couldn't be a quieter evening during the year.

Sean reckoned dragging himself to Mass and attending Easter dinner fulfilled his holy day obligations for the year of our Lord 1916, and he'd managed to extract himself before Mam brought out the pudding. Easter Sunday evening was dead dull, so he and Martin Gavin, the only one of his friends also able to escape family obligations, knocked about the streets for a little diversion. They ranged over to Stephen's Green to take the piss out of young couples in furtive embraces on benches in shadier parts of the park, but they'd tired of that and ambled up Kildare Street to Trinity College. There they'd smoked and lounged against the closed iron gates at Parliament Square. Since there were no students or university porters about on Easter Sunday, they took turns tossing pebbles at the statue of that old Tory toff Burke, seeing who could ding one off the general area of his willy.

When they'd run out of cigarettes and pebbles, the boys wandered across the O'Connell Bridge to see if there might be anything interesting north of the river, along the quays or up Sackville Street. From the middle of the bridge, Sean spotted a crowd downriver, milling about in front of the old Northumberland Hotel.

Martin slapped him on the shoulder and motioned to the commotion. "What do you suppose all that's about?"

Sean spit over the bridge rail and said, "Only one way to find out."

Martin fell in beside him as they jogged across the bridge and down Eden Quay.

"That's where Larkin's union has its meetings," Martin panted. "The transport workers' place." The Transport and General Workers' lockout back before the war, led by employers terrified of anything with even a whiff of unionism, was still fresh in the minds of workers and families who nearly starved over those long five months.

They could see that most of the men gathered in the street were in the bottle-green tunics and turned-up slouch hats of the Irish Citizen Army, one of the Republican militias that paraded on weekends to tweak the noses inside Dublin Castle. Some leaned against the facade, beneath the long legend painted the width of the building with *Head Office Irish Transport and General Workers' Union.* Below that sagged a fading canvas banner that had hung since the first weeks of the war: *We Serve Neither King Nor Kaiser, But Ireland.* A variety of rifles were stacked in clusters along the pavement, muzzles protruding in uneven arrays.

It was easy enough for a couple of eager young lads to melt into the crowd. Some of the men were in immaculate complete uniforms, smart enough to stand parade with any army. Others had only a hat and bandolier, some not even that. There was nothing about Sean and Martin that would make them stand out, including their age since many of the volunteers weren't more than a few years older. Milling through the crowd, Sean picked up snatches of conversation.

"Thought the maneuvers were canceled before the message arrived?"

"Lord, I've a full head from too much of the Easter drink taken…"

"Connolly says we're to spend the night here for a road march tomorrow mornin'."

Martin grew anxious about the number of guns in plain sight and badgered Sean. "Let's head back to my house and get clear of this lot. We don't want to get caught out in any Republican nonsense."

Without turning, Sean said, "You go along. I've a mind to stay. I'll find some place to spend the night or I'll sleep rough."

Martin sighed and tugged down his cap. "You're daft, Sean Brannigan. This looks like nothin' but trouble to me." With that, he headed back down the quay to find the nearest bridge to more familiar streets south of the Liffey.

A pair of volunteers in oversized green uniforms, each with a bandolier slung across his chest and an arm band with the Red Hand of Ulster, stood a little apart and whispered with nervous cigarettes twitching in their lips. They didn't appear to be more than sixteen, not more than a year or so older than Sean.

"Don't suppose I could beg a fag?" Sean said, looking for a way into their conversation.

One of the young volunteers looked Sean up and down, then extracted a packet of Woodbines and shook one out. Sean nodded his thanks and extracted the cigarette, lighting it from the glowing end of the fag held out by the volunteer. He took a long drag and exhaled through his nose, providing his bona fides as a genuine smoker.

"Quite a to-do, 'specially for Easter Sunday," Sean said.

Figuring he was too young to be an informant or a spy from the Castle, the taller sentry assumed a patronizing tone and replied, "If you're part of the Irish Citizen Army, you have to be prepared to make sacrifices, even on Easter."

The shorter one added, "Even if it means sleepin' in the HQ tonight and missin' the Easter Monday holiday, too."

"Some doings planned tomorrow?"

The taller looked round to ensure no one else was within earshot and said, "Rumour has it we're in for more than a road march." He closed the space between them a little farther. "My da's a pressman at *The Evening Mail* and helps print *The Irish Worker* upstairs here in his off time. He's been in there for hours. They've never printed the paper on a Sunday before."

The shorter stubbed his cigarette under the toe of his boot, then appraised Sean anew. "Don't recall seein' you at any musters."

"I'm from over in the Liberties—my mam keeps a pub on the Coombe." A woman running a public house was still rare enough to raise eyebrows, so Sean hurried to add, "My da was lost at Gallipoli, so she's had to make her own way."

"The bloody war," said the shorter, patting Sean's shoulder and shaking his head in sympathy.

"The fuckin' war," said the taller, cocking his head back over his shoulder at the banner above them. "Another chance for Irishmen to die for an English crown, the more fools they be who take the King's shilling."

Realizing what they'd just said to the son of a man who'd given his life, they looked uneasily at their shoes. Sean rescued them, saying, "I'll not soon forgive the English for sendin' my father off to die. Nor for taking my brother's leg, not that he sees naught but glory in it, least when he's into the drink."

Seeing Sean held kindred views on both the war and the English, the volunteers rejoined with gusto.

"There's never been an Englishman did a good turn for an Irishman," said the taller.

"We'll have no peace in this land 'til we empty Dublin Castle of all the English and the gombeen men and drive them into the sea," said the shorter, spitting at the pavement as indignant punctuation.

Each was mouthing sentiments they'd learned from older men, no less sincere with the ardor of youth. Sean thought to press his newfound friends, so continued, "I've had a mind for some time to join the Volunteers or the Citizen Army, but figured my age wouldn't allow it."

"Hang about tonight and we'll see if we can get you on as a messenger," offered the taller. "You know the streets?"

That was something Sean could answer with sincerity. "I was born in the Liberties and I've wandered every street and alley south of the Liffey since I was old enough for my parents not to notice." Stretching the truth, he added, "I know the north side as well. If you're in need of runners, I'm your man."

Quite satisfied with their men's discussion and having come to a man's conclusion, they headed into the converted hotel in search of someone with enough authority to enlist Sean in the Irish Citizen Army.

A gruff clerk with a suspicious face was convinced by the two young volunteers that Sean could be of service as a message runner, so the newest recruit was sent to the mess, a room in the back taken over by the ladies of the *Cumann na mBan* and stocked with endless gallons of strong tea and hampers of buttered sandwiches made with Easter hams. Sean gobbled two sandwiches and washed them down, then picked a heavy wool blanket from a pile near the door. He threaded his way through the crowded rooms to the back of the building in search of a place to make up a pallet for himself. As he wandered down a dark hallway, lined either side by what had been hotel guest rooms before the Transport Workers' Union took over the hotel four years ago, he picked up the thick smell of printer's ink and the thrumming of unseen machinery.

Snick-thump, snick-thump.

Drawn by curiosity, Sean crept down the narrowing passage that led out of the old hotel, the walls shedding their plaster and turning to unfinished bricks. Squinting down the gloomy corridor, he could just make out the turned-up hat of a Citizen Army soldier.

As Sean approached, the sentry snapped his rifle up and barked, "Stand fast and identify yourself."

"New messenger, just joined up," Sean said, noting the jumpiness of the guard. "Lookin' for a place to sleep, out of the way."

The volunteer ordered his rifle and relaxed. "They'll be needin' you soon enough, but they told me not to let anyone in 'til the printin' is done."

"Maybe I could take the corner here, have a nap while we're waitin', yeah?" Sean was beyond curious as to what type of printing required an armed guard. "Or at least we might keep each other company."

The sentry didn't object, so Sean slid down the rough wall and draped the musty blanket over his shoulders. One of the *Cumann na mBan* ladies had been passing out small five-packs of cigarettes and Sean managed to circle back in the commotion and pick up a second. He held one out to the sentry, who hesitated, not sure if this was allowed. After a covert glance down the dark corridor, he nodded and took the packet.

Leaning on his aged Mauser, a souvenir from the Boer War inherited from an uncle who'd had his fill of King and Empire at the siege of Mafeking, the sentry smoked in silence. A swaddled Sean sat against the damp wall, waiting for an opportune moment to restart the conversation. The corridor filled with their blue smoke while the steady sound of the press paused from time to time, indistinct voices filtering through the heavy metal door.

"So why do you think they're keepin' you..." The guard's eyes narrowed with suspicion. "I mean... *ourselves* here all night? Suppose it must be something big tomorrow?" Sean studied his hands while the guard weighed whether this new boy was trustworthy or not. He reached some resolution, cigarette dangling from his lips, and shifted his rifle to the other side before recommencing his lean.

"Suspect it's to do with what's going on in there." The mechanical rhythm started up again. Between the cigarette and the overpowering smell of ink, Sean's head had gone groggy. The sentry seemed in no hurry to continue the conversation and Sean's chin began to sink to his chest, cigarette still burning between his fingers.

The sound of a thrown bolt followed by the screech of uncooperative hinges startled the guard back to his parade-ground posture. Sean shook away the cigarette that was nearly burning his knuckles. He squinted into the sudden flood of light spilling through the doorway. A man with a full mustache, sleeves rolled above his elbows, stepped through the doorway with a thick sheaf of papers draped like a waiter's towel over his arm. As he turned to close the door, half the papers slipped and scattered across the floor.

"Shite! For the love o' God! Shite!"

On hands and knees, Sean hurried to help the disconcerted man gather his spilled papers. The sheets were flimsy like newsprint and the size of the playbills from the Royal or the Gaiety he'd seen plastered all over town for as long as he could remember. He couldn't very well stop to read one, but he glimpsed the largest letters near the top...

IRISH REPUBLIC.

After a few hours of fitful sleep, disrupted by the comings and goings from the pressroom, Sean was roused by the toe of a woman in a tidy green *Cumann na mBan* uniform. As he rubbed the sleep from his eyes, she said, "You're a messenger? With me, boy."

Sean let the musty blanket fall to the floor as he rose to follow her through the pressroom. Three men sat slumped on a bench against one wall, copious amounts of ink and fatigue visible on each. Sean nodded, then skirted round a scratched and dinged printing press, close on the woman's heels. She pulled another heavy fire door and they emerged into the back of a shop stacked with children's clothing, baby blankets, piles of nappies, and a few sticks of furniture. The strong wardrobe smell told of the well-used nature of the goods.

A dozen or more people clustered near the service counter, a few teenage boys like him and the rest women of various ages. Two uniformed women were busy behind the counter rolling or folding sheafs of the posters he'd helped gather off the floor a few hours before, wrapping them in brown paper and tying them with string. Stacked at the end of the counter, they made a tidy pile of parcels.

Once the flurry of wrapping and tying ended, one of the women strode from round the counter and stood arms akimbo and feet apart. In a steady voice, she gathered the curious mix of boys and women milling about the used clothing store.

"All right then, here are your instructions for this morning." She scanned the group as they clustered round her. Her sharp, almost crystalline, blue eyes pierced each of them in turn. Sean smoothed down his disheveled clothing.

She wore the same bottle-green uniform as the other women, hers finer and better tailored, cinched with the wide belt and thin shoulder strap of a Sam Browne. Her pressed woolen skirt fell to mid-calf, over the tops of shiny-black buttoned boots, but her tunic was almost identical to the men's of the Citizen Army. The big lower pockets and the sharp-flapped upper ones were ironed as stiff and flat as a sandwich board, not intended to hold much of anything. She wore a well-knotted necktie and was topped by a broad-brimmed hat with a wide ribbon of dark green. She was every inch the soldier, more so than many of the men in Citizen Army kit he could see through the store windows, smoking and rubbing the night's rough sleep from their faces.

"Now, I won't describe to you what's in these parcels—you've no need to know more than what you'll be carrying is of the gravest importance to our future," she said, silencing the murmuring with a gloved hand. "And that of our children and our grandchildren, too."

The two women behind the counter picked up parcels and handed one to each of the couriers.

"I'll be at the door to give you your destinations. You're to deliver a parcel to your assigned places with the greatest care and diligence, no matter what you see or hear on the streets. Do you understand the importance of what I've said?"

There was a mumbling of affirmation, but this would not do and the woman said, "I'll have each of your answers, in turn. Clear and loud." She looked from face to face, searching for hesitation and any traces of dissembling, informers and traitors having long bedeviled past struggles.

"Yes, ma'am."

"I'll do my duty, as will my man next door."

This continued round the tight circle, ending with Sean. The woman looked him over and said, "How old are you, boy?"

Knotting his cloth cap in sweaty palms, Sean mumbled to his scuffed brown brogues, "Fourteen, ma'am. Fifteen in two weeks."

She raised his head with her hand, the black leather of her gloves warm and smooth under his chin, and gave a reassuring smile. "Then you'll have a good long life ahead to tell tales of this day." Sean nodded and returned a tentative grin. The brown paper crinkled as he gripped the parcel tight under his arm.

Turning back to the group, she said, "Now, be quick about your deliveries, but not so fast as to draw attention. You're out for a stroll on this fine Easter Monday, nothing more." She paused for the little wave of nervous laughter. "You'll say you've a delivery from Liberty Hall and hand over the parcel to whoever asks to take it. When you've finished, right back here for another parcel—we have near forty." She gave another sharp nod for emphasis.

"Miss Molloy?" one of the assistants said, handing over a sheet of foolscap with neat writing in two columns while the older woman made for the front of the shop.

As the couriers filed to the door, she read out destinations from the list.

"Main gate of the South Dublin Union in James Street. You'll be met there, but don't loiter if no one appears. Right back here." The young wife with a husband in the Citizen Army nodded, tight lipped, then pulled her shawl over her head and turned right outside the door.

"Kingsbridge Station, the tobacconist just to the right, inside the main entrance." A boy a little older than Sean and near a head taller trotted outside.

"Round the tradesmen's entrance at the Shelbourne Hotel." An older woman, looking very much like one of the street vendor shawlies who gathered in the back of The Gallant of an evening, placed the parcel in a market basket over her arm and left without a care in the world.

"The Brazen Head on Usher's Quay, just over the Whitworth Bridge. You'll need to knock this early." A younger woman with ruddy apple cheeks and fly-away ginger hair, eyes wide as saucers, licked her nervous lips and nodded in acceptance of her assignment. Miss Molloy patted her arm to steady the girl and sent her on her way.

"The ironmonger's shop on Thomas Lane, just round the corner from the Pro. Like you're going to serve at Mass." Another young teenager, better dressed than Sean by half, grinned and skipped off up the quay toward Marlborough Street and the Catholic cathedral.

"Bookseller at No. 3 in Chancery Place." Sean didn't recognize the street name and looked puzzled.

"Up behind the Four Courts?" Miss Molloy said. Sean nodded recognition.

Relieved at not being sacked for his shaky knowledge of the geography north of the river, Sean shot out the door before the formidable Miss Molloy could change her mind, pulling up his collar against the wind gusting from across the river.

The first delivery was uneventful, the parcel accepted by a man with owlish glasses and a scholar's dusty demeanor who'd taken the time to introduce himself as Mr. Conway. After winding his way back to the children's clothing store next to Liberty Hall, Sean picked up a second parcel and delivered it to a sweet shop at the foot of the O'Connell Bridge, only three or four minutes away. Then he dropped a third across the river at the second-floor flat above a haberdasher's shop on the Temple Bar. He'd still not had the chance to read what he was carrying, swept up in the excitement of something important, not knowing just what.

When he returned a fourth time, Miss Molloy rewarded his keenness with a day-old sandwich, some cold tea, and another parcel with a paper bag containing a thick brush and a pickle jar filled with wheat paste. She glanced at the gold watch pinned to her breast pocket and told him to hurry off to the General Post Office across from Nelson's Pillar and wait there for instructions.

He wandered Sackville Street near the Post Office—although everyone Sean knew called it the GPO—since Clerys' clock had read eleven but hadn't found anyone likely to give him instructions. He circled the base of the Pillar watching Easter Monday shoppers as an excuse for his lingering. When showery rain started to fall, he loitered under the Post Office portico, leaning against one of the big Ionic columns until a Metropolitan Police sergeant gave him a few wary glances. Once the rain let up, Sean walked back over to Clerys and made himself inconspicuous among the bustling holiday shoppers and the sprinkling of people waiting on agreed rendezvous beneath the big bronze clock.

By the time the Pro-Cathedral's bells rang out the Angelus at noon, Sean had all but resolved to return to the used-clothing store. Then he noticed that people walking the pavement or stepping from the trams that converged at the Pillar were looking with quizzical interest down the broad street toward the river, some craning for a better view. Clutching his bag and bundle, Sean threaded through the gathering crowd for an unobstructed look.

A hundred or more of the men whom he'd seen lounging about Liberty Hall were marching up Sackville Street in disciplined columns. As they approached, Sean saw a big brush of a mustache under a slouch hat, marking a Scotsman pointed out to him the night before—James Connolly, a leader of the Citizen Army and a notorious trade unionist. Sean had heard the name discussed in disapproving terms by some of the regulars in his mother's pub.

The squadron of green-clad men, most with rifles sprouting bayonets, commenced wheeling once they'd passed Clerys, forming up in the street before the GPO's main entrance. The people surrounding Sean murmured, wondering why the Irish Volunteers or the Citizen Army would make one of their road marches up the busiest street in Dublin on Easter Monday. A few began laughing outright.

After standing in place for what seemed a long time, Sean heard Connolly's rolling Lothian r's as he yelled, "Charge!" Some children squealed with delight at the exciting scene they were sure had been arranged for their holiday entertainment. Their parents now weren't sure how entertaining this scene was meant to be.

A few people flushed out the Post Office doors. Sean heard a ragged volley of muffled shots from within and the flock of exiting people thickened, cutting off in random directions. He threaded through the crowd toward the GPO, looking to report to someone in an officer's uniform.

Smaller armed groups barged into buildings adjoining the GPO, soon followed by shattered glass showering onto the pavement. Heads and rifles appeared at upstairs windows behind furniture shoved forward to barricade the openings. Sean was starting across the street when a pudgy man in an Irish Volunteers' uniform, flanked by a shorter man in an ordinary suit and Connolly in his Citizen

Army kit, stepped into the street. He stopped in the middle of the road with his back to Lord Nelson on his high pedestal and turned to face the black statue of Daniel O'Connell, the Liberator of Catholics, presiding over the river end of Sackville Street from a much more modest plinth than the Hero of Trafalgar's.

"In the name of God and of the dead generations…"

With a jerk, Sean realized the short man was reading one of the papers he'd been delivering all morning. He tore open the parcel, unfolded the papers, and shook one out.

"We hereby proclaim the Irish Republic as a sovereign state…"

Two men standing nearby jeered and hooted, soon joined by others, and Sean was surprised how much offense he took at the heckling.

This'll show the King and the English what we think of their bloody war, Sean thought, jaw tightening as he read along.

The children assumed taunting was part of the pageant and joined in with their higher voices. Most of the women shook their heads and clucked their tongues, dismissing the rebels with the backs of their hands. Once the reading was over, the pudgy man shook hands with each companion. All three turned and retreated into the occupied GPO.

With the proclamations draped across a forearm, Sean made his way to Nelson's Pillar and began pasting them every three or four paces along the base. It was slow going, given the flimsy paper and damp stone. With a half-dozen remaining, he trotted across to the Post Office and, the suspicious constable having fled with the patrons, stuck the rest on the granite front. He set the paste and brush at the foot of one of the big columns, then approached a sentry at the main doors. The young soldier was one of the two who'd recruited him the night before.

"Well, you've managed to find some diversion." His smile was a little nervous but all the more genuine for it. "You best stick here. There'll be need of runners and messengers. We've garrisons all over the city."

Glancing into the big foyer jammed with anything that could serve for cover, Sean grinned at the sentry and said, "So, this is what all the doings was about, keeping everyone at Liberty Hall last night?"

The sentry slapped Sean's shoulder and said, "We've got ourselves a Republic, so. And the Brits are like to be mad as hornets when they find out we've taken the South Union, the Castle, Stephen's Green. Places all over the town. Up and down the country, too."

"Who should I report to?"

The sentry hooked a thumb over this shoulder and said, "Ask for one of the commanders' aides. They'll be the ones sending out messages and such."

Once inside, the acrid smell of the earlier gunshots bit Sean's nostrils. He asked a uniformed woman setting out a typewriter on a small table where he could find one of the aides. She directed him into the high-ceilinged main gallery.

Sean passed along the line of phone boxes where he'd once come with Mam to make a call to a rectory in Donegal after she'd had a letter about her Aunt Colleen's death, only to learn the poor woman had been put in the ground two days before. A big man in a Volunteers' uniform was lugging a British officer whose hands were lashed together with telephone wire. As Sean approached, the officer stuffed the officer into the last phone box and clattered shut the door.

"You'll stay until you learn to act a proper prisoner, Captain," the big man said, barking a single loud laugh before turning with a self-satisfied grin.

Sean approached and said, "Excuse me, sir."

The big man fixed his wide, happy eyes on Sean and said, "What are you doing in here, lad? Can't you see we've a rebellion underway?"

"I was told to find one of the commanders' aides," Sean said, clearing his throat, tight with nerves. "I'm to run messages and the like."

Although nearly fifteen, Sean was small, destined to be a late sprout if he ever sprouted at all. Working his cap in his hands, hair sticking out like sprigs of a blackthorn, he appeared all the more diminutive next to the big man.

"You've found the aide-de-camp to Joe Plunkett himself, the man who planned this chivaree." Sean looked up into eyes that promised all manner of devilment. "Mick Collins, from the south of the County Cork. And who might you be?"

"Sean Brannigan, sir," he said, then added with a twitch of a smile, "From the south of the River Liffey." There was sufficient mischief in Sean's eyes to make Lieutenant Collins of the Irish Volunteers throw back his head and bounce a laugh off the vaulted ceiling. Sean staggered from the backslap that rewarded his cheekiness.

"You stay close, Sean Brannigan. There'll be work aplenty this day."

Even a teenage boy knew soon enough the Rising was doomed to failure. After the first heady excitement at the GPO, Sean traipsed over Dublin carrying messages to a half-dozen other rebel positions sprinkled willy-nilly both sides of the river. At City Hall, he'd encountered Miss Molloy, who now carried a holstered revolver on her impeccable Sam Browne belt. He'd then made several more trips across the river, Lieutenant Collins discerning that the young lad from the Liberties knew the south side much better than the north. He visited the hastily dug trenches on Stephen's Green, right across from St. Vincent's, the charity hospital where his sister Deirdre had worked before leaving to nurse in a very different sort of conflict in France.

When he'd been dispatched to the garrison occupying part of the huge poor house that comprised the South Dublin Union, Sean went several blocks out of his way to avoid his mother's pub on the Coombe. By mid-afternoon, the flow of arriving Volunteers stopped and sporadic fighting flared as the Government realized there was serious trouble afoot. A policeman had been killed when the Volunteers tried to enter Dublin Castle. Fierce fighting was taking place near City Hall, where they'd retreated when the Castle's gates had been locked against them.

As the daylight waned, Sean's early excitement soured to fearful resolve. His free range of the city was circumscribed by shooting at a dozen places as platoons and companies from various battalions of His Majesty's Forces stationed in and near Dublin began to rally. The O'Connell Bridge was uncrossable on foot, rebel and Army snipers peppering the lodgments at either end.

Returning from the South Dublin Union, he'd dashed half-bent across the narrow Ha'penny Bridge, since the keepers weren't much interested in collecting the pedestrian toll, what with bullets in the air. Knowing enough to avoid besieged Sackville Street, he meandered through the back alleys and cut over on Henry Street to the north side of the GPO. There he saw two dark outlines, one large and one small, lying in the street. He crept along the wall of the Post Office, inching on fingertips across the damp granite, curious as any frightened boy of fourteen to see what the shapes might be.

Sean had never seen a real corpse before. Sure, he'd stood beside the coffins of a few old relatives and one young neighbor who'd died from the scarlet fever. Those were fussed over and dressed up and laid out to look like they were sleeping. With all the talk of how peaceful and natural the dear departed looked, Sean had thought of them more as large dolls than people who not long before had laughed and loved and suffered.

What lay on the slick paving stones wasn't some poor soul laid out in a polished wooden box before the drawn curtains of a front parlor. In a disorienting mix of horror and fascination, he moved toward the smaller figure, a crumple of wet khaki with one arm flung out, a white hand clutched below the wide brass guard of a saber. A few yards beyond the dead trooper, his horse lay still and glassy-eyed in a congealing puddle of purple that drained from a pair of ragged bullet holes in the big bay's neck. A stirrup was flung back across the curved saddle, its well-tended leather shedding raindrops. The horse's broad flank lay still, ribs creasing the glossy brown hide, no exhausted breath disturbing the eerie tableau.

When he came near the dead trooper, Sean saw the head was turned toward him, chin tucked under his extended arm and obscured behind a woolen sleeve. His round, flat hat rested on edge between him and the dead horse. He'd come dressed for parade, not battle— no need for a helmet.

Thought the rebels… thought we'd just cut and run? Only needed to wave their swords?

There was no shooting near the GPO for the moment, nothing to break the magnetic pull of this scene of violence. He went down to one knee and pulled up the sleeve, revealing the face of the trooper.

Lord, he's no older than Francis, is he?

He looked along the body, from the short brown hair down to the heel of an ankle-high brogan. One of the trooper's puttees had come unfastened in his fall, six inches of the unraveled legging wicking up muddy water from the street. The other leg was twisted back, the impossible angle sending a shiver through Sean.

Not a mark on him. Must be shot in the front. Sean noted the unnatural set of the young soldier's chin. *Maybe broke his neck.*

This was no peaceful sleep. The trooper's one visible eye was open, but not wide in shock or surprise as Sean expected. He seemed to be staring off, but it was emptied of the man behind it, like looking into the eye of a pigeon or a dog. Unable to break away, Sean didn't hear shouts from one of the barricaded windows behind him, urging him to clear off the street.

A silent tear slid down his cheek as he closed his eyes and the street turned to a sandy strand in a faraway place called Gallipoli.

Capital City of Dublin in Ruins

Parts of Irish Capital Looted by Rebels

DUBLIN, April 27—Dublin has been brought under the guns of British warships that have anchored in Dublin Bay. It is believed, however, that the military authorities have the revolutionary situation so well under control in the Irish capital that it will not be necessary to fire on the city.

Reports that rebels had sacked part of Dublin were given official cognizance when Prime Minister Asquith announced that there was no reason to believe that the banks were unsafe. The government and financial institutions of the Irish capital are guarded by troops and machine guns have been mounted upon the roofs of many buildings to sweep the streets.

The proclamation stating that the civil law has been suspended makes evident that the Sinn Feiners who took part in the uprising will be tried for sedition and some of the leaders may be tried for treason.

The military authorities have made progress in putting down the uprising. The troops are making many arrests and all of the county of Dublin is being disarmed.

Wide swaths of Dublin had been laid waste by the soldiers called to quell the Rising. The Government had been caught unaware, not sure what to make of it. Even after the shooting had begun, the official response was chaotic and ineffective. However, by Tuesday night when the size and breadth of the rebels' operations were starkly apparent, the Lord Lieutenant declared martial law and handed over his civil authority to the military. Reinforcements streamed into train stations inexplicably left unoccupied by the rebels. Soon, field artillery arrived and began battering the rebel strongholds, along with bombardments from a gunboat that made its way up the Liffey.

By the early hours of Friday morning, from the river to well past the Nelson Monument, the wide expanse of elegant Sackville Street was a shambles, huge mounds of rubble piled where buildings had stood undamaged on Monday. The General Post Office had caught fire from the shells lobbed into it, tendrils of black soot rising from a few gaping window frames, while the men and women within held out in grim resolve. Hundreds, thousands of bullet marks pocked the classical facade.

Late Friday afternoon, Sean and the other two messengers who'd stayed to the end, along with four of the youngest Volunteers, were ordered by the wounded Commandant Connolly to save themselves by making their way out through the tunnels the rebels had chopped through the walls of adjoining buildings. Sean knew them well, having snaked his way through all parts of the network, building to building, running messages out and carrying ammunition back to the GPO these last four days. Having hidden in plain view under the noses of the Irish Constabulary and the Royal Army as just another street waif gleaning what he could from the destruction, Sean looked over his fellow youngsters in their filthy, sweat-stained green uniforms with great concern.

"We can't have you leaving like that," he said, herding all five toward the stairs that led to upstairs offices. "You'll be shot or pinched. There're coats and hats left by those runnin' out when we marched in on Monday. Shall we do a little shoppin', gents?"

They jogged up the wide staircase, excited at the prospect of some scavenging. Upstairs, they made their way from room to room, picking up overcoats, suit coats, all manner of headgear, a few umbrellas and briefcases. When they gathered up again at the foot of the stairs, they sported a ragtag lot of oversized clothing and odd hats.

"Well, you're an unruly sight. And that's grand."

One of the young Volunteers still wore regulation green breeches, sticking out from below a charcoal-grey tweed coat and a cloth cap. Walking over to a sandbagged window where a small fire had burned a few days before, Sean picked up some remnants of blackened wood. He handed the charred pieces to the others, keeping one for himself.

"Now, stand still while we scuff you up."

Sean dropped to his knees, rubbing charcoal into a front leg of the Volunteer's breeches, then nodded to the others to join in. After a few minutes of blackening and piss-taking at the expense of the recipient of their ministrations, Sean stood and circled the lad to assess their work.

"Long as you stay out of any hard rain, this ought to get you past the Brits." Sean smiled at the nervous Volunteer and tugged on the lad's jacket lapels to fit them to his narrow shoulders. This seemed to reassure the skittish young rebel, so Sean turned back to the others.

Doesn't seem like anyone else is in charge, he thought. *Might as well be me.*

"All right lads, the shelling's likely to start up again, so we'll make ourselves cozy until dark, then head out the south tunnels, one or two at a time. That'll put us closest to the river. I reckon that's our best chance of gettin' clear of this part of town and makin' our way either home or out of Dublin altogether. That's a decision each'll make on his own account. Agreed?"

Heads nodded all round the tight circle, some more certain than others. Sean had watched the officers bucking up the men, encouraging them, giving them strong words, something to pull them past their fear. Seemed these lads could use some of that stiffening.

"We've been ordered out because we're the youngest, and we've no choice but obey. The rest can't hold out much longer, that's clear enough, and there's no tellin' how many more will die or what'll become of them that fall into the hands of the British." Most of the lads were staring at their dusty shoes, one looking back wide-eyed with shock. "We may be all that's left, least 'til others smarter and older can put things right. We need to get free and stay free, carry on the fight any way we can, big or small."

It all went off so easy, at least for Sean. He'd been roaming the city with his friends for almost two years, ever since his father left to rejoin his old regiment. Even though he'd already done his bit in South Africa, his da had gone again. Some days, if things had gone hard at work or the weather turned damp, Sean noticed his da's limp from the Afrikaner bullet a surgeon had dug out below the knee. Daniel used to joke with the neighbor men that Sean was his bonus baby from the Boers, born nine months to the day after he returned home on convalescent leave. Eda was forever grateful the war in faraway Africa had ended before Daniel could be returned to the fighting. But now he was gone.

Fuckin' English king and his fuckin' daft war. And all the fuckin' daft Irishmen who went to fight it.

He was the last one out of the tunnels and he went alone. Slouching along the battered quays, no one paid him any attention. There wasn't much fighting once off Sackville Street, if you stayed away from O'Connell Bridge.

He'd picked his way through the dark streets, staying within sight of the river all the way out to North Wall. After sleeping rough against the tiny deckhouse of an abandoned coal barge lashed up at the quay, he wolfed down some potted meat, stale bread, and a can of condensed milk he nicked by smashing out the side window of the deckhouse when it was light enough to see inside. Restored by an ill-gotten breakfast, he made his way back toward the center of town with a caution he struggled to disguise as nonchalance.

With the daylight, clusters of poor children appeared on the piles of debris that cascaded from shattered facades, picking firewood from splintered rafters and floorboards. A few held some trinket they'd stumbled across. All watched Sean with listless stares, numbed past crying by hunger and fear. Their filthy clothing was a mishmash of baggy charity hand-me-downs and patched breeches or dresses, most too short for their lengthening arms and legs.

Sean joined these random gatherings of tenement children whenever an Army or Constabulary patrol passed by in a sputtering truck or an armored car. None patrolled on foot, the streets still in the thrall of rooftop snipers or rebels holed up inside buildings. At least in a vehicle, there was metal between the soldiers and the rebels as well as a motor with which to retreat.

No one in a uniform paid him any mind and Sean gained confidence as he moved about unnoticed. He decided to make his way back along Eden Quay to Liberty Hall, where his irregular service as a volunteer to the rebel cause had begun not six days before.

He bundled up some scraps of wood with a length of frayed lamp cord as a kind of disguise and shuffled along the quay. He was surprised to find the building mostly intact, the long union placard still affixed to the front, although someone had pulled down the anti-war banner. Most of the glazing was shattered and soldiers wandered in and out with armfuls of papers and files, two standing sentry duty on either side of the entrance.

The little charity clothing shop from which he'd been dispatched with copies of the Declaration of the Republic was gone, a gaping slice taken out of the block of buildings. The structure on the other side of the shop was more damaged than Liberty Hall, but still stood intact. The clothing shop was simply missing, reduced to jumbled bricks and shattered lumber. A musty smell permeated the street, mixed with the taste on his tongue of tart plaster dust. Random articles of tiny clothing turned over in the wind gusting off the river.

The abandoned baby clothes brought to mind a clear image of his mother and his breath caught with a knot tightening in his stomach. Thoughts of her had come in snatches throughout the days he'd been out, but there'd always been another message, another reason to keep his wits about him and his thoughts on the task at hand. Besides, there had been no way to get a message to her without tipping Francis as well. Sean was sure his brother would've locked him in a room or sent for the Constabulary, so full of King and Empire, trying to convince himself the loss of his leg wasn't for naught.

One of the soldiers guarding Liberty Hall hallooed to move him along. Sean sniffed and dragged a sleeve under his nose, then tugged his cap and nodded in pantomime subservience before trotting off up the quay, an unneeded faggot of firewood tucked under his arm, heading for home.

CHAPTER FOUR

Eda

"I'm terrible sorry, Mrs. Fitzmorris, but we've had no sugar since Wednesday," Molly said in her quiet way from behind the little grocery counter.

A stout woman with rowan cheeks sighed and clucked her tongue. "With no one knowin' how long this fightin' would go on, they stocked up, I suppose. More's the fool I am for not doin' likewise."

"We've a bit of tea," Molly said, proffering a battered green tin by way of consolation. "And salt. I'm afraid there's naught else."

The customer fished a little leather change purse from her coat and said, "You best give me threepence of tea, then. We'll drink it black." She gave Molly a wry look and added, "Unless you reckon my man would like his tea with salt? Might serve him right, the lazy codger."

Molly returned a smile and handed over a small paper packet with loose tea folded inside. She laid the three pennies without a sound into the pasteboard box Eda kept supplied with a little change. The box sat behind the short counter from which Eda dispatched her publican's obligation of selling a few necessities to the neighborhood families. The counter was right next to the door so respectable women wouldn't have to step into the pub proper. It didn't bring in much profit, but Eda knew it was expected and she'd already rankled the Liberties with all her cleaning and renaming.

The rising by the Irish Volunteers and the Citizen Army had triggered a run on every greengrocer and pub along the Coombe and right across Dublin City. The milk and eggs went first, even though farmers had arrived Easter Monday before the fighting to resupply shelves laid bare by the great quantities of food an Easter weekend demanded. Eda's meager inventory of staples went nearly as fast. First the flour and sugar, then the coffee and cigarettes—even the matches. She still had plenty of postage stamps, no one seeing much purpose in sending letters with the General Post Office aflame. She'd bought a few pounds of tea on Holy Thursday morning, but that supply was dwindling fast since word got round that she hadn't raised her prices to profit from the general misfortune, as others had done.

Putting the tea and her change purse into a pocket, the customer pulled her shawl up over her hair and leaned close to Molly. "Have you any word of your Sean, so? I mean, since he went missin' Monday?"

Biting her lip, Molly steeled herself, determined to remain steady for Mam's sake. But it was so very hard, she and Sean raised almost as twins. "We've not heard a thing, Mrs. Fitzmorris, but thanks for the asking. He knows the streets better than most, so I've no doubt he's kept himself clear of danger."

"Well, I'll say a decade or two for him just the same. Our Lady will look after him, if any help's needed."

"That'll be a comfort to Mam."

The older woman squeezed Molly's hand, then looked with pity into the girl's ice-blue eyes filling with tears.

Unlike her grocery inventory, Eda's cellar was full when the shooting started and had never risked running dry. The brewery only shut for a few days and was soon delivering on the south side of the river, at least to the places that hadn't seen much fighting. The big wooden barrels began arriving regular as clockwork at The Gallant by Friday morning. And there was plenty of whisky and gin stacked in wooden crates on the shelves below. Truth be told, the Sinn Feiners had been good for business, with so many men unable to get to their work. And what else was an Irishman with idle hands to do but share his opinions on the dire situation in his local?

Not that Eda thought much about the state of her earnings. Sean hadn't been home since Easter dinner and she'd had not a word of him since the shooting and shelling began on Monday. She'd been to the church half a dozen times to light candles and kneel with the Altar and Rosary Society, who'd kept up a steady vigil since the first sounds of battle on the streets.

But it was work that provided her comfort, as it had since she was a girl in Donegal. In that hard and poor place, it was a matter of day-to-day survival. Here in the city, even with her husband making a fine wage and providing a warm house with plentiful food, she'd found useful work to occupy all her waking hours. Her daughters inherited her diligence, with Deirdre in France nursing the war-wounded and dying and Molly with her studies. The younger daughter sat on her stool behind the little grocery counter, devouring a book and lost in her faraway place, oblivious to the men at the bar.

"Give us a song, Lieutenant!" bellowed Francis, standing more drinks than the pub's accounts should have to bear.

Johnny O'Fallon downed his whisky and slapped down the glass on the bar's polished wood. He leaned his weight on his cane, took a few steps away from the rail, cleared his throat, and commenced his party piece.

They were summoned from the hillside, they were called in from the glen…

Peter Conway took the opportunity to slide behind the bar and help Eda wash and dry pint glasses and whisky tumblers. Engrossed in the song and awaiting the chorus, none of the others noticed.

"Customers aren't allowed behind the bar, Mr. Conway," Eda said, handing him a clean towel and dunking her hands back into the greying wash water. "But you're a gentleman and welcome just this once."

And the country found them ready at the stirring call for men, the baritone filled the pub.

His round glasses were half-fogged from steam coming off the washtub, so Peter removed them for a wiping while his towel still had a dry corner. He placed them back with practiced care and said to

Eda, "You're wearing yourself threadbare with work and worry, Eda. It's a pleasure if I'm able to assist in little ways like this."

"*Go raibh maith agat*," she said, thanking him with a weary, crooked smile. "Francis hasn't been much help these last days, at the whisky all of his waking hours."

"It must be difficult for him. And all the others who… gave so much… of… well, of their youth to the war. It's understandable they find the… this rebellion a kind of… slap in the face." Although a learned man who could lecture students with great precision in two languages, Peter Conway wasn't so eloquent in the presence of Eda Brannigan.

Let no tears add to their hardships, as the soldiers pass along…

"And perhaps he's… using the drink to cover his… his worry over his brother?" He looked into the glass he was drying and said in a scarcely audible voice, "Much like yourself, with your work."

Eda splashed a pair of glasses sticky with tawny remnants of porter into her wash tub. "Bah, what else would I do with myself? 'Tweren't for the pub, I'd be destroyin' myself with the fear and wearin' out my knees worryin' the beads down at St. Nicholas."

And although your heart is breaking, make it sing this cheery song…

There was a general shuffling as the others prepared to join the chorus.

"You've a right to be concerned and there's no shame in it. There are many mothers missing their boys who'll be overjoyed when they're home safe… now that the fighting in the streets is over." Peter pursed his mouth and turned away from her.

Eda noticed his odd expression and thought to comment, but decided it best to return to the glassware. She'd a fondness for Peter Conway, she'd not deny that, but didn't know him well enough to intrude on all his private thoughts.

Keep the home fires burning, while your hearts are yearning… A swell of voices boomed out the chorus.

Peter and Eda's heads turned up from their work, looking over the room in the soft light of the dim electric bulbs back-fitted into the pub's old gas fixtures. Many of the men standing near the lame Johnny O'Fallon could now be called regulars. Eda saw her Francis, an arm thrown over the shoulder of another veteran, the one with the big black patch over one eye and half his cheek. They both joined the singing with lusty voices and misty eyes, still tenderhearted Irishmen despite the suffering they'd seen and endured.

Though your lads are far away, they dream of home…

Peter removed his round glasses a second time, looking to wipe away the steam again. With a sideways glance, Eda saw him dab at his eyes before attending to his spectacles.

There's a silver lining, through the dark cloud shining…

Over the crescendoing voices, Eda heard—as only a mother would—a single sharp gasp from her Molly. But with the crowd of singers between them, Eda couldn't see her daughter by the door.

Turn the dark cloud inside out…

The singing dropped off until there wasn't a sound from any of the two dozen drinkers. In the sudden quiet, everyone heard the soft sobs. As if by silent command, the crowd of men parted, giving Eda and Peter an unobstructed view.

In the open doorway, Sean stood with Molly sobbing into his shoulder. With his free hand, he slid the stained cloth cap from his head. The grimy exhaustion etched on his face was accentuated by wide eyes brimming with relief at being quit of the recent horrors.

Sean met his mother's dazed stare and gave her a little nod of recognition. Her hands flew to her mouth and tears coursed over them. She wobbled from the sudden lifting of the constant fear of the last five days. Peter grabbed her by the waist and she collapsed against him with weary relief.

Francis staggered as he moved toward his younger brother, a result of both his artificial limb and the copious amount of drink. He grabbed onto the shoulders of a few men who steadied him and passed him on toward the door.

"Hello, Francis," croaked Sean, choked by exhaustion.

"I'd have expected more than that," Francis spat back at him. "You've near killed our mother with grief, thinkin' you were lyin' dead in the gutter somewheres. What in God's name were you about, then?"

With nothing left in him to muster a lie and little desire to do so anyway, Sean straightened himself and closed the distance between him and his big brother.

"I was runnin' messages and carryin' ammunition for the Citizen Army. The Volunteers, too. At the GPO and all about the town." Sean paused as a thick ripple of gasps and rumble of disbelief spread across the room.

"Jayzuz, are you daft? You were out with those traitors to the Crown? The very Crown your own da gave his life defendin'?"

Several of the men—all the veterans and a few who weren't—stepped behind Francis, menacing the disheveled and dejected boy standing slump-shouldered before them. The rest wandered back to the bar, suddenly finding this no longer their concern. A few examined their shoes with obvious discomfort. Loomed over by the others, Sean held firm.

"The very Crown that took my da from me, you mean? And your leg, Francis?" Sean glared up at Francis, despising the drunkenness and crippling weakness he'd brought home from Gallipoli.

"And to what purpose, can you tell me, so? There's never an Englishman did a single good deed for an Irishman, includin' the King himself." Sean gave a half-hearted spit at the floor.

Peter Conway moved from behind the bar and round the crowd until he was standing beside Molly at the door. He was just able to throw himself between the brothers as Francis reeled forward swinging at Sean. Caroming off Peter's shoulder, Francis fell in a pile to the floor. Two men helped raise him to his feet while Peter hustled Sean toward the tidy flat above.

Rushing up the stairs, Sean looked up into the face of his rescuer, confused with the sudden familiarity of it.

"Your mother will be right on our heels, lad," Peter said as they pushed past Danny sitting at the top of the steps watching the commotion below.

"You're from the bookstore, over behind the Four Courts," Sean whispered as Peter dragged him to the little kitchen at the back of the flat. "I took a bundle of the proclamations to you on Monday."

"Aye, that you did. And it will do neither of us any good for that to become widely known at this moment."

Two sets of footfalls clomped up the steps and Peter said in a rush,

"We're both of us in this, but precious few know that. The men below will assume you were only a rash boy out for some adventure. Those of us left free need to keep the cause going, build things back." Sean nodded his understanding in the dimness.

"So we mind each other's secrets from here out?"

Sean nodded again, then jerked his head toward a movement in the darkness at the back of the kitchen.

As Eda burst in, Molly flicked on the single bulb suspended above the middle of the room. Peter had grabbed a tea towel and was making a show of cleaning up Sean. Eda glanced across the room through swollen eyes and saw Danny half-hidden beside the press that held her dishes.

Surveying Sean in the better light, she found him a filthy mess.

"Molly, you come with me to fetch hot water and clean towels downstairs. Your brother looks to have been drug through all the streets and half the sewers of Dublin." She cupped Sean's cheek with her hand, gave him smiling reassurance that she wasn't as angry as she'd every right to be, then disappeared down the stairs.

Molly stood staring at the brother she'd loved for as long as she had memories. She smoothed his unruly black hair, the whiteness of her hand stark against it, and whispered, "Why did you do it, Sean? You could've been killed. Was it so important to you? To set yourself apart from Francis?"

He jerked her hand from his hair and said, "What difference does it make now? We were beaten in the end."

She turned away in confusion, following her mother down to the pub.

Peter rung out the cloth he'd wet under the single cold-water tap and began dabbing at Sean's filthy cheek. He turned the lad's chin toward him with the icy cloth and said in a calm and quiet voice, "Being beaten doesn't greatly matter in Ireland. Not fighting does."

Danny's impassive face watched from the shadows behind them.

CHAPTER FIVE

Thomas

Town garrison duty, police duty, relief convoy duty—any kind of duty but a real soldier's duty. That's what was left to them. Occupation, the brass hats named it. A daily bollocks, the troops called it, and proved it with surliness and petty misconduct.

Currently, their obligation was distributing endless sacks of corn. Or rather *wheat,* as the Yanks insisted, it being their produce. That and filing endless reports on tonnage of foodstuffs moved from Point A to Point B, incidence of malnutrition among the German population, and whatever else piqued the interest of the American relief administrator, Herbert Hoover. On the one occasion when his soldiers had been tasked to transport Mr. Hoover himself, along with his sacks of wheat and cases of bully beef, Lieutenant Thomas Piers-Musgrave found him an unremitting prig. The administrator had been raised within the Society of Friends and after three hours in a staff car with this particular Quaker, the lieutenant was convinced the Crown had been quite justified in shipping them to Pennsylvania two centuries ago. Mr. Hoover was also some variety of engineer, and more of a crashing bore than even the average Scot of that profession.

His mother's family—the Piers half of his double-barreled name—had an ancestral heap in County Tyrone where he'd been dragooned into spending summers as a boy. As a result of this unenthusiastic connection to Ulster, he'd been commissioned in the Royal Inniskilling Fusiliers in September 1918, just in time to contract the Spanish influenza. Out of consideration for his family's feelings, he'd decided not to die, but instead endured a six-week convalescence, finally joining his battalion in France on the 14th day of November, 1918. Lieutenant Piers-Musgrave then passed exactly one night sleeping in a trench dugout, after which his commanding officer decided the Germans had no interest in overrunning their lines, having recently agreed to an armistice, and called off manning his portion of the trenches through the simple expedient of not bothering to do so. The battalion commander had been with the colors since early 1915 and with a gassing, some shrapnel in his thigh, and a Military Cross to show for it, no one at General Headquarters was in a mood to court-martial him.

Perceiving no imminent combat, the commander had placed the grass-green Lieutenant Piers-Musgrave in command of a company of 150-odd Irishmen, each believing in his heart of hearts he deserved to be home rather than making the impending march into the Rhineland. Thus had the lieutenant passed a perfunctory four months since the guns fell silent.

Brushing off the accumulated light rain or dense fog that comprised the bone-penetrating perpetual dampness of a depressing slate-grey German winter, the lieutenant stepped into an adjutant's office occupying the front parlor of a fine townhouse requisitioned from an angry but tight-lipped German lawyer and his weepy wife. The British had been kind enough to let them remain on the premises, displaced to the servants' rooms above the garage. The lieutenant had glimpsed the owners on a previous visit, wrapped in their tatty overcoats and huddled against a biting wind, clutching food aid parcels with furtive glances as they disappeared up the staircase of the garage.

He shook out his trench coat, still so-called even in the absence of trenches, as he stood before a jolly coal fire of a type only the occupying Allied forces could afford to keep stoked. He unbuckled the leather map case he carried under his arm and extracted a neatly folded pair of typewritten pages.

"My report on yesterday's convoy, sir," the lieutenant said, handing the sheets with their crisp creases across the cluttered desk that sat facing the fireplace. A single clerk, huddled at a narrow mahogany secretary shoved into the coldest corner of the room, produced a listless clacking from a banged-up Corona typewriter that had been at war much longer than Lieutenant Piers-Musgrave.

The adjutant, a captain with a look of soul-crushing boredom, sat staring outside, his eyes foggy as the glazing in the long front windows. His fingers were yellowed to the knuckles by endless cigarettes, smoking being his only comfort and diversion. He'd been promoted when all the other captains returned home, his three weeks' combat service before the Armistice making him the most experienced junior officer. That had been enough reason to slap another pip on his shoulders and plop him down behind a desk to run the battalion while the commander slept late, drank early, and whored often.

The captain glanced at the report and tossed it into the battered wooden tray at the edge of his desk, then lit another Woodbine before forcing himself to converse with as few words as propriety allowed.

"Old Man wishes to see you, Piers-Musgrave."

That was unusual enough, the battalion commander having become a phantom to his junior officers and a perfect myth to the private soldiers.

"Any idea what it's concerning, sir?"

The languid, almost flaccid, adjutant gazed with lifeless eyes at the lieutenant as he exhaled an unnaturally long stream of smoke from his nostrils. He blinked once and said, "How do you suppose I would know that? Perhaps in regard to your incessant whingeing about your tragic underutilization?"

The lieutenant flushed hot up the back of his neck and glanced away, only to see the clerk's shoulders convulsing with stifled laughter. He looked into the mackerel-eyed stare of the adjutant, who telegraphed his perfect disdain for the overly keen subaltern standing red-faced before him.

"When would the commander wish to see me, sir?" the lieutenant said, in a voice not as confident as he'd hoped, while straightening his back.

The adjutant's nasal exhalation came faster this time. "How in bugger-all bloody hell would I know?" The put-upon adjutant crushed his cigarette in an overflowing tin that once held pears, if the tattered label was to be believed. Without taking his disdainful stare off the lieutenant, he called across the room to the clerk, "Corporal, nip up stairs and see if the colonel is among the living." With icy insincerity, he added, "There's a good chap."

Not knowing what was expected, Lieutenant Piers-Musgrave stood at attention for an uncomfortable length of time. As perspiration soaked through under his arms, the corporal's footfalls sounded on the half-turned staircase before he reappeared in the doorway.

"Colonel's compliments, sir. Says to send the lieutenant up to his room. Says he'll have a palaver with him there." The corporal slouched back to his frigid desk and began his clacking again.

The lieutenant didn't move, waiting to be dismissed. The adjutant lit another cigarette and looked up, stupefied that the younger officer was still there.

"You heard the man, Piers-Musgrave. First floor, big room over the front. Now, bugger off. And see yourself out when the commander's done with you."

The colonel's bedroom, all chintz wallpaper and floral fabrics, must have belonged to the lady of the house. Now the only woman in the chamber was lying on her stomach across the crumpled bedclothes, sound asleep and stark naked. When the lieutenant entered after a pair of quiet knocks, he pulled up at the sight of the woman on the bed.

Standing a few steps inside the room, he stammered, "Sir... Lieutenant Piers-Musgrave... reporting as... ordered." He threw up a slow salute above a wide-eyed face.

The commander had managed to pull on his drawers and an unbuttoned shirt while sitting on the side of the bed. He stood, wobbled, and then looked over at the lieutenant.

"Ah, Piers-Musgrave." He waved the back of a hand in reply to the junior officer's salute, then noted him staring at the naked woman. The colonel reached across the bed and pinched the curving backside. The woman grumbled, rubbed the heel of a hand into one eye, and rolled toward the commander, propping herself on an elbow. Her mousy hair was wild and loose, hanging down far enough to cover one breast, leaving the rest of her revealed.

"*Komm zurück ins bett… Es ist noch so früh,*" she said, not wanting to leave the clean sheets or the warm room. When she noticed the young man gaping at her from across the room, she flashed a jerky smile, unfurled a showy sigh, and slid to the edge of the bed.

"Best get dressed and on your way. Appears I'm forced to do business this morning." Noticing the red welt he'd left on her bum, he patted the spot a few times and gave it an indifferent rub.

The lieutenant noticed the woman was quite thin, her legs long and lean as she sprawled on the bed. When she rose and bent for something to cover herself, each of her vertebrae and ribs was countable as she fumbled about. She stood up with the colonel's khaki service tunic bunched over her breasts with one hand, a single sleeve held between her legs with the other. Her collarbones were as sharp and defined as her cheeks. She scampered behind a folding Chinese screen and the lieutenant heard the rustling of fabric sliding along limbs as she dressed.

The commander crossed the room and reached for the tunic she'd flung back on the screen and laid it over a straight-back chair near the door. He buttoned his fly as he spoke.

"You've not been particularly happy with our little endeavor here, have you? Not enough excitement? No enemy to machine gun or stick with a bayonet?" He went to the nightstand and picked up a random glass. Finding it clean enough in the weak light filtering through the window, he poured three or four fingers of whisky.

He took a long drink and turning with an abstracted look said, "You don't know how bloody lucky you are. I had four long years I'd give my last good leg to forget. You were fortunate to avoid the whole cocked-up show." He downed the remainder and refilled his glass without it occurring to him to offer a drink to his subordinate.

"I understand, sir. But you in particular, with all you've done, can appreciate how frustrating it is for me. Never having had my chance, as it were."

Another large whisky went down the commander's throat and, thinking he should set some minimal example, resisted going for the bottle a third time and set the glass back on the nightstand. He searched a trouser pocket and produced a packet of cigarettes, extracting one with his lips. It dangled unlit from his mouth as he tucked in his shirt and fished a necktie from beneath the bedstead.

"Your people have estates in Ireland?" The colonel turned to a full-length mirror, angled up on its brass stand, and commenced knotting the tie.

"Yes, sir. The pater has distant relations all over Westmeath. My mother's family has holdings in Tyrone. I spent most summers at my grandparents' estate there."

The tie completed, the commander lit his cigarette and went to the dressing table. He uncapped a long-necked bottle of brilliantine and shook it a few times into his left palm, rubbed it into his right, and ran both through his disheveled hair. Taking up two tortoise shell hair brushes, he returned to the long mirror and smoothed down his glossy hair.

"My wife's family has a pile in the countryside outside Cork City. She's passed every summer there since I've been away, as she did when she was a girl. I swear she's more Irish than a bloody Fenian."

The young German woman stepped out from behind the screen, fully clothed and tugging down a brown cloche. She crossed over to the colonel, pushing some hairs up under the hat, then stretched on her toes to kiss his cheek.

He gave her an oddly self-conscious smile. "My batman has a parcel for you in the kitchen. Some cans of bully beef and a few packets of biscuits. Believe a little coffee, too."

"Kafee?" Her eyes widened and she kissed him again, this time on the mouth. He patted her shoulder and pushed her toward the door. She left without a backward glance, her heels sounding on the wooden stairs.

The colonel snatched his tunic from off the chair and shrugged it on. Leaving it unbuttoned, he slouched into an arm chair and pinched a shred of tobacco from the end of his tongue.

"So you know Ireland well? The people as well as the geography?"

The lieutenant hesitated for a moment, then said, "Yes, I'd say I do. There were all those summers with my grandparents. Mother hires her chamber maids from the villages near the family estate in Tyrone and her lady's maid is from Belfast. Our nurse was from Fermanagh and my first tutor was a young graduate from Trinity in Dublin." He paused to consider all he'd just said and added, "I'm much like your wife, I suppose. My sisters and I even have a little Gaelic, from our nurse."

The colonel sat in silence studying the young officer through the haze of his cigarette. After a minute of uneasy silence, he rose to his feet and went back to the dressing table.

"I've an old schoolmate in Dublin who's working military intelligence, involved in something or other to do with the Sinn Feiner nonsense that's been going on there." He fished through the little drawers in the dressing table, finally stopping to extract an envelope.

"Just had a letter from him. Most of it's the usual nattering," he said, handing the envelope to the lieutenant. "Toward the end he mentions that he's desperate for some trustworthy English or Scottish officers who might pass themselves off as Irish. Says it's all very hush-hush and sneaky-peaky. Sound like something that might interest you?"

Turning the envelope over in his hands, the lieutenant was unsure whether the commander intended for him to read it immediately.

"Dash it all, take the bloody thing with you! His name and address are on the envelope. Nothing in the letter you can't see otherwise. If you're interested, write him yourself and mention that I recommended you. Better yet, send him a telegram. He sounds rather keen to find men as soon as possible."

Lieutenant Thomas Piers-Musgrave smiled despite himself, holding the ticket to his deliverance. Of course he'd send a telegram—it might cut days off his time in this purgatory of the Rhineland.

A decent interval of as long as five minutes having passed since his last drink, the colonel strode to the nightstand and poured himself another large whisky. He turned and held the glass up toward the lieutenant and said, "I'll gladly sign your transfer, Piers-Musgrave, if it'll help root out those Fenian bastards. Stabbed us right in the back with that ludicrous rebellion back in '16. Right before the bloody Somme. We should have shot the whole lot then. Give them what's coming, I say."

And with that, he saw off the lieutenant with a dismissive wave.

CHAPTER SIX

Eda

Eda had shooed all the regulars out for the Holy Hour. She knew some owners subscribed to the unwritten rule that as long as a customer was inside at two o'clock, he could carry on drinking throughout the mandatory two-hour closing. But she thought it not too much to ask of a man to go home to his family for a few hours of a Sunday afternoon, although she was certain a few nipped out of her establishment early enough to get themselves locked inside some other pub. That wasn't her bother.

Molly carried up an old whisky crate from the back, the one she used for restocking sundries sold from the little counter next to the door that had become her special domain. She set the crate on the counter and filled the empty spaces on the shelves behind and below, careful to rotate the oldest stock to the front, just as Mam had shown her when they'd taken on the pub more than three years ago.

Since Sunday was always busy for last-minute dinner needs, Molly had sold quite a lot of flour and sugar, coffee and tea, cigarettes and pipe tobacco. She'd brought out the battered cash box and the little green ledger that contained all the purchases on tick, as too many were wont to do. It was the hardest thing Eda had learned, how to collect what was owed her on credit for these little essentials. So many of her customers scraped by on precious little. The young war widows with their children and meager pensions the Crown begrudged them. Ancient ones scraping by on ten shillings a week from the old-age allowance they collected at the post office. Women with husbands who spent their wages on drink or wagering, oftentimes both. There was a similar ledger behind the bar, with a longer list of names and sums owed.

While Molly counted out her morning's receipts at the bar, her sister, Deirdre, slipped in next to her. She draped an arm over the younger girl's narrow shoulders, kissed the side of her head, then left her nose nuzzled in the soft hair, so shiny and bright it seemed metallic. Molly closed the lid on the old pasteboard box and leaned into her sister, taking hold of the warm hand over her shoulder.

Behind the bar, Eda suspended her perpetual wiping and polishing, giving out a long sigh at the tableau of her daughters. Peace and quiet were rare enough, between the opening hours of the pub and the arguing of her two eldest boys, Francis and Sean. But she'd not let that spoil this small moment.

Molly pulled away with her distant smile, a look often puzzling to both her mother and sister. She slid the ledger across to Eda, neat piles of pennies and shillings atop.

"I've some revising to do for Latin, so I'll be up to my room while it's quiet," she said. Before heading to the stairs at the end of the bar, she turned back to her sister and kissed her cheek. "It's grand havin' you home with us. We won't have to worry ever again, will we?"

Deirdre smoothed the back of her hand against the girl's porcelain cheek, raising a faint blush.

"No, never again, Molly-o." Her voice caught on the name their father had always used for his youngest girl. Deirdre dabbed a surreptitious tear while Molly floated up the stairs, light as a bit of thistle down. Eda knew Deirdre still ached from the loss of her father, but she was relieved to her bones that her eldest daughter's time in the military nursing service was at an end.

"She'll have to know soon that you're going to your Aunt Nola in Canada. Which of us will be the one to tell her?" Eda whispered.

There was a little scuffling as Molly reached the top of the open staircase, silencing their conversation. Deirdre glanced up and noticed

Danny perched at the stop of the stairs, pressing himself against the wall to let his sister pass. When the door to the upstairs closed, the boy disappeared back into the shadows.

"I suppose it'll have to be me," Deirdre said. She straightened herself, shoulders pressed back, and worked both hands into the small of her back. "Seems only right, since I'm the one away and gone again."

"You're a thundering herd, the lot of you," Eda said, smiling across the bar as she served up the drinks. "You'd think you'd not seen a watering hole in days. And it only being the two hours."

"It's a perilous time at my house of a Sunday, what with the mother-in-law underfoot after Mass!"

No telling which of the men that was, not that it mattered. The others pealed with laughter.

"'Tis the very staff of life, a man's pint, Eda! You'd not deny such a necessity, would ye?"

Another burst of laughter bounced from the pressed-tin ceiling.

"Liquid bread!"

"The black elixir itself!"

"Unless a man prefers the amber stuff."

This last was in a voice Eda would always know. Francis seldom came behind the bar if there were any from his old regiment about. She gave the crowd a quick scan and spotted him amidst a knot of four or five standing off the end of the bar near the stairs.

As she watched, her son threw back the tall whisky in his hand and passed the empty glass to one of the men. Francis gave him an encouraging nod and the man turned with a sheepish look upon the unscarred portion of his face. He stepped to the bar and Eda made her way over.

"For Francis, Mrs. Brannigan," he said in a half-whisper, not that he was hiding anything that wasn't a well-known fact within the walls of The Gallant Fusilier. Eda swept the glass off the bar and poured another large whisky from the bottle she kept in the corner of the lowest liquor shelf, the better to keep an eye on how much her son was drinking. But she never denied him, with all he'd been through.

Francis never asked his mother for a drink, fearing her disapproval. So a kind of ritual developed, one that all the men knew, in which he'd have one of them ask for his drinks. It was a little sham in which they all engaged, sympathetic to Francis's sensitivities. His mother played along, too.

After the scarred veteran handed over the replenished glass, Francis raised it to nose level and said in a clear voice, "To the Regiment!"

The gathered men raised theirs in turn and replied in unison, "The Dubs!" From across the pub, older men and those younger ones who hadn't served, followed the ex-soldiers with a mixed bag of toasts.

"Hear, hear!"

"To the fallen!"

"The King!"

These regulars, as well as a few faces to which Eda hadn't yet put names, had stepped over the threshold of The Gallant within seconds of St. Patrick's Cathedral striking four o'clock. This was the authoritative signal along the Coombe, it being assumed that Protestant bells must perforce be most accurate.

The scrum at the bar included many veterans, some who'd been early regulars at the pub since being invalided home by gas or shrapnel, blindness or amputation. Others had come home after the Armistice, intact on the exterior. Eda knew of their unseen scars as she served up their drams and pulled their pints. She couldn't explain the few who'd returned none the worse for wear, a bit thinner and older to be sure, but no more troubled than if they'd been on holiday by the sea. There were precious few of those.

At five o'clock, the heavy front door opened and a neatly dressed man with round steel-rimmed glasses slipped inside. He removed his hat and headed to the end of the bar near the two enclosed snugs at the back. Most of the regulars avoided that end of the bar. The tiny private rooms with just a table and a few chairs were for women, allowing them to slip in the back door with little notice. Clutches of men looking for privacy sometimes used one of them when unoccupied by the ladies.

Any man at that end of the bar was expected to take drink orders for the ladies, since—Saints preserve us!—they couldn't be seen loitering at the bar awaiting service. Peter Conway didn't mind the additional duties, so as he took up his accustomed post, several of the regulars hallooed to him.

"Ahh, I thought the place looked brighter! We've a scholar in the house!"

He nodded and gave a twitchy smile in reply.

"Well, a good Sunday to you, Mr. Conway!"

Turning his hat in his hands, he said, "And to you, Mr. Donahue."

"Mister, is't? The wife will accuse me of puttin' on airs!" The ensuing slap on the shoulder made Peter tense, much as he tried to suppress it. He pressed a book wrapped in brown paper tighter under his arm while hanging his hat on one of the hooks outside the second snug.

"You've some catching up to do, bookseller! We've been in an hour or more already!" Another nod and uneasy smile, which seemed enough for the greeter, who turned back to the bar and gave his empty pint a little wave in Eda's direction.

He supposed he was a regular now, although he'd never been one anywhere else, making him quite a rare male of the Irish species. He was still a little awkward, even after the few years he'd been coming to the pub, with the easy familiarity and good-natured nosiness that came along with acceptance into the regular crowd at The Gallant. He'd initially dragged Johnny O'Fallon along whenever he came, but Johnny had begun objecting to the trek over to the Coombe from Trinity when there were so many adequate pubs much closer at hand. And if anything, Johnny's craving for the liquor had only gotten worse, as had his attendance at tutorials.

Eda had noted the first time Peter came in alone, skittish as a newborn lamb on trembly legs. She'd not made mention of it then and thought it best to continue this indulgent conspiracy of silence concerning the subject. He'd become a special friend to her, one upon whom she could rely for sound advice or a sympathetic ear. And as a man who kept his own counsel, she'd known early on that he'd keep her affairs private, too.

She was certain he was sweet on her. Women have a way of knowing, even with the awkward ones like Peter Conway. This was confirmed by the leery manner her son Francis spoke to him, overprotective of both his mother and his father's memory. Sean and Molly liked him well enough, as did Danny—as much as Danny warmed to anyone. He'd even gotten Sean reading again, bringing him all manner of books on Irish history and the new poetry by Yeats and all the scribblers from Dublin and beyond.

Her second son left the Christian Brothers' school soon after turning sixteen, it being mutually agreeable to both himself and the holy brothers. Eda appreciated his help after the apprentice pubman she'd inherited with the premises went off to the fighting, never to return. Sean was willing to do the sweeping out in the morning, as required by the Corporation, allowing her to do a bit of housekeeping and get soup or a stew ready for their dinner. He helped unload the barrels that arrived from his father's old brewery and he kept the cellar stocked and tidy. He always unlocked the doors promptly at eleven o'clock—twelve on Sundays, of course—and pulled the odd pint for the early arrivers. All that Sean wanted in return was his bed, board, and a little pocket money.

He also asked to be free of the pub by noon every day. This arrangement suited Eda, considering that her eldest son was unlikely to rouse himself before that time. This was a blessing, keeping Francis and Sean apart. Their terrible rows had continued apace, a few times descending into shoving and the odd fist before she or Molly or one of the regulars could separate them. So it had been since the Volunteers and Citizen Army upended the town on Easter Monday three years past, Sean out with the rebels for days while Francis and the other veterans huffed and fumed over the disloyal stab in the back, what with so many Irishmen fighting and dying in France then.

She'd not a notion where Sean disappeared after the noontime crowd thinned, sometimes out all night and not returning until it was time to start his morning's work. Oftentimes he'd come upstairs just to wash and change his shirt and drawers. Still, he was doing a man's work and deserved to be treated as such, just as she'd allowed Francis when he apprenticed at the brewery cooperage, back before the war.

From time to time, Sean would bring one or two friends to The Gallant, disappearing into one of the snugs at the back, staying clear of Francis. Although open at the top, the little private rooms had walls that ran well above eye level, with frosted glass in the doors to admit some light without allowing for prying eyes.

The first snug, the one nearest the rear door that opened onto Hanover Street, was by unspoken tradition reserved for the exclusive use of the more successful shawlies, the street vendors along the Coombe that sold everything from ribbons to mussels, sometimes from the same basket. These women, each with a black shawl over her head, slipped into the back door and into the first snug, generally unnoticed by all but Eda. On one memorable occasion, some young rakes from University College were out on a tear and adversely possessed the first snug. When the shawlies came in for their usual porter and pipes, they stood in the open door of the snug, shortest to tallest, staring daggers at the students. When their derisive hoots had no discernible impact on the women, the students slunk away defeated into the night.

The second snug, the one under the stairs running up to the flat, was open to all comers. Possession being nine-tenths of the law, you were welcome to stay for as long as you'd a mind to linger. That's where Sean and his companions took up residence now and again.

"Well then, Peter Conway, and how are you this fine day?" Eda set down the lightest pour of whisky she could manage and allow Peter his self-respect, then placed a soda siphon between his drink and the crowd at the bar to provide a little camouflage. Peter filled the glass near to the rim with soda.

"An mhaith. Agus tu fein?" Although they often conversed in a patois of Irish and English, Eda gave him a warning look with a taut shake of her head. Speaking Irish was considered a very Republican affectation in loyal circles these days, what with the shootings and bombings erupting all over the city and across the country. With so many of the men in the crowded pub former soldiers, he understood and switched to English on the trot.

He replied again, a little louder to be heard by those nearest, "I'm quite well. And yourself, Mrs. Brannigan?"

She flashed a thankful smile and patted the back of his hand. It seemed an ordinary thing, but this had become a special kind of intimacy, sending a pulse through him whenever she repeated it. He slid the parcel from under his arm and placed it on the bar, masking his thrill at her touch.

What Peter Conway, a man of great learning, did not know after three years' acquaintance with Eda Brannigan was whether she ever felt the same thrill.

He glanced up to the little landing and the door to the flat above. Danny, Eda's last-born, sat perched there with arms about his bare knees, at nine years old still in short trousers. Peter raised a hand and waved his fingers at the boy. Danny turned his head toward the wall and buried his face in his arm.

"Is Sean about? I know he's seldom in this time of day, but I've brought a book he'd especially asked for. I could leave it."

Eda busied herself with her ubiquitous towel and said, "Oh, he's knockin' about upstairs. Like God Almighty, our Sean rests on the seventh day. Go right up—you know the way."

Leaving his hat on the hook near the snugs and his untouched weak whisky on the bar, Peter took up the wrapped volume and threaded his way through the crowd toward the foot of the stairs. Francis gave him a terse nod and a cold glare in minimal recognition as he passed through the cluster of old Dubs and turned up the open staircase. When Danny saw him coming, he flattened himself against the wall, cheek pressed against the cool plaster.

Fruit drops were the only known vice of Peter Conway and he always had a little tin in an inside pocket. He'd shared them with Danny in the past, thinking it a good thing for him and the timid boy to have a harmless secret. It was clear the youngster had missed his father more than his mother would admit these last four years.

Snapping open the candy tin, Peter palmed it so only Danny could see and held it before the boy's face. When Danny glanced up, Peter gave him a wink and shook the tin. A little puff of sugar powder wafted under the boy's nose and he dug into the candies with two fingers, extracting a tangerine one. Peter snapped the tin closed and winked again.

Barely audible above the hubbub below, Danny said, "Thank you." Peter nodded and slipped through the door, opening it just enough for his narrow frame to pass through. A few moments later, when he was sure Peter would be in the dining room or kitchen with Sean, Danny did the same.

"The kettle's still hot. Will I wet the tea?" Sean slid the old iron kettle back onto the front of the coal stove, then leaned against the sink edge, taking up a small plate with bread and butter to continue eating.

"Thank you just the same, but I'll be getting back downstairs. I'm only meant to be dropping off a book for you."

Sean shrugged and slid the kettle to the back of the stove again. Through a mouthful of bread, he said, "Suit yourself. You've a parcel for me, so?"

Peter handed it over to Sean, who wiped his buttery fingers across the back of his trousers before accepting it. It weighed more than he'd expected from a book that size. He set the parcel on the drainboard and untied the string. The brown paper fell half-open, the edges standing up along the creases, revealing an octavo-sized volume of old Protestant sermons.

"You thought I'd need divine inspiration? Or is it converting me to the Church of Ireland you're after?" Sean said with a little laugh. He hadn't darkened the doors of any church, Catholic or Protestant, since Easter in 1916, having lost a good deal of religion in the rubble of the GPO.

"It was a size fitted for purpose. Couldn't very well be a law text and it had to be in English, since you don't read the Irish, as your mother well knows."

Flipping open the utilitarian brown cover, Sean's smile disappeared. Inside, set flush into a recess cut within the thick pages, nestled a blued revolver with a walnut grip, and below it, an indentation holding two dozen bullets.

"I was only told you'd be needing this," Peter said in a low and unnecessary whisper. "You're to receive further instructions in the usual manner. When they've a need for you."

Removing the gun from the book, Sean fumbled a little but managed to extend the cylinder, then snapped it back into place.

"I wasn't about to carry it about loaded," said Peter.

"Well, I'll not be able to say the same." Another little laugh. This time, Peter noticed the darting eyes that accompanied Sean's show of indifference to the danger they were both begging, a reminder that Sean Brannigan had just gone eighteen. He wasn't yet the hard man he pretended and that Peter would never be. Still, they'd both do their bit.

"Where will you keep it?" Peter said, noticing Danny sitting at the end of the dining table through the open doorway of the kitchen. He was doodling aimlessly in the back of an exercise book with a big blue pencil.

"Let's have a look, back in my room," said Sean. As he walked through the dining room toward the hall that ran to the back of the flat, he mussed Danny's hair a little and the boy swatted his hand away. At nine years old, he was of an age to resent having his hair tousled, especially by his own brother.

In the big back bedroom he shared with his brothers, Sean motioned to his corner with a narrow bed along the wall and a bookshelf running above. Peter recognized some of the books he'd given Sean filling one end, perhaps a third of the shelf all together. Sean slid the sermons between a pair of similarly sized books and stepped back. Nothing seemed out of the ordinary with the arrangement.

"I'll bring more books over the next few weeks. Best bring quite a few. You'll want that one to get lost in the clutter. Maybe bring you a few more religious tracts, so that one isn't the odd man out."

The two stood side by side, studying the bookshelf. "We'll need to think of what to tell your mother, you becoming such a sudden scholar."

Early Sunday evenings were a special time for Eda. With only a sprinkling of regulars lolling about, she and Peter Conway lingered at the end of the bar speaking Irish for a few hours. These sessions had begun upon an awkward request from Peter, seeking to improve his ear by speaking with someone born to the tongue, so he said. And Eda was a Donegal girl, with the unique and somewhat harsh way of speaking that came from her wild corner of the island.

Not that Eda ever ventured from the bar, such a thing being too frivolous to her way of thinking. So she kept up the pretense of work, giving the odd glass a twist in her towel or stacking a few beer mats now and again. The only exception to this self-imposed rule was when Eda sang in Irish. Early on, Eda had mentioned to Peter one of the dandling songs her mother sang, bouncing her younger sister, Nola, on her knee. When her mind wandered as she nursed her own firstborn in the small hours, Eda sang the old tunes, soft in the darkness so as not to wake her husband. Then she'd catch herself and switch to one in English picked up from Daniel's mother or the other women of the neighborhood. By the time Sean was born five years later, the Irish songs were fading like an old photograph and it cheered her to have a reason to reclaim them before they vanished entirely from her memory.

The men at the bar overheard her singing some bit of nonsense for Peter as part of a story she was sharing. As was right and proper in any pub, they demanded she sing for everyone. This seemed so much silliness to her, grown men wanting to hear a child's song. But with cajoling and encouragement from the patrons and little nods from Peter—him with the shameless adoring look about him—she relented.

The crowd of drinkers listened in rapt attention that first time. One or two wiped away tears for their own grannies who'd sung to them in the old tongue. She was near knocked to her knees by the thunderous clapping and cheering. Now a song or two from her in what Peter called the *sean-nós*—it being just singing to her—became the toll she paid to be left to her conversations with the quiet scholar at the end of the bar.

One of the regulars, an old mate of Daniel's from the brewery cooperage, called out from across the room, "Eda! Give us a song now! We won't be denied a moment longer!"

Another replied from the opposite corner, one of the wounded men from the regiment who often sat at the end of the long bench so he could leave his crippled leg extended. "Give us *A chuisle mo chroí*!"

"Get on with yourself, Charlie Maguire—you ask for that one every Sunday!" The others hooted poor Charlie down and he returned to his pint with an embarrassed smile.

"I've another that's just been given back to me in a letter from a dear old auntie in Donegal regardin' the flight of Bonnie Prince Charlie. It's an *aisling*, a kind of vision or a dream, called *Bimse buan ar buairt gach lo.* Which means 'every day I suffer grief'—or that'll be near enough for you ignorant heathens!"

Taking her accustomed spot in the center of the room as the men's laughter calmed, Eda smoothed down her apron and crossed her right arm over her chest, grasping her left high up by her shoulder, a pose that helped her with her nervousness when called upon to sing.

"*Sé mo laoch mo ghile mear…*"

The high nasal sound of her singing the haunting chorus seemed to Peter so unlike her speaking voice in Irish, but he knew it was the way these songs had long been sung. Hers was a strong voice, plain and straightforward, with none of the flittering ornaments he'd heard from singers up from Waterford or over from Connemara.

"*Sé mo Chaesar, ghile mear…*"

With a coat over his arm and a cap already on his head, Sean threw open the door at the top of the stairs. When he heard his mother singing in the Irish he understood not at all, he sat himself down on the third tread, below his little brother on his accustomed perch at the top stair.

"*Suan ná séan ní bhfuaireas féin…*"

Francis glanced up at Sean's broad smile as he nodded along with the song. Looking back to his younger brother again and again as Eda worked through five wistful verses, the tight-jawed look on Francis only deepened and reddened. The contrast between the brothers would have been all the more stark had either known how the tune lionized an earlier rebel seeking to topple an English king.

"*Ó chuaigh i gcéin mo ghile mear.*"

As Eda finished the chorus a final time, the men clapped their hands—some hardened with labor, others softer—with Sean adding whistles and cheers from the top of the stairs. Francis limped with angry purpose toward his mother as Sean gamboled down the staircase.

"You've a dozen and more thirsty men here, Mam. You're needed behind the bar," Francis said, taking his mother by the forearm. Some of the men at the back called for the forestalled *A chuisle mo chroí* and Sean joined with them as he made his way toward his mother.

"Come on, Mam. Give us just the one more?" he said, easing his brother's grip from her arm.

Peter Conway threaded his way through the knot of men surrounding Eda and stood behind Francis.

"That's enough of this nonsense," Francis said, elbowing Sean in the ribs to separate him from their mother. "She's work to do."

Sean pushed away Francis's arm and said, "Because you aren't able to lift a hand to draw a pint? Which is it, Francis? The peg leg or the gallons of whisky you throw down your gullet?"

"You don't understand a single word she's singin', but there you sit with your big Fenian grin. That's what you're about now, isn't it, Sean boy?"

Francis hitched round on his artificial limb, squaring up. Sean didn't give an inch, glaring back at his taller brother. The smell of whisky on Francis's breath infuriated Sean all the more.

"And what was it you were about, Francis? Runnin' off to do the biddin' of the bloody English? Gettin' Da killed and yourself butchered?" He pushed Francis's chest with one hand, tipping him back into Peter's arms. The quiet man helped Francis get his legs under him again.

Francis lunged at Sean, grabbing his sleeves and holding himself tight against him. Spitting with anger, he shouted, "You were out with those goddamned Sinn Feiners! Stabbed the men off to the fighting right in the back, you ungrateful bastard! I wish they'd stood you up against that wall in Kilmainham Gaol and shot you along with the rest."

"Francis! For the love of God!" Eda's words carried sharp as a flute over the rumble of muttering men.

His face twisted in unthinking rage, Sean threw a wide punch that caught Francis square on the left cheek, knocking him sideways. A couple of men caught him before he hit the sawdust-strewn floor.

"It's not over, Francis. Not by a long shot. We'll have our nation yet. And the English out for good!"

Peter Conway grabbed Sean by the arm and hustled him toward the door, saying in an uncharacteristically loud voice, "Best out the door with you, Sean. There's no call for you to distress your mother as you've done."

As they reached the door, Peter hissed into Sean's ear, "We can't have another scene like this. You mustn't draw such attention to yourself."

And with that, Peter shoved the new gunman out the door.

CHAPTER SEVEN

———◆———

Ned

The speck on the ordnance maps known as Glenador consisted of a police station with two Royal Irish Constables, a mouldering fieldstone post office, a tiny pub just large enough to hold the resident drinkers, a single-room schoolhouse, and an unremarkable parish church built in the decades following the Catholic Emancipation. A half-dozen houses of various sizes and degree of upkeep filled the spaces between the public buildings.

Jesus, what've I let myself in for?

Ned Tobin was a Boston man born and bred, and therefore accustomed to the crowds and smells of a big city. But Glenador was where his father had been born and, more to the point, his grandfather's farm lay less than a mile to the east. That's where he'd determined to go, trying to shake the restlessness and irritability that had followed him home from the war.

Not knowing a better place to start, he walked toward the post office carrying his battered valise, the one he'd bought after being made an officer in 1916. A man of forty—perhaps more, possibly less—sat on a wooden bench that hadn't seen a touch of paint in years, puffing on a short pipe. The man glanced through his smoke at Ned, then returned to his musings.

Ned set his suitcase outside a break in the low stone wall, a blank space where a gate might have once swung, and stepped through. The man smoked on.

"Morning."

The smoker glanced up again and said, "'Tis that, indeed." He extracted the pipe from his lips, examined the bowl for longer than seemed necessary to Ned, then tapped it against the end of the bench. A little shower of ash and sparks settled onto the packed clay.

"But what else would it be, not yet gone half ten?" He slid the pipe into his coat pocket and stared up at Ned with an impish quizzical face, quite pleased with his little joke. "What might I do for ye, friend?"

"I'm Ned Tobin, just arrived from America."

"Tobin, is't?"

"Yes, sir. My father was born here about. Emmett Tobin."

"Well now, that makes you altogether more interesting," said the man, heaving himself up and extending a hand for a proper greeting. "Jimmy Clancy. Of the Clancy clan, the half of this village you'll not be related to. But don't get any designs on my sisters or nieces, if you please."

Ned took the offered hand and said, "Did you know my father, before he left for America?"

"Bah! How old do you take me for? Or do you not age so fast as us in Amerikay?" The postmaster slapped Ned's shoulder with a rolling laugh that must have originated far below his knees. "But I do recall my da and my uncles mentioning an Emmett Tobin they used to run with as lads, before he went away over the sea. Course, I knew your granddad right well. I was one of the pallbearers carried him to his rest behind the church there. I'll show you his grave, right next to your grandmam, if you've a mind."

Ned took out a packet of Woodbines, the harsh English cigarettes he'd grown accustomed to smoking in the trenches after he'd rushed north to volunteer with the Newfoundlanders in 1914. He offered one to Jimmy Clancy, who shook his head and patted the pipe in his pocket.

Ned drew on his cigarette and looked over the village.

It'll take some getting used to.

He exhaled a slow stream from his nostrils and turned back to the bemused Jimmy. "I'd like to see my cousin Kevin Tobin, if you know where I might find him? My father wrote ahead and I'm hoping he'll help me get settled with the farm."

Jimmy's bemusement bloomed into outright chuckling and he said, "You'll be takin' up the farm, so? If you don't mind me sayin', you seem a little citified to make much of a farmer, Ned Tobin."

Ned drew again on his cigarette to quell his rising annoyance. "We'll find out soon enough. Where can I find my cousin Kevin, if it's not too much of a bother?"

"Well, in addition to bein' a cousin, yer man Kevin is the schoolmaster. This bein' a Tuesday, I'd expect he's at the schoolhouse yonder." Jimmy motioned across the small village green. "I'd suggest you go have a few pints and a ploughman's plate over to the pub. I'll send Kevin along, soon as he dismisses the children."

Ned crushed his cigarette against the mossy stones of the low wall and said, "I'd be very grateful, Mr. Clancy." He reached down to grip the suitcase, reseated his fedora, and turned toward the pub a few doors down.

"You'll need to give a good pound on the door. Owner's deaf as a stone and it's not quite openin' time. I don't reckon the coppers will give him much trouble about it, what with you bein' a Yank and new to our ways."

The ancient owner of the nameless pub was as hard of hearing as the postmaster had promised. What little he comprehended triggered responses rendered unintelligible to Ned by the man's thick accent and paucity of teeth. There being little chance of meaningful discourse, Ned contented himself with a few pints while picking at the tired meat and stale bread that constituted his lunch.

He'd moved from the bar to a small table under the single window, its mullions filled with wavy glass from some earlier century. Pushing away the ploughman's plate half-eaten, he languished like an old cat in the late morning sunlight, watching the smoke from his cigarettes twist and swirl with the pub's dust.

Ned was snapped from his pleasant stupor by the universal sound of schoolboys released from their confinement, shouting and laughing as they dodged and wrestled on the little green outside the window. The girls followed in two tight clutches, giggling and pointing as the boys acted out all the more for the girls' sake. After all the children had flushed from the schoolhouse like startled sparrows, a slender man a few years older than Ned and with the same black hair and pale skin of Ned's father stepped through the open schoolhouse door, then pulled it closed behind him. He didn't fish for a key, there being no call for such distrustful ways in east Tipperary. He stepped across the green toward the post office where Jimmy Clancy was once again ensconced like a baronial lion on his ramshackle bench.

The men conversed a few moments—or rather Jimmy talked and Kevin nodded—the postmaster gesticulating toward the pub and Kevin's impassive eyes following the stabs of Jimmy's pipe stem. Kevin waved a backhand parting as he ambled over the green. Encountering a pair of boys whose wrestling had grown a little testy, he separated them and continued toward the pub.

When he entered, the deaf publican said in a loud voice that startled in the close space, "Well, here y'are, then, Master Tobin!" The old barman gave Ned a deliberate look, then pointed Kevin over with raised white eyebrows and a long sideways nod.

The schoolmaster stood staring at the American for a long few seconds, then set himself on a nearby stool and resumed his silent inspection. More awkward seconds past while Ned sat, back against the window frame and legs crossed, smoking his latest cigarette.

"You're my cousin Edmund?" said Kevin, more declaration than question.

Sitting up, Ned stubbed his cigarette in a rusty jar lid, then reached his hand across the table with a wide smile.

"I am, though most call me Ned."

The newfound cousin shook Ned's hand and said, "Kevin." Neither his gaze nor his unsmiling lips varied while he spoke the two syllables.

Couldn't be from the same blood. No Tobin's this stingy with words, Ned thought.

"Well, you're well met, Cousin Kevin. As I'm sure was the same with you, I grew up hearing endless tales of our fathers' incorrigible childhood."

"Somewhat," said Kevin. As if fulfilling minimal good manners for the occasion, he forced out, "Condolences for your granddad—he was good to me and mine."

With an entire sentence between them, Ned expanded the conversation. "You've had a letter from my father, explaining my plan for taking up the farm?"

A slow nod.

"I'm hoping you've someone in mind who can help me work the place, get the stables stocked again?"

"Aye."

"Would he be another cousin?" Ned hadn't the slightest notion, but thought this might chivvy up a more informative reply.

"No. A McNamara."

Jesus, like pulling teeth with this one.

Ned reached for the cigarette packet and his old trench lighter on the table. He tapped a few halfway out and offered one to Kevin, who shook his head.

Lighting his cigarette, Ned noticed through the smoke that Kevin was distracted by something outside the window. Whatever was outside was far less interesting than watching the change creeping over his cousin's face. The stony expression, cold and impenetrable as a funerary statue, unknotted and melted into a little smile. Nothing big and toothy, but coupled with the wrinkles of delight at the corners of his dark eyes, a dramatic change nonetheless.

As someone pulled on the iron handle, Kevin rose and turned toward the heavy plank door. With a big heave against the weight, in stepped a short woman topped with a riot of flyaway nut-brown hair.

She smiled up at Kevin and squeezed his arm, then turned to the barkeep and shouted, "How's she cuttin' today, Neill?"

Showing a gummy smile, he said, "Oh, well enough, Maire. No use in complainin' regardless."

"Right enough, Neill. Right enough," she bellowed back.

Pleasantries dispensed, she turned her full attention to Kevin. "Brian McNamara's just been by with one of his sons—those boys are longer every time I see them, I swear—says he's some matters to discuss regardin' Charlie Tobin's farm—God rest his soul. With no tellin' when that cousin from America will turn up, you'll need to…"

She stopped when Kevin nodded her attention toward Ned.

With bottom lip out and eyebrows knit, Maire sized up the seated man leaning against the window frame, scrutinizing Ned with forensic intensity. Realization returned her face to its previous reckless animation, relaunching her conversation.

"Saints preserve us, this must be the man himself! I'd know the look of a Tobin anywhere. You're not one of the black Tobins, like this quiet one here, but a Tobin, sure as I'm standin' here! Edmund, is it?"

Ned rose and said, taking her hand lightly, "Please call me Ned. Only my ma called me Edmund, and only when she'd a need to take a strap to me."

Maire studied him a little again and said, "You've the look of your granddad about you—not his twin, mind you, but you take after him well enough."

She set herself on the stool vacated by her husband, then glanced at the table. With a look of mock outrage, she turned on her taciturn husband and slapped at his leg. "Why, you didn't even offer the man a drink? You'd do as much for a total stranger, let alone a long-lost cousin!"

Although women were still a rarity in town pubs, even after loosening the old rules during the war, that sort of city fussiness never penetrated to tiny pubs in rural places like east Tipperary, so Maire wasn't the least hesitant to order drinks. Shouting at the old publican again, she said, "I'll have my half cider and my man will have a small whisky, this early in the day. I'll wager, bein' a Tobin man, Cousin Ned will have a whisky, too?" The last she said over her shoulder with an eye on Ned.

"A whisky would suit me fine."

Kevin joined her at the bar to carry back the drinks. Ned saw no money change hands, although the barman scribbled in a little book on the back shelf. Maire returned to the table with her cider, Kevin in step behind her with a whisky in each hand.

After they'd settled, Maire raised her glass and said, "Here's to the whole Tobin clan, whichever side of the ocean or the turf they might be!"

Maire took a healthy sip, set down her cider, and slapped both palms into her lap. "Well, since it's as certain as the sunrise you got little useful information out of this one"—she patted her husband's knee, then jabbed a kissed on his cheek—"what might I be answerin' for you?"

Ned was growing fond of this new acquaintance, so much like the women of his own family in Boston. He sipped his whisky and said, "Kevin mentioned he'd found someone to help run the farm. Would that be the McNamara you mentioned?"

"The very man—Brian McNamara. And he's two strappin' boys near to manhood, though the Lord knows how he keeps them. They feed like locusts. Pity the girls they marry, havin' to fill those bottomless pits. Two hollow legs, the each of 'em."

Kevin sat silent, the airiest smile creasing the corners of his mouth. His eyes remained fixed on his wife, noting every word. With a little pang of sadness, the pair conjured in Ned a memory of his parents, back before the war, before his mother had taken ill the last time. His father was never as quiet as Kevin, but he'd the same adoring look about him whenever she was near at hand.

"Are you listenin' to me at all, Ned Tobin?"

Snapped back, he realized he'd wandered longer than was polite. He flashed a smile and attended to his whisky, eyes purposefully on Maire.

"So we'll fetch Brian McNamara, if he doesn't stop for a pint first, before he heads home. That's his horse and wagon, other side of the church."

"I've been out to the farm myself and tidied the house," Maire said. "We've turned the mattress in the front bedroom and you've fresh linens, so there's a place to sleep. I put a basket of turf on the kitchen hearth and some tins in the cupboard. You'll need to nose about and see what's what—plenty of daylight left for that. We'll sort your cookin' and cleanin' later."

With no more reason than that she'd stopped talking, Maire poked another kiss onto Kevin's cheek. He reached into her lap and squeezed her hand, leaving it covered with his own. She looked up at Kevin with an altogether different smile, comfortable and deep, then smoothed down a few hairs protruding from a cowlick at the back of his head.

Ned was content to watch, lighting another cigarette and filling the companionable silence with his smoke.

Maire peered over her husband's shoulder and out the little window. "There's the very man himself."

Ned glanced through the glass and watched the broad shoulders of Brian McNamara, beside one of his lanky and ravenous sons, striding across the village green.

CHAPTER EIGHT

Eda

Eda had become quite adept at spotting a military man whenever one found his way to her pub. Of course, The Gallant Fusilier was a favorite of veterans from the Dubs, her husband's and son's old regiment. Men from other units soon discovered the place and came in search of a sympathetic ear or a few of the old songs. They'd tidied up the lyrics, her daughter Deirdre having informed Eda many of the tunes had the most profane words in their native form. With this secret out, Eda chuckled at the many insertions of "bloomin'" and "blessed." The men knew full well she wouldn't tolerate the originals in her respectable establishment.

They were well into the high summer of 1919 when, on a Thursday afternoon, Eda noted a young man step through the door whom she pegged as an officer. The place wasn't crowded with evening regulars, just a few of the more needy or bored. The new arrival looked about the place, then walked to the bar, removing his hat as he made his unhurried way.

"Well now, welcome to The Gallant, Lieutenant," Eda said with a touch of devilment. "Or is it Captain?"

The newcomer pulled up short.

"I beg your pardon?"

"You're not old enough for a major, even in the terrible war just finished," Eda said. "What will you be havin' today?"

He hung his hat on one of the hooks under the bar and, still thrown a little off-kilter, said, "A small whisky… and the soda siphon, please."

She poured the drink and hooked a finger under the spout of a green-glass siphon, setting both before the young customer. "That'll be ten pence, but we'll settle up before you leave."

Eda took up her habitual wiping. The newcomer pulsed soda into his glass then took a long sip.

"What gave you the idea I was an officer, if I may be so bold?"

The glass in her hand squeaked dry as she twisted. She set the clean glass in line with a dozen others on a shelf behind the bar.

"I've seen quite a few of your comrades pass through here, all ranks. It's the stride and the set of the shoulders give it away. And officers have a particular walk, unhurried like. They must've taught you to move as if you weren't afraid. We'll see if you still walk the same in 1940, when I'm old and grey and you've a fine paunch."

The new patron watched Eda through narrowed eyes, his smile tentative, until he could determine if she was taking her fun at his expense. After a long pause, he gave a soft chuckle and said, "Lieutenant, I'm afraid. Lieutenant Desmond O'Connell. I was with the Royal Inniskilling Fusiliers."

"With a last name to conjure with—that of The Emancipator himself!" As was ever her custom, Eda reached across the bar and introduced herself. "Eda Brannigan, proprietress of The Gallant Fusilier. And you're always welcome here, Desmond O'Connell, even if the pub is named for the Royal *Dublin* Fusiliers. My son and late husband both served with the Dubs at Gallipoli."

She'd refilled his glass while they talked. He took up the siphon again and said, "A terrible thing, Gallipoli."

"A tragedy for this family. My Daniel fell on the beach and lies in the rocky ground there still. My son lost his leg as well. Thanks be to God, he came back to me, luckier than his own dear father." Having recounted her sad history many times over the four years since her husband fell to the Turks, it had lost much of its sting. In the small hours of the morning, she might still shed a tear for her Daniel. Not so often now.

The front doors flung open and a pair of men stepped through.

"Fine day, isn't it? After the showers this morning?" said the first.

"And not over-warm for July," she replied to the one who always commented upon the weather.

"I smell a change in the wind, and we'd a red sky at sunrise, so it's like to change to rain soon enough," the man said with great seriousness.

"I'm sufferin' a powerful thirst, Mrs. Brannigan! Save me before I turn to a very pile of dust!" said the other.

"Ach, there's little chance of you dryin' up this side of the grave, Joe," she threw back, knowing of his prodigious tippling.

There was no need for orders—she knew theirs and they never varied. As she bustled about drawing a pint of porter and pouring a large navy rum—the Weatherman having spent a few years before the mast in the Merchant Marine—Eda said, "And this fine young gentleman is Mr. Desmond O'Connell, or rather Lieutenant O'Connell, late of His Majesty's Royal Inniskilling Fusiliers. I'll leave you to make your introductions, before you commence extracting free drinks from him."

The two new arrivals lifted their glasses to Desmond, who returned the honors. They slid down the bar and settled on either side of the newcomer.

Again the door opened with deliberate purpose and, with an even gait, in strode a man in a dark jacket and a blue window-pane waistcoat. The two regulars turned in silence as their eyes followed him to the far end of the bar, nearest the front windows.

The Weatherman leaned close to Desmond and muttered, "That's the Pintman. The light is best near the windows."

Eda drew a pint of porter with conspicuous care and set it with ceremonial flair before the new arrival, then turned back to her chores without a word. The man in the blue waistcoat stared off in the direction of the back wall, but in truth he was a thousand miles away. Small tan bubbles slid up the inside of his glass, clouding the dark beer and disappearing into the lathery head.

"Patience is the mark of a true pintman," said the Tippler.

"No pint must be touched before its time," added the Weatherman.

Desmond glanced down the bar with bemusement and whispered back, "Does he ever speak?"

The Weatherman took a long drink of his rum, then wiped a wrist across his mouth. "Oh, he's right friendly after a pint."

"But that first pint is his religion," said the Tippler. "And none dare disturb him 'til he's done with his prayers."

The Pintman took up the glass and held it at eye level as he scrutinized the head and determined that the beer was well settled. He then held the glass up to the light coming through the front windows.

"Now, many a man will tell you that porter—or your stout, as some would have it—is black or the darkest brown," whispered the Weatherman. "But as the Pintman himself has proven, your authentic Irish porter is the deepest shade of a ruby red."

Desmond's curiosity overcame his breeding and he stared down the bar in unvarnished delight.

Setting the glass back down in the exact spot Eda had first placed it, the Pintman gazed upon it for what seemed a very long time. Then pulling back his shoulders, he placed the tips of his fingers on the barrel of the glass and lifted it to his lips.

"He claims," said the Weatherman, "you should never allow your palm to touch the glass. It overheats the beer, so."

As the glass reached the Pintman's lips, the two commentators fell into a reverent silence. The Pintman took a long, deep draught, closed his eyes, and swallowed. A third of the beer was gone. The Pintman loosed a deep sigh and opened his eyes, a languid, beatific look about him. He set the pint down and stared off again.

Desmond shook his head in smiling disbelief. The Tippler noticed the newcomer's skepticism and said, "The pint is a thing of powerful importance to your serious pintman, lad, and 'tis not something to be made sport of."

Desmond rushed to say, "Of course... I didn't mean... he just seems so content with something as simple as a pint."

"We'll introduce you, then, once he's done with his prayers," said the Weatherman with a paternal wink and slap on the shoulder, "now that you've demonstrated the proper respect."

The two regulars raised their near-empty glasses again and Desmond returned the salute, receiving the intended message that the price for their commentary would be to stand a round.

Waving over Eda, Desmond said, "The same again, for myself and my new friends, if you please."

Near the bottom of his second pint and thereby reducing his risk of spontaneous combustion for another few hours, the Tippler said, "Now that you've a drink or two in ye, lad, we'll be hearin' yer story— life, death, and miracles." Both men stood waiting for the immediate intimacy any Dubliner would provide under similar circumstances.

Now's the test, he thought.

"Well, Mam's people are from Cork City," he said.

"You've not the sound of a Corkman, boy-o," said the Tippler, studying him a little closer.

"Indeed you do not," said the Weatherman with pursed lips. "I'd pin you as an Ulsterman."

Not going to make this easy, are they?

"Well, you've a fine ear," said Desmond. "Da's folk are from north Tyrone and that's where I came up."

"Ah, well that explains it, then," said the Weatherman with a satisfied nod.

"Indeed," said the Tippler, flicking an ash into the sawdust, then draining his third pint. Wacthing the residue lacing down the sides of his glass, he added, "Not so many O'Connells up north, I'd have thought?"

Desmond caught Eda's eye and twirled a finger. The older men's faces brightened, wiped clean of lingering suspicions by the prospect of another round.

"Da worked the farm my granddad left him, and taught school as well. Mam came into some money when an old auntie of hers passed down in Youghal. She divvied half to Da for a fine breeding bull and half to send me to four years of boarding school in England."

He looked each man square in the face without so much as a blink. "So, there you have it. Mam thought to make an English gentleman of me and all I got was a commission in the trenches and a bit of posh sneaking into my speech."

When the next round arrived, the others seem to lose interest in further interrogation as they attended to their drinks. Having successfully buried Thomas Piers-Musgrave for the time being, the newly minted Desmond O'Connell lifted his glass and settled in for the afternoon. He was certain he could match watered-down whiskies with these two for hours.

The routine at The Gallant continued apace, as familiar and comforting to its owner as an old worn chair by the fireside. Francis had limped in just past five with his jerky gait, throwing his artificial limb forward with each step. He joined his mother behind the bar, giving her a little surge of relief that he hadn't gone for the whisky right off.

"If you'd wipe down the bottles on the shelves, Francis, that would be grand," Eda said, extracting a clean towel from a shelf under the till and holding it out to him. "They're dusty as a miller and we can't have that in The Gallant, can we?"

"No, Mam," he said, flashing his mother a smile. "Inspection order at all times."

She draped an arm round his waist and pressed against him. He patted the back of her hand, then shook her off by reaching for a green bottle of tawny port and turning it in his cloth. Francis leaned a hip against the back counter, easing a little weight off the stump of his leg. It always throbbed when he'd been out walking, pressing down into the ill-fitted prosthesis with each step.

Eda turned and surveyed the room. More men had arrived in twos and threes, a few seated on the red horsehair bench running along the wall opposite her. The upholstery was faded from its original deep crimson, but the material was hearty as boot leather and cleaned up well enough.

Danny had crept in after a few hours back with his friends in the old neighborhood. Eda glimpsed him back on his perch, sitting in the shadows above the illumination that spilled from the light fixtures. She reckoned the flat was lonely during opening hours and the boy seemed to be doing little harm to himself watching the activity in the pub. Besides, having him nearby was reassuring, knowing he wasn't mixed up in any Sinn Fein nonsense like his brother. Danny was surely too young for that sort of thing, having just turned ten.

She ran a palm across her forehead and round the back of her neck, then tucked a few loose hairs behind an ear. One of the men from the bench made his way to the bar and handed over two empties just as Eda heard the snick of the door latch above her. She took the two pint glasses and began filling one with a long draw on the polished handle of a beer pump, glancing up as she worked.

Danny scooted down a few steps and pressed himself against the plaster. Molly stepped through to the landing, a small book tucked in one elbow, and pulled the door closed. She touched Danny's dark hair with the tips of her fingers as she stepped past, scratching his scalp until he looked up and gave her a crooked smile.

Desmond O'Connell, feigning attention to some lie being spun out by the Tippler, watched with noticeable intensity as Molly descended. Eda watched his eyes jerk downward with each fall of Molly's boot on a tread. The shorter skirts brought on by the war still remained the fashion, with half of Molly's dark-stockinged calves visible.

The regulars had learned not to stare when Eda's faerie-daughter appeared. Even the younger ones who came to drink with Francis knew better. But all of them, young and old, admired their Molly, who raised a smile and a sigh whenever she floated down the narrow stairs and brightened the smoky barroom. She was seventeen now, with so many good years ahead of her—even mention of university, if you can imagine such a thing. But hadn't the war turned the world upside down?

With her hair in a haphazard chignon and the faraway half-smile she often wore, Molly slipped behind the bar and weaved past her brother. When she reached the squat brass till, she bent at the knees, as the sisters had scolded her to always do since her first days at school. She slipped a slender finger, almost translucent in the weak yellow light, through the metal ring pull in a small cupboard door.

Being a newcomer to The Gallant, Desmond was unconstrained in his staring. He watched every move of the young woman who'd appeared behind the bar, gentle as a night fog creeping in off the river. As she fished into the small cabinet, he saw a quick flash of the polished brass ring encircling one slender finger. He raised the watered-down whisky to his lips and swallowed the lump that had risen in his throat.

Desmond offered cigarettes to the two regulars with philanthropic rapidity. At the third succession, he finally came up short.

"Well, I'll be needing to buy more fags," said Desmond with the easy and confident look of a man who knows he has the much fatter wallet. "Where can a fella find some tobacco?"

It was an unnecessary question, since he'd watched the fair-haired girl sell cigarettes in packets or loose twos and threes to a half-dozen customers. He'd also noted after each sale she turned back to a pocket-sized book bound in royal-blue buckram, the late summer sun backlighting her through the windows.

The Tippler hooked a thumb over his shoulder toward the door. The Weatherman, with greater sobriety than his companion, said, "Why, just ask our Molly, there by the door. She always has the Woodbines." He then added with helpful self-interest, "And always something finer, too. Usually the Player's Mediums." He punctuated this by tapping his finger alongside his nose, manifesting his opinion as to which would be the proper choice.

"Molly would be the fair colleen at the counter?" Desmond said, grateful for the knowledge of her name.

"The very one," slurred the Weatherman, the strong rum reeking from him. "Younger of the two handsome Brannigan girls." He stole a look down the bar to confirm Eda was not within earshot of his impertinent remark on her daughters' persons.

Taking temporary leave of the boozy conclave, Desmond tugged at the cuffs of his suit jacket to pull out some of the wrinkles from two hours' leaning on the bar as he strolled over to the little counter behind which Molly sat, her nose and all her attention inside the small volume open in her palms.

"That must be a story of great interest."

Molly startled at his voice and a rapid flush bloomed in her cheeks, but her airy smile returned as she closed the book. When she looked up, her eyes widened and darted in small glances, not sure where to settle, as she pulled in her lips and swallowed.

"I... I like to read while I'm at the counter," she said in a voice that carried to him and no farther. She held up the book in both her hands, as if making an offering to the comely stranger standing so close.

Desmond leaned in to read the engraved title on the cloth cover. His closeness renewed her pink flush.

"Shakespeare? And no less than *Hamlet*?"

She nodded, encouraged by his interest.

"Mr. Conway lets me borrow his books. He has all thirty-seven of Shakespeare's plays in these pocket editions," she said all at once, holding the book a little closer. He reached for it, brushing the back of his fingers in her palm as he lifted the book. Her face burned crimson.

"It's finely crafted." He riffled through the pages and added, "With some engravings as well."

She retrieved the book taking care not to touch his hand. "Yes, they're lovely. Although the artist doesn't see Ophelia as I do," she said in a throaty whisper. "In my imagination, I mean."

"Is Mr. Conway one of your masters?"

Setting the book in her lap, Molly took a deep breath to clear her head and cool her cheeks. She settled herself and said, louder this time, "No, he is not." This gave her a boost of confidence, and she continued in as businesslike a tone as she could manage. "Mr. Conway comes to The Gallant quite regularly. He speaks Irish with Mam—with my mother—and has become quite dear to my family as a result."

She gazed back at Desmond with all the appearance of placid composure. She couldn't still the throbbing in her chest, but he wouldn't hear that through all the hubbub in the pub.

"Your mother is an Irish speaker?"

"Mam came up in Donegal. She made her way here to Dublin when she was near to my age. She was in service with a grand family in Merrion Square when she met my father. They married and she never gave another thought to leaving."

Hoping her knees would support her, Molly rose from her creaky stool and folded her hands at her waist. "Is there something you need, sir? That brought you to my counter?"

"I don't require your name, Molly, since the gentlemen at the bar provided that already." She willed away the blushing as he gave her another wide and lovely smile.

"Then you have me at a disadvantage, sir," said Molly, straining to sound like her cocksure sister, Deirdre, away in Canada.

"Well, there being no one at hand to do the honours, I hope you'll not take offense," he said, bowing from the waist, "Desmond O'Connell, at your very service, Miss Brannigan."

She blinked several times, then bowed her head in reply. "I'm pleased to make your acquaintance, Mr. O'Connell. Like The Emancipator?"

"The very man, as your mother noted earlier," he said, cocking an eyebrow. "Sadly, him having such a fine statue and bridge, we are of no known relation."

"'Tis a grand name nonetheless, Mr. O'Connell. Now, what would you be needing?"

"To call me Desmond—or Des, as my sisters do." He tipped his head toward the shelf, not taking his eyes from hers. "And a packet of cigarettes, if I must buy something to keep this conversation from ending."

Refusing to be flustered like a silly schoolgirl—although she was just that, albeit of a more serious stripe—she replied, "I've Woodbines, four pence for ten. Or you might prefer Player's? They're ten-and-a-half for twenty."

"Well, seeing as how my new friends…"

He couldn't have seen Eda steaming across the crowded pub after catching a glimpse of the goings-on at the sundries counter. And Molly had no desire to see anything but Desmond.

"Molly, I'll be needin' you to make your little brother's tea," Eda said, with a notable absence of good humor. "Upstairs."

Her disappointment evident from the pouting round her mouth, Molly said, "Yes, Mam. Mr. O'Connell here was needing cigarettes." She wedged the blue book in her elbow and padded up the stairs. She took Danny's hand and lifted him to his feet, then disappeared behind the door.

Molly had left a packet of Player's Mediums on the counter. Eda studied the sailor's head on the label and traced a finger round the ring buoy. Desmond stood rubbing a shilling between his thumb and finger. He noticed it was a Victoria coin, the old queen's profile and coronet worn and indistinct. When he flipped it, the shields were unrecognizable, the denomination and date faint but legible.

After standing too long in awkward silence, Desmond said, "Molly said they're ten-and-a-half, Mrs. Brannigan."

Eda continued tracing the cigarette pack, running her fingertip over the waves and round the lettering. Then she stopped and fixed Desmond with an inscrutable stare.

"You shouldn't let those two take advantage of your good nature, Mr. O'Connell," she said, more formal than she'd yet been since he first walked through her door. "Unless you're heir to the throne, they'll drink your pockets empty, if you allow it."

"I'll watch myself, ma'am, and thank you for the warning. I thought, being a new boy, that I ought to stand a few rounds. 'Twas what we did to each new arrival in France, I'm afraid, shameless as we were." He gave Eda the same endearing smile that had melted her daughter moments before.

"My dear husband died a sergeant-major, Mr. O'Connell, and I'm certain he'd not have allowed such foolishness on his watch," Eda said, reminding him her family had done their part, too.

"And now that I've kindly warned you off buying endless drinks for the regulars," she said, "I'd like you to give my daughter a wide berth, if you please."

Snatching the shilling from his hand, she tossed it into the cash box and slapped the lid closed with no intention of making change. Before Desmond could protest his innocent intentions, she was back behind the bar pulling a pint.

The chastened Desmond returned to the company of his well-lubricated new friends, and Molly resumed her duties at the front counter after leaving a mug of tea and two slices of bread with potted meat for Danny. With her nose back in *Hamlet*, she stole glances at Desmond whenever the expanding group of drinkers shuffled and rearranged itself, leaving quick gaps with a clear view to the bar. Eda's attention was on Desmond, too, and rather less fawning. When she'd satisfied herself he'd gotten her message and would behave, she returned to her wiping and pouring, totting and collecting. With a new small whisky and large soda, Desmond submitted himself with good humor to the inevitable commentary on his chatting-up Molly and brush with Eda.

The Tippler set his pint down after a pair of long gulps and said, "You've received your baptism by fire in The Gallant, lad. Best mind yourself for a few days, but Eda's not one to hold a grudge. Assuming, of course, that we'll be seein' you again?"

This perked up the Weatherman, shaking off his inebriated lassitude to reinforce the Tippler's interest in making the young man with the deep pockets a regular of the establishment. Squinting through his rummy haze, he said, "Course he'll be returnin'! Haven't we been... so very..."

"...very hospitable this fine day," said the Tippler.

He turned and revealed the Pintman, who'd slid beside him unnoticed by the others. Having long finished his lonely prayers over two glasses of porter, the Pintman was quite sociable and added his expert opinion, "'Tis a fine pub for the pint. You'd do worse in many another."

Desmond knew this bonhomie was steeped in self-interest, but as both the newest and soberest member of the group, he played along.

"I've every intention of being a regular, gentlemen," he said, jerking his head over his shoulder toward the front door, followed by a showy wink. He stole a glance down the bar to ensure Eda hadn't seen.

The other men's agreement came in forced and throaty chuckles to prove they hadn't lost all prurient interest in a pretty face or a fine ankle. The Tippler slapped Desmond's back with a big, heavy hand while the others nodded concurrence. The mild ribaldry was interrupted by a syncopation of greetings weaving through the crowd of men behind them.

"Look what the cat's dragged in!"

"Yer man, Sean Brannigan himself!"

Desmond turned to watch the new arrival. Like an unassuming Moses parting a sea of thirsty bodies, a young man of slight build, shorter than most of those round him, ran the gauntlet of backslaps and off-hand greetings, making his way to the end of the bar opposite Desmond. His workaday smile broadened as he reached his mother and kissed her cheek. Eda smoothed down his dark hair as she'd done most every day of his life, while Sean twisted a cloth cap in his hands with the residual embarrassment of an eighteen-year-old passing into manhood.

"Now, here's a fine surprise to brighten the day," Eda said. "I don't suppose you're here to help at the bar?"

She didn't mean much by this, since Sean was diligent in his morning duties and never complained about the dirtiest chores left from the night before. He'd even taken on replenishing the sawdust in a big biscuit tin the shawlies had stashed in their usual snug. Since the jacks at The Gallant consisted of a single porcelain pan over the drain in the middle of the open cellar, even the men hesitated to use it after dark, preferring anonymity in the back alley. The ladies had by necessity devised their own facilities, hauling in a foot-square Jacob's biscuit tin and half-filling it with sawdust scraped from off the floor. Tucked into the corner of their snug, they could squat with skirts draped down and relieve themselves with a little modesty and much convenience. Sean added the biscuit tin to his morning routine and never spoke a word about it.

Sean treated his mother to another unaffected grin. She kissed his cheek and said, "Danny's just had his tea, but the kettle's still warm, I'm sure, and there's a tin of potted meat opened. Go fix yourself something, so at least I'll know you've not gone hungry all day."

"I could use a mouthful. Maybe have a chat with Danny, too."

This brightened Eda and she said, "That would be grand. He sees so little of you, Sean. And you know how he looks up to you."

He nodded, kissed his mother's cheek a third time, and trotted up the narrow stairs, disappearing into the rooms above.

Down the bar, Desmond asked the Weatherman, "That was Molly's brother?"

"Aye, that it was. Sean Brannigan, Eda's second son," said the Weatherman, producing a pipe from an inner coat pocket, there not being cigarettes currently on offer. "He was just shy of fourteen when his father fell. Terrible age for a lad… to lose his da… like that." He drew a fat pinch of tobacco from a leather pouch, stained black with years of handling, and tucked the flakes with some effort into the bowl. "Not that there's any good age… for losin' a father."

Having achieved a loose-tongued but intelligible stasis in his drinking, the Weatherman seemed the most reliable source. Desmond closed the distance between them, leery of Eda overhearing. The other drinkers were too deep in their cups to care or remember what was spoken.

"Must have been a terrible age to live through all that fighting in '16, too? What with the shelling and sniping?" Desmond sipped his watered-down whisky and looked over the glass as the teetering Weatherman struck a lucifer under the bar edge and struggled to introduce it to his pipe.

The older man pulled hard and a long blue flame from the wooden match disappeared and reappeared with the exaggerated bellowing of his inebriated cheeks. The Weatherman spat into the sawdust, having sucked down some tarry residue with his prodigious puffing. He gulped a little amber rum to clear the foul taste.

"Oh, 'twas a terrible time for all... every man, woman... and child in... in all of Dublin." The Weatherman gave a few slow, deep nods. "And young Sean... caught up in it. Near killed his... his dear mother there." He pointed at Eda drying glasses by the beer pumps. Desmond noted that Francis had left off dusting bottles and was back amidst a group of four or five men, whisky in hand, conversing with animation.

"Our Sean... well, he fell in with... with the rebels at the Post Office," said the Weatherman. "Bein' so young and... and... what's it they say? Impressable?"

"Impressionable?" said Desmond.

"The very word! Young Sean bein' so... impressable as he was. But wouldn't many a boy... what with the excitement and... and the thrill of danger?"

Desmond nodded agreement and waited to see if the older man would continue, but he stared off and puffed at his pipe.

"He must've gotten clear of all that soon enough, once the Army arrived and the real shooting started?"

Withdrawing his pipe long enough to down the remaining rum, the Weatherman said, "Not our Sean... made of sterner stuff... his father's son, that one. No, no. He was out on... on Easter Monday and no one saw hide... nor... nor hair of him. Not until... oh, when did he return? Friday was't?"

"'Twas Saturday... in the afternoon," said the Tippler in a burst of lucidity, settling back on his elbow with half-closed eyes.

Holding off for the moment on another round, Desmond said, "What would the Fenians be doing with a boy for what, five long days?"

"I hear tell all manner o' things... Runnin' messages and... and carryin' the ammunition and such. Never heard our Sean went about... with a rifle or pistol. Least not so as the Castle... or the Army would've known."

Desmond signaled to Eda for another round. She soon arrived with a whisky and a small rum in one hand, a pint of porter in the other, omitting a drink for the barley-conscious Tippler. She gave Desmond a knowing look and flashed a glance at the Tippler. "The better for his health and your wallet, Mr. O'Connell."

"That was your son?" he asked.

"Yes, my Sean."

"He looks to be the same age as your Molly—are they twins?"

Eda stiffened at the newcomer's bringing Molly into the conversation and said, "Only of the Vatican variety. Sean is the older, by just under a year." She turned to answer the beckoning of another drinker, but stopped and added, "That making my Molly the younger." And with that, she showed him her back and marched down the bar.

CHAPTER NINE

Molly

October was a drier month, if there could be such a thing in Ireland. The days were still warm enough, with crisp nights that made for good sleeping. Children whose families cared enough to bother were back at school and the streets were the less hectic for it. It was a fine time to walk out with a handsome man of an afternoon, and Molly Brannigan felt every inch a sophisticated lady on the arm of her gentleman.

"Your mother's come round?"

Molly squeezed Desmond's arm tight to her side. "As long as we're together during the daylight and in public. That's something, isn't it?" She skipped a step, matching his longer strides to keep from bouncing as they walked. That felt childish and she so wanted to feel like a woman.

"No more stealing a few moments after your classes?"

The reminder of her schoolgirl studies raised the blooms in her cheeks, which Desmond found quite alluring. This was not the hardest duty he'd ever drawn, and Dublin was a far more congenial place than a grey border town full of surly Germans. And if Molly was his way in? Well, that wasn't so tedious either.

They were walking the pavement round Stephen's Green, the

interior of the square park having a deserved reputation for illicit petting on the shadiest benches under the big sycamores and limes. They couldn't chance anyone spotting them near one of those and reporting back to Eda, Dublin being as much gossipy village as city.

Pointing over the arrowhead tops of the iron fencing, Desmond said, "Isn't that where the rebels dug their trenches? During the trouble in '16?"

Molly craned her neck to peek through a break in the low bushes. "Farther down, I think. Closer to the hotel. You can't see a mark in the grass anymore. The gardeners patched everything."

"Was it frightening, that time?"

"Not frightening exactly," said Molly. "The shooting and shelling never came so close to us. The South Dublin Union was awful, I heard tell. And Jacob's factory. We could hear the shelling across the river, from the gunboats and at the GPO."

"One of the men at The Gallant said your brother was out for days? With the rebels at the Post Office?"

"That was the worst of it, Mam so frantic with worry. She tried not to show it, working herself half to death for distraction. But I knew Sean would come back."

As they turned up the east side of the Green, Molly stopped and placed a hand on one of the slender wrought-iron lampposts, spaced like tapers in a candelabra right round the edges of the park. It felt cool, almost cold, to her touch, the slanting late afternoon sun not reaching this part of the square. She stood silent, appraising a nondescript building across the street.

"What do you see?"

She let out a deep exhalation and turned toward him with a forced smile. "That's St. Vincent's. My sister, Deirdre, worked there. As a nurse, before she volunteered."

"She served most of the war?"

"From autumn in 1915," said Molly. "She was on the Somme. Then at a general hospital in London after she hurt her back in France."

Falling silent again, she studied each divided-light window, those of the lower floors long and narrow like a proper Georgian townhouse, shrinking to squat squares by the top floor. The dark front door opened between faux Doric columns and a sister in the long black habit and starched wimple of the Daughters of Charity stepped out and turned down the street.

"What are you thinking? Of your sister?"

She didn't turn to answer him, her thoughts searching back to some earlier place. "This is where everything changed," she said, her voice strangely disembodied.

She ran her hand up the lamppost, the coolness calming. "Mam sent me here, to fetch Deirdre. I must have been twelve. She'd just found out from one of the neighbourhood busybodies that Da had enlisted. Gone back to his old regiment. Francis, too."

She pushed away from the lamppost and folded her fingers into her palm to warm them. When she turned back, her look of loss and longing startled him. He licked his lips, about to speak, but Molly continued.

"That was when it began. So many people going away and not coming back. Or coming back in pieces. Francis without his leg. But Deirdre, too. She wasn't the same—taking so much medicine for her back, especially at night. She tried to hide it from Mam and me, but we knew. I think that's why Mam sent her away to Canada."

He had no idea what needed to be said, having missed the terrible violence of the war, so he stood searching her face with uneasy glances. There were no tears coming, rendering her hurt all the more profound.

"The war took Da. He was the first man I ever loved, wasn't he?"

Desmond studied the pavement, unable to bear the accusation in her words, as if he stood for all the soldiers of all the armies who took so many fathers away from young girls. She noticed his sudden dejection and placed her hand, still cool from the iron post, along his jawline and lifted his face toward hers.

"After I learned Da was never to return, I wondered if I'd ever love another man."

The hurt cleared as she examined Desmond the way she'd studied the building. At her unflinching look and the feathery feel of her fingers against his cheek, warmth spread outward from his constricted chest and he swallowed hard.

"And have you found such a man, Molly Brannigan?"

She let her hand drop from his face and said, "That remains to be seen. He'd have to love me back, wouldn't he? Else what's the point?"

Brushing away her unsettling trance, she slid a hand through his elbow again. The spruce-green brim of her hat just cleared his shoulder. With a gentle tug, she led him toward the north side of the park and the flow of fashionable people arriving at the Shelbourne for high tea.

"Well then, Mr. O'Connell," said Eda, "thank you for bringing my Molly back so prompt. She always makes tea for her brother and herself, which is a great help to me."

She was still a little stiff with him, not having warmed to the idea of her daughter walking out with any man. His distracting Molly from her studies and filling her head with romance was an annoyance. But as long as they kept to her rules, there couldn't be much harm in it. And wasn't she not much older when she'd met her Daniel?

Writing to Deirdre in Nova Scotia was a tonic for her. The letters took a few weeks going back and forth, but even if she knew before licking the stamp what her eldest daughter's reply would be, setting down her concerns about Molly was therapeutic. And as expected, Deirdre cautioned her against smothering the poor girl and urging her to give Molly a little freedom to grow.

But Eda knew her firstborn was made of tougher stuff than Molly. From as far back as Eda could remember, Deirdre was set in her opinions and stubborn in having her way, able to bend her father and most others to her will. Molly would never have the brass neck of her sister, for better or worse.

"Fine day for a stroll, Mrs. Brannigan," said Desmond, squirting his accustomed dollop of soda into his usual small whisky. They'd eschewed the familiar use of first names by unspoken agreement once Desmond sought to regularize his budding interest in Molly, thinking it proper to keep a little formality between them. "Once the sun went low, Molly became a little chilled, so it was best we returned anyway."

"You've shown yourself a proper gentleman," said Eda. "So far at least," she added with a flat voice and arched eyebrow. Unable to play the hardened widow for more than a few moments, she flashed him a quick smile. She missed having her Daniel to see their girls safe through this dangerous territory of handsome young men.

"My mother would be over the moon hearing that, Mrs. Brannigan." He lifted his glass and took a small sip, having established a reputation among the regulars as a man who sought the conviviality of the pub more than the bibulousness. Had they stopped to think on it, none of them had ever seen Desmond with a full head of drink. That he continued to stand far too many rounds no doubt greased his acceptance.

He'd grown to expect a clot of regulars to congeal round him within minutes of his arrival, having adopted both him and his wallet as their own. By another of the unspoken rules that abound within the close community of a Dublin pub, the regulars allowed Eda her moment of private conversation with the prosperous young man who'd an eye for their dear Molly. With Eda having spoken her piece and polished her way down to the opposite end of the bar, the Weatherman and the Tippler were drawn to Desmond like iron filings to a magnet. They ensconced themselves at Desmond's elbows with back-slapping gregariousness.

The Pintman had been meditating on his second stout when Desmond and Molly returned from their stroll. Having completed his adoration of the sacrament, he slid down the bar to join the others gathered round the young man in the fine suit, adding his greeting to those already underway.

"Well now, aren't you the fine thing today, Desmond O'Connell? With your best suit and a lovely maid upon your arm."

"A perfect day for stepping out, to be sure." Desmond caught Eda's eye down the bar and signaled with a twirl of his index finger.

As had become ritual between them, she shot him a raised-brow smile, tut-tutting with a shake of her head, then set about pulling pints for the Tippler and the Pintman, a rum for the Weatherman. There was no need to fetch a second whisky for Desmond. She was wise to his ways and appreciated that he wasn't overfond of the drink. Her own man hadn't been much of a drinker either and she wished just such a man for each of her daughters. Since buying the pub, she'd seen too many of the other kind. Eda placed the drinks before the waiting men, then returned to her busy work at the other end.

"Ohh, I believe our Molly's smitten," said the Weatherman.

"Aye, that she is," said the Tippler.

"Watch yourself," said the Pintman with an exaggerated wink, "or it'll be a pram you'll be pushin' down the pavement." The three men unleashed a wave of guffaws with renewed backslapping, then tucked into their fresh drinks.

Over the rim of his glass, Desmond's eyes wandered about the barroom. The counter by the front door was unoccupied, Molly having gone to make her little brother's tea. Her older brother Francis was inserted within a cluster of men, a rotating group that never seemed the same twice. Desmond reckoned many of the men from the Dublin Fusiliers dropped by out of a sense of obligation, the Brannigan family having contributed much to the glory of the regiment. A few had the dress and bearing of officers, but most appeared to be working men who'd done the hard fighting and returned without complaint to a laboring life back home.

"Eda's husband, he was a cooper at the brewery, wasn't he?" Desmond studied each man round Francis as he spoke.

"Not just a cooper, lad."

"A cooperage foreman was Daniel Brannigan."

"Yet he never lost the common touch," said the Tippler. "I knew the very man for many a year before the war. Me and the missus, didn't we live just across the street from the Brannigans in New Row?"

The other two, neither of whom had been acquainted with Eda's husband, nodded their silent second-hand agreement in deference to the Tippler's superior knowledge.

"And couldn't he still craft a barrel better than any man in Dublin?" The Tippler paused to drain the bottom half of his pint and Desmond signaled for another round to keep the story flowing.

"I heard tell of a time when a new journeyman scoffed at Daniel's skills, thinkin' a foreman of several years' standin' wouldn't still have the stuff. Daniel thought to teach the upstart a lesson and didn't the other men make a right duel to the death of it? I've heard tell near twenty pounds in wagers changed hands that day. Even the managers came down to watch and have a flutter."

Eda had wiped her way back down the bar when she heard snatches of talk about her dead husband. "Now, stop pullin' the leg of this young one, Joseph Gavin. There was no such thing. My Daniel was only workin' the bench next to that new man because so many were out with the grippe."

"Ahh, I remember that well enough," said the Pintman. "The winter of '11, it was. I had a bad dose myself. Laid up a fortnight."

Undeterred, the Tippler said, "Well, didn't your man show all his skills, Eda? 'Twas the talk of the neighbourhood."

"And his skills grow with each retelling," said Eda with a confidential lean toward Desmond, patting the back of his hand. He'd seen her do the same to many at the bar, a recognized sign of her affability. But she'd never patted his hand before.

He smiled into his glass.

"My Francis would've been as fine a cooper as his father, had the Lord granted him the very chance," said Eda, glancing over to the group surrounding her son, as she did with increasing frequency after each whisky he consumed. "He'd only been a year at his apprenticeship when he joined the regiment with his father. With just the one leg, he couldn't abide the heavy work and the long hours on his feet, could he?"

She wasn't looking for an answer. Desmond noted a flicker of the preoccupied drift he'd seen in her daughter earlier. Eda shook herself as if scolding her own foolishness. "But that's all in the past and I've a public house to run."

The Tippler raised his glass before Eda could turn away and said, "To the memory of Daniel Brannigan, as fine a man as ever trod the streets of Dublin." The other three raised their glasses in solemn reply, each having ample practice honoring fallen men these last five years.

When the glasses went back down on the bar, Eda patted the Tippler's hand and said, "That's kind of you to remember him, Joe." The two shared a companionable silence of shared memory, then Eda straightened her shoulders and said to the others, "And you'd be the better men for having known my Daniel, too." She gave a pursed-lip glance to the Tippler and said, "Not that the acquaintance has done much to improve your man here."

Leaving a burst of laughter at the Tippler's expense in her wake, Eda steamed out from behind the bar toward the little round tables lined up the length of the long bench, producing a chorus of clacks and clinks as she gathered up empty glasses.

With Eda out of earshot, Desmond asked, "What about Eda's boy, Sean? Surprised he hasn't apprenticed at the brewery cooperage like his father and brother."

"Oh, Sean's always been the wild one," said the Tippler. "Over in New Row, he and my boy Martin used to run the streets from dawn 'til dusk, always in one sort of mischief or another."

"And Sean hasn't come up as tall or broad-shouldered as his brother," said the Weatherman, pleased to have something useful to add. "It's frightful heavy work."

"Get on with yourself," said the Pintman. "What do you make of Art Rooney, so? The man can't be but five feet tall."

"But thirteen stone, if he's an ounce," said the Weatherman. "Strong as a bull."

With the conversation staggering off into another endless dispute over a bit of nothing, Desmond corralled them back. "So where does Sean work, then? Molly said he left school two years ago. He seems in and out of the pub at odd times."

"Why, he works right here," said the Weatherman.

"Does all the morning chores for his mother," said the Pintman. "A great help to the poor woman he is."

"And without a word of complaint," said the Tippler, having the last word as the recognized expert on the Brannigan family. "Of an early mornin', you'll see him on the street out front, scrubbin' the pavement and polishin' the windows, his mother bein' most particular about the cleanliness of this place."

"Not like old Paddy Shanahan, eh?" said the Weatherman. "You'd have thought it was twilight all the day through, never introducin' rag nor water to those windows in all the years he owned the place."

"Don't be slanderin' poor Paddy," said the Pintman. "Didn't his wife make him clean the windows when they had the wedding breakfast here for her niece?"

"That would've been eighteen hundred and ninety-two. Perhaps ninety-three," said the Tippler. "I hear tell Paddy's niece is a grandma now, this past spring."

Although his affable smile never faltered, Desmond found it

tedious keeping these men on point. It was all the more maddening when they'd information he needed. His boss wasn't pleased with the pace of the investigation and wanted Desmond to either produce the goods on Sean Brannigan's rebel activities or move on to a new assignment. But Desmond wasn't inclined to give up on the Brannigan family just yet, neither Sean nor his sister.

"You know, my boy Martin was out after Easter Sunday dinner with Sean, just before the trouble began in '16," said the Tippler, the utility of this piece of information breaking like a shaft of light through the meandering cloudiness.

Latching on to the Tippler, Desmond said, "Didn't I hear Sean was out all that week? But not your son?"

The Tippler drained the latest in his long train of pints and studied the brown residue with a wistful look. Desmond had learned to read the signs.

"Will you have another, then?"

"Ah, sure, go on," said the Tippler. "In case there's no porter in heaven, we better have another while we can, eh?"

Desmond signaled again to Eda, who arched her eyebrow and shook her head and pulled another pint, the ritual complete.

"Well now, my Martin's a decent lad, though not above a little devilment. But what he saw over to the Citizen's Hall threw a scare into him," said the Tippler, pausing as his pint arrived and waiting until Eda departed. "Enough to convince him he wanted no part of that rebel nonsense. But Sean stayed with the Sinn Feiners and wasn't seen until the donnybrook was over."

With the conversation taking a turn more interesting than usual, the Pintman and Weatherman closed in round the other two.

"Wasn't I right here, this very spot, when young Sean staggered in through that door, looking as if he'd been through the fires of Hell itself?"

"That was a holy show, right enough," said the Pintman. "And didn't they upend the whole town with their nonsense?"

"Now, don't be talkin' down them poor rebels," said the Weatherman. "Sure, they were fools takin' up the fight when they did, what with the war ragin'. But weren't they a brave lot? The women, too? And they made their stand, didn't they? Like Robert Emmett and Wolfe Tone." He gulped back his rum and added, "More'n any man here can claim."

Desmond noted to check the files back at the office, maybe send to London for Merchant Marine records on the man next to him. Then he turned back with studied indifference to the Tippler and said, "Does your son still run with Sean?"

"Yeah, sure. They'll pop in here for a jar now and again, with the rest of their crowd, but they mostly take to one of the snugs or sit back in the corner." The Tippler extracted one of the cigarettes Desmond offered and leaned into the proffered match, tilting back his head and loosing a long stream of smoke.

"My boy says Sean's uneasy drinkin' in front of his mother, what with his poor brother's weakness and all the pain that brings her." He took another long drag. "My Martin's a butcher's apprentice now and doesn't have as much freedom as Sean. Not like when they were chiselers, runnin' the streets like a pair o' gypsies."

"Yer man himself," said the Weatherman, pointing his chin toward the front door. "And Joe's boy Martin as well."

Sean was exchanging words with his brother, who was a full head taller even leaning on his crutch. Desmond guessed Francis favored the father, since Sean was all his mother. It was a little odd how Molly didn't seem to match any other family member.

The brothers manifested no signs of pleasure, but they appeared civil. Francis was still sober enough to mind his tongue and Sean went to extraordinary lengths not to distress their mother. Desmond saw Sean wave up toward the top of the stairs and watched his face brighten when Danny Brannigan waved back. Then the boy slid back into the shadow, shoulder against the wall and only his legs visible dangling over the first few steps.

Sean turned to a pair of men behind him, spoke a few words, then motioned to the back. The two worked their way toward the snugs, Martin Gavin stopping to exchange a few words and chuckles with his father and the others, then slid through the door and disappeared inside the snug under the stairs. A few moments later, Sean approached holding three pints of stout and kicked the brass plate at the base of the door twice with the toe of his boot. One of his companions opened, relieved him of a pint, and closed the door behind him.

With the small of his back against the bar, Desmond looked over to the snug with hooded eyes. Through threads of smoke, he glanced up to the landing at the top of the stairs. Danny had moved to the edge overlooking the open top of the snug where Sean and his friends had sequestered themselves. The walls of the snugs stopped at about eight feet, a full three feet below the dingy arabesques and fleurs-de-lis in the yellowed plaster mouldings topping the walls. The boy's taciturn face and intense eyes were illuminated by a frosted light fixture that hung from a long downrod that once carried coal gas to the lamp below. Now the long pipe was entwined like a caduceus with insulated electric wire.

Pressing his luck, Desmond returned his attention to the Tippler. "That other fellow, did he run with Sean and your Martin, too?"

The Tippler said, "No, no. He's a Cavan man, new to Dublin. I met him just the once, when he was here maybe a month ago with Martin and Sean." He stopped and pursed his lips, knitted his brows, struggling to call up more information. "Name of Barry. Can't recall the first name, not for the life of me."

With a loud clack, the door at the top of the stairs opened and young Danny scooted close to the banister, thin legs dangling between the spindles. Molly mussed his hair as she always did and trotted down the stairs, her footfalls masked by the hum of conversation and bursts of laughter. Desmond watched as she placed an arm round Eda and pulled against her for a moment, then bent to retrieve the small ledger and battered change box. Eda smoothed the girl's ash-blond hair with one hand while making entries in the larger credit ledger kept next to the till.

While he was admiring this unaffected moment between mother and daughter, Desmond didn't notice a quiet bespectacled man whom he'd seen a few times before had slipped up to the bar on his left.

By the time Desmond went looking for her again, Molly was halfway through the tangle of drinkers. The men parted with respectful nods and smiles as she floated through the rough gathering. None were tempted to say anything cheeky or lewd, she being the daughter of a fierce and protective mother who controlled their supply of alcohol. Molly gave a nod and a smile to each one, touching a few she knew well on the arm as she passed.

His attention was pulled back by Eda's voice, chatting with animation to the man with the steel-rimmed round glasses who held a small wrapped parcel under his arm. They spoke rapidly in Irish, out of which Desmond could only pick the odd word.

Then Eda switched to English and said, "Mr. O'Connell, have you met Peter Conway? Or have I been so rude as to never introduce you two gentlemen?"

"No, I don't believe you have, Mrs. Brannigan." Desmond stepped round the slumping Tippler and offered his hand. Looking startled behind his spectacles, Peter took his hand. It was dry and firm, not what Desmond had expected.

"Peter Conway. At your service, Mr… O'Donnell?"

"O'Connell, Desmond O'Connell. A pleasure to meet you, Mr. Conway." Desmond turned the radiance of his smile on Peter to no obvious effect. The older man stared back in somewhat confused silence.

"I didn't mean to eavesdrop, but my nursemaid was an Irish speaker and it gives me pleasure to hear it again. I only have a few words now, not having kept what I learned as a child."

"And more's the pity, Mr. O'Connell," said Eda. "Be a fine thing for all to know the mother tongue, if you were to ask me." She looked to Peter for agreement and, after a little hesitation, he nodded.

"Another book for Sean?" Eda pointed to the parcel Peter had set on the bar. "You've made better work of gettin' that one's nose in a book than the Christian Brothers ever managed."

"Yes, well, he seems a keen student," said Peter. "Often boys discover their love for learning later than we would hope. Not like the girls." He looked toward the door where Molly sat perched on her stool reading a small book and gave Eda a tentative smile.

"Perhaps I'll just give this to Sean, then have a small whisky," said Peter. "Is he upstairs?" He turned toward the staircase.

"Ach, don't trouble yourself," said Eda. "Sean and a few of his mates are in the snug just behind."

Peter Conway nodded, then walked over and rapped on the doorframe with his knuckles. The door separated a crack. The Cavan man appeared in the narrow opening, looked the bookseller up and down, and said something over his shoulder. The door swung wide to admit Peter, then shut again.

"Now Mr. O'Connell," said Eda as if dismissing some tradesman or delivery boy, "you'll be finishing your drink and settling up. Molly's moonin' and glancin' over here more than's good for her, and I'd have you gone so she can attend her work."

CHAPTER TEN

Sean

They'd set up their offices a few blocks from headquarters. Everyone assumed the Fenians—or the Irish Republican Army as they'd styled themselves since their farcical insurrection in 1916—had spies all over Dublin Castle. They couldn't very well traipse in and out of the very center of British power in Ireland day after day. As it was, the story about this being a business office dealing in vague sorts of commerce was already wearing thin among the suspicious neighbors.

The chief had a separate office, but the others occupied a large room that once held the stenographers and typists of a long-abandoned underwriting firm. With its north-facing windows looking down on a narrow side street, the dinginess alone might have driven the insurance men into bankruptcy. The perpetual pall of smoke that hung over the desks whenever the big room was occupied did nothing to dispel their torpor.

A chair moaned as the occupant shifted and resettled, piercing through the low hum of conversation and the clacking of a typewriter pecked with two unskilled fingers. All languid activity ceased when the private office door opened with a brisk click and a burst of air.

"Davidson and Piers-Musgrave," said a slender man with a regulation mustache and unruffled demeanor. "If you would, in my office?" He disappeared behind the door, silhouette receding from the translucent glass.

Two younger men at desks abutting back-to-back sat up in unison. One stubbed out a cigarette while the other rose and hooked the suit coat off the back of his chair, sliding an arm through a sleeve.

Two sharp knocks on the boss's door and the even voice said, "Come." The junior men stepped inside and took the chairs before their chief's larger, cleaner desk. The window was open a foot, a token breeze cleaning out a little of the must and smoke. The more pleasant workspace relaxed the two younger men into their slat-backed chairs.

"Well then, tell me how you're getting along with these new persons of interest," the chief said. "Davidson, what about yours— Gavin, is it?"

"Martin Gavin. Not a great deal to report, sir," he said, the trill of his native Edinburgh doing battle with years of public school posh. Long days pretending at Strathclyde Irish confused his accent all the more. "I've made his acquaintance at the butcher shop where he's apprenticed and I've managed a chance encounter at a tram stop. I promised to stand him a pint after he gave me directions to the Custom House. Believe I've identified his local pub in Hanover Lane, although he drinks round a wee bit."

The chief leaned back and extended a leg under his desk, the knee torn by shrapnel and rebuilt after a fashion by Royal Army surgeons.

"Any sense he suspects you?"

"Not that I can determine," said Davidson. "He seems to accept me as a shipping clerk for a Glasgow firm's office here. He's not asked since I mentioned it. He works morning hours in the shop, so I've dropped in on my way to work every other day or two. I've already bought enough rashers to last six months. Told him I live with my old grandparents here."

"No sign of IRA activity?"

Davidson shook his head and said, "No, sir. Seems the butcher he works for isn't keen on the Republican cause, so Martin keeps any rebel activities well clear of the premises. I'll pick up the scent once we start socializing after hours."

"Good, well begun. Keep your shoulder to the wheel," said the chief, wincing a little as he rearranged his bad leg. He'd willed away the limp, but sitting for any length of time stiffened it. "Now Piers-Musgrave, what do you have with your new subject? Friend of this Gavin, yes?"

"Sean Brannigan's the name," said the agent. "Father was a sergeant-major with the Dubs, killed at Gallipoli. Older brother in the same battalion—came home without a leg. He'll be easier to watch than Gavin, I suspect. Works before opening at his mother's pub on the Coombe. I've seen him, confirmed he's the man in the photograph from Intelligence. No chance to speak with him yet though."

"You say he works before opening in the pub? What's your approach, then? Is he around much during opening hours?"

"Doesn't seem to be. And the mother's a formidable one, but she'd have to be, running a pub on her own." He fished a packet of cigarettes from his coat and looked for permission from his superior, who nodded approval.

"What are the Intelligence chaps' suspicions about your Mr. Brannigan?"

Piers-Musgrave leaned forward and dropped a blackened match into his boss's ashtray. "A bit murky, other than he was out with the rebels in '16. Wasn't much more than a boy. He's eighteen, so would've been fourteen, perhaps fifteen then. One of the regulars at his mother's pub said he ran messages and ammunition at the GPO. He was out the entire week of the rebellion."

"Young or not, in the thick of it."

"There's something else the regulars mentioned, about his father dying in the war at a bad age for Sean," said Thomas Piers-Musgrave, a lieutenant seconded from the Royal Inniskillings, seated next to a captain from the Royal Scots, across from a major late of the Coldstream Guards. "That may explain his allegiance to the Republican cause. He'd hardly be the first to blame the Crown for such a loss."

"What about the brother? The one who lost a leg at Gallipoli? What are his politics?"

"Staunch King-and-Empire man. And a drunkard. The pretense is he runs the pub with his mother, but really spends his time drinking with other veterans. Rather pathetic, really."

Piers-Musgrave crossed his legs and ran a finger along his upper lip. "I've been working myself close to the family through Sean's sister Molly. She's a year younger—seventeen—quite a lovely thing."

Cameron Davidson stifled a laugh.

The chief smiled and said, "Well, no reason our duties can't be as pleasant as possible. You think the girl might be interested in a romance?"

"The way she looks at me, I fear she'll lick me like a candy apple."

Mirth overcame discipline and Davidson let out a barking guffaw. The chief's chest heaved with laughter, too, albeit more self-contained than the big Scotsman.

Thomas Piers-Musgrave blew self-satisfied streams of smoke from his nostrils and said, "By the way, I'm calling myself Desmond O'Connell."

"O'Connell?" said the chief. "Isn't that laying it on a bit thick?"

In the exaggerated voice of a musical hall Paddy, he replied, "Well, sure'n doesn't sweet Molly Brannigan and her dear mam admire the name well enough?"

All three laughed.

So there it was, tucked inside a rubbed and worn copy of Swift's *Directions to Servants*, chosen for thinness rather than content. He'd known it was only a matter of time. The letter ought to be on parchment, he thought, with a big red seal, but here it was. A stranger's death warrant, scribbled on a torn sheet of lined foolscap, like some schoolboy dashed it off and stuffed it in his primer before the Latin master could catch him out.

When Sean read the order, the churn of excitement and revulsion in his guts almost knocked him off his pins. Peter Conway suggested they all sit down.

With some color back in his face, Sean handed the note over to Martin Gavin, who scanned it, then glanced back and forth from Sean to Peter, hoping someone would laugh it off as a prank. The man from Cavan eased the note from Martin's moist hands, read with indifference, then handed it back to Sean.

Tucking the order back inside the book, Sean said to Peter, "You know what it says?"

In a steady voice, Peter replied, "I do. They asked me to gather intelligence for you, so it was necessary." He gazed back through his round glasses at the younger man, just out of his sad and eventful boyhood, who'd have to do this dirty work of the rebellion.

Taking a slow and deep breath to steel his nerves and steady his voice, Sean said to Peter, "So what do you have for us on him?"

"His name is William Hallock, aged 62 or 63, a magistrate in Tullamore. He's caused trouble for the boys down in King's County. South Tipperary and Queen's, as well. Locked up quite a few. Now he's cooperating with a new initiative from Dublin Castle to seize our bank funds."

The close room was filling with smoke as the younger men listened, cigarettes doing little to settle their nerves. They'd write down nothing that could be found if captured or killed. Sean would burn the order upstairs after he'd studied it a last time.

"What about the proper place for... the work? Any suggestions from the lads in King's County?"

Peter cleared his throat and said, "He works from the police barracks and is escorted to and from his home. They've too few men in Tullamore to leave a constable at his door every night, so it'll be catch-as-catch-can in that regard."

"We'll maybe need to hold over for a few days, 'til we catch an unguarded night?"

"They'll see to that in Tullamore. The brigade's in disarray in King's, so the Galway lads will support you. There's money for your tickets in the back of the book. Make sure you take separate trains and are not seen together."

The three nodded.

"You're to contact P.J. Moloney. Go to his house separately and after dark. Well spaced in time, too. His house is in Maryborough, right at the top of Church Street. It's two stories with twin chimneys—has the side of an abandoned church tower as a back wall, so you shan't miss it. It's three doors up from the gaol."

Pausing to look over the others, Peter noted the nervous eyes of Martin Gavin, although Sean and the Cavan man, whose name he didn't need to know, looked well enough collected.

"I'll hear each of you repeat that name and address. You must be able to conjure it on your own."

"Moloney, top of Church Street, Maryborough. Two stories with twin chimneys. Up against a church tower," said the Cavan man as he crushed his cigarette in a chipped yellow ashtray. He flicked a little ash off the green rim, then ran a fingertip under *Bulmer's Cider - Cider Maker to His Majesty the King*.

"Mahoney... in Church Street," said Martin, "Maryborough."

"That's *Moloney* in Church Street," said Peter in his calmest tutor's voice, although this was a more serious tutorial than any he'd overseen. These boys weren't puffed-up Trinners either. And they'd be harder men when this business was through.

"Yeah... yeah, Moloney... in Church Street," said Martin. "Maryborough. Up against a church tower."

Peter nodded and turned to Sean.

"P.J. Moloney, top of Church Street, two stories and two chimneys. Right up against a ruined church tower."

"Grand," said Peter. "I suggest you repeat that to yourselves until it's familiar as your own address. Hallock's children are grown and gone, so it's just he and his wife. They've a day maid and cook, so there are no servants sleeping in. With no guard, it will be the two of them."

Peter took off his glasses and produced a clean handkerchief with crisp creases. They didn't need cleaning, but this was one of his nervous habits when he wanted to avoid unpleasantness.

"I have no information as to whether they sleep in separate bedrooms." He put the glasses back on the bridge of his nose, looking down at the table while he looped the curved metal ends behind his ears.

Martin Gavin's attention was still careening from face to face, cueing off reactions from the others. "Yer not sayin' we should do the wife as well?"

As leader of the team, Sean said, "We'll not set out to harm her, but you know this is a dangerous business."

"I'll not have her seein' me and passin' it on to the Constabulary," said the Cavan man.

"We'll mask ourselves, so there'll be little chance of that," said Sean. "Make sure you each bring a big kerchief. Wear it round your neck, like farm workers."

Peter rose from his chair. "I've been away too long. We don't want your mother suspecting. You'll receive a final order from the Galway commander when they want you to go, after coordinating with the Tipperary lads. They'll be getting you out after… this business."

The bookseller smoothed the front of his trousers and stood for a moment, changing back to the countenance of a distracted and bookish scholar.

That there were far fewer people on the Green in winter emboldened Molly and Desmond to venture over to one of the benches. Deep in a corner under the droopy bare boughs of a weeping ash, their seat was invisible in the slanting sunlight that did little more than deepen the shadows. They'd returned several times since their first electrifying embrace back in November, and Molly couldn't go more than a few minutes without thinking of Desmond's mouth on hers. Each return to St. Stephen's Green intensified that first crash of pleasure, and their chaste kisses turned hungry, searing with heat.

Molly shoved him back with a half-hearted push, panting as their mouths separated. Her face burned bright red, her neck blotchy pink over tensed tendons. Desmond rubbed his lips together and heaved a sigh, desire banked for the moment.

"I don't believe I've ever seen anything as lovely as you."

There was nothing left to redden, but Molly's mouth turned up and she ran her palm along his cheek. He'd shaved several hours before, so the smoothness was gone. She caught a distant scent that clung to his suit of lavender and lemons from the *eau de toilette* he used each morning. She searched his eyes, dark cobalt in the gloom. They appeared somehow cold in the deep shadows, like dead water between ice floes breaking on a river.

"I love you, Desmond O'Connell, with everything that's in me," she said, stroking his cheek again. "But do I even know you?"

He pulled her hand to his lips and closed his eyes as he kissed the center to create a diversion from her unsettling statement. "What an extraordinary thing to say," he said, speaking into her palm while he kissed it.

She pulled back her hand with the lightest tug, laying it on the woolen gloves she'd placed in her lap. "You seem to have dropped from the sky, just for me. Perhaps you're a demigod, like Orpheus?"

He turned his eyes back to hers, having recomposed himself. Wielding the fetching smile he knew would dispel any doubts, he said, "But you're alive, so you couldn't be Eurydice," he moved to kiss her again, "now, could you?"

The last words were smothered by her lips on his. He opened his mouth and flicked his tongue against the tip of hers. She arched her back, pressing hard against him, while he ran his hand inside the open front of her coat and up under her jumper. Her mouth crushed against his bottom lip as his thumb ran over her nipple, the hardness pressing through layers of shift and blouse. He drew a sharp, sudden breath as her hand found his hardness through the wool of his trousers.

Martin Gavin was coming off the rails from all the waiting. Sean knew it, could see the deepening lines in his friend's forehead, the darkening under his eyes. The sunken look of too little sleep—hollow and haunted, like a starving animal. Martin's bluff bravado only accentuated his jumpiness.

Two months on, they hadn't done the job yet.

Sean knew it would be him and Barry, the man from Cavan. He'd tell Martin as soon as he arrived. There'd be simpler work for him soon enough.

He flipped the book over a few times, its brown cover trailing wispy threads from the spine. Caesar's *The Gallic Wars* this time. He wondered if Peter Conway sent subtle messages with the titles he chose for secreting notes sent from the higher-ups. There must be others, more men to whom the unassuming bookseller carried orders and pistols, emptying his bookshelves for the sake of deception. This was the first time Peter had left a book with Eda, hadn't delivered it into Sean's hands himself.

Caesar's memoir carried yet another order to kill the magistrate, Mr. Hallock of Tullamore.

Visit your uncle at home. Soon as possible. His health is failing.

It was the fourth time his uncle had taken a turn for the worse.

He'd rallied three times, on account of the Galway Brigade having other priorities or the magistrate's mother-in-law dying in East Anglia or someone somewhere getting cold feet.

The wave of nausea Sean had felt when he read the first of these abortive orders—maybe a little with the second, too—had been displaced by shrugging skepticism. This one was as likely to be countermanded as the others, so there was little use getting his bowels in an uproar.

He jumped a little when the door to the snug swung open. "Might you knock, then, Martin? You frightened the shite out of me."

Two men pressed into the snug, a tightly smiling and swaggering Martin Gavin, followed by the taciturn Barry from Cavan.

"Lookin' a bit nervy there, Sean boy," said Martin, slapping him on the shoulder and plunking down in a chair across the scarred table. His pantomime confidence had started to grate.

Barry took a chair facing the door, cigarette dangling from his lips. Sean had noticed weeks ago that Barry was smoking like a fiend, never without a fag, lighting a new one off the butt of the last.

"Another note from uncle?" said Barry, pointing with his cigarette to the book under Sean's hand.

"We'll get to that soon enough," said Sean. "There's somethin' of importance I've to say first." He centered the book in front of himself, then placed a hand on either side, palms flat on the table, staring at the half-worn gold lettering on the cover. Barry watched through his haze of smoke, legs crossed and an arm thrown over the chair back.

Sean looked as if he were nursing a wound while he searched the flushed face of his boyhood mate. When their eyes met, Martin began his habitual jerkiness, glancing from Barry to Sean, then to the door, before settling on his hands that were wringing away nervous sweat.

"It's no good, Martin. You know it, too."

The wringing accelerated and Martin said, "What are you on about, Sean Brannigan?"

"You know you're not up to it, to this job," Sean said with slow precision, so there'd be no misunderstanding. He wanted this over as fast as possible. "Have you had a decent night's sleep since this whole thing began? You look a holy wreck."

"There'll be other jobs," Barry added, disguising his pleasure behind a hand holding the cigarette to his mouth. "Some aren't cut from the right cloth for this work."

Tense silence hung in the close room. There was no angry shouting, so Sean let Martin have the time he needed to puzzle through this sudden change in his young life.

Finally, Martin looked up at Sean and said, "Yeah, maybe 'tis best I pass on this one. Wait for the next, so."

"There'll be other work," Barry repeated.

"Aye, important work, too," Sean said.

Martin Gavin rose with the aches and pains of an old man, his false assurance draining away as his shame grew. He nodded to Barry, then to Sean, and mumbled, "Well, good luck to you both." He slipped out the door without another word.

Barry lit a new cigarette from the one he'd not yet finished, lounged back in his cross-legged looseness, and said, "Smartest thing I've yet heard from you. You've known right along he's an awful risk."

"What's done is done. It's our show now. We'll leave for Maryborough tomorrow morning, you first. Take the 6:05. No later than the 7:18. I'll follow on the 10:40. It's dark early, so you make your way to Moloney's between seven and eight. Tell him I'll be in before ten o'clock."

CHAPTER ELEVEN

Sean

March of 1920 came in like a lion, if lions were all over soggy and grey. It was the dreariest and dullest time of the year, Lenten self-denial coupled with a winter refusing to pass into spring. It would end soon enough, sure as the Lord would rise from the dead in early April, but the pub had grown sour with the sullen attitudes of the patrons and the dank smell of their clothing.

What worried Eda and her rosary the most, however, was the inevitability of Francis's drinking growing as the anniversary of his father's death and his own dismemberment approached. Far from fading, this period of profoundest drunkenness started a little earlier each year, as if the pain of his memories was sharpened, like sheered rocks slipping down a cliffside with the turning season. This would make five years since the horrors of that morning on the beach, yet Francis was as far away from her as he'd been the day he arrived by taxi from the military hospital where the doctors could do no more for him.

Between two and four was the quietest time most days. The earlier mealtime crowd was gone and she'd cleared the remnants of sandwiches—potted meat or cheese, even cold sliced bully beef for those who'd gained a taste for it during the war. She bought the sandwiches by the trayful from the grocer's in Patrick Street and sold them for a halfpenny over what he charged her. One of the grocer's apprentices delivered them at ten o'clock, every morning but Sunday, and Sean stowed them under tea towels on a shelf beneath the bar.

Three men sat in close conversation on the bench near the back, but they hadn't ordered a drink in half an hour. Taken with their lack of laughter, Eda reckoned they were discussing business. One of her regulars leaned against the bar near the front windows, smoking his pipe and nursing a pint while he leafed through the *The Irish Times*. Eda was strictly ecumenical in her newspapers, having arranged with the newsboys for daily delivery of the unionist *Irish Times* and the nationalist *Irish Independent*, plus the *Examiner* from Cork on Sundays.

With arms crossed and a towel dangling from one hand, Eda surveyed her domain with satisfaction. She'd made a fine go of it for nearly five years now, cared for her family, and made a place for herself as a respected publican and pillar of the community at her end of the Liberties. And The Gallant Fusilier had become known throughout the town as a place where you could find an honest pint and good company without the gambling and coarse language of those shabby places along the quays. There were men who remembered her husband from the brewery cooperage and tradesmen from along the Coombe, students over from Trinity and shawlies from their stalls and barrows. Some days she felt all of Dublin passed through her doors, and that lifted the heart of a Donegal woman who'd first come to the city a terrified girl with country ways.

Lost in her thoughts, she didn't hear the door open. Most of the regulars sought to fill the room with their loud welcomes upon entering. Peter Conway wasn't such a voluble sort.

He stepped inside with a dripping umbrella flapping in his hand, stopping to fasten the strap that held it wrapped tight. Glancing about with his habitual look of half-startled puzzlement, he spotted Eda behind the bar and grinned like an awkward schoolboy praised for a fine recitation. Without a thought, she wandered down to the end of the bar nearest the snugs, the unobtrusive spot to which the equally unobtrusive Mr. Conway gravitated.

"Well, fancy seein' you here in the midst of business hours. Will you have a small whisky?"

Leaning the dripping umbrella against the brass foot rail, Peter said, "No, I think not today, Eda. Perhaps a half of cider instead?" He glanced down at the man and his newspaper, then back over his shoulder at the group across the room on the bench. When Eda returned, she set the half-pint glass in front of him and stood smiling.

Their conversations had become a curious mix of languages, switching back and forth with seamless ease, sometimes in mid-sentence. It drove others to distraction, but it had become their way. Since she'd said nothing in Irish, Peter continued in English.

"I'd hoped to find you in a quiet moment."

"And so you have, Peter," said Eda, taking up her towel, without which she would feel naked behind the bar.

"I was wondering..." he coughed a little, then went on, "...if perhaps we could have a meal sometime."

Polishing the spotless top as unnecessarily as ever, she said, "Why, of course. You can join us for tea tonight. Sean might even pop in, since we're havin' the cold ham from Sunday. And haven't you eaten with me and mine a half-dozen times before..." She tensed when he ceased her polishing with a hand over hers, flabbergasted by the interruption.

"I rather meant... that perhaps you and I... might have meal at a proper restaurant," he said, then swallowed hard. "Just the two of us... if you thought that proper."

For the first time since girlhood, Eda Brannigan was seen to blush, bright as a beet.

They'd bought the little gimcrack Ford truck before the war for making deliveries. After Barry arrived round half seven at the tidy house at the top of Church Street, Mr. Moloney instructed his boy to drive the truck through Tullamore as if he were delivering to some farm, then lay by outside town. After nine o'clock, he was to drive past the magistrate's house to see if there was a Constabulary guard on duty there, then make his way back home.

Sean slipped in the front door of the house before ten o'clock, just as the pudda-pudda sound of a truck rounded the corner and slipped into a backstreet.

"That'll be my boy, back from Tullamore," said Moloney. He'd asked neither Sean's name nor Barry's. Some things were better left unspoken in these times and he was worried enough that two young strangers knew his name and address. He took Sean by the elbow and directed him to the kitchen at the back where Barry sat at the table with an agitated Mrs. Moloney fussing about him with a teapot and a biscuit tin. No amount of anxiousness would have anyone saying the Moloney house wasn't as hospitable as any in Maryborough.

P. J. Moloney was in shirtsleeves, his grey waistcoat straining against a prosperous stomach. He ran a hand over his damp forehead and balding head, smoothing the few remaining hairs. His wife returned the biscuit tin to a press near the sink and disappeared into the dining room. Just as she'd faded into the unlit front of the house, the Moloneys' son slipped through the door.

"This is the second of the lads down from Dublin," said Mr. Moloney as the younger man stepped into the dim illumination. Sean nodded and mumbled a greeting.

"Best not ask names, son," said Moloney. "Best for all concerned."

The lanky lad nodded to each of the visitors before turning to the business at hand.

"No sign of any RIC men, front or back. I saw the lights go out in the front parlor when I passed by about half nine."

"They're abed, then?" asked Barry, tapping ash into a battered sardine can a testy Mrs. Moloney had produced after Barry lit his first smoke without so much as asking her leave.

"Aye, reckon they are," the lad said as he poured himself a cup of tea from the tepid pot. He splashed in some milk, then grimaced at the coldness as he slurped.

Moloney smoothed his sparse hair again and said, "Right. Turn on the hall light, then." His son set the teacup down in the sink and trotted to the front of the house. Sean heard a loud pop as he twisted the switch, producing a dim spill down the hallway.

"That's the signal agreed with the Galway lads. They'll drive past each hour from half ten to half one. If they see the glass above the front door lit, they're to pick you up at the top of the next hour in the street behind." Talking it through calmed Moloney enough to cease his pacing and sit. His son returned and leaned against the frame of the hallway door.

"So you've forty minutes to wait," said their host, followed by a resigned exhalation. He produced a nickel watch from the pocket of his waistcoat and nodded at the face, confirming the time.

Sean used Barry's cigarettes as rough timekeeping, not wanting to ask Moloney and appear edgy. He figured about seven minutes each. Just after Barry lit a fresh cigarette from the glowing butt of his fourth, Sean heard the sound of a motorcar easing its way down narrow Church Street.

"After the job, then," said Sean, "where are we to meet the Tipperary men?"

"Ahh, didn't I forget to tell?" said Moloney, with spread palms and a nervous chuckle. He smoothed his hair again with both hands and Sean saw the sweat soaking through under his arms. The son shifted from one foot to another, then settled back against the doorframe.

"You're to make your way from Kilbride Street where yer man himself lives, down to the canal. The Tips will meet you on the quay, at the distillery warehouse. The Galway lads will point the way when they drop you off, but you can't miss it. Big stone building, three stories high and right along the canal. None about but a single night watchman." Moloney gave another tense chuckle. "And him likely asleep or drunk."

They fell into agreeable silence as Barry filled the kitchen with smoke. Three cigarettes later, Moloney nodded to his son. The two went to a large china press at the back of the long kitchen and heaved it up. When the cupboard was perpendicular, Sean could make out the dark outline of a small door not more than three feet high that had been concealed by the furniture.

The son pulled hard on a sliding iron bolt. It didn't budge, so he gave it a few kicks with his boot heel, breaking it free. The little door swung open and Sean felt a damp and musty chill flow in.

"My boy will see you outside. That'll take you through Old St. Peter's bell tower, just the other side of that wall. Then out into the churchyard."

Moloney motioned them to the opening as his son stooped low and disappeared into the blackness. The father stuck out his hand to Barry, then took Sean's.

"God bless you, lad." He squeezed hard and said, "You're doing your bit and we'll not forget that."

"And yourself as well, Mr. Moloney," said Sean. Barry was already through, so with a final glance and nod to P.J. Moloney, Sean moved into the tomblike darkness.

The younger Moloney waited just inside the old church tower. When Sean came out, the boy said, "You'll need to stay right close, so grab my coattail. It's cursed dark with the clouds and there are headstones and toppled monuments all about."

When they emerged from the far side of the tower, patchy starlight produced a few silhouettes, forming fantastic and eerie shapes. Sean's imagination might have run away, had his thoughts not been occupied with the grim task of laying another man beneath such a stone. He pushed the pistol a little deeper into the waistband at his back.

The churchyard wall loomed ahead in the darkness. The gate was nothing but a patch of charcoal grey in the long inky shadow of the wall. When they neared it, young Moloney said, "Best stay along the wall. We'll see their headlamps when they make the turn up the street."

Banned from smoking by circumstances, Barry fidgeted with a box of matches in his trouser pocket.

The wrought iron gate to the street illuminated with headlamps moving along at a crawl. The Moloney boy lifted the latch on the gate and opened it far enough for the two men to slip out, but not enough for the groan of rusty hinges to alert the neighbors.

"Good luck," he whispered into the darkness and then was gone back among the toppled headstones.

A black touring car stopped before the gate and the driver reached over his seat and swung open the back door. Barry was first in and slid across. Sean jumped in and closed the door with quiet care. The tires crunched on loose gravel, the engine barely audible as they crept out of the deserted street.

Once onto the main road, the driver sped up and the front passenger turned back to Sean and Barry. "Welcome gents. Make yourselves comfortable. It's near twenty miles to Tullamore, so we borrowed this fine automobile from a doctor over in Ballinasloe.

Gave him a proper receipt and promised we'd leave it somewheres conspicuous when we was done. Unless he went to the RIC, in which case we swore we'd burn it." The shadowy figure threw back his head and let out a belly laugh.

"You see how wide that old doctor's eyes was? He's like to be under his bed cowerin' as we speak. He'll not go for a constable," the driver said.

The passenger gave another big guffaw and the driver's shoulders shook with laughter, too.

A burst of a match pierced the darkness as Barry got a smoke going. He tapped the passenger's shoulder with the end of the packet.

"Well, don't mind if I do," he said, taking one. The driver shook his head. Barry struck another match and held it forward, close to the passenger's face. Sean could see ginger hair under a cloth cap and a lined face that put him well into his forties. He disappeared into the darkness as Barry shook out the match.

They rolled north along a macadam road that bisected a handful of tiny villages, most just a farmstead and a few cottages, perhaps a forge. Sean sat silent, watching Barry's and the Galway man's faces glow orange with each drag, then recede into shadows.

"Damn it all, Piers-Musgrave, I expect results. I've allowed more time than the likely value of Sean Brannigan deserves."

Desmond O'Connell—as he'd begun to think of himself all his waking hours—watched his boss's back at the window, both hands deep in his pockets and rocking on his heels.

The Castle was after them to show something for the time and money they were chewing through while chasing what seemed phantoms. The intelligence section hadn't even turned up a usable photograph of that devil Mick Collins who was responsible for ordering up the worst of the Sinn Feiner atrocities in Dublin. Now he was extending his assassinations and intimidation right across the country.

London, in turn, was pressuring the Castle. Lloyd George had outlawed the Fenian assembly, the Dáil, in September. Then Churchill concocted a scheme to stiffen the Royal Irish Constabulary's officers who, living among the population, were subject to constant threats. Whether Protestant or Catholic, Loyalist or a man only trying to feed his family, it made no difference. Recruiting had begun a few months ago for a special reserve force and the first few had appeared in Dublin a week ago in Army-khaki breeches and RIC bottle-green tunics. As a result, the pressure for Desmond's special unit to penetrate the IRA networks was increasing.

The commander turned from the window after an uncomfortable silence and said, "You've one more month, Piers-Musgrave. You'll need to press Brannigan's sister more vigorously. Either she'll start providing information or she'll get suspicious and cuts ties with you. Either way, so be it. We'll move you on to something else if she goes to ground."

"That's unlikely, sir. She's quite devoted to me."

Cameron Davidson snorted and slapped his thighs. Switching to musical-hall Scots, he said, "Och, ye've nae bedded tha' braw wench, hae ye? Trouble wi' yer wee soldier, laddie?" Davidson slapped at Desmond's crotch, then laughed uproariously at his own joke.

The commander, suppressing a smile, said, "Press her, Piers-Musgrave. Press her."

"Is that what you English call it? Pressing?" said Davidson. "I've had a good look at lovely Molly Brannigan—wouldn't mind having my own breeches pressed by that sweet lass."

Desmond laughed along with every appearance of sincerity. He knew it was past time, too.

The house hulked over Patrick Street, a mass of dressed grey stones punched through by double-sash windows. No lights inside, but the windows rattled in the light breeze and threw off flashes of reflections from houses occupied by more nocturnal neighbors.

Parked in front of an ironmonger's up the street, Sean slid close to Barry and peered out the back window as the Galway man in the front seat gave them final instructions. Much was left to the last minute to avoid too many knowing too much for too long. If there was a consistent theme running through all the failed rebellions of five centuries and more, it was an abundance of informants and turncoats. And there was a risk of spilled secrets if anyone got lifted by the Constabulary or the Army or the new Auxiliaries.

"We believe yer man sleeps in the bedroom at the front of the house, with the windows over the door there," the Galway man said, pointing down the street. "These big houses have a staircase right on the main hall. The front door's locked at night—we had one of our boys try it a few weeks back—so you best go through the kitchen entrance. There's a gate off the side lane through the garden wall."

He reached under the seat and produced something heavy wrapped in a piece of hessian sacking and handed it over to Sean. "Here's a smith's hammer to use on the back door, if it's locked. You can use it on the glass or to punch out the lock. Best to decide when you get a look at the door."

Sean unwrapped the battered hammer and hefted it. "We'll need to move fast if we have to break our way in. He's sure to wake from the ruction."

"Sure look it," said the Galway man with a resigned shrug. Sean glanced at his partner Barry who gave an equally indifferent shrug.

"Which way's the canal?"

"You'll want to go out the way you came in, head down the lane away from Patrick Street. Keep straight on and you'll come to the canal." The Galway man didn't ask why they needed directions. This was the end of his responsibilities and someone else had the more dangerous matter of getting the gunmen away once the deed was done.

"Let's get on with it," said Barry.

Sean handed over the hammer to his partner, then stuck a hand over the seat and said, "We're grateful for all you've done." The Galway man shook the offered hand in a more perfunctory manner than would be polite in most circumstances.

The driver stared straight ahead as Sean and Barry slid out the back. Well before they reached the narrow lane beside the magistrate's house, the noise of the motor car disappeared round a corner, leaving only the unsettling sound of their own footfalls on the pavement of the deserted street.

Once they ducked up the alley, the only illumination came from slender moonlight peeking through thin scudding clouds. It was enough for them to spot the break in the stone wall surrounding the back garden.

Barry was first to the gate. He turned to make sure Sean was behind him, then pushed. It swung easy on its iron hinges, giving off one sharp squeak. They crept into the garden with the crunch of gravel biting at the soles of their boots, the white stones marking a pathway through the darkness.

When they reached the short flight of steps up to the back door, Sean caught Barry by the elbow and stepped past him. Reaching the door, he ran his fingers along the jamb and felt the cold hardness of a brass knob. He looked back to see Barry's shadow a few steps below. When he gave the knob a careful twist, it rotated a quarter-turn.

"Leave the hammer," he said, leaning down toward Barry to make his raspy whisper heard. "Unlocked."

The hammer swished through an unseen bush, ending with a quiet thud as it hit the mossy ground beneath. Barry came up right behind Sean, revolver ready. Sean drew his own pistol from his waistband and twisted the knob again. He let his shoulder settle against the door and it gave way.

A little greyness filtered down the long hallway from the fanlight over the front door, ambient illumination from the houses across the street and the pub a few doors down. They could make out the features of the kitchen and the light grew as they crept round the table into the hall.

Sean looked along the wall to his left and saw the spindly silhouette of a balustrade. He leaned back and whispered, "Stay to the edges. Less chance of squeakin'. Pull up your kerchief." Barry's shadow nodded, the pistol held near his head pointed at the ceiling.

Fishing two fingers inside his collar, Sean tugged the twisted kerchief up over his nose. With his left hand on the wooden globe atop the newel, he turned to face up the stairs. His own breathing seemed so loud, even through the blood pounding in his ears, he was sure anyone within a block could hear.

He stopped at the foot of the stairs. How many times had he gamboled, light on his feet, up the stairs at The Gallant Fusilier, or even in their old house in New Row, back before his father went off to die for the English king? Inhaling twice, deep and cleansing, he placed a foot against the edge of the first stair and pushed down. Silence. He placed his other foot along the edge of the next tread and shifted his weight. Nothing. A third step, then a fourth. He could hear Barry moving behind him in the murk.

When he reached the top, Sean followed the banister as it turned back into the upstairs hall, toward the front of the house. The bedroom door was ajar, the same light from the street giving weak illumination to the room beyond. Barry slid in behind and placed a light hand on Sean's shoulder to signal he was in place.

Sean's vision narrowed to the vertical line of grey light leaking through the crack in the bedroom door. He blinked away some sweat running into the corner of his eye. His thigh touched something hard in the deep shadows and he reached down to the edge of a small table, running his hand round it. His sleeve brushed something—a hollow wobble, then a crash as brittle china exploded at his feet.

Startled murmurs came from behind the door.

"Bugger all," hissed Barry. Then realizing the futility of whispering, he yelled, "Get in that fuckin' bedroom!" He heaved Sean through the doorway.

The whole scene flickered, a jerky cinema picture. A middle-aged woman in a blue satin sleep cap clicked on a bedside lamp with a beaded shade, turning to Sean with a confused, then disbelieving, expression. Next to her, a man with dark hair and a neat grey mustache leaned sideways into the shadows.

When Sean raised his revolver, the woman's confusion dissipated and she shrieked in abandoned terror. His eyes followed down the sleeve of the man's pajamas that ended in a hand hidden within a drawer in the nightstand.

"Shite! He's goin' for a gun!"

Sean aimed at the center of the magistrate's chest.

He'd only fired the pistol once before, in the countryside outside Dublin where he and Barry had hiked for practice. With so little ammunition, they'd each fired only three bullets at some old brown stout bottles, missing every time. The trigger felt so much heavier in the horrible intimacy of the bedroom. He pulled harder, jerking the gun a little. The sound was softer, less echoing than when they'd shot their three rounds in the woods out past Clontarf.

The wall behind the magistrate blossomed in a maroon chrysanthemum as the back of his head disintegrated.

He seemed unreal, like a painted mannequin. A single dark ruby hole above his right eyebrow. Not where Sean had been aiming at all. The magistrate slouched down in his half-sitting position, head lolled sideways towards his wailing wife. His eyes were open, glassy as a dead eel's. Not a drop of blood was on the front of his crisp cotton pajamas with the indigo stripes. It puzzled Sean, all of it done with just one poorly aimed shot. But here was the magistrate that had been causing such trouble for the lads, his life snuffed in an excruciating instant.

The smoke from the shot hung in the air, fulsome, almost sweet. Not like before, out in the countryside. Then it seemed acrid and bitter, contrasting with the rich smell of manure from the nearby fields.

The second shot didn't seem very loud either. Like a pop or a slap within the draped and upholstered bedroom. And the shrieking stopped.

The wife crumpled back against the pillows and her flannel nightgown wicked a bright crimson pattern from the hole in her chest. Her breathing was ragged and raspy while the life dimmed in her wide eyes, returned to their startled expression. Barry cocked his revolver again and Sean turned. The first thing he noticed was that Barry hadn't bothered to pull up his mask.

The third shot was thunder in his ears.

Sean and Barry dashed down the hallway, pounded down the stairs leaning on the banister, then stumbled through the kitchen to the back door. They ran out into the garden, following the white-gravel path back to the gate, then turned down the narrow lane while forcing themselves to slow to a walk. They were panting like blown racehorses when they reached the canal in what seemed seconds.

The big bond warehouse for the local distillery sat on the quay close to the narrow waterway's edge, just enough space for a truck to pull up. Four lamps protruded from curved posts set right up against the exterior walls, leaving discrete pools of light beneath.

In the shadows beyond the last circle of illumination, Sean saw a man's face in an orange-red glow as he puffed on a cigarette, leaning against the side of another nondescript automobile. Sean turned to Barry and motioned to the waiting vehicle. They broke into a run. The driver heard their slapping feet and flicked his cigarette into the canal. He opened the passenger door before dashing round to the driver's side. Jumping behind the wheel, he revved the idling engine as Sean and Barry jammed themselves into the front—the only seat in the tiny runabout.

The driver was calm enough to make their escape seem nothing more than a return from a late pub night. They hadn't gone a hundred feet before Barry lit a cigarette.

They were soon out of Tullamore and rolling south through the dark countryside, the headlights picking out the curving boreen and stone hedgerows either side of the dark surface.

"What in hell were you thinkin'? You couldn't be bothered to pull up your mask? There was no call to shoot the wife, too."

The driver began to whistle under his breath, thinking it best neither to hear nor remember what was said six inches from his ear.

Barry stared out the side window at the nothingness. Without turning, he said, "There was every reason. Just like there was no reason to mask myself. Either the magistrate was sleepin' alone or the wife wasn't goin' to live through this night."

"If you covered your face, there'd have been no need."

"This war is like to be a long and nasty piece of work. The Brits aren't leavin' all gentle like. We can't be takin' unneeded risks. And that means no witnesses to our work." He lit a cigarette off the old one and returned to studying what little he could see of the passing countryside.

Sean sat in a sulk for some time. But when the driver stopped whistling, Sean asked, "Where are we bound?"

"Down into east Tipperary, a village called Glenador. I'm to deliver you to the schoolmaster between seven and eight in the mornin'." The driver gave a quiet chuckle and added, "Not that I expect he'll be hidin' the two of you in the schoolhouse, mind. We'll lay by for a few hours when we reach a big woods, beyond the next village. You boys should take some rest. The Lord only knows when you'll have your next sound sleep."

CHAPTER TWELVE

Sean

Kevin Tobin had made a vague excuse to his wife as to why he needed to leave early for the schoolhouse. She didn't give it much thought and he was relieved for that. His son and daughter weren't up, but they would be soon. Neither was old enough for school, so they hadn't lost the pure joy of waking each morning to a day that might bring all manner of new things.

He wasn't one for waiting, although few but his wife would know how anxious he could be. He'd cultivated a taciturn and aloof reputation so parents wouldn't fear he'd spill any secrets their children might share. Not even his wife knew of his other activities, and he intended keeping it that way.

It was only important that the intelligence lads in Dublin knew. He got his orders from them and sent back reports through a bookseller near the Four Courts. He'd only met this connection once, on the trip to Dublin back in 1918 when he'd volunteered through an old college mate to collect information in the eastern reaches of Tipperary and assist where he could.

The bookseller was a mousy kind of fella with round glasses, almost as reserved as Kevin. They'd exchanged the minimum words needed to establish procedures and codes, agreeing to secret their communications in the leaves of Irish-language books. That was how Kevin had received instructions to assist a few IRA men on an operation in these parts. He didn't know what operation—didn't care to know—only that he was to hide them until the West Cork Brigade could pick them up. He wasn't sure when that would be, so he'd have to find someplace other than his cousin Ned's farm where he intended to stash them tonight and maybe tomorrow. Ned was due back from a visit to Dublin the day after.

Nothing to do but wait. He'd already washed the chalk boards, swept out the classroom, and stirred up enough coals to restart a slow fire in the little stove that scarcely heated the room. If they came, they came. If not, it would be just another day teaching the children of Glenador. He was jerked out of his pondering by the sound of an automobile entering the village, stopping near the school. A door slammed and before he could reach the front, there was a sharp knock at the entry door. When Kevin swung it open, two men—neither much more than eighteen or nineteen—stood in the doorway, haggard and unkempt.

He greeted both with a single nod and opened the door wide, motioning inside.

Barry spotted the wooden pail and dipper near the stove that provided water for the students. "I could do with a drink."

Kevin nodded again but his expression never varied. He walked over to the other man and said, "I'm to hide you until the Cork men collect you."

The shorter man slid off his cloth cap and rubbed his fingers through his hair several times like a dog scratching, then gave Kevin a tentative smile.

"I'll be seein' more of Ireland than I'd expected, so."

Kevin stood silent, studying the young man. Dubliner, that much couldn't be hidden.

Strange how you come to miss things that once annoyed. The clopping and honking of the jumbled traffic in Dublin soothed Ned, so familiar and comfortable, although in the Boston of his younger days it had been mostly horse-drawn. He thrilled to the smells that wafted up from the filthy river or belched from the open doors of butchers and fishmongers. Much as he'd grown to love the rhythms of his grandfather's farm, how they relieved some of the baggage he carried from the war, sometimes the quiet was stultifying to a man raised in the noise and rush of a city.

An overdue holiday, even if only a few days, was doing Ned Tobin a world of good. With reason to dress in other than trousers with shiny knees and shirts stained under the arms, he felt like Major Tobin again. Like a man demanding and deserving respect. His walk lost the exhausted slouch from long days working the fields and horses. The heels of his polished shoes tattooed the pavement as he made his way from the brick hotel with the elegant fanlight in Molesworth Street, over to Grafton and up toward the river.

A little intoxicated from the hubbub, he'd zigged and zagged behind the Castle and found himself at the foot of Winetavern Street looking over the Richmond Bridge at the big copper-topped dome of the Four Courts. It had been years since he'd let his mind lose track of time and wander away from him. Not something you could've done in France, let yourself forget where you were.

Pushing aside the taut twine, he glanced again at the address on the brown-paper wrapping. With a break in the traffic along Merchant's Quay, he dashed to the bridge, then slowed to a stroll, enjoying the sights up, down, and above the River Liffey.

The son of a self-made businessman who'd never had a kind word for a lawyer, Ned wouldn't choose to be in the heart of legal Dublin without a purpose. In this case, he was to deliver a parcel for his cousin. Kevin had said it was just a few volumes in the Irish language he'd borrowed from a bookseller behind the Four Courts. Once Ned crossed the bridge and landed on Inns Quay, he glanced along the front of the courthouse with its six tall columns. Under the ceremonial archway of the east arcade, a half-dozen barristers fussed like a congress of crows, gowns flapping as they clutched briefs and horsehair wigs.

The address was in Chancery Place and the hotel doorman had told Ned it was straight off the bridge and right along the east side of the Four Courts—but sure aren't there only the two courts now, and a fine thing that was, since they were taxed a scandalous amount,

Saints preserve us, and sure you'd not stand for a blessed minute of that nonsense in Amerikay, would you? It was only after several attempts that Ned extracted himself from the doorman's urgent need to educate him.

In the first block of Chancery Place, Ned located a small storefront, the ground floor framed in wood and divided-light windows. It was painted glossy black, even the mullions in the windows, with fading gold letters above the door reading *P. Conway — Bookseller.*

To forego buying rounds and enduring the endless patter at the bar, Desmond made a show as he walked into The Gallant of patting down his pockets in search of the cigarettes he knew were inside his coat. He shrugged toward the bar, where several pairs of thirsty eyes were already upon him, and turned to the short counter next to the door behind which Molly Brannigan sat on her stool. She hadn't seen him come in, absorbed in a slim volume she held in both her palms.

When Desmond placed a hand on the countertop, she looked up to see who had the temerity to intrude upon her reading. The sight of her beloved blew away her tetchiness like a feather on a gale.

He'd never seen a face so pleased to see him, not since he'd left his old nurse when he went off to boarding school and she'd died during his first term. Molly looked at him without a shred of judgment or expectation, her pale skin and clear eyes shining from his presence. He drew in a long breath to dispel the tightening in his throat.

"Well, Miss Brannigan, I find myself in need of a packet of Navy Cuts," he said louder than necessary, giving her a twitch of a wink. She smiled back, then turned to the shelves as much to hide her burning cheeks as retrieve his cigarettes.

"And some matches, if you please." Although he hadn't looked back at the bar since he first came through the door, Desmond could feel the sharp eyes of Eda on his back. He'd felt her protectiveness radiate across the crowded barroom enough times before.

Molly set the packet on the countertop, then bent to fetch a box of lucifers from underneath. When she looked up again, he'd placed a folded one-pound note on the counter, a finger keeping the bill from opening.

"Oh, I don't know that I've the change to break that."

Pushing the quid note closer, he slid it open a little, revealing a scrap of paper concealed within the fold.

With a quick glance at his imploring look, she swept up the bill and, screened by the counter, hid the small paper in the pocket of her skirt.

Holding up the white bill with its black and red printing, she said, also louder than necessary so the nearby men were sure to hear, "Well then, Mr. O'Connell, you havin' such an open-handed way with your money, I'll have to fetch more change from behind the bar, won't I?"

Desmond grinned at Molly's perfect mimic of her voluble mother, watching her long yellow braid sway above her slender waist as she walked away. The thought of loosening that braid and holding that waist, bare under his hands, aroused him in a rush.

He'd know exactly what that would feel like tomorrow afternoon, if he knew his Molly.

"Over at the window," Kevin said to the taller of the gunmen who was lighting a cigarette. Barry shot the schoolmaster an annoyed glare, then trudged across the room and slouched against the wall next to a square window, blowing smoke out the side of his mouth at the raised sash.

Motioning Sean toward the blackboard with a terse nod, Kevin took up a piece of chalk as he passed his battered desk. Barry didn't seem concerned enough to join them, so Kevin sketched a simple map for Sean.

"Here's the village green. We're here." He drew an X on the south side of the green. "You'll walk to a farm, few miles east. Take the Ballysloe road here." He added a double line from the green, running off to the right. "Stay to the road. It twists and turns."

Sean nodded and said, "What are our chances of being seen along the way?"

"You'll not go unseen. You'll pass several farms." Kevin went to a narrow closet at the back of the schoolroom and fished round inside. He returned to the big desk with two bundles wrapped in shirts with their sleeves knotted together. He looked over at Barry, who tossed his fag out the window and wandered over.

"There's bread and cheese and bacon, an old jumper each. It's chilly at night," said Kevin. "Walk the road without a care, farm laborers headed for work. Common enough sight." He handed a bundle to each man in turn, one threadbare and white, the other a worn greyback flannel from some Tommy lucky enough to come home from the war.

"You look like you've been sleeping rough. More's the better," said Kevin. "You'll cross a stone bridge over a shallow stream, the road rising the other side." He drew a rectangle for the bridge. "Once you're on the downhill, look for the next lane on the right. It's lined with ash trees." He drew in the lane and added some asterisks for trees.

Sean nodded and stepped a little closer, committing it to memory. Barry glanced at the drawing from time to time, but otherwise looked bored and in need of another smoke.

"At the end of the lane, you'll be in a farm court." Kevin added a large square to his sketch. "There's a house here, and a stable across. Half-dozen mares in there, so keep away." Adding a final rectangle, Kevin said, "This side's a hay barn with a thatched roof. Hide there."

"Horses in the stable?" said Barry. "Why don't we just find the farmer? He must be with us, yeah?"

Kevin looked over at Barry and said, "He's away to Dublin. Won't be back 'til Thursday. If the Cork men don't come before then, we'll move you along," He added, his bluff expression unwavering, "Next choice is a cave."

"Who's mindin' the horses while the farmer's away?" said Sean.

"One of the neighbors and his boys help work the place. The farmer's a bachelor and a city fella like you." Sean looked a little surprised at what he took for a backhanded insult, but Kevin went on. "He's my cousin. From America. Not his fight."

At that, Barry moved back to his post at the window and lit another fag.

"He keeps a dog, but the beast wasn't about yesterday. Must be with the neighbors," Kevin said, then leaned back against his desk, waiting for questions.

Sean studied the chalky drawing with close-knit eyebrows and said, "What're we to do if this neighbour and his boys come to turn out the horses?"

Kevin stood and drew a clutch of X's to the north of the farm buildings. "There's a woodlot, behind the hay barn. Thick with trees and underbrush. Hasn't been cut for five years or more. Plenty of cover. One of you keep watch during daylight. Out the back and into the woods with your bundles should anyone arrive."

Sean turned back to his partner. "Anything on your mind?"

"Not a thing," said Barry. "Hardly a perfect situation, but better than a cave."

Kevin walked Sean to the front door and Barry fell in behind, cigarette dangling defiantly from his lip as his smoke wafted up to the schoolroom's rafters.

"Better be off. Time to ring the bell for the children," said the taciturn schoolmaster of Glenador.

CHAPTER THIRTEEN

Molly

Since she was now a scholar studying for university entrance examinations at the Sisters of Mercy school, Molly no longer had to wear a uniform. For the girls in their itchy tights and pleated wool pinafores, Molly Brannigan was the height of sophistication as she wandered their cloistered world in the clothing of a grown woman. She dressed simply, albeit a cut above what most of the girls were used to seeing on their own mothers and aunties. A successful pub owner like Eda Brannigan could provide better for her daughter. Nevertheless, Molly wore everyday skirts in navy or grey with simple blouses and plain sweaters. She owned two fancy frocks. One she wore for Mass. The other she'd inherited from her sister, Deirdre, and with some taking in suited well enough for parish dances and occasional shopping excursions when her mother treated her to cream buns at one of the tearooms on the resurgent Sackville Street.

In exchange for her envied scholar's privileges, she helped by tutoring the odd girl who'd fallen behind. Mostly she was left to prepare for the arduous examinations she'd soon face. The sisters treated Molly like a farmer's prized heifer, she only the second girl from the school attempting university, not just a nursing course like her sister or Our Lady of Mercy teacher college down in Blackrock.

Before leaving in the morning, Molly had told her mother she'd be home late since she had a tutorial with one of the struggling girls. Eda Brannigan was nothing if not tenderhearted and told Molly to take as much time as needed. Francis would have to mind the pub while she saw to making Danny's tea.

The fabrication had come so easily to her lips. She'd not lied to her mother, not about anything of importance, since she was a little girl. Even then, she'd not been able to keep the guilt from her face. Her sister could always catch her out in a fib, but she was away in Canada.

No matter, she was off to meet her Desmond, to fall into his embrace with no one else to see. Away with the secret kisses and groping under a tree in Stephen's Green. She was treated as a woman by the men in the pub, by the sisters at school. Now she'd have the pleasures due a woman in the arms of the man she adored.

She'd had the same whispered conversations as any other teenage girl, seasoned with the knowledge of a Dublin girl who'd grown up seeing doxies along the quays or flushed from the stews of Monto to wander the streets on evenings with slow trade. Her sister, Deirdre, gave her the medical facts and a little advice from her own limited experience, but there was no way for Molly to know the truth of what it was like to lie with a man.

And Desmond was waiting for her. Her stomach tightened and her legs weakened with the thought of him, the smell of him, the taste of his mouth on hers. She walked faster, almost skipping toward the address. *Henrietta Street No. 12.*

She couldn't have refused him. *You will come if you love me.* She wouldn't have wanted to anyway. *Knock and say my name to whoever answers.*

No. 12 was one of many once-grand Dublin houses fallen upon harder times. The wealthy Protestant families had abandoned the city for greener and more fashionable suburbs fifty years ago, leaving their brick Georgian heaps for the working people to divide into one- and two-room flats with shared kitchens below and communal toilets behind. No. 12 was reclaimed from the overcrowded squalor of the street as a self-styled hotel, with dirty white paint peeling from round the windows and yellowed newspaper stuffed into a missing pane in the milky fanlight above a garish vermillion door.

With fingers trembling, Molly lifted the weathered knocker and rapped three times against the door. She pulled her hand away as if scalded and placed her fingers across her throat. She felt rushes of blood pulsing beneath her skin as she waited.

The door opened a crack and an old woman's craggy face appeared. She looked Molly up and down with a myopic squint.

The name came out in a cracked and tentative voice. "Desmond O'Connell."

The old woman's expression melted from a suspicious glare to a leering toothless grin. She opened the door wide and motioned the girl inside.

Molly stepped through and the old woman slipped a dry, wrinkled hand through her arm. "Yer gentleman will be expectin' ye, dearie. In No. 7, just to the left, top o' the stairs." She squeezed Molly's arm with her swollen-knuckled hand and cackled her way down the hall.

The wide stairs told of young ladies descending for callers and departing for balls, but now the treads were scuffed and gouged, the dark paint of the handrail worn to bare wood along the top. The appearance of a lighter swath running up the middle of the wooden stairs revealed where a carpet runner had once muffled the feet of children running down to greet arriving relatives. A single sooty gaslight halfway up cast jaundiced shadows down the drab red-silk wallpaper, its brocade pattern erased by age and poor illumination.

It didn't matter, not at all. Molly strode up the creaking stairs, trembling with excitement. At the upper landing, she scanned the three doors to the left, spotting a tarnished brass 7 on the door at the end of the short hall. She hurried on, pulling off her gloves, and knocked twice.

The door flew open so quickly she knew he was overflowing with equal anticipation. She stepped into the bright room and threw her arms round his neck. Without a word spoken, she sealed her mouth over his. Not knowing how it got there, her coat was in a heap on the floor.

They pulled apart and he held her almost at arm's length. He opened her cardigan, gaping at each button he loosed like a child with a holiday gift. He slid his hands up her sides, feeling the ribs under his fingers. Pushing the sweater off her shoulders, he tossed it across the bench at the end of the iron-framed bed and turned his attention to her blouse.

She grabbed his wrists and stopped him, then stepped in close and did as he had done, running her hands up his sides and pushing off his suit coat with both hands. Laying it across the low bench next to her sweater, she smiled at the homely still-life of a married couple undressing for sleep.

When she turned back, the look of him frightened her. There was a hunger, his breath coming in short bursts and his face flushed hot. His fingers fumbled with the small abalone buttons of her blouse and he tugged at them in frustration. She grasped his wrists again and moved his hands to her waist. His eyes never left her as she carefully released each button, fingers moving in graceful patterns as if she were tatting lace. She gazed at his face, wondering why he didn't look up at her.

She slipped out of the cotton blouse and laid it over her sweater, then unhooked her waistband, heeled off her shoes, rolled down her stockings, and stepped out of her skirt and underskirt together. She pushed the shoes and stockings under the bench with her bare foot, standing before him in her camisole and drawers.

He finally raised his eyes and looked into hers, desire burning in his cheeks. She found it intriguing and exciting, the raw power she had over this man, perhaps any man she chose. She ran her hand up his thigh and pressed it hard against his crotch, squeezing the hardness. Flinging off his shirt, he grabbed her hand and rubbed it up and down, eyes closing with a low moan.

Then he snatched away her hand and looked down into her face. He reached for the hem of her camisole and began to lift, slow and tentative, as if fearing a slap. She raised her arms and he slipped the white cotton over her head. The cool air of the room raised gooseflesh on her bare skin.

He stared—almost gaped—at her breasts. Her chilled nipples were stark against the whiteness of her skin and he stroked the back of his fingers downward from her neck. She gasped as he ran over her breast, then stood on her toes to reach his mouth and tongue. While they kissed, she slid the waistband of her drawers to her knees and was startled by the wetness that had soaked the fabric between her legs. They fell to her ankles in a wrinkled pile.

He stepped back, taking in her complete nakedness in the late afternoon light filtering through the yellowed gauze curtains. She was flawless he thought, like a diamond of the purest water and finest cut. As he loosed the plaiting of her braid, he looked back and forth from the growing plume of flax in his palm to her alabaster skin. The hair at the junction of her legs was golden and downy, not the straw yellow of her braid.

As her hair came free, he let it fall over her shoulders. When she looked up, a sharp pang shot through her. He seemed hesitant, a little wild, and she wasn't sure what to make of it. He looked like someone else, not her Desmond. She ran her hands over her arms to smooth away her silly fears.

His braces dangled loose, so she reached to unbutton his fly, finding it awkward with men's buttons backward of women's. She'd felt his erect penis before, both through his trousers and on the taut flesh when he'd once slid her hand inside his underwear, but she'd not yet seen it.

She pushed his trousers over his hips and he shimmied them off. He began undoing the large buttons running along the front seam of his union underwear, but after the third impatiently shoved the underwear down to his feet.

She was transfixed. It looked so much bigger than it had felt.

Then she let out a giggle, pointing down at the long hose and garters he still wore. He followed her finger and reddened, embarrassed and annoyed, then shook his head and laughed, too.

"I look a right fool."

"You're a lovely, handsome man," she said and knelt at his feet, biting her lip to silence any more tittering.

It wasn't obvious what to do with his hose garters, having only worn stockings herself a few times, borrowed from her sister or mother. Tugging at one of the shiny metal clasps, she flinched when the elastic flew free and dangled. She opened each clasp in turn, then rolled down the black hose, her loose hair brushing his erection.

She delighted in the breathlessness of their anticipation. There were no thoughts of anything but utter fascination with the man exposed before her. She traced the musculature of his arms, his chest, down his back and across his buttocks. She'd studied marble nudes by the Greeks and Michelangelo in the glossy plates of art books. The sisters allowed them for her university exam preparation but kept them locked in a little office.

Here was her David. She crumpled into his arms as he lifted her onto the bed.

CHAPTER FOURTEEN

Sean

There was clean hay, unlike places Sean had slept during his first Eastertide with the IRA. He'd bedded down on floors or in doorways during those horrible days—declared glorious now by their leaders and scribblers—when he'd been out with the rebels in '16. No time to think about the quality of accommodations then, especially once the Brits brought up artillery and gunboats. Accidental, that had been—just a young lad out for a bit of excitement at the expense of the British. The bastards that took his father. No politics in him then, all restless rage.

He kicked the boot of Barry, stretched in the patchy sunlight snoring soft as a self-satisfied dog. The sleeping sentry didn't react, so Sean gave him a harder kick.

"Jayzus, can you not stay awake for ten minutes all together?"

A hand came up to Barry's face rubbing it all round, lips smacking over a dry mouth. He opened one eye and looked up at Sean, then raised himself on an elbow, his free hand going to his coat pocket for a packet of fags. He'd bought six at the tobacconist in the station back in Dublin. He was down to his final one.

"Don't be so fuckin' skittish," Barry said. He slid open the cigarettes and sighed at the diminishing rows. "We're out where God lost his fuckin' shoes. The neighbour and his boys have already come and gone. What's up your arse, then?"

"The Royal Irish Constabulary, seein' how we just shot two people." Sean said. His exasperation with Barry from Cavan was boiling over with regularity since they'd hiked out from Glenador. He'd also noted their language turning profaner by the hour. But that wasn't the worst sin on Sean's immortal soul.

"Finish that fag and get back inside," Sean said. "I'll take watch. Wasn't sleepin' much anyway. And don't be smokin' inside—you'll set all that hay afire." He paced in small circles near the open door of the barn, not risking going farther into the open courtyard. He could see straight up the lane rising to the main road from here.

"Settle yerself, boy. What's done is done. And we're clear and away from the RIC." Barry twisted his cigarette on the sole of his boot, careful not to bend the remnant. Pulling a spent packet from another pocket, he placed the butt with the others he'd saved.

Everything the man did grated now and Sean said, "Are you a factory chimney, Barry? Shite, can you not go half an hour without a fag?"

"Waste not, want not, my dear mam always says." He slapped Sean on the arm as he ambled back into the dusty darkness of the hay barn.

It was all so different, almost four years since that chaos and fear in the General Post Office. The first generation of leaders were gone, lined up against a high wall in the Stonebreakers' Yard at the back of Kilmainham Gaol. Only Dev had escaped because he was born in New York City and the American ambassador intervened at the urging of his mother. What had been de Valera's lucky accident of birth hadn't helped the others. Although they'd Irish parents, James Connolly was a Scotsman and Tom Clarke an Englishman, so there were no ambassadors to rescue them. The rest were Irish born and now all of them lay beneath the exercise yard at Arbor Hill Prison, dumped without ceremony.

The younger men rounded up and sent off to detention in England and Wales rebuilt the IRA after their release in the general amnesty a year after the rebellion. The big lieutenant who'd taken up Sean as a runner at the GPO was now his boss, not that Sean dealt with him often in person. Bold as brass,

Michael Collins, hiding in plain view all over Dublin, with the Castle not able to lay a hand on him. He'd even been to the snug at the back of The Gallant a few times, although Sean was only allowed to mind the door and keep his mother's suspicions at bay. Otherwise, whatever Collins had to say to Sean Brannigan came in anonymous notes stuffed between the leaves of musty books delivered by the unexceptional Peter Conway.

The squad of hard men Mick Collins assembled in Dublin was making life bloody difficult for the police and military intelligence men, as well as the odd recalcitrant civil servant not able to take less lethal hints. The magistrate of Tullamore had been one of these, much to the misfortune of himself and his wife. Sean was too well known round the Liberties to disappear into the crowd like the Corkman Collins, so he'd been detailed for work in the countryside to earn his spurs as a gunman.

The day dragged on without rain, a rare occurrence in the last days of an Irish winter. The in-and-out sun had taken the chill off the breeze. Perhaps Barry was right, Sean thought. They'd gotten away clean from Tullamore and made their way to the farm, being seen only by one man tightening the ropes over his haystacks and two women bent under heavy peat creels. They'd passed with waves and big smiles, Sean greeting them with the only words of Irish he knew, hoping to conceal his Dublin accent. It would have raised more suspicion if they'd said not a word. They didn't need gossip in the village about two surly strangers on the Ballysloe road.

He needed to calm himself so he sat in the packed dirt and bits of straw with his back against the barn's south wall. The radiated warmth from the stones seeped through his jacket releasing his tensed shoulders. The last of the bread and bacon was wrapped in waxy paper in his pocket, so he opened it and chewed the hardening bread while he looked over the buildings again.

It was a tidy place. Everything with fresh whitewash, the door and gate and window frames of the house glossy with new green paint. The horses had been turned out behind the stable and were browsing grass at the far end of the pasture without a care in the world. The neighbor would be back before dark to bring them in, but that wouldn't be for three or four hours yet.

They'd crept over to the pump beside the farmhouse, filling a bucket hung on a peg above some sacks of grain in the barn. He'd go have a drink, he supposed, with a little of the dry bread and salty bacon stuck somewhere between mouth and stomach. But the heat of the wall was grand and he'd not been truly warm for days.

"Well now, what have we here?"

Sean jerked awake and sat straight up against the barn wall, looking with wide eyes into a pink face bearing a not altogether welcoming look.

"Who might you be, young fella?"

Sean began to mumble, his thoughts knocked akilter by the proximity of the stranger's head, bent at his ample waist and almost nose to nose.

Barry materialized from inside the barn to rescue Sean. "Ach, I'm just a cousin of the owner's, down from Cavan to watch over the place while he's away," he said with deliberate exaggeration of the rising pitch found at the end of an Ulsterman's sentences. "And my mate here came along for a wee bit of diversion, having naught else to do with himself."

This was a time to let Barry do the talking, Sean knew, since the very map of Dublin City was in his own voice. That wouldn't help with Barry's story, so Sean slid off his cap as he rose and nodded to the big man who'd straightened and taken a step backward.

"Now, who knew the owner had family up in Cavan?" said the man. "I've known his father since we were boys, runnin' these very fields together, and never heard tell of any relations up that way."

Barry never blinked or stumbled. "I'm a cousin from his mother's side."

The man's forehead relaxed a little. "Ahh now, that would explain it. Emmett married an American girl, but Irish just the same, so I've been told. And couldn't her people be from anywhere?"

"Well, they're from up in Cavan," said Barry, calm as you please. Sean feared he was pushing the lies too far. "My old gran, may she rest in peace, was Ned's mam's auntie." To Sean's relief, Barry had finally dredged up the name mentioned in passing by the schoolmaster back in Glenador.

"Well then, your mam must hear from her still, being cousins like they are?"

"Didn't she have a letter just this last Eastertide," Barry said, "telling how everyone was hale and hearty over in America?"

The big man held out a thick-fingered hand to Barry and said, "Eamon Nugent, at your very service." After pumping Barry's hand a little longer than politeness required, he turned and offered the same hand to Sean, who took it with another silent nod. The big stranger's wide smile struck Sean as a bit too ingratiating.

"I was agent for the farm here, after my old friend Emmett's father passed. Then his grandson—a Boston man, born and raised—got a hankering to try his hand at farming back here in Ireland," said Eamon to Sean. "The war did many a curious thing to men who went through what these young ones did."

He gave Barry another of his unctuous grins and added, "I was about discussing some particulars with the owner regarding a fine stallion I've heard tell over in Mayo."

"We'll be sure to pass that on to my cousin Ned when he returns," said Barry. "Nugent, is it?"

"Nugent, Eamon Nugent," he said, producing a big handkerchief and wiping it across his face and across his neck. "He'll know the name. And I hope you'll forgive my suspicions."

Barry dismissed the apology with a magnanimous back of his hand. "Long forgotten, Mr. Nugent. Who can blame a man for bein' careful these days, what with all manner of wild rebels causin' mischief here, there, and anywhere."

There were only the two telephones in Glenador, although the Government had run cables out through this part of Tipperary more than a year ago. The ancient pub owner had considered having one, but the general consensus was that the phone box in the post office was sufficient for all purposes, few people having someone to call anyway. The tiny police barracks had its own dedicated line, sad necessity these days with rebels robbing and shooting respectable people like that poor magistrate and his wife over in Tullamore.

The tiny Royal Irish Constabulary barracks in Glenador consisted of two rooms, with the jakes in a rickety shack behind. The squad room was in front, the squad consisting of one affable sergeant and one eager young constable. Behind was a smaller space, separated by a door that was left open, since the only fireplace was in the squad room. This back room served as a bedroom for the officer on occasional night duty. It also served as a holding cell the few times someone had been arrested for a crime that warranted detention. In recent memory, the only person who'd been held in the back room was old Sweeney, caught for the umpteenth time distilling *poitín* in his abandoned cowshed. They'd let him go after a day or two, the magistrate in Clonmel sending word to bind him over for trial on a one-pound bail.

The police telephone wasn't used more than once or twice a week, often not even that. Sergeant Boyle was suspicious of the device and avoided using it entirely. The young constable was fascinated by the tall black telephone and Boyle was happy to let him make whatever calls were required.

While the fresh-faced constable spoke in his lower-registered telephone voice, the two other men sat on opposite sides of the desk. Both were large but in different ways. Sergeant Boyle was the son of a big father and an even bigger grandfather, all the Boyle men characterized by barrel chests and lantern jaws. Eamon Nugent, by way of contrast, had come to a flabbier largeness not through inheritance but from modest prosperity and an expansive diet. His own mother couldn't have been an inch above four-foot-ten. They'd hardly needed the four pallbearers to put her in the ground.

The young constable returned the earpiece back to its hook and said, "That was the barracks in Clonmel. They said a couple of men from Dublin who've been working the shootin' of that magistrate over in Tullamore want to have a talk with Mr. Nugent. They left soon as they heard, so won't be long."

"Right then," said Boyle. "It does seem passin' strange, those two lads lookin' after the Tobin place, seein' as Brian McNamara helps work the farm."

Eamon sat with the same self-satisfied look he'd worn since entering the tiny barracks an hour ago, insisting that Sergeant Boyle notify his district headquarters of the strangers' presence. It seemed a lot of trouble, but Eamon insisted and Boyle saw no harm in it. The Clonmel barracks would probably think Eamon some manner of crank.

Having overheard the telephone conversation, Eamon was now a very cat among the pigeons, smiling and relaxed in his squeaking chair. Had Sergeant Boyle been born with anything other than an utter lack of curiosity, he might have pumped Eamon for information. When the sound of a motor car filtered up from the village green, Boyle walked over to the single window next to the front door. A long Crossley touring car pulled up in front of the barracks and two men, the passenger wearing a dark wool overcoat and the driver a tan trench coat, emerged from either side. Both wore black fedoras pulled low, half-covering their eyes. Boyle couldn't imagine why they'd need to hide their faces out in east Tipperary, but those Dubliners were quare particular sometimes.

The older of the men entered first and took in the room at a glance, his gaze settling on Boyle's sleeve rank.

"We're here to speak with Eamon Nugent," he said. His posh public school manner showed even in those few words. Boyle was unnerved by these Dublin toffs, Protestant to a man and looking down their noses at honest country people.

"Yer man himself, right here," said Boyle, his nerviness showing in the forced joviality.

Eamon pulled his bulk to standing, the old chair complaining every inch of the way. "I'm Eamon Nugent," he said.

The younger man in the trench coat circled round to the back of the room. The older Dublin man gave a nod and the younger fished a coin from his trouser pocket and put a convivial hand on the junior constable's shoulder.

"Why don't you nip over to the pub for a pint or two on me, mate?" said the younger, the sound of Liverpool in his words. "And take your sergeant with you. He looks in need of a drink, too." He passed a big silver crown to the constable and patted his shoulder again, a little more insistent the second time.

The young constable's mouth opened, then closed mid-word. He looked to Boyle for guidance. The Sergeant heaved a resigned sigh and said, "I could do with a pint of the black."

He fetched his cap, then glanced back at Eamon Nugent's smirk and was glad to be shed of whatever mischief was afoot.

The older of the Dublin men stood at the window with hands deep in his overcoat pockets, watching the two local constables cross the green. Eamon found the intervening silence disconcerting and retrieved his big handkerchief to wipe his face and neck.

The man turned from the window, having puzzled through some problem. He sized up Eamon Nugent with the same practiced glance he'd used on the room when he entered.

"My name is Hastings, from G-Division at Dublin Castle. I was assured you'd know what that is?"

Putting his handkerchief away, Eamon said, "Oh, that I do. I've had… a relationship, shall we say, with your colleagues since before the end of the war. I don't flatter myself too much by sayin' I've provided them useful information."

The Liverpool man standing behind Eamon scoffed and said, "And you've been paid bloody well for it."

The older man silenced his colleague with a withering stare. "Please sit down, Mr. Nugent. We're keen to hear what you might tell us about these suspicious strangers you've encountered."

Hastings offered Eamon a cigarette, then took a seat. The two sat in their entwining smoke, the sweat reemerging on Eamon's broad forehead.

"About these two strangers?"

Never more at ease than while talking, Eamon spun out his information with growing enthusiasm.

"I drove myself out to the Tobin place to see Ned, the American who runs the farm now. Ned's da and me were boys together, but Emmett Tobin went off to seek his fortune in America, thirty years ago or more. Ned's granddad passed in 1917, and I was asked to act as agent and let the place to a respectable tenant."

"Which you were able to do?"

"I was able. We never had the conscription here, so there was plenty of young men looking for farms. Younger sons from big families and such."

Hastings sat deep into his chair, looking with disdain at Eamon, despising him as representative of all Irishmen who'd failed to rally to the colors.

"Simmons, you were with the King's Liverpool Regiment, weren't you?" Hastings said.

The younger man came round and leaned on the doorframe, joining Hastings in casting a gimlet eye over the fat Irishman.

"That I was, sir, 8th battalion," said Simmons. "And remind me, sir, wasn't you with the 2nd Ox and Bucks?"

"Yes, I was. We were both at the Somme, Mr. Nugent," said Hastings, "while so many of your countrymen were turning traitor back here."

Out came the handkerchief. Eamon swabbed his forehead again and didn't bother returning it to his pocket, worrying the linen between his hands.

"And right proud we were of all you lads who beat the Hun, myself more so than most." Eamon forced a weak chuckle that faded in the threatening atmosphere of the squad room.

"This American, Ned Tobin. What do you know of him?"

Eamon sat straighter, warming to his story again. "Ned's a Boston man born and bred, if you can imagine a city fella takin' on a farm. He was in the war, and long before the Americans came in official, fair play to him. He volunteered with the Newfoundlanders as a private soldier, then was made an officer after their terrible losses on the Somme."

Both men blinked a few times, Hastings looking out the window for a moment, before returning his attention to Eamon.

"Then the Americans wanted him after they came into the fight, needin' back all their men with experience in France. So Ned was made a major and finished the war with the Yanks. Had another hard time of it with his American regiment, I'm told. All Negroes, except the officers. Can you imagine such a thing?"

Hastings ground his cigarette under his toe and crossed his legs. Eamon sensed his impatience, but was determined to prove his worth to the Dublin men.

"When Ned got home, he couldn't settle himself and thought takin' up his granddad's farm might be just the thing. His father had done right well with shops and property, so Ned arrived with more than enough to get the farm all done up and the stables filled with fine mares."

"He's first-generation American, raised in an Irish family? I'm told there's not much love wasted on the English among the Irish in America?" Hastings was more interested in this farmer now.

Seeing a chance at ingratiation, Eamon jumped at the opening. "Didn't the Republican Brotherhood come out of America fifty years ago? And the Clan na Gael as well? And where do you suppose this current batch of rebels are gettin' their money, now that the Germans are well and truly beat? Oh, Amerikay's a very nest of Fenians, and those in Boston the worst of the lot, so I'm told."

"You said there were two strangers at the farm. Where's Tobin, then?"

"Isn't he off gallivantin' in Dublin? Felt he'd earned a holiday, bein' American," said Eamon. "Always last in and first out, the Yanks, just like in the war, eh boys?" His chuckle again rang hollow before the two expressionless men. Eamon regretted it as soon as it left his throat.

Hastings rose and returned to the window, staring across at the little schoolhouse. "About these two men?"

"The one who did the talkin' claimed to be a cousin of Ned's down from Cavan. He had the sound of an Ulsterman. When I said I didn't know of any Tobins in those parts, he said, nice as you please, he was a cousin through the mother's side."

"What made that suspicious?"

Eamon's confidence was building again and he relaxed back in his squealing chair. "His mother was born to Irish parents in America."

"They could still be cousins, through their grandparents perhaps?" said Hastings.

"And isn't that just what he said, the Cavan man?" Eamon said. "A cute hoor, that one. Hands as soft as a priest's, too. Never done a day's work on a farm, I'll warrant you that. Same with the quiet one."

"That doesn't answer the question of their being cousins or not," said Hastings, his impatience rising again.

"He said his mam had a letter from Ned's mother, just last Eastertide. Wrote that the whole family were doin' just fine." Eamon spread his hands and gave the Englishman an irksome grin.

Hastings stuffed his hands deeper into his overcoat pockets and turned back to Eamon, "Which is exactly the kind of tripe one would expect in a letter from a cousin you've never met."

"Now, that's the curious thing," said Eamon, about to burst with self-satisfaction. "Seein' as how my old friend Emmett Tobin's poor wife passed to her everlasting glory in the year of our Lord nineteen-hundred and eleven."

Hastings shot a glance at Simmons, who stood ramrod straight for the first time since entering.

"You're sure of this?"

Eamon patted his thighs with his thick sweaty hands and said, "As sure as these are my own two legs. She's been in her grave nine years."

Simmons went behind the big desk and snatched for the telephone.

It wasn't a long walk back to their shared flat when sober, but it was more of a challenge in a drunken stagger with two fuddled women in Spanish-heeled pumps. But Dubliners wouldn't pay any mind to two young couples out on a tear, headed God knows where and making a laughing spectacle of themselves.

"How much farther is this gaff of yours anyways, Cam?" said the dresser for an ingenue actress at the Royal.

"What do you reckon, Lieutenant Piers-Musgrave?" said Lieutenant Cameron Davidson. "You had some use for land navigation marching into Germany with the Inniskillings, unlike some of us who spent our war sitting and shitting in the trenches."

"How far, then? I'm legless in these fuckin' shoes, Tommy!" said the aspiring actress who'd recently ended her run as a harem girl in a burlesque at the Queen's.

"Oh, not more than a few blocks, I should say," said Thomas Piers-Musgrave, who as Desmond O'Connell had developed quite a facility for pacing his drinking while others overindulged.

"Says the plummy Englishman who wouldn't know shite of Dublin," said the wobbly ex-harem girl, answered by a burst of laughter that bounced off the buildings either side of the empty street.

"Janey Mac! Sure and ye're not speakin' o' me, a daycent Irish b'y?" said Thomas. Another peal of high and low laughter echoed. The dresser stumbled a little. Cam pulled her up and held her tight against him.

The girl brushed her skirt smooth and said, "Fuckin' frightenin' how easy you take that Irish on and off, Tommy. Gives me the willies." She stopped Cameron and tugging on his hand, pulled him toward her. She wrapped her arms about his neck and slapped her mouth against his, rolling an open-mouthed kiss side-to-side across his face while reaching down for his erection and giving it several long squeezes. Cameron emerged from the kiss and looked about with heated furtiveness, then walked her backwards into the recessed doorway of a shoe shop.

"Christ, that one's a regular bitch in heat," said the ex-harem girl. Thomas pulled her to a halt and pressed her to his chest, placing an equally sloppy kiss on her mouth. She didn't recoil, pushed her tongue hard against his while he squeezed her breast.

Cutting off the kiss, Thomas said, "A bit of privacy wouldn't go awry just now. What say you?"

"You're the fuckin' English lord of the whole fuckin' manor, Tommy." She leaned in against him for support and leered up into his face, her boozy breath twitching his nostrils.

The store behind them had doors flush to the pavement, so they backtracked with exaggerated tiptoeing past the groping couple in the shoe store entry. The girl giggled into her hand as they crept back up the street until they found the deep shadow of another recessed doorway.

He put his finger to his lips with wide eyes in a call for quiet, then leapt round the corner with her in tow. They both pulled up when Thomas stepped on something soft, followed by a sharp squeal. In the tussle of startled bodies, Thomas grabbed the arm of the shortest and yanked him out onto the pavement. The boy struggled like a hooked fish, trying to free his sleeve from the tight grip.

With only the light from an anemic bulb in a single lamppost across the street, Thomas saw snatches of the boy's face as they struggled. Something about the intensity and sadness of his look unnerved him. He loosened his grip and the boy jerked away.

Watching the youngster run off up the street, Thomas stood mulling what unsettled him about the urchin. The ex-harem girl tugged him into the darkness again.

"Little bugger scared me half to death," she said. "Now, come here and let's see what's in them trousers."

Shaking off his unexplained concern, he stepped back into the entry and squeezed the girl to him, grinding against her hip.

The only sounds in the street were the throatiness of excited breathing and the fading sound of Danny Brannigan's footfalls as he ran back toward the Liberties.

CHAPTER FIFTEEN

Ned

He couldn't see the back of Ireland fast enough. Headed across the sea and home to Boston, tail between his legs, so Ned considered it. The Auxiliaries, they were called. Thuggish gangs the Irish Government recruited from the throngs of desperate veterans, workless for a year or more since the guns had fallen silent, willing to take up arms again to do the hard policing of the unruly Irish that their own feckless Constabulary was loathe to undertake. He'd heard an earful about them over three drunken nights spent in a Republican-leaning pub in Queenstown while awaiting departure on the next steamer for America.

Ned Tobin had just returned from Dublin when they'd arrived. A prig of an English captain and his driver in a touring car, followed by a Crossley tender stuffed with an ex-sergeant-major and a half-dozen demobilized soldiers, itching for trouble. Ned stood in impotent rage as they set alight his house, his barn, and his stable.

He'd walked into the village, begged a ride to Thurles from his father's old agent, Eamon Nugent, and withdrew all the money he had on deposit at the Bank of Ireland branch there. He checked into a hotel, bought some clothes and a suitcase, took a long bath, then commenced drinking. The next day, he continued drinking

on the train down to the port at Queenstown, booked passage on
a steamer leaving in four days, and reported to the nearest pub to
carry on with more boozing. Just like his old man had done every
day since word came in 1918 that Ned's big brother had died from
the Spanish influenza. The Tearin' Tip, Bobby Tobin had been
called in the boxing ring, the pride of the Boston Athletic Club
toffs who loved nothing more than watching other men beaten
senseless.

His father had turned into a fine example of an Irish drunk and
Ned had seemed determined to follow in his footsteps. But aboard
a White Star liner, the endless blue-grey sea that put Ireland farther
and farther behind calmed him. With no smoking allowed in the
second-class stateroom he shared with an American machine-tool
salesman, Ned split his time between the bar, the smoking lounge,
and a deck chair he'd paid the cabin steward seven-and-six to rent
for the voyage. The chairs either side of him in the long line of
teakwood and striped canvas remained unoccupied since departing
Queenstown, so it was an unwelcome distraction when a tall man
with a thick head of steel-grey hair and matching eyebrows sat next
to him. The older man smiled and touched the brim of his hat when
he approached, then sat in silence, riffling a days-old copy of *The
Times*. After a few minutes, he folded his paper and set it on the
small drinks table between them.

"Fine weather again. Looks like it won't be a hard crossing," he
said, the missing r's and jumbled vowels of a true Bostonian shining
through.

"It does indeed." Against his better judgment and desire to ignore
all sober humans, Ned added, "You're from Boston?"

"Brookline, which stubbornly refuses to become just another
Boston neighborhood. But I'll forgive the insult. You?"

With rueful amusement, Ned said, "Boston man myself, from
Southie. And had I known you're from Brookline, I might've found
better ways to insult you."

The older man laughed with the heartiness of one comfortable
in the company of a compatriot, then extended his hand. "Aloysius
Pendergast. But call me Al, as all but my dear sainted mother have
long done."

Ned's edginess dulled in the face of this new acquaintance's affability. He gripped the hand and said, "Edmund Tobin. But call me Ned, since I've never answered to the other, even to *my* dear sainted mother."

Al Pendergast chuckled at the riposte and nodded with a crinkly-eyed smile. He settled back into his chair and looked out over the horizon.

Finally, the older man spoke again. "Did you board at Queenstown?"

Ned produced a packet of cigarettes and offered it to Al, who extracted one. The old trench lighter Ned had carried since France was a handy thing on a breezy deck. He held it out to Al, then lit his own smoke.

With a long exhalation, Ned replied, "Yeah, at Queenstown. You?"

"The same," said Al. "You don't sound much like a Southie man."

"I've been away all but a few months since 1914," said Ned. "I joined up with the Newfoundlanders to get in on the adventure before the war ended without me."

"You needn't have hurried, son."

"No, I needn't have. And my dear father, a Tipperary man to the bottom of his boots, has not yet forgiven me for taking the King's shilling. Even of the attenuated Newfoundland variety."

"Bit of a Fenian, the old man?"

"Why he ever left I'll never know." The bitterness creeping into his voice made Ned testy, as always when discussing his father, and he took a long drag hoping to expel his peevishness with the smoke. "He's done well enough for himself in America."

"What brought you to Ireland? Yearning for a look at the Old Sod?"

"Repulsed by running a candy store for my father on West Broadway," said Ned. "That is no place for an old soldier."

"Must be hard, finding a normal life, after all that."

"Indeed it is," said Ned. "And my dear sister, who has assumed the mantel of my dead mother, banished me to our late grandfather's farm in east Tipperary."

"You went from a candy store in Southie to a farm in Munster?"

Aloysius Pendergast found that quite amusing, smoking and chuckling while Ned replied, "Turns out I had some talent for it. Until the English intervened of a fine morning. Six days ago."

The older man stopped chuckling and listened with intensity, pretending to occupy himself with his cigarette until he'd heard the full story of Ned Tobin.

"Seems a few rebel lads on the run spent the night in my hay barn while I was away in Dublin. A group of special auxiliaries showed up after I'd returned. They burned it all—house and outbuildings—but not before bolting the doors of the stable to ensure my mares died in the flames." Ned extinguished his cigarette in the ashtray on the little table, grinding it with a deliberateness belying his wish it were in the English captain's eye. The older American felt the waves of cold, steely anger that emanated from Ned.

"No friend to the British, then?"

"That, Aloysius Pendergast, would be a colossal understatement," said Ned.

"Well, Edmund Tobin, when we reach Boston, I've a few men I believe you should meet."

CHAPTER SIXTEEN

Sean

A Chara,

We were pleased to hear that you are away and safe. I've had permission to write a short note to assure you your family is well but you are missed. I want to tell you what's transpired in the place where you had your near escape from capture. The school master who assisted you has been arrested and tried in a military court. He is to be executed in Roscrea. The Auxiliaries who you narrowly missed burnt the farm. The owner has returned to America.

I write this distressing news only so you will not be surprised when you inevitably hear it from some other source. You must not blame yourself for these sad events—the schoolmaster knew the risks he was running and his name will be added to our roll of heroes. The Auxiliaries have perpetrated many outrages across our benighted land. You must keep yourself safe and stand ready to obey future orders, so that we may carry on the struggle.

Not knowing where you are being kept, I entrust this to our comrades to put into your hands.

Beannachtaí leat,
P.C.

The smell of cattle didn't bother him. After hiding him on a remote dairy farm for three months, the Cork brigade turned Sean over to a railway switchman sympathetic to the cause. There were a few empty cattle wagons being repositioned, inserted in the long string of cars filled with mooing and stamping. The empties hadn't been cleaned out, so Sean kicked at the filthy straw, turning the bedding with his toe until he found a dry spot in a back corner. He carried a bundle the dairyman's wife had packed for him. By the heft of it she must have thought he was on a passage to India rather than a train to the livestock market at the edge of Dublin.

He nodded in and out of sleep for most of the trip, even after the sun came up and he could see green countryside and snatches of houses and shops as the train pulled through villages and towns with its cargo of Cork-raised beeves. It was early afternoon before the buildings came closer together as they entered the outskirts of Dublin. They'd been slowing steadily for some time and weren't moving much faster than a man could run when the piercing screech of brakes all along the line of wagons rose in a discordant chorus.

His instructions were to stay in the empty car until someone came to fetch him, so when the train came to its final stop on the siding, he stayed in his shadowy corner finishing a pint of milk and a currant scone. The last of the food gone, he listened as the cattle wagons were unloaded, the beasts objecting and wailing as if they knew what fate awaited. Time dragged on without anyone coming and he mulled over the worst eventualities that might befall him. He fretted that a railroad guard would turn him over to the RIC or that he'd have to make his own way across the entire city from the North Circular Road where the livestock yard sat all the way across the river and into the Liberties.

Once his mind began careening over thoughts of arrests and firing squads, the spray of blood across the bedroom wall behind the dead magistrate emerged in vivid detail. There was nothing to chase away such thoughts now—no exhausting work on a dairy farm or the terrified thrill of sneaking through the night from one hiding place to another. Alone in the silent interior of an empty cattle wagon, he finally confronted the enormity of what he'd done.

The poor magistrate's wife, her fish-eyed stare into nothingness with her blood dyeing her nightgown crimson—she didn't need to die. Who was Barry to decide her life was less valuable than some unknowable risk to their own? All she'd done was run her husband's household, pay his bills, keep him company at night. Surely that didn't merit what they'd done? He was as responsible for her death as Barry. There was no denying that.

A moan of disgust rose in his throat. He clamped a hand over his mouth, only to find it shaking like some old one's with the palsy. Swallowing back his sobs, tears and snot soaked his cheeks and upper lip while his shoulders heaved with his silent contrition. Not since his youngest years had he cried himself to sleep, not even after word of his father's death had come from the War Ministry. But he hadn't killed his father, hadn't watched him die.

Jerked awake by a boisterous conversation between a pair of passing yardmen, he watched a spill of lantern light pass the open doorway, keeping time with the crunch of feet on the gravel. He pressed himself flat against the wooden wall of the wagon, willing himself to vanish into the thickening darkness.

As the nighttime hours crept onward, Sean brightened a little with the prospect of being retrieved soon. The bitter weeping had relieved some of the creeping wretchedness that he'd pushed back since the night of the shooting. His purpose was clearer—to stay free and occupy the thoughts of men in the Castle pursuing him and a hundred others. The more of them at large, the more trouble for the RIC and the Army. This was his next role, and he was determined to perform it to the rafters.

A raspy whisper echoed inside the empty wagon. "Sean! Sean Brannigan!" The voice, throaty and low, was familiar.

"Martin?"

A silhouette heaved up into the doorway and whispered again, "Sean? Where are ye?"

Leaving the remnants of the food parcel, Sean walked through the inkiness and reached for Martin's shoulder, who jumped like a frightened hare.

"For fuck sake, Sean. Don't be scarin' the shite out of me," he said, but Sean heard the smile in his voice. Martin grabbed Sean's forearm and pulled him into a tight embrace.

"You've made quite a ruction, you and that surly gobshite Barry. Half the country's hidin' you and the other half's lookin' to hang you."

The memory of their last parting stabbed Sean. "Martin, I know I hurt your pride, takin' you off that work up in Tullamore, and I'm sorry for that."

"Ach, there's naught needin' an apology. I've kept myself busy doin' odds and ends. Like fetchin' sacks o' shite like you." He swung a hand at the shadow of Sean and hit him in the ribs. "What was it like, then?"

"Numb, not thinkin'. Seein' your own hand holdin' a gun and not even feelin' it in your palm. Then the noise, not loud like you'd think. Somehow… personal," Sean said in a flat staccato voice, then added, "The blood is terrible."

"Well if I was you, I wouldn't go confessin' that to any but the Christian Brothers. No tellin' who one of the archbishop's priests might tell. Or some shifty Jesuit," said Martin. He slapped Sean on the back a last time and said, "Out with you. I've my orders, so."

With a drop of four feet to the gravelly track bed, Sean fell when he hit the ground and slammed his shoulder against a creosote-slathered sleeper. He pulled himself up, boots sliding in the stones, and grabbed the edge of the wagon while he rolled his shoulder to check for damage.

"Dust yerself," said Martin. "We'll be leggin' it down to the Four Courts, but it'll be ziggin' and zaggin' all the way, you bein' such a famous outlaw and all."

The bookshop hadn't changed in four years, not since Sean had placed a parcel with a dozen copies of the Declaration of the Irish Republic into the hands of Peter Conway. They'd shared many a secret since, secrets they managed to keep from Eda Brannigan.

Peter was waiting in the darkness, sitting in a chair he'd dragged from the cramped office at the back and placed against a bookshelf just inside the glass-paned door. When Martin knocked, the door opened almost before he'd lifted his knuckles. The surreptitious bookseller dragged them inside by an elbow each.

"To the back. You can see the light under the door. Watch the counter on the left."

All three scurried like church mice to the rear of the store. After they'd crammed themselves into the office lined with ledger books and brown files tied with ribbons, Peter closed the door. He'd thrown a handkerchief over the small shaded light on the edge of the crowded desk.

He looked over Eda's middle son, not having seen him for more than three months. He was filthy enough, sticky black creosote down one arm and strands of straw stuck here and there. He looked none the worse for wear otherwise, although Peter sensed a new hardness about him.

"Martin, you've done fine work," said Peter. "Be off now and mind you don't draw attention."

Nodding to the older man, Martin shook Sean's hand and slid out the office. A moment later, the little bell over the door jangled as Martin stepped onto the street. Sean hadn't noticed the bell when they'd come in.

"There's someone here for you," Peter said. "Upstairs, in my flat. You can have a wash and a bite as well, before we move you along. We'll put you in one of my old shirts. Might be too long, but at least it'll be fresh."

A childlike feeling of safety crept through Sean—the warmth of the closed-up office, someone looking after him, the familiarity of the city after so many desolate places. "That's grand, Peter. I'll be grateful to be clean again."

He pulled at the hem of his coat and looked down to inspect himself in the light. "Mam wouldn't be pleased with me bein' on the streets lookin' like this, would she?"

Out came an immaculate folded handkerchief and off came the round steel-framed glasses. Sean smiled, having long known this was Peter Conway's way of postponing uncomfortable subjects. He waited in the warmth and bookish mustiness of the little room, rather enjoying the bookseller's manifest uneasiness.

"Before we... before we go up, Sean," Peter said, "there's a matter of which I'd have you aware." On went the glasses, with the careful placement on the nose and the rethreading behind each ear. "Your mother…"

Sean's chin snapped up and his amusement drained away. "What of Mam?"

Peter reached for his handkerchief pocket again, but caught himself. "Oh, no, no. There's naught wrong. She's healthy and prospering as before. But there's a… a… more personal matter I'd have you know."

With cleaning of his glasses already accomplished, Peter commenced restacking a pile of books on the crowded desktop. Sean grabbed his hand to still the fussing.

"Out with it, man. Jayzus, you're nervous as a schoolboy. I'm not the Latin master askin' you to recite Virgil." The amused smile was back, enjoying a little tease at the scholar's expense, comfortable in the normality of it.

Reaching some kind of resolve, Peter straightened himself, shot the starched cuffs of his shirtsleeves, and squared his shoulders. At full height, he was a half-foot taller than Sean.

"These few months you've been away," he said, pausing to clear away the last of the reluctance stuck in his throat, "I have been walking out with your mother. We've enjoyed several meals together, just the two of us, and we've attended plays and readings in Irish. And sometimes in English." His resolve was draining with each word as he stumbled through to the end, "And… and we've enjoyed… strolls in the parks on some days with fine weather."

Sean wasn't gobsmacked at the news. Perhaps a little startled, not being long out of boyhood and carrying residual notions about parents and their separation from the ways of normal people. But he'd seen them together at the end of the bar often enough.

The startled look didn't remain long and he sensed Peter Conway's relief in the long exhalation he tried to hide while studying his shoes. Placing a hand on the taller man's shoulder, Sean said, "Well, that's a fine thing, Peter. Really a fine thing. Mam hasn't had much of that kind of happiness, not since Da was taken."

With enough nerve summoned to face Sean, Peter left off scrutinizing his shoes, raised his head, and said, "That comes as a great relief."

"Bah, who'd object to Mam gettin' a little spoiled with attention from a fancy man such as yourself? Molly must be thrilled with the romance of it, her nose bein' in the poetry and the Shakespeare for hours on end."

Peter's face darkened and he took up studying his shoes again.

"I'm afraid your brother Francis isn't... supportive."

Peter navigated to the stairs from the little cramped office in the pitch dark while Sean followed the bobbing shadow to the stairwell. They made their way toward the slit of yellow light showing under the doorway to the flat above. When he reached the top, Peter waited for Sean to crowd in behind. He edged inside, pulling Sean along by the sleeve.

The rooms were lit by a single lamp on a small table next to a wing chair. Two legs protruded from the chair, as did two arms with slender-fingered hands, one holding a cigarette. The owner of the limbs was indistinct, lounged back into the shadows cast by the deep sides of the chair. Once the two men were inside and the door closed, the visitor stood.

"You've created quite a fuss down in Tullamore." The sulky look of the man's mouth chilled Sean, since he'd been present when that mouth delivered a flogging to an inept IRA man in the snug at the back of The Gallant. Sean stood in silence, not daring a word, with only Peter's sliding of the dead bolt puncturing the smoky stillness.

The wide-set grey eyes—which few men and no women forgot once encountered—betrayed the devilment bubbling behind them. The man stepped forward with a hand extended and, as Sean reached to grasp it, Mick Collins pulled him to his chest with a clamping arm round his neck, tousling Sean's hair like a puppy's fur.

After a loud laugh, Mick released Sean and said, "You did us all proud. That was the first, for both you and Barry, and I know that's a difficult, sometimes terrible thing."

Bending to retrieve the cap he'd dropped in the roughhousing, Sean smoothed his hair on the way back up. Having tagged along behind Michael Collins since the rising in '16, this praise meant everything.

"I was glad to do my bit, Mick," said Sean, hoping he didn't sound prideful. He slapped his cap into his palm and looked toward the double windows with curtains pulled tight over them. "The wife was somethin' I'd hoped to avoid."

Mick drew a long breath and exhaled, not bothering to raise the fag still burning in his fingers. "This is a war, Sean. Nothing less. The great tragedy of war is the innocent suffer. Like that old one in Tullamore, God rest her soul."

He gripped Sean by the shoulders and gave a gentle shake. "We're to have our nation, in our time, lad. After 800 years. And you'll have tales to tell your grandchildren." The mercurial expression changed to a sad graveness, and Mick added, "But we've much more of this hard business before us. The English won't leave with polite asking."

Having smoked little of it, he turned to the crowded little table and stubbed his neglected cigarette behind the pile of books into what Sean assumed must be an ashtray. Then Collins stood to his full height. Although not much taller than Peter Conway, he gave the impression of a much bigger man. He glanced about the room as if he were its proprietor, gave a wide grin that accentuated his large nose, and said, "I could do with a drop, Peter, it having been a long day and not yet over for me. Would there be a bottle about the place?"

Peter wasn't a man to insert himself into conversations uninvited, so he turned to a narrow escritoire next to the meagre fireplace without a word. Reaching into the shadowy recess of the desk, he produced a squat bottle, then reached into the darkness again, his hand returning with the stems of three port wine glasses interlaced in his fingers. He stepped back to the table and placed the glasses on the stack of books. He filled two right to the brim and handed one to each of his guests, then poured less than a half for himself.

"I trust a glass of port will suffice," he said as he restored the bottle and lifted his own glass. "I don't keep whisky about the place."

"You're a wise man, Peter, separating yourself from such a near occasion of sin," said Mick. He gave a sharp laugh, then downed his port. Peter raised the bottle a little by way of inquiry, but Mick shook his head.

Sean drank half his port and some of the tenseness drained away as the warmth spread outward from his throat and stomach. He drank the remainder and nodded his thanks to Peter.

"I've one more stop to make, then off to today's resting place. I thank you for the drink, Peter," Mick said. Retrieving his plain grey fedora from a hook next to the door, the man in the ordinary overcoat turned to Sean and said, "Barry's been lifted by the Auxiliaries, you should know. They caught up with him in Galway and gave him a rough time of it. We were moving him up the west coast, you up the east. He drew the short straw."

He shook Peter's hand and said, "See if you can get the lad tidied up, feed him, and let him get some sleep."

"Certainly."

Looking about the place a last time, Mick Collins said, "We'll send you instructions in the morning where to move him. No longer than one night here regardless. He's right under the nose of every high court judge in Ireland."

He shook Sean's hand and slapped his shoulder harder than most men would. The devilment returned to his eyes, melting off some of his thirty years, and he threw back his head and roared with laughter. "But isn't that a grand joke, Sean boy?" He opened door and said, "Right under their noses? A grand joke indeed!"

They could hear him skip down the stairs with surprising lightness. He whistled a quiet ditty neither of them recognized, followed by the distant sound of the little bell over the door.

No instructions came. As the day wore on, Peter wished there was work at the University to serve as a distraction. But Wednesdays were sports days, so no tutorials were scheduled, although most of his students limited their midweek athletics to pint-lifting.

Where to move Sean would be Peter's decision. As the afternoon crept on and the shadows of the hulking Four Courts fell across Chancery Place, he came to a decision. Perhaps not the best solution, but it would have to do.

Sean had left Dublin without a word to his mother, who'd been sick with worry. The apprentice barman she'd taken on in the new year found an unsigned note that the right-handed Peter had printed with his left and slid under the back door of the pub five days after Sean disappeared. It told her Sean was alive and well, working all over the country for a road haulage company. It left her puzzled why he'd taken up this new work without telling her, but Sean had always been an impulsive and wandering sort, all the more so since he'd lost his father. He'd turn up safe in the end, just as he had after that wretched week four Easters ago when the Army reduced so much of the town to rubble.

Truth be told, she missed him, even as little as he'd been about the place most days. Sean's flying in and out at no telling what time added some playful mystery to her days and his appearances always gave her a flutter of excitement.

The new apprentice had done the morning work enough to know the routine, but Eda found him not as fastidious as her son. She spent time each day buffing the odd stretch of brass he'd missed with the flour and vinegar polish. She always gave the doorways another sweep, clearing away the last of the old sawdust and dried mud, real or imagined. The apprentice was a quiet and decent young man, but he wasn't family.

The apprentice's granny had passed and he was home in Stonybatter for a few days to attend the funeral and wake. Eda would close and do all the morning chores, too, knowing Francis wouldn't be good for a blessed thing before noon, so burning had his need for the liquor become. And Molly was too occupied with revising for her examination and all the tutoring she was doing for that poor thing who was failing her classes at the Mercy Sisters' school.

"You'll finish those drinks now or they'll find their way down the drain," she said, threatening the last of the dawdlers right at closing time. "I've a long few days ahead, what with Sean off at his new work and the apprentice away."

The Pintman looked wistfully into his dwindling porter, then drained the glass to the dregs. The Weatherman left his rum on the bar in a brief protest, then emptied his glass, too. The Tippler was too bleary-eyed to manage the full pint before him, so the Weatherman put aside his disdain for anything but spirits and finished the porter in three giant gulps. He set down the empty glass, trailing globs of tan foam, back in front of the Tippler, who looked quite surprised having not recalled drinking it.

"I'll take this one and clear away," said the Weatherman, tossing one of the Tippler's arms over his shoulder and hefting him toward the door.

"I'll see you tomorrow, then, Eda," said the Pintman. With a last sigh and a forlorn glance at the empty beer glass, he turned and shuffled out into the night as well.

After retrieving the glasses from the bar and stacking them in the sink below, Eda strode to the front door and snapped down the flush bolts top and bottom, then spun the knob of the main lock. She glanced up and down the street through the leaded glass, noting a few stragglers ambling or staggering their way home from other places along the Coombe. She turned and surveyed her empty pub, relishing the quiet if not the sour smells. She let her shoulders unknot and, like every other night, she could finally exhale.

It was hers, The Gallant Fusilier, such as it was.

She walked with less determination toward the back entrance, kneading the pulls and strains of a long night from her lower back. She reached for the sliding bolt that secured the door opening onto Hanover Street along the side of the pub. Before she could shoot the bolt home, a tiny rap on the windowless door shocked her hand away and she gave a little yelp of surprise. Eda opened the door a few inches to shoo off the would-be drinkers seeking after-hours entry. She didn't abide winking at the law, unlike some of the other pub owners. She was tired enough most nights as it was.

The person on the other side pushed the door open another six inches.

"Off with you! This is a law-abiding public house that doesn't allow after hours…" Eda cut herself off mid-sentence as Peter Conway pushed inside and closed the door. He took stock of the barroom, ensuring the place was empty.

"Why are you skulkin' about this late, Peter?" she said. "You weren't in earlier, so I thought you'd something on at the University."

He blinked a few times, edgy and furtive, not like her Peter at all.

"No, not the University," he said. He took her hand and led her inside a little farther, but didn't remove his hat. "I have a surprise for you. Someone you'll want to see."

Motioning her to one of the stools by the last round table along the wall, he said, "He's out back in the alley. Shall I fetch him in?"

Eda sat herself down, not averse to the relief it gave her feet, and said, "If it'll put an end to this secretiveness, fetch in the Pope of Rome himself."

He nodded and rushed out the door. Within seconds, the door opened again and in stepped Sean. Eda shot from her seat and ran to her son, smothering his head in her arms.

"*Mo buchail*! My own boy!" She pressed her cheek against his hair and squeezed the breath from him. He peeled her arms away gently and smiled back at her beaming face stained with tears.

"Hello, Mam. I'm sorry for leaving without a word."

She squeezed him again and said, "'Tis over and done. My heart's so full of joy with the sight of you, there's no room for anger." She squeezed the breath from him again, then looked him over.

"So how long are you home from your work with the haulage company? Is it good work? Do they treat you well?" She produced a handkerchief from her apron, wiped her eyes and blew her nose, tsking all the while at her silly sentimentality.

Sean had no good answers, having just that moment learned he'd been duly employed in the road haulage business. Peter Conway stepped in to end the awkwardness.

"Eda, *a chuid*, perhaps you should sit again? There's something I must tell you and it's weighed on me for some time."

She sat dutifully back on the stool, a little disturbed by the earnestness in his voice.

"That note you had, the one slipped under the door, about Sean and his work with the haulage company?" Eda nodded, exhausted after her long day and confused as to where this was all headed. "I'm afraid I wrote that note."

"Why would you do such a thing?"

"Because I was concerned with how grieved you were at Sean's sudden disappearance," said Peter. "I wanted to allay your worst fears."

Eda looked from her son, who studied the floor, to her beau, and said, "So he wasn't working in haulage? Then where was he and what was he doin' all this time? And how would you have known he was alive and unharmed when his own mother knew nothing of him?"

Her voice rose with each question as her confusion and ire grew in tandem.

Now Peter looked to Sean and said, "She has a right to know. Dangerous as it may be, you know she'd never betray her own son."

Sean looked as if he'd been stabbed and said, "Peter, no... no you mustn't. She's my mam and... and you mustn't."

Eda hauled herself to her feet, past confused and well into livid. "One of the two of you will tell me what this is about or I'll send the both of you packin' this very night." The fire in her glare was something Sean had seldom caused but well remembered. Peter had never seen her in such a state.

"Eda," he said, reaching for her arm. She slapped his hand away. "Sean was off performing duties for... for the Republican cause."

"For the love of God, Sean Brannigan! Didn't you get enough of that foolishness those days you were out in 1916?"

Peter raised a hand to silence Sean before he could protest. "Eda, I need you to know that I'm a part of the Republican movement, too."

He didn't see the slap coming, quick as her anger flashed. His head snapped to the side and the heat rose in his cheek before he understood what had happened. Readjusting the glasses dangling from one ear, Peter stood in silence, burning with embarrassment and shame at his long deception.

Then Eda rounded on him and hissed, "You brought my son into your foolhardy, murderous... *movement* you call it? Suicide, I call it. How could you live such a wretched lie, all this time?"

Sean went to his mother and, taking her by the shoulders, turned her away from the stricken Peter. There was such a deep look of affection and care on his face, it snuffed her anger.

She put a hand to her son's cheek and, shaking her head and spilling fresh tears, said, "Oh Sean, what have you done?"

He leaned to her and brushed her cheek with his lips, gentle as a falling leaf, then licked her briny tears from his own lips.

"Mam, it wasn't Peter who brought me to the IRA. I never really left after the rising. With our leaders shot and so many in detention, it fell to the youngest to keep things tickin' over. Mostly, we spied on the Castle and the Army, reportin' to whomever we were told."

She hadn't stopped shaking her head, but she took aboard all he was saying.

"I didn't know Peter was involved until I was added to the list of those he ran messages to and from. They were in the books he lent me."

Motioning Peter over to her, she gripped his upper arm so hard it made him wince.

"Is that true? You did no recruitin' of my son?"

Placing a hand over hers, her grip loosening a trace, he said, "It's true. And I only wrote that note because I knew he was safe, because of the messages I'd carried. I couldn't bear to see you suffer, so I crafted the story of Sean's working for a haulage company. An excuse as to why he might be anywhere in Ireland and away for long periods."

No one said a word for a considerable time. The pub was still as death, the silence punctured only by Eda's subsiding sniffs. She blew a last time and stowed away the crumpled handkerchief.

"I should've known you'd never take up readin' as a pastime, Sean Brannigan. And wasn't I braggin' to Brother Michael from the Christian Brothers outside the fishmonger's just last week, fool that I am."

Wrapping her in his arms and clinging to her as if he were a toddler hugging her leg, Sean said, "I'm so sorry I grieved you, Mam. I'd have done anything to spare you, and I know Da would've expected that of me." He sniffed a little as he spoke.

She still held Peter's hand and squeezed it as a sign of apology and forgiveness. He returned the pressure, then released hers.

Holding her son's face, she forced him to look directly at her and said, "You'll hear this, Sean, and you'll take it to heart. Your father was as fine a man as ever walked this town, but he held powerful beliefs about what was right and what was wrong. And he was as pigheaded as could be should you try to dissuade him. It got him killed, fightin' in what he thought a righteous cause."

Shaking Sean's head side to side, she added, "'Tis my burden to be mother to a son who has the same kinds of wild notions as his father." He smiled back and placed a kiss in one of her palms before she dropped her arms.

"And I'm not at all sure which side your father would've landed, were he here to choose." She motioned the two men to the bench and took up her stool on the other side of the table. She smudged at some wet rings with her hand, then wiped her fingers in her apron.

"The English haven't won themselves any affection with their heavy hand since shootin' those poor men in '16. It's only gotten worse, the Castle bringin' over all those old soldiers and officers, desperate for a pay packet, to bully and beat."

Peter looked as relieved as a man who'd cheated the firing squad, like de Valera. "I don't expect you to agree with what we're about, Eda, but it encourages me that you see the injustice we're struggling against."

Eda patted the back of his hand, the old familiar gesture calming him all the more. She scooted her stool in close and laid her hands in her lap, looking across the table. "Now, what's Sean's situation?"

The anxious glances careening between Peter and her son told her all she needed to know. "There'll be no more of that. Sean's my son and I'll do everything I can to help him."

Sean leaned in, elbows on the table, and said, "Mam, I was out on a job. Doesn't matter where or who with. It went off as planned and I've been on the run and in hiding ever since. Most of the time down in Munster, on a farm with two fine old ones who were grateful for the help I could give."

"Explains why you look a little fleshy for an outlaw. What is it you're bein' sought for? Is it somewhat bad?"

Working a thumb into his palm, Sean said, "Bad enough, Mam. I'm a soldier with the Irish Republican Army and I've done a soldier's work. That's all I can say. It's safer if you don't know the details. In case something should go… amiss."

All she could see were the last tatters of innocence stripped from her boy, the dark one who looked so much like her. He and little Danny were the two she could claim as her own without anyone to deny it. And Sean just gone nineteen—they'd missed marking his birthday while he was away and how that had distressed Molly. But hadn't his boyhood fled him years ago? He's the one took his father's death the hardest. Turned in on himself, found something he needed on the streets, so she'd given him license to wander with his mates. Perhaps she'd missed the neediness, but he'd long been one to keep his own counsel—his little brother all the more so.

Eda snapped back—there were problems needed solving. "What's to be done, then? I mean tonight?"

Peter said, "We need to keep him moving, no more than one night in any location. I didn't receive instructions for tonight, and he stayed with me last night."

"Right next to the Four Courts? Are you daft?"

"There's no one about at night with the courts shut up tight. He stayed hidden during the day, then we made our way here. We've been outside in the alley for over an hour."

She thought for a long minute in silence, running her mind over all the possible problems and best solutions. The two men let her work through matters in her own way.

Finally, Eda said, "You'd best keep in the back room. That apprentice boy you'll remember?" Sean nodded. "He's away with his family 'til Friday. You can sleep on his cot."

"What'll we tell Molly and Danny? Francis, too?"

"We'll take up Peter's lie and make it our own." Peter flinched at her choice of words. Eda went on, "You're just back for the night before you head out on the next trip with your haulage job. You came in so late you slept downstairs so as not to wake Francis or Danny by comin' upstairs."

Sean pursed his lips and ran over the story to himself, then nodded and said, "Yeah, I can tell that straight enough."

Eda took her son's hand and froze him with an intense stare. "And you're not to breathe a word of your... involvement to anyone in this family after me. Do you understand? I'll not have them drawn into this."

"Of course, Mam. I'd not want that either."

She turned to Peter and said, "You're about the place most days. Do you suppose the pub is bein' watched? I hear tell the Castle and the RIC use all manner of detectives, dressed like any man on the street, tryin' to find out the rebels."

"I've observed everyone who comes and goes with any regularity as close as I dare," said Peter. She noticed how the awkward and bookish demeanor she found so endearing was nowhere to be seen.

"I haven't noted anyone suspicious, from my observations. Still, we'd best keep Sean out of sight during daylight, until we can move him on tomorrow night."

Eda chewed her bottom lip as she pondered the situation. "Francis will be the problem, Sean. After you've had breakfast with us upstairs and seen your brothers and sister, you can say you've friends to meet and blow out the door, as you've long done. That won't seem suspicious. Then down to the cellar and into the storeroom. There's a door, so no one going down to use the toilet will see you."

Peter said, "That might be best. Perhaps you could actually read a few of those books I've lent you."

Neither Eda nor Sean had ever heard the bookseller make even the mildest joke and both burst into laughter. As they sighed into soft chuckles, a startled gasp came from above, then slapping feet on the stairs. Sean looked over his mother's shoulder and saw his sister flying down and rounding the bar. He jumped up and dashed toward her. She slammed into his chest and he wrapped her in a tight embrace.

CHAPTER SEVENTEEN

Molly

With Molly knowing of Sean's return, there'd be no hiding it from the rest. After the tearful reunion with her brother, Molly turned to her mother. "I'll wake the others. They'd not want to miss this moment. May I?"

Eda rubbed a hand down the sleeve of her daughter's nightgown. With aching tenderness and some reluctance, she said, "Go on, but I doubt you'll have luck rousing Francis."

Molly headed for the stairs, stopping as she passed Sean for another tight embrace, then scurried on her toes to the flat above.

"Francis might have a full head of liquor," said Eda, "but he's no one's fool. He's like to see through your tale of this new job. Especially with precious little love lost between you." She went back to the stool, exhaustion in every joint and limb. "He'll think the worst straight off."

Peter wandered back to the bench opposite her. "There's no changing now. We'll have to keep up the bluff, best as we can."

With the energy of Molly's welcome dissipated, Sean looked more tired than a man of nineteen should be as he plopped down next to Peter. He ran a hand through his hair a few times, then slouched back, letting himself melt against the pale upholstery.

"Francis'll think what he will. He's not trusted me since I was out in '16. I'm sure he's had all manner of suspicions over where I go and who I see." Looking for a little reassurance from his mother, he said, "But we're still brothers. And that has to mean more than the Crown or the Republic, yeah?"

She couldn't force out the heartening reply Sean needed to hear, examining her chapped hands and willing them to cease their wringing. Finally, she said in a murmur, "Brothers you are and brothers you'll always be."

The door at the top of the stairs opened again and Molly gamboled down, still in bare feet although the empty pub was chilly and damp as a crypt at midnight. She didn't care, dropping down next to Sean and threading her arm through his, head alternating between his shoulder and snapping up to glance toward the door she'd left ajar. The minutes dragged with no sign of life from above.

Then the steady slap-clop of Francis on his crutch sounded as he made his way down the hall from the bedroom at the back. When he appeared in the doorway, silhouetted by the light in the sitting room, he appeared steady enough, although he could hardly be sober. A much smaller outline appeared at his hip. There would be little he could do if a man of twenty-five was determined to topple down the stairs, but Danny closely attended his brother's unsteady descent.

He'd taken the time to strap on his leg. Painful as that was after a long day in the prosthesis, his descent was stiff and slow. Strange how much more agile he was on just the one good leg and his crutch, Eda had long thought, but she knew he wouldn't appear before his younger brother or Peter Conway without two feet to stand upon, even if one was sanded and polished.

No longer able to contain her glee, Molly leapt from the bench and dashed to the bottom of the stairs, holding out her hands to Francis as he struggled down the last few steps. Reaching the floor, he looked at her upturned palms with practiced derision. Undeterred, she entwined her arm through his, staying close at his side as they crossed the room.

"See? Sean's back to us," she said, hoping to hurry the transit a little. She pointed to the bench in the dim light. "There he is, right by Mr. Conway, safe and sound. Isn't it grand?"

Hearing his sister's sing-song, Sean looked over to the trio in their nightclothes. Danny, barefoot like his sister under his oversized flannel nightshirt, disappeared behind the older ones as they walked. Francis glared at Sean, his scorn and half-drunk rage evident to all.

Eda pulled up another stool for Francis. She hovered and fussed while he let himself down with painful deliberateness and jerked the hinged knee joint up to a right angle. Molly returned to Sean's side on the bench while Danny balanced on his haunches next to his eldest brother.

"Hello, Francis. How've ye been keepin'?" Sean said, mustering as much nonchalance as he could through his exhaustion. His older brother sat with an impassive stare.

"Here's a grand thing, all of us together again," said Eda. "It gladdens my mother's heart." She reached across to pat Sean's hand on the tabletop, while doing the same to the one with which Francis was gripping his knee. She could smell the whisky on him, but his face looked alert enough, well-versed as he was in functioning at all levels of inebriation.

Francis turned his hooded stare to the bookseller and said, "Mr. Conway here isn't family, Mam." She jerked her hand away from his, reddening at his slow bitter words. Peter patted his pockets in search of his handkerchief, then removed his glasses, clearing his throat once, with only the smallest sounds escaping from him as he polished.

"Although he loiters about enough, I can understand the confusion," Francis said, his hand tapping the tabletop in an unconscious plea for a drink. "And what's he doin' here at this hour, anyways?" Francis waited for Peter to return his glasses to his nose, withering him with another cold glare.

Sean could see that Peter was caught on the back foot by his brother's question, and hurried to interject, "I was dropped at the east end of City Quay and was leggin' it home and bumped into Peter here just comin' out the Trinity gates, turfed out by the librarians fearful of him takin' up residence if he stayed later. I asked him along, thinkin' he'd be a welcome addition to my homecomin'." He slapped the scholar with too much hardiness.

"Isn't that right, Peter?"

"Yes… yes. Just that… I was researching a paper… a new paper I've been meaning to write… on the semiotics of… of Irish illuminated manuscripts." The very effort of this off-the-cuff fib appeared to exhaust Peter and he willed himself to vanish into the shadows.

"Ahh, that's right, Sean boy. You've got that fine job with the road haulage concern, criss-crossin' the island for months on end," said Francis. "And how's that, what with you not knowin' the first thing about drivin' a lorry?"

Sean had thought this question out and said, "I help with the liftin' and carryin' of the crates and such. And my driver's teaching me a bit of the knowledge, even lettin' me drive some lonely stretches in the countryside."

"Well, that's grand, much as we miss your work here at the pub," said Eda, struggling to move the conversation past the most brazen lying. "The new apprentice is workin' out well enough, although the poor lad's gran just passed and he's away for the wake and funeral."

Francis's jittering hand slapped the table with a report that echoed off the high ceiling. Molly gasped and grabbed at her throat while the others flinched. Only Danny seemed unsurprised, looking up at Francis with expressionless dark eyes. The crippled brother pushed up from the table, balancing on his crutch while he steadied his artificial limb. After poising himself from the rapid rise and residual tipsiness, Francis rounded on his mother.

"If he's workin' on a lorry, I'm the winner of the fuckin' Galway races," he said, anger with his mother and disgust for his brother radiating from every word.

"You shouldn't use that language in front of me and Mam. Nor Danny neither," said Molly, seeing that her stunned mother was in no condition to correct Francis. Her meek scolding fell impotent in the gathering tension.

Francis grimaced at the bite of the prosthesis on the sore stump, slapping at it as he moved toward Sean and Peter. He was wide awake and sober now, by the look of his building rage. Francis placed a hand on Danny's shoulder to steady himself. The boy winced at the crush of the angry grip.

"You've been out again, haven't you? You disloyal bastard, you're out with those goddamned Sinn Feiners again?"

"Francis!" said Molly, cheeks burning.

The sound of his name riled him all the more and he jerked his head toward his sister. "Shut your gob, Mary Margaret," he said, spitting her christened names at her with stinging condescension. "You'd believe your precious Sean here if he said he'd been to the moon and back. Open your silly eyes for once, can you, girl? He's a traitor, in league with a band of murderers. He's one himself—I'd wager a hundred quid on it."

Her hand moved from her throat to her mouth as thick tears welled. That was enough to get Sean to his feet, his own anger ending any ability to keep this elaborate tale spinning out. He shook off Peter's insistent grip on his sleeve.

"Yeah, all right then," Sean said.

Peter Conway rose and grabbed Sean by the forearm. "Sean, you mustn't." Sean brushed him off.

"No, Peter. This has been growin' between me and him since he was sent home without a leg. Holdin' court with those other broken and busted men who thought they were great patriots, marchin' off to fight the Germans. And he's drunk as a fiddler's bitch every night, leavin' all the work to Mam."

Sean took a step toward Francis, squaring his shoulders. "I've been with the IRA since the Easter fighting. Never stopped. And we young ones kept things together while those captured were shipped off to English prisons and camps in Wales. I've gotten more responsibility since, much more."

"You're a goddamned traitor. You deserve to be shot against a wall at Kilmainham, just like Pearse and Connolly and the rest of that disloyal mob." Danny winced as Francis squeezed his shoulder harder.

"For the love of God, Francis! Don't say such a hateful thing!" Eda choked out the words between gulping sobs. Neither brother paid her any heed.

"If there's disloyalty to be had in this family, it lies with you," Sean threw back. "You're an Irishman, born and bred, like every one of our generations before. Yet you cling to the bloody Crown like a squallin' babe on a sugar tit. What has any Englishman brought us but grief these 700 years and more?"

Francis pushed the table aside and it crashed to the floor, rolling back and forth on the wooden boards. "You've swallowed all their guff, so? The whole feast of nonsense about Perfidious Albion and all their shite? Well, that isn't what Da thought when he went off to the fight, was it?"

They were squared off and would've been nose-to-nose had Francis not been a head taller. Eda's shock passed into abject grief at the mention of her dead husband, not wanting his memory dragged between the brothers. She sobbed into her red hands, rocking on the low stool. Molly sat choked with horror, tears coursing and nose running to her mouth.

Sean glanced his mother's anguish, but there was no stopping the long-simmering grievances. He looked back to Francis and let go a loud, mocking laugh.

"For King and Empire, is that what you think took Da back to the regiment? You're more a stupid arse than I'd ever imagined," Sean said, shrugging his coat and stepping back while he spoke. "He went to keep you out of trouble, you bloody fool. You and your daft friends, rushing off half-cocked to enlist. That was a condition he gave the commander, that he'd have you under him."

Francis wobbled on his crutch, ferocious tension seizing his body, stiffening his limbs. Danny stepped up and took his arm.

"That's a goddamned lie, Sean—and you're a soulless coward to even say it!"

Sean tossed another taunting laugh at his brother and said, "Believe what you will, but I heard Mam and Deirdre speaking of it, after you and Da were gone. And Deirdre was powerful angry at Da for his foolishness in chasin' after you, since he'd already done his bit in South Africa already."

Francis's face pinched with the blows of Sean's words, looking to his mother for contradiction. "Mam, is that true, what Sean says?"

Eda sobbed harder into her hands and nodded her head twice. The wild anger creasing and twisting Francis's features slipped into confusion, eyes darting to his mother, back to his brother. Sean didn't appear triumphant, but rather stricken with sorrow at this terrible truth hanging in the stale air.

In the agonizing silence, Eda dropped her hands from her mouth and folded them in her lap. Still rocking with short rhythmic motions, her eyes were squeezed tight. As her lips moved, a few words of Irish were audible under her breath. Peter Conway was the only one to recognize she was praying to the Virgin.

When Danny felt the grip loosen on his shoulder, he sensed the collapse of his brother and slipped his thin arm round Francis's waist to steady him. Peter joined in, moving him to the bench. Sean stood panting with adrenalin and made no move to sit, pacing in short turns behind his mother, realizing in a rush the enormity of the danger in what he'd just revealed to his brother. Molly slid next to Francis and pressed herself against his arm, wiping at her nose with the back of her hand.

"Molly dear, you take Danny upstairs and try to get back to sleep as best you can," Peter said. "Tomorrow will be another day." He smiled with patient kindness at the two youngest Brannigans. "Now, off with you both."

Danny was too young to talk back and there was no argument left in Molly, so she rose and hugged the boy to her as they crept with bare footsteps across the room and up the stairs.

Peter retrieved a stool and settled before Francis. He sat ramrod straight and looked over the stricken brother, assessing his ability to hear any more. After a few moments, he leaned forward and rested a hand on Francis's good knee.

"Look at me, lad. There's no time for shock or confusion," said Peter. "Look at me."

Francis raised his head and saw someone he didn't fully recognize. The furrows of confusion deepened in his forehead as Peter continued.

"Your brother is sought by the Constabulary. The Auxiliaries and agents from the Castle as well. We need him to stay here and stay out of sight tomorrow. He'll be moved on come nightfall. Do you understand?" He squeezed Francis's knee to get his attention.

"Yeah, yeah," he stuttered. He blinked several times, dispelling some of the haze of confusion, then said, "We? Jayzus, are you one of them, too?"

"I am," said Peter, the gravity of what he was admitting freighting the words.

Francis hazarded a glance to his brother, still turning and pacing behind their mother, not paying attention to what was passing between the others. Eda had, with some intercession from the Blessed Mother, steadied herself and attended to Peter and Francis's conversation in sniffling silence.

"What's he done, then?" Francis said, nodding at Sean. "It must be serious, if the Government wants him so much that he's on the run like this. And all that time away, too?"

"Yes, most of that time, too, but he was hidden in the countryside. We've only recently learned the Castle was closing on his whereabouts, so he had to be moved in a rush." Peter's voice was louder and more authoritative than any of them had ever heard before. It was strangely calming.

Peter squeezed Francis's knee harder and said, "You must keep this secret. Regardless of your differences, he's still your brother. You mustn't tell anyone, not even your closest friends." He bore down harder on the shaken man's knee and added, "You must stay away from the liquor today. Not a drop. If anyone asks, you're a little unwell and thought it best to abstain."

Running a hand over lips already parching, Francis nodded his agreement. He looked over and saw Sean standing behind Eda, a hand on her shoulder.

"It doesn't matter what happens to me, Francis." Sean said, stepping round their mother. "I'll face whatever befalls. But think what the Castle would do to Mam. She'd lose her license sure—she and Molly and Danny would be turned out on the street," he said, plaintive in his plea to protect the three people they both loved most.

Mam said they were to go on as if it were any other day, not change a thing—but not to say a word to a living soul about Sean being home. It being a Thursday, Molly left off her studies at three o'clock and hurried to the dingy hotel in Henrietta Street. Desmond might already be there, or he might arrive a little after her. No matter.

The old housekeeper answered her knock, never missing the chance for a leering cackle at what this innocent-looking maid in the clean and proper clothing would soon be doing above her head. Molly gave up caring about the old woman's prurience months ago. And hadn't she been stunned by her own boldness? Meeting her lover in a part of town she hardly knew existed, throwing off her clothing and reveling in her wantonness. She loved him and would do whatever he asked, in bed or out, now and forever. Amen.

Finding that Desmond hadn't arrived yet, she had leisure to daydream. What need had they of a ceremony with mumbled words or the droning priest reading the banns out on three Sundays? She felt married to him already. Having drunk the potion of their desire they could no longer help themselves, she thought, like Tristan and Iseult. Or perhaps they were Abelard and Eloise? Desmond should be relieved she'd no father to castrate him like the star-crossed monk. She giggled into the silence. This tatty little room above the front door—the only place they'd ever made love, ever seen each other naked, ever abandoned themselves to their passion—this was their home. A place they alone had made and would always be their first, no matter where else they wandered together.

She heard the knocker bang on the grimy wood of the front door—three times, with a pause before the third. Perhaps it was a code he'd worked out with the old one below. Perhaps it was just his way. She'd find that out, along with so many other things, in the months and years ahead. Kicking off her shoes, she twisted the key with the stained tasseled fob and opened the door a tiny crack. She removed her blouse and dropped her skirts, peeling off her camisole and stepping out of her drawers as she listened to his footfalls on the stairs.

He saw the door was a little ajar as he was raising his hand to knock, her habit being to lock it from the inside if she arrived first. Opening enough to slide into the room, he flushed with hungry excitement when he saw her standing amidst a pile of garments, combing her fingers through her unbraided hair like Botticelli's Venus. He crushed her against his chest, covering her mouth with his while tearing at the buttons of his own clothing.

Three-quarters of an hour later, she lay with her head in the hollow of his chest, below his collarbone, a spot she'd claimed as her own each time they'd exhausted themselves. He'd been ravenous with her, climaxing three times with little pause between. He'd spilled inside her all three times, but she didn't care. She was almost certain it was beyond mattering, having missed her monthly twice.

Her older sister, trained as a nurse before the war, explained it all when she'd gotten her first menses a few months before her thirteenth birthday. Deirdre cautioned her not to listen to foolishness from prattling girls, then proceeded to horrify and fascinate Molly with the clinical details of female menstruation—and what might cause it to stop—with more practical advice as to what to expect from boys or men in that regard. With Da just taken from them and Mam so vacant during those sad days, Deirdre, with her disregard for any kind of nonsense, had taken her little sister in hand and equipped her with all the facts she could absorb. For weeks afterward, until her sister left to nurse for the Army, they'd privately giggled over all Deirdre had revealed that memorable evening in their shared bed.

"You seem far away."

She shifted her head and brushed some hair from her forehead. "Was I gone for long? I was thinking of my sister."

"She's off in Nova Scotia, isn't she? With your aunt?"

Lacing her fingers through the patch of dark hair in the center of his chest, she said, "Yes, with Aunt Nola. I miss her so very much. I was remembering when she told me all about... about what we do here together. It all sounded so... scientific. And frightening."

"Am I so very frightening?"

She laughed into his warm skin, still moist with sweat, and kissed his arm. "No, Desmond O'Connell, you're not frightening. Neither is your little companion." She reached down and squeezed his softening penis through the threadbare and greying sheet.

He flipped her to her back and tickled along her ribcage, then silenced her laughter and thrashing with a long kiss before rolling back to his side.

"So is everything well with your family? Your mother? I haven't been into the pub since last Friday."

"And you've been naughty staying away," she said. "You know I hate going a day without seeing you. Where have you been?"

"Some business down in Munster, but nothing important came of it. I managed to see my mother and she insisted I stay the weekend," he said, relaxed as he could manage spouting nonsense about a fictitious mother in Cork City. "I should've sent a note or a telegram, and for that I'm most sorry." He kissed the side of her head absently.

"Your brother Francis keeping well? Minding his drinking at all?" he said, without any genuine concern for the welfare of Francis. He thought the crippled brother a self-pitying wretch who couldn't accept his fate and get on with his life.

Molly raised onto her elbow and with a mischievous look said, "The most wonderful thing happened last night, but you mustn't tell anyone. Mam made me promise, although I can't imagine why."

He gave her an encouraging smile and said, "Of course I won't tell anyone. Now, out with it before you burst like a ripe peach."

"My brother Sean, he's home from his work on the lorries. Just for a night or two, but it was such a grand surprise when I heard his voice—I flew down the stairs and there he was! He seemed tired but looked like he'd put on half a stone. Imagine that?"

"That's a grand surprise indeed."

He kissed the side of her head again, spitting an annoying strand of yellow hair from his mouth while considering how he could best extricate himself from the cloying, needy arms of Molly Brannigan.

CHAPTER EIGHTEEN

Sean

Although the family knew he was back, Sean thought it best to leave the shared bedroom to Danny and Francis. Before he flopped on the cot in the back room, exhausted and drained, he organized a bolt-hole for himself in the storage room at the back of the cellar, having the advantage of access to the doors that opened up onto the pavement at the side of the pub. It had no electric light and the cellar was dank at the best of times, perfect for barrels of lager and stout but inhospitable to the warm-blooded.

In the morning he carried down a chair and a paraffin lamp from the back room, lifted a few packets of fags and matches from the sundries counter, and quietly pulled some books from the bedroom shelf. His mother gave him two lap rugs, fed him a cooked breakfast, and made up a basket with two bottles of cider, some potted-meat sandwiches, and an apple from the four she'd bought to make a tart for Sunday dinner.

Down in the cellar, he smoked and read, dozed off and on, ate a little, and stomped round the storeroom to warm his feet when the dampness penetrated all the layers of wool. He stuck his head out now and again, checking for sunlight through the narrow cracks in the heavy cellar doors.

These checks had grown more frequent as the tedium of his captivity dragged on, yet the daylight was slow to fade. He hustled back to the storage room when he heard feet on the stairs descending in an urgent rush. There was a sharp flurry of raps on the door and the voice of Peter Conway, filled with uncharacteristic anxiety.

"Sean, it's Peter. Come out now, lad," he said, opening the door as he spoke. Sean was jolted by the agitated look of the man.

"Leave everything. I'll clear this up," he grabbed Sean under the arm and pulled him into the main room of the cellar.

"What are you on about?" Sean said, the worry in his voice turning to fear.

"We've a man inside the Castle—you must have suspected. He just got a note out, says the G-section is on to you, knows you're hiding here. They're just waiting to get a squad together, since our man convinced them the place would be full of hard men and explosives, to buy you some time."

"How could he have done this?" said Sean. "Is he drinking? Was it Francis tipped them?"

"No knowing. He's not left the pub, but he could have sent word to the Castle." Reaching inside his coat pocket, Peter extracted a letter-sized brown envelope, bulging from its contents. He shoved it into Sean's hand.

"That's money to carry you through. You need to get to George's Quay. There's a coal barge, painted blue with the name *Peggy Gordon*. The owner crews it himself with his sons and they're friendly to the cause. They're leaving tonight, down the coast to Cork. You have that?"

Taken aback by the suddenness with which his situation had turned, Sean struggled to focus. "Yeah, yeah. Coal barge, the *Peggy Gordon*, at George's Quay."

"There's a second envelope inside the first. It's addressed to the captain of a ship, a freighter with a Dutch captain who's friendly enough as long as we pay him." Peter pushed Sean toward the cellar doors as he spoke. "He'll carry you without questions, if you give him that envelope. His name and the ship's are on the outside."

"What about Mam? Will they molest her?"

"I'll watch over your mother. When they find nothing, they'll leave her be. The City Corporation wouldn't dare revoke the license of the widow of a sergeant-major. And the Castle wouldn't have the nerve to order them."

Peter grabbed Sean by both arms and, through his owlish round glasses, stared with pitying intensity at the young man, grown up too soon in this bloody fight.

"The freighter's headed for New York. Make your way north from there, to your sister." Seeing the grave look of sadness mixed with fear, Peter added, "You'll be back one day soon. When we've finished this business."

He released Sean and shouldered open one of the cellar doors. Halfway out, Sean paused as he heard pounding feet and shouts from above. Peter shoved him up and onto the street, then slammed shut the doors.

Scrambling to clean out any signs of recent habitation, Peter stuffed the food wrappings into the stinking drain that served for a urinal, then folded the books inside the lap rugs, placing them on a shelf with odds and ends of pub hardware. He slammed the chair against the floor to break a leg and chucked it into a corner. He stood bolt upright as he heard gunshots from the street above, paraffin lamp in his hand.

When a plainclothes man from the Castle burst down the stairs with two uniformed constables at his heels, Peter was peering through his glasses at the shelves of spirits, lamp held high to aid his search, a confused and absentminded Diogenes.

"Is that you, Eda?" he said, calmer than he'd any right to sound. "I can't seem to find that bottle of Pernod you asked for."

"He's given us the slip, Piers-Musgrave," the boss said, back at the window where he always headed when displeased with one of his subordinates. "How many months did you spend with his sister? And now he's given us the slip."

"We should have moved sooner, sir."

The boss turned and sniffed, "Said with perfect clarity of hindsight. The G-section had information the pub was stuffed to the gills with IRA sympathizers, even explosives in the cellar."

Desmond—or he supposed he was Thomas again—sucked in his

cheeks and studied the floorboards to suppress a flash of anger, then said, "I told them there was no possible way that was true. I've spent days in that pub."

"It seems you were right, since they found exactly one nearsighted Trinity tutor in the cellar, the publican's beau apparently, searching for a bottle of spirits."

"Peter Conway?" said Desmond. "He was in the cellar when they raided the pub? I've never seen him that side of the bar, not once. There was always something a little too innocuous about him."

"He sells law books to barristers from a shop next to the Four Courts and tutors medieval Irish literature, for God's sake!"

The boss returned to his desk, situating himself in his chair while Thomas remained standing, and said, "Take a few days, Piers-Musgrave. Clear your head, get drunk, go whoring. Forget the Brannigan matter. I'll expect you back on Wednesday to take up that railroad inspector we suspect may be running fugitives." With an indignant sniff, he added, "Perhaps he'll have a daughter to your liking as well."

With the sudden and complete return to his old persona, Lieutenant Thomas Piers-Musgrave stood stiff at attention before his superior, burning with the shame of his failure as Desmond O'Connell.

"Will that be all, sir?"

CHAPTER NINETEEN

Sean

How had his sister found herself in Newfoundland, married to a man she'd loved during the war but had resigned herself to never seeing again this side of the grave? Deirdre—Mrs. Oakley now—

told Sean she pinched herself a dozen times a day, half-certain she'd awake from this topsy-turvy dream of a life into which she'd fallen like Alice down the rabbit hole.

Deirdre's new husband was content enough with the addition of his wife's troublesome brother to their new rumrunning enterprise. The first few voyages down the Maine coast had been very lucrative, proving that a bet on the unerring thirst of Americans was a sure thing, despite their Prohibition law. That Jack had readily accepted Sean as the fourth member of the crew on his grandfather's old schooner was a great relief. Sean knew his sister and Jack Oakley had traveled a long and meandering road with too much heartache already. He'd no desire to knock them off the rails again with his sudden arrival on their doorstep.

The first mate on Jack's schooner was a large and amiable fellow named Geordie King, a childhood friend who'd carried Jack to a field hospital the first day of the Somme. It didn't matter to Jack or Geordie that two of their crew were city raised and without experience at sea, figuring they'd learn quickly enough. Sean was a Dublin lad whose only knowledge of the ocean came from childhood trips to the beach at Sandymount.

The other, a Negro fellow named Chester Dawkins, had been a solicitor—or whatever the Yanks called them—in New York City before the war. His seafaring experience extended no further than watching the odd ship making its way up or down the Hudson. He'd been brought to the rumrunning by an American named Ned Tobin, beside whom Chester had fought in France late in the war. The New Yorker had served as a lieutenant in the colored regiment where Ned had been assigned when he'd gone home to join the American forces in 1917. Chester's quiet and contemplative nature was far from Sean's talkative gregariousness, but they'd grown into an easy friendship.

Sean had learned from his sister soon after his arrival that this Ned Tobin was the very reason for the remarkable changes in Deirdre and Jack's lives. The Bostonian had ambled to Aunt Nola's Halifax establishment one grey day in early May and Deirdre had struck up a conversation with this man she'd pegged as a Yank the moment he opened his mouth. He'd said he was heading for Newfoundland to look up some old mates from the first regiment he'd joined back in 1914 in his rush to get into the fight.

Deirdre had made herself indispensable to Aunt Nola and her husband. Through long days working behind the bar and poring over accounts, Deirdre admitted to Sean she'd managed to push back most of the lingering ache from the man she'd fallen for while he was a patient at the London hospital where she'd been reassigned after the Somme. He left her without a word of farewell, invalided home while she'd been down with flu, and shattered her heart.

So they'd each had a particular reason for heading up to St. John's—Ned to propose a rumrunning scheme to his old comrades, Deirdre to settle up with Jack Oakley, and Sean to avoid an English rope or firing squad. In the end, Jack was the man they'd all needed, since he had claims to both Deirdre's heart and his deceased grandfather's old cod schooner, the *Ricky Todd*, upon which he'd so often sailed as a boy.

Sean wagered that it had taken very little for Ned Tobin to convince Jack, who had fallen into bored and desultory drinking since his return, to throw in with an illegal enterprise that promised both excitement and profit. After what they'd seen and suffered in France, the dangers seemed remote and petty in their flush of reclaimed acquaintance with a thrilling new endeavor. After his months living in hiding and on the run in Ireland, Sean was cut from the same cloth and thought little of the risks, too.

Deirdre had told Sean the marriage happened so fast she'd not had time to write their mother a proper letter telling of her changed circumstances, sending only a short telegram. The ink had scarcely dried on their marriage license when she'd had word from their mother about Sean's imminent arrival. Another two months would pass before Sean jumped down from the back of a lumberman's wagon in front of the tidy white house into which Deirdre and Jack had only just settled.

With a voyage every few weeks, the rumrunning had accumulated cash at an astonishing rate. Their high-quality Canadian and French products were bought up by Negro speakeasy owners in New York City who gladly paid top dollar, since the Italian and Irish gangs demanded extortionate prices from the colored owners in Harlem and Brooklyn for rotgut moonshine mixed with caramel to resemble whisky. Ned had determined the best way to avoid both the established gangs and the Coast Guard cutters was to run their cargoes into a dozen sleepy outports in Maine and New Hampshire, unload onto trucks for the last overland leg into New York, then head into Boston to load legitimate cargoes. They didn't make much on these legal goods, but a northbound unladen schooner riding high in the water would attract notice from the Coast Guard.

Sean had yet to meet the near-legendary Ned Tobin about whom he'd heard endless stories. Now the man himself, if Geordie King's loud shouts of greeting were to be believed, stood on the Oakley Premises's quay beside Jack's father. The *Ricky Todd* eased alongside with sails furled, chugging in under the power of the diesel engines Geordie had fitted belowdecks. Sean stood at the bow and tossed a line to Jack's father who lashed it to an iron bollard while one of his warehousemen handled the stern line thrown by Chester. Ned kept well clear until the warehouseman propped a narrow gangplank through an open section in the ship's rail.

"The sailors returned from the sea," said Ned, shouting above the creaks of the ship straining at its moorings and the rumble of trucks and wagons working the waterside.

Jack limped up the deck from the helm, having sent Geordie below to shut down the idling engines. He checked Sean's knots with an unobtrusive glance, then hollered ashore to the American, "Ned, b'y! What're you doin' this far north? Why didn't you let us know you were comin'?"

"Didn't know myself until the last moment. Thought I'd see how you cod haulers are faring."

Sean bounded down the gangway, then stopped to let his legs adjust to solid ground again. He walked over to the American in the fine suit and hat, extending his hand.

"You'd be that Ned Tobin, then? I hear my dear sister owes you for one genuine husband and one prosperin' business."

The sound of Sean's voice brought an involuntary smile from Ned. "'Tis I who owe your dear sister the greater debt," he said, letting a little Tipperary creep into his voice. The two grasped hands with hearty friendliness, then stepped aside so the others could come ashore.

Jack's father greeted his son with a handshake and an arm about his shoulders. "What did you bring us back this time, b'y?"

Jack glanced back at his crew, all smiling with devilment at their captain's father, then said, "Why, we've fetched you back two hundred cases of the best tinned Boston beans… and twenty-five crated lady's bicycles." The men behind Jack broke into laughter at the older man's dumbfounded expression.

"We'll shift the beans to crews heading out for the fishing banks, but I've not sold a bicycle in my life. What do you expect me to do with two dozen of them… for ladies?" Rick Oakley shook his head and chuckled.

With Jack safe ashore—always last off his ship by both habit and superstition—his father signaled to his workmen at the waterside to pull the canvas off the main hatch and unload the return cargo of beans and bikes. All of Jack's crew knew his father's business was not to be involved with the outbound cargoes—this being Jack's one non-negotiable condition when he agreed to the rumrunning scheme. He'd convinced his father and uncle to sign over title to him of the old schooner without many questions asked.

"We'll get her unladen, Jackie. You and the b'ys be off for a bath and a hot meal."

A truck painted with *King Haulage Company* idled up the quay, the driver from the family company waving from a running board to Geordie.

"There's our ride. Who's with me?" Geordie said. Chester and Jack nodded and headed toward the waiting truck. Jack yelled over his shoulder to Ned that Deirdre would expect him for supper with the rest of the crew.

Sean was about to take his leave, too, when Ned said, "I could do with a drink or two. What say you give your sister and her husband a little time alone? Care to join me?"

Geordie King loosed a big guffaw. "Fine idea, although those two need no encouragement in the direction your mind's runnin'." He headed for the truck, shouting back, "See you at supper, b'ys!"

Sean knew a smoky diner a few blocks up from the quays that served a variety of liquors in coffee mugs, Newfoundland having extended its own ineffective wartime ban on the sale of spirits well past the Armistice. Fortunate to their enterprise, the Newfoundland government, however, had no objection to transshipping liquor from Canada and elsewhere, it being excellent for the island's maritime trade.

Ned motioned for Sean to lead the way, and the two men stepped off uphill. Walking in silence until they were well away from the bustle of men at the waterfront, Ned said, "I've heard you and I have some mutual friends in Boston."

"Well, that's a grand coincidence, isn't it?" said Sean, thinking the American was just making conversation.

"Perhaps not such a coincidence," said Ned, "our mutual friends having a certain interest in the current woeful situation in Ireland."

Sean missed a step in his surprise. "Doesn't seem likely I'd know them, Ned, seein' as how I'm a proper Newfoundlander now without a care about who does what to whom back there."

Ned stopped and grasped Sean's arm. The knowing sureness of Ned's placid smile made Sean a little uneasy.

"Let's respect each other, shall we?" said Ned. "I had a long talk with our mutual friend Aloysius Pendergast the day before leaving for St. John's. It was the very reason for my hasty departure from Boston, in fact."

"Yeah, so? I met Al Pendergast while I was looking for work in Boston, to earn my passage up here. He was good enough to give me some odd jobs," said Sean, studying Ned with the suspicion that had become second nature from the months on the run in Ireland.

"He told me your entire story. All the trouble back home and your work with the IRA," said Ned. Sean felt his face redden, although he wasn't sure whether it was with embarrassment or anger.

"Let's trade, then," said Ned. "I know your story, so here's mine. The English took something of great value from me, something I loved dearly and miss fiercely. I organized this rumrunning business to make the money to pay them back in kind."

They stood without speaking. Sean noticed the eyes in Ned's otherwise nonchalant face burned with furious resolve. Sean pursed his lips and let out a loud exhalation.

"All right, I'm here to avoid bein' hung by the bloody English. What's your revenge to me?"

Ned turned to continue their uphill stroll. "We've the same ambition—drive the English out of Ireland. You for your grandchildren's sake, me to settle my own accounts." They stopped at an intersection to let a smoky Ford chug past. "Which is why every other dollar I make purchases rifles, ammunition, explosives, whatever we can get to send to the Republican lads. It gives me great satisfaction that bullets bought with my ill-gotten gains might end up in the bodies of the Auxiliaries that wronged me."

"Why did Al tell you all about me, so?"

Ned placed a hand on Sean's shoulder and squeezed harder than would be amiable. "Al and his associates would like me to keep an eye on you while you're here and see you home safe when you're called back. Also, I would like half of your share to add to mine. There's always more need than we can fulfill."

Sean pointed across the street and they crossed mid-block, making for the café.

"Of course. Done."

Ned offered a hand to seal the deal and Sean gripped it without hesitation.

"Here ends the first meeting of the St. John's chapter of the Fenian Brotherhood," said Sean. He shoved against the brass push bar and stepped into the hum of conversations and clatter of plates.

CHAPTER TWENTY

Eda

Young women can be altogether tragic when a romance ends, Eda knew, having been a teenage girl once upon a time. Still, her Molly was holding on to her sorrows longer than most. It wasn't for lack of attention from other young men, but she gave no encouragement and took no interest. Her face looked gaunt to her mother, although she seemed to have gained a little flesh, her skirts and blouses tighter on her.

If the sudden disappearance of that cad Desmond O'Connell wasn't enough, the poor girl was denied a place at Trinity after slaving over her studies for the last eight months. She refused to discuss other possibilities, perhaps the teacher's college, so distraught had she been from her double disappointment.

More grey hairs and a few more brow lines, Eda thought, then shushed her vanity. Every mother knew they'd take on the suffering of their children and this was no burden that she couldn't bear, although heaven knows she'd already seen enough grief within her family. Two far across the sea and one without a leg—now poor Molly. At least Danny hadn't known much tragedy, too young in 1915 to remember the loss of his father.

"Did you check the stock at the counter?" said Eda.

Molly didn't reply right away, then looked up a little confused.

"Molly, I was askin' if you'd checked the stock at your counter?"

"Aye, Mam... I mean, not yet... today," she said, rubbing the thin volume of Shakespeare she held. The gold lettering was worn, but Eda could still read *Hamlet* as her daughter lifted her hand from the faded cover.

"That's one of your favorites," Eda said.

Glancing about the pub with a puzzled look, as if she weren't sure how she'd ended up there, she said, "It always comforts me."

Eda wasn't much for books, but she liked to listen to Molly or Danny read aloud when she was washing up or darning socks. "Well, those Danes and their horrible misfortunes would make anyone feel better, by way of comparison."

She hugged her daughter against her with one strong arm, a towel dangling from the other resting on her hip. When she let go, Molly gave a weak smile and walked to the backroom.

Francis hadn't set foot behind the bar since he'd come down after the lunchtime crowd and was standing in his accustomed place amid a scrum of veterans and a few men too old to have served but allowed on sufferance. The faces rotated from day to day, all except Francis's. They'd been drinking hard for a few hours and the rising volume of their discourse was punctuated by the occasional soldier's song.

"So is that scurrilous brother of yours still hiding away, Francis?" asked one former Dub who'd come back from Gallipoli with all his limbs but his health ruined by fever. "He'd be wise to stay away, what with the Auxiliaries givin' no quarter to them Sinn Feiners."

Francis threw back the whisky he'd been holding no more than a minute and said, "Our Sean's never been one you'd call wise, Dick. Not a great one for the thinking."

Eda alerted to Sean's name, straining to make out what was being said ten feet away.

"Disgraceful, him dishonorin' the memory of his own father," said an ex-soldier with a glass eye set in a matrix of hardened scars. "Disgraceful."

"Sure, but he's still your brother, Francis," said one of the old ones who'd never worn a solider's coat. "That has to count for more than..."

Francis pounded his crutch against the floor, cutting off the old man, and bellowed, "He's no brother of mine that makes common cause with murderers and traitors! Doesn't the Castle believe he shot that magistrate over in Tullamore? And his poor wife? No brother to me, any man who'd do such bloody acts."

Eda heard her son and darted out from behind the bar, elbowing aside a few men blocking her way. She jerked Francis by the elbow, nearly toppling him, and hissed in his ear. "Get yourself behind that bar while I go see after your sister. And don't you make a spectacle like that again or you'll be out on your drunken ear, Francis Brannigan."

The other men studied the floors or walls with sheepish glances as Francis limped off, planting himself behind the bar with a stormy look. The apprentice barman scurried to the far end, hoping to escape the tense vortex swirling round Francis and his mother.

Satisfied she'd put an end for the moment to his horrible attacks on his brother, Eda went in search of Molly.

In the dimness of the back room, Eda heard muffled sobs. Squinting, she saw a crumpled form prostrate on the apprentice's narrow cot. She hurried back to her stricken child and sat at the end of the little bed, swaddling Molly's head in her arms.

"*Ach, stórin*," Eda said, rocking the limp form in her lap. "I know your heart's broken, but there are other men waiting, better men than Desmond O'Connell."

Hearing his name spoken, Molly wailed as if stabbed. Eda held her tighter.

"Shhh, shhh," she said, soothing the girl as she had when she was a colicky baby, so tiny and fair. "You don't believe me, I know, but there will be another. One who deserves your goodness."

Molly's wailing grew to a keen and, through her grief, she sputtered, "I'll never be free of him, can't you see that? I can never be free now."

The desperate frantic edge to her daughter's voice froze the very blood in Eda's veins. Carefully, she lifted her daughter up from her lap, supporting her under an arm. It felt as if she were playing with an old rag doll, threadbare and worn. She turned Molly's face toward hers.

"This is beyond an abandoned romance, isn't it?"

She couldn't look at her mother, teetering on the edge as she was. Her mouth gaped, but nothing came out except silent agony. Her head lolled, chin to her chest.

"Molly, what's happened between you and Desmond?" Eda asked, already knowing the answer but needing to hear the admission from her daughter's lips.

"I've his child in me," she whispered. Her shoulders heaved as she sobbed and gulped air.

Eda knew this was a moment of great danger and bit her lip until she tasted blood, scrabbling for time to organize her careening thoughts. She rocked her stricken girl a little and rubbed the center of her back.

"We'll face this together, the two of us. I'll stand by you no matter what, Molly," Eda said. Then, with a long sigh, added, "You mustn't hold out hope he'll marry you. You must let that go."

Then she joined in her daughter's sobs, fearing what these next months would bring.

CHAPTER TWENTY-ONE

Molly

Eda found comfort sitting at the big table brought from their old place when she'd moved above the pub, the one she and Daniel had purchased when they'd moved to the terrace house in New Row. It was rubbed and oiled by her husband's rough cooper's hands and those of each child as they'd grown. Tiny hands with chubby fingers, smearing jam and butter. Then bigger, busier hands, puzzling over schoolwork or conjuring grand fantasies with whatever plaything they'd found at hand. Later, Deirdre's in exhaustion from long days at the charity hospital, before she exiled herself to the war as penance for her awful parting with her father. Of course, Molly's slender hands, far away in her books, idly caressing the smooth wood, lost in her thoughts. Poor Francis's, too, with circles of slopped whisky ringed by the glass that was seldom empty as he drank his sorrows over the loss of his father and his leg. And her own chapped hands, long accustomed to scrubbing and polishing since her days as a chambermaid at the big house in Merrion Square where she'd started her life in Dublin. Before she'd ever met Daniel Brannigan or imagined bearing his children.

So there it was, Eda thought. Not that hers was the first family with a teenage daughter fallen pregnant. And wasn't a baby always a gift from God? She wouldn't send her daughter away to the Magdalene

Sisters and their squalid laundries. Too many girls who went in never came out. Lord only knows how many of their babies never left.

Danny and Francis were still asleep in their room at the back. She'd not noticed when Danny came home from a friend's house over in the old neighborhood, but it had been after she'd put Molly in bed to sob herself asleep. Must've been past midnight and she wondered for a moment why no one had sent him home earlier.

The flat was quiet as a church, the only intrusions some clopping and morning shouts from the street or the rattle of a dropped spittoon by the apprentice below. She lifted her mug, letting the steam wash over her face and up her nostrils. That had always helped sort her thoughts.

She'd send Molly to Donegal, to live with her cousin Brigid's family. They'd concoct some bit of nonsense for a veneer of respectability— that Molly had a young soldier husband (Saints be praised) off on garrison duty in Hong Kong (if can you imagine such a thing) and Eda too busy (poor widow) to care for her, what with the pub to run (God give her strength). No one would truly believe it, but everyone would conspire in the lie, not knowing when one of their own might require similar consideration.

It was the disappointment that stung. Such high hopes for her Molly, with a chance to learn things Eda couldn't imagine. The Mercy Sisters encouraged Molly to persevere, told her it wouldn't be shocking to require two attempts—especially for a woman, and a Catholic at that—to gain admission to the Protestant bastion of Trinity. They'd offered to keep Molly on as a tutor, pay her a modest wage. That was the farthest thing from the girl's mind now.

Eda had long brewed tea so strong it was black, the way her husband liked it. With a little milk, it took on the rich brown of coffee. Blinking the steam from her eyes, she gazed at the fine photograph of her husband and son, smart in their uniforms, that came in the post after they'd shipped out for Egypt, on their way to that terrible beach and the waiting Turks.

Such a handsome man...

Hadn't she fallen for a fine smile and lovely eyes, just like her daughter? Sure, they'd managed to control themselves until well and properly married. Most of the time at least. She smiled recollecting that it was only by the blindest luck or the intercession of the Virgin

Mary that she hadn't landed in the same condition as her daughter. And her employers would've sent her packing with neither reference nor second thought.

There was something queer about Desmond O'Connell. Not just the education or the fine speech or the endless brass in his pocket. She'd never quite put a finger on it. From the very first, something about him unsettled her. Her Daniel had thrown himself over with a kind of wild abandon she'd long hoped for her daughters, too. But Desmond held back parts of himself. She'd never settled in her mind what those parts might be.

No matter, since he'd disappeared like a thief in the night after putting her Molly in a family way. That made him an all-too-familiar sort of man, known to every mother the world over and given out as a warning to every daughter. She'd as soon Molly not have anything from him, neither money nor attention. They could afford to care for the little one, and any who thought ill of that could go straight to the Devil.

A good chin with Peter Conway would strengthen her resolve. She couldn't think of the last day he'd missed at the pub. He was a fine companion and she'd enjoyed stepping out with him the dozen or more times they'd done so. It was such a comfort to have someone with whom she could converse in Irish. All the years she'd been married to Daniel, she hadn't realized how much she missed her native tongue. Except, of course with the Lord, who was sure to hear prayers even in Irish, although He'd a manifest preference for the Latin variety.

Wouldn't Daniel have thought it a fine thing, him a grandfather?

She glanced at the portrait on the sideboard again, then pushed away from the table and gathered herself for another day in the pub below.

TWO JUNIOR OFFICERS ASSAULTED, ONE DEAD
VICTIMS OF IRA "MURDER GANG"

Dublin murder, 25th September, 1920.—At about 7 a.m. on the morning of Saturday, 25th of September, 1920, there occurred a vicious attack upon two junior officers of the Royal Army, committed by cold-blooded and cowardly assassins of the I.R.A. Attacked in a flat they shared, the two officers were sleeping when four gunmen burst in and fired shots into the men in their beds. One of the officers died where he lay, while the other survived the initial assault and languishes in hospital, clinging to life. The gunmen escaped on foot, scaling a garden wall and last seen running down a back alley in the direction of the river.

Although no details as to the identity of the victims have yet been made available, sources in Dublin Castle assure this newspaper that both young officers had served in France with distinction.

NAMES OF DEAD AND WOUNDED RELEASED

27th of September, 1920.—The War Office today released the names of two junior officers attacked on Saturday by gunmen of the I.R.A.—

Name.	Rank.	Regiment.
KILLED.		
Davidson, C. ..	Lt. ..	5th Royal Scots (Qn's Edinburgh Rifles)
WOUNDED.		
Piers-Musgrave, T. ..	Lt...	9th Inniskilling Fusiliers

Francis tottered on his crutch struggling to keep himself upright in his drunken indignation. Every new rebel outrage gave him fresh license to turn to the whisky with a clear conscience. And the IRA was giving him any number of reasons.

"Shot 'em in their beds... in their bloody beds," he repeated for the tenth or hundredth time since he'd taken to drink after seeing the first of the Monday morning papers. "They served like us. Did their bit. Gunned down by Fenian cowards." He swept his free arm wide, threatening to slosh whisky over his interlocutors, a few of whom were equally shattered. To avoid wastage, Francis emptied the glass and handed it to the man nearest the bar.

Slapping the back of his hand against the chest of a drinking companion, he said, "Comrades of my dear brother, no doubt. Long may he rot in Newfoundland. And my sister Deirdre, too, for having him under her roof."

The apprentice was alone behind the bar and Francis wasn't too drunk to have noticed. He well knew his mother wouldn't tolerate such talk. The more sober of the men knew it, too, and shot glances at the front door through which Eda had exited with a market basket on her elbow more than an hour ago.

Molly had retreated deeper into her books, the only means she knew of escaping her unfortunate circumstances, if even for a moment. Anything to fill her thoughts with something other than foolhardy daydreams of Desmond walking through the door and sweeping her off to the St. Nicholas rectory for a quick marriage in the pastor's study where such delicate matters were dispatched so as not to distress the faithful.

The waistbands of her skirts were tightening, but her blouses still fit. The weather was cool enough most days she could wear a jumper without attracting attention, but there would be no way to hide her pregnancy much longer, even with the deficient amounts of food she forced down only when urged. Eda had written a few weeks ago that Molly would be arriving in Donegal in early October. The note Mam received back from her cousin Brigid struck Molly as more resigned than enthusiastic, even with the half of it in Irish. She'd have an honorable story to tell of her pregnancy and her phantom soldier husband. She could at least be seen on the streets without shame in tiny Bunbeg, far out in the west of Donegal, a place that might as well have been on the moon to a girl who'd passed every one of her eighteen years on the streets of Dublin. So far away she wouldn't feel every face judging her, as would surely be the case if she stayed in the Liberties while she grew big as a house.

She closed the volume of Robert Browning, leaving a finger stuck in the page where she'd left off, then shifted on the stool behind the counter. Her back had started to cramp and ache the last few days, not for any particular reason she could discern, although Mam said there'd be all manner of odd changes as the baby grew.

Some of the older regulars offered a few comforting words to her after it was evident Desmond had deserted her and the pub. When after a week she'd stopped appearing downstairs with red-rimmed eyes, the men decided by general consensus that she was best left to herself and they turned to mourning the loss of Desmond's liberality instead.

"A terrible thing, when a man abandons his pub," said the Tippler. "It doesn't bode well."

"He should've been decent enough to end things with our Molly outright, then come and stand his rounds like a man," said the Weatherman. "I knew men with a girl in every port acted more the gentleman than yer man Desmond O'Connell."

"A man shouldn't throw over the pub where he hangs his hat for light causes, to be sure," said the Pintman. "But he was a whisky man, you'll recall, and not one for the pint, making him somewhat untrustworthy, to my way of thinkin'."

Francis had teetered to the bar and again grabbed a folded *Irish Times*, waving it like a member of the Commons with an order paper. He staggered back to the knot of old soldiers and hangers-on, jabbing the paper under a few men's noses.

"Shot them in their beds! An officer of the Crown, shot dead in his sleep," he repeated. "Brave comrades of my brother, Sean." He handed over the paper to the man next to him when the apprentice produced a new whisky for him.

Watching Francis's raging, the three regulars down the bar shook their heads in ragged unison. They each paused to lift their various glasses, then set them down again.

"Terrible thing, terrible these shootings and bombings," said the Pintman. "But isn't rebellion always a terrible thing?"

"But Francis wouldn't be going on so about Sean if his mother was here," said the Weatherman.

"That he would not, or she'd have him by the ear and up those stairs," said the Tippler. "Like she did when he was a naughty boy over in New Row."

"You can't rightly call them Fenians cowards," said the Pintman. "Takin' on the might of the British Empire with next to nothin'. And their leaders back in '16, didn't they go to their deaths brave as any man could? There'll be no denyin' that."

"Don't let Francis hear your blasphemy," said the Weatherman. "He'll bar you for life." To emphasize the gravity of this ominous peril, he drained the tall rum sitting at his elbow.

"These are strange events that bode ill," said the Tippler, likewise punctuating his concern by emptying the glass he was holding. "I can feel it in my bones, worse is comin'. Far worse."

The front door swung open and Eda Brannigan's brisk return snuffed Francis's bitter ranting, leaving him to mumble and smolder among his friends.

She pushed back the shawl from her head, letting it drape her shoulders, then swung her market basket atop the counter next to the door.

"I had them parcel out the sugar for you at the grocer's, Molly," she said, pulling small, tight-folded brown bags, one after another, out of her basket and lining a dozen on the counter for her daughter to stack on the shelves. "It's three days 'til payday at the brewery, so many will be wantin' small lots until then."

Molly didn't react until Eda touched her arm. She raised her head and, realizing it was her mother, set aside the book and gave Eda a distant smile. She moved the sugars two at a time to the shelf, lodging them between larger packets of flour and the big tin of pipe tobacco that anchored the end.

Eda watched the odd slowness with which her daughter moved, her motions as detached as some arcade's mechanical fortune-teller. Maybe things would be better once she was through the train journey up to Letterkenny. Getting clear of the city might be just what she needed, clean air and new faces.

As her daughter settled and reopened the book of poetry, Eda gathered her basket and squeezed her daughter's hand. As she turned toward the bar, the door cracked open and a tentative-looking man in a porter's uniform stepped inside and looked about with nervous glances, turning his cap in his hands.

"Beg pardon, ma'am," said the burly man about the same age as Francis. "I was told… to come here… to The Gallant Fusilier… and ask after someone. I've a message."

"Well, you've found the very place," said Eda, good-natured with any new customer. "And who might you be lookin' for?"

He nodded a little, turned his cap again, and said, "I've come from the Royal Dublin Hospital… over in Baggot Street, so." Eda smiled and nodded encouragement.

"I was told… by one of the nurses… to give a message to Molly."

The two Brannigan women turned as one to the broad-shouldered young man in the dark blue uniform.

"I'm Molly." The effort of speaking to a man of any sort flushed her face and she looked back down at her book.

"The nurse says to tell you that… that you should come right away, quick as you please," he said, then licked his lips while making sure he had the message correct.

"She says to tell you Desmond is asking for you… and to say he's in a bad way, so you ought to come along with me and we're to make haste."

Setting her basket on the counter, Eda said, "Go fetch your wrap, Molly, we'll be off with this young man."

Molly came from behind the counter and stood before her mother, the sudden blush drained away, leaving her deathly pale. With both hands, she gently removed the shawl from her mother's shoulders and wrapped it about herself. Unsure in the face of her daughter's chilling resolve, Eda didn't resist.

"No, Mam. I'll go alone."

An unlikely sight they were, the burly porter and lissome Molly, her striding with determination while the porter rushed to stay close, like a reluctant boy pulled along in the wake of his busy mother. She'd no idea what brought her Desmond to such dire straits and she wasn't interested in slowing her progress to take up the topic with the huffing porter, her head pulsing with erratic emotions and disjointed thoughts.

Straight up the Coombe through a few changes of street name, then diagonal across Stephen's Green and out the north side, right onto the lower end of Baggot Street. After that, she'd not need to think at all, straight on to the Grand Canal, although it didn't look so grand sliding through Dublin on its way to the Shannon and the sea.

She'd let her mother's shawl fall to her elbows on the Green when a fist constricted in her chest as they hurried past the bench under the big weeping ash tree where she and Desmond had started down the path that had led to this. She gave a reflexive glance toward the charity hospital where her sister had nursed and recalled her stricken mother sending her to fetch Deirdre five years ago. The lovely park would always bear painful reminders of the two men she'd most loved.

Even at a good clip, it was twenty minutes by foot to the hospital. By the time they'd reached the little one-arch bridge across the narrow canal, Molly had sweat through her blouse and was panting near as much as the porter. Having passed the hospital only a few times and never with reason to give it much notice, Molly wasn't prepared for the tug at her arm by the porter after they crossed the canal bridge. She turned halfway toward him but carried on sideways, desperate to keep moving. He was so winded he couldn't gasp a word, so he nodded her toward a large building. The brickwork was the orange-red of an overripe persimmon, peaking through grimy streaks of coal dust and city dirt. Dingy tan trim interrupted the mass of masonry at each story, framing five floors of windows.

Molly ran up the half-dozen stairs and slammed her weight against one of the heavy double doors, then halted in the lobby twisting in confusion with no idea which way to go. Frustrated tears welling, she turned to the put-upon porter, who took her by the arm and led her up the central staircase to the second floor. An efficient-looking woman of about forty manned an oaken counter that controlled access to a long corridor with high ceilings. Her bleached-white uniform glowed in the subdued light of late afternoon.

Having managed to modulate his panting, the porter said, "This here is that Molly you was askin' me to fetch, Sister. For that fella." The nurse dismissed him with a curt jerk of her chin. The porter was relieved to be shed of Molly and disappeared down the stairs, back to the more mundane duties of manhandling unruly patients and unloading ambulances.

"Your name is Molly?"

Fighting for composure, the near-stricken girl said, "Yes, Sister. Molly Brannigan."

"When he was conscious earlier, Lieutenant Piers-Musgrave asked for you. It's good you've come straight away."

Molly flushed with relief at the obvious error and said, "Sister, I was told to come see Desmond. Desmond O'Connell."

The nurse eyed Molly closer and understanding the young woman's cluelessness was genuine, said, "Desmond was the name Lieutenant

Piers-Musgrave told me to send you, though I haven't the foggiest idea why. His given name is Thomas."

The reprieve from her worst fears had proved fleeting and Molly struggled to make sense of what this woman was saying, unable to put together enough words to dispel her confusion.

"Follow me," said the sister, rounding the end of the counter and marching off down the corridor, certain the puzzled Molly would follow.

Just before reaching the tall single window at the end of the hallway, the nurse cut left as if on parade, whisking past a soldier keeping post by the door. The soldier tracked Molly with his eyes as she followed into the room, but didn't challenge her.

The antiseptic smell that her sister often brought home on her clothing from the charity hospital hit Molly's nostrils, so much stronger in the room than the hallway. There were two white-painted iron beds, the nearest to the door with its mattress rolled up at the head. In the other lay the father of her unborn child, the man she'd loved as Desmond O'Connell. An older man sat near the window in a dark wooden arm chair. He had the trimmed mustache of an officer, although he wore a dark worsted suit with a regimental necktie in a neat four-in-hand knot.

Seeing Molly trail in behind the nurse, he sighed while crushing out his cigarette and rose to his feet, his good breeding overpowering his manifest lack of enthusiasm at the sight of her.

He crossed to the older woman and said, "This is her?"

"Yes, she claims so, Major," said the sister. Having delivered her charge, she went to the side of the occupied bed and felt the stricken man's wrist, checking his thready but persistent pulse. She bent down to examine the bottle under the bed, a long ochre tube running from the man's chest, draining a thick pinkish fluid.

"Please leave us, Sister," said the major.

Once the nurse had departed, the major turned his attention to Molly, who stood frozen five or six feet from the bedside, sobbing into both hands with tears flowing over her knuckles. She feared to move, waiting for any indication this was some tragic prank.

"Miss... Brannigan, is it?"

Molly gave a few frantic nods but stood rooted in place.

"Lieutenant Piers-Musgrave, whom I believe you know as Desmond O'Connor..."

"O'Connell," whispered Molly. "Desmond O'Connell."

"Yes, quite. Desmond O'Connell," said the major, staring at her with unblinking and undisguised disdain. "You might be interested in knowing his actual name is Thomas Piers-Musgrave, late of His Majesty's Inniskilling Fusiliers. You read of him in the papers, no doubt?"

Molly shook her head, eyes transfixed on Desmond. "I don't read the papers much."

"Then you wouldn't know how four cowardly gunmen of the so-called Irish Republican Army shot Lieutenant Piers-Musgrave and his flatmate, Lieutenant Davidson, in their beds Saturday morning." The major sniffed and turned toward the window, attempting with little success to hide his disgust.

Composing himself, he looked back to Molly and continued. "Your Desmond is much more fortunate than Lieutenant Davidson, who died in his bed. He was brought here, where the surgeons removed three bullets from his chest. He has been in and out of consciousness ever since."

Over her gathering sobs, the major added, "In his few moments of lucidity earlier today, he asked that you be sent for. Although I cannot fathom why."

Molly reached a hand toward the bed, then turned to the major with an imploring look.

"Go on, then," said the major.

Molly rushed over and took up Desmond's hand in both hers and bent close to his face, pressing his palm against her cheek. She stood like this, wetting his inert hand with her tears, for some time while the major retreated to the window, studying the traffic on Baggot Street below.

"Desmond, it's me. It's Molly."

He stirred almost imperceptibly but didn't open his eyes. She had no way of knowing whether he could hear her.

"Who did this to you? Who could have done such a thing?" Her pleading words were met only by raspy breathing.

From the window, a surer and angrier voice answered for him. "Were I to offer a wager, Miss Brannigan, I would say your rebel brother, Sean, and his traitorous comrades."

Molly stood confounded and let Desmond's hand fall back to the bed.

"He's in Newfoundland. He left Ireland months ago. How could he be responsible for such a terrible thing?"

The major moved back to the chair and sat, unconcerned by the presence of a woman left standing. His relaxed menace chilled her with fear.

"Come now, Miss Brannigan. America is shot through with Fenian sympathizers. Half of Newfoundland is from the Irish dross that washed up there. The Irish Americans send arms, money. How difficult would it be to send a letter, perhaps a telegram?"

"Sean wouldn't do such a thing," she said, "not to me."

"But you would do it to Sean, wouldn't you?"

She didn't understand, but the disgust in his tone assured her there was more to come.

"After all, you provided Lieutenant Piers-Musgrave here…" He paused and corrected himself with a contemptuous little smile, "… I mean, Desmond, of course, with the whereabouts of your brother, hiding in your mother's public house. I assume you heard the gunshots in the street outside your door?"

"No! I did no such thing nor would I!"

"But you did, Miss Brannigan. What does one call it? Intimate secrets? I'm well aware of your trysts at that pathetic hotel. I received weekly reports on them," he said, abandoning any semblance of a gentleman, a cat torturing a helpless mouse.

"What are you? Desmond was a businessman, with family in Tyrone and down in Cork," she said with an attempt at firmness unconvincing even to herself.

With a barking dismissive laugh, the major's eyes narrowed as he looked at Molly in amused disbelief. "He was an intelligence officer for Dublin Castle. His family is in England, although they've some summer heap up in Ulster. And he's an officer in the Royal Army."

Molly stood in stunned disbelief, beyond tears and sobs, and snapped, "That's not true! You're a liar! Sean says all Englishmen are liars."

The major rose and came at Molly. "We should have lifted your whole bloody family. Even your one-legged brother and that insipid bookseller. We've suspected him for months. The Castle wouldn't have it though. Can't be seen harassing poor war widows and maimed veterans." He waved an arm over the unconscious man. "And this is what that sort of sentimentality brought us! One of my men dead and the other likely won't see another morning. Sister!"

Heels clacked down the corridor as the major said, "You're a pretty bit of fluff. Easy enough for him to shag for information about your brother's activities. Sister!"

Molly withered under his cruelty, her knees turning to rubber. She stared at him with stunned eyes and a tortured mouth as she teetered by the bedside.

The major scoffed again and said, "You don't imagine he actually cared for you? Loved you even? Gawd, what a gullible thing you are."

The door flew open. The nurse grabbed Molly by the elbow and pulled her out of the room, the major's overwrought laughter following them down the corridor as she hustled Molly to the stairs.

They'd not even had the decency to call a taxi, leaving her to stagger about the south side of the river, somehow finding her way back to the Liberties, although she'd never recollect how.

It wasn't until near closing that two mothers from the old neighborhood brought Molly through the door of The Gallant. There weren't many left in the pub and fewer who were sober. That included the diehard regulars, as well as her brother Francis, swaying within a small cluster of boozy veterans awaiting the time bell. Peter Conway had remained later than his usual time, hoping to calm the woman behind the bar fretting over her youngest daughter and what unknown strife she might be enduring at the hospital.

The smoke of all the evening's pipes and cigarettes was turning stale, so the blast of fresh air through the doors that followed behind the stricken girl turned all heads, including Eda's. The sight of their dear Molly hushed every man in an instant and launched Eda from behind the bar, dropping her towel into the dirty sawdust as she ran for the front. The garish yellow light from the ceiling fixtures, bouncing off the mirrors on the long side walls and flashing from the brass fittings, accentuated the wild look of the poor girl.

Her hair was loose, dank and limp as flotsam kelp. Dirty streaks followed the lines of tears down her cheeks and her upper lip and corners of her mouth were crusted. She'd fallen more than once, with a ragged rip near the knees in her skirt. Dried blood had seeped through and there was more blood on her blouse where she'd rubbed her lacerated palms.

Pivoting on his crutch in his wooziness, Francis lost his balance and lunged for the shoulder of the man next to him. Steadying himself, he said, "Molly, what the devil… you're wrecked." Eda pushed past and Francis grabbed a companion's shoulder for support a second time as Peter Conway brushed by, too.

The two women relinquished their charge and stood back tut-tutting and shaking their heads in sympathy, only the good Lord Himself knowing why He'd needed to visit yet more sorrow on poor Eda Brannigan.

Wrapping Molly in her arms, Eda pressed her to her breast. Molly fell disjointed into her mother's embrace, as if someone had dropped the strings of a marionette. Eda ran her reddened fingers through the stringy yellow hair, cooing to her distraught child as if she were a fussing infant. Faint mewling sobs came from deep within the encircling arms.

"*Seoithín seo hó, mo stór,*" Eda said in a whisper, oblivious to all those gathered round her. "*Fuist, fuist, mo chailín milis.* Hush now, you're safe at home, my sweet girl." As she rocked back and forth on her heels, Peter Conway sniffed and dabbed at his eye with a knuckle. One of the neighbor ladies produced a rosary and moved her lips silently, while her companion carried on tutting and shaking her head.

The Pintman had taken it upon himself to produce a clean towel from behind the bar, a place he wouldn't dare venture under normal circumstances, where he'd soaked it in hot water and wrung it. He made his way over to Eda and stood with steamy towel in hand, not sure what more to do. The Weatherman had weaved across the room and procured one of the stools from the small tables along the wall and brought it up behind Molly. When he set it down a little abruptly, Eda glanced over her daughter's head and flashed him a tiny smile of thanks.

She eased Molly down onto the low stool while the Pintman extended his arm to Eda. Taking the warm towel, she nodded once and set about cleaning her daughter's face, then her bloody hands.

Once she'd cleaned through the worst of the grime and seen there were no serious injuries, she handed the towel over her shoulder to Peter hovering at her side. Eda gathered Molly's hair in her palm, then looped it into a loose knot to keep it off her face.

"Now child, can you speak a little?"

Molly nodded and drew in a deep, shuddering breath, then looked into her mother's fretting eyes. Fresh tears welled as she said, "He lied, Mam. The whole thing was a terrible lie."

"Who lied?"

Molly glanced across the faces of the gathered men, hesitating on those who'd befriended him. "Desmond. He wasn't Desmond."

There was a little rumble of monosyllables round the room, then Eda said, "What do you mean? Who was he if not Desmond O'Connell?"

"They told me his name is Thomas. I don't recall the last. And he's English and works at the Castle." She rubbed the back of her hand under her nose and Peter handed over his handkerchief for her to blow.

"And they said he was an Army officer, too."

"Why would he need to lie about his name?" Eda said. Tongue clucks from her two old neighbors reached her and she gasped, "Holy Mother of God, he's a wife and family already?"

Molly looked confused, then shook her head while studying her injured palms, as if seeing them for the first time.

"No, Mam, he was after Sean," she said. "The Castle wanted Sean and his friends."

Francis staggered forward on his crutch, standing beside his mother and looking over his stricken sister.

"And they nearly got the wee bastard, too!"

"Francis," said Peter Conway. "Now is not the time for this."

Molly's face cringed and wrinkled as if she'd been slapped, and she said, "I told him Sean was home. I was so excited—I wanted to share it with him." Her mouth gaped and she choked out, "I nearly got him killed, Mam!"

Wanting to keep her daughter's wits about her, Eda smoothed back a few of the girl's stray hairs and said, "We'll hear none of that. Sean is safe and away across the sea, with your sister, Deirdre. You did no harm, at all, at all."

With a relieved smile, Molly nodded at her mother's kindness.

"But why did they fetch you to the hospital? Has Desmond... or Thomas, if that's his true name... has he been hurt? Is he ill?"

Just able to keep herself from sobbing anew, Molly said, "He... he was shot. In his bed. One of those men the IRA attacked on Saturday morning."

This revelation triggered a burst of discussion among Francis and his mates.

"Must be that Royal Inniskilling officer, the one that survived the slaughter."

"Aye, there's still a Sunday paper about," said another. The paper was duly produced and creased above the fold on the front page, the story of the assassination being lead news.

"Lieutenant Piers-Musgrave, it says," read Francis. "First initial is T." Molly nodded her recollection of the name and blew again.

Another man at the back of the group, having arrived just before last call, inched through the knot of ex-soldiers, extending a late edition paper. Francis snatched it with his free hand and glanced at the front page. The angry scorn twisting his face melted into confused pity as he handed the evening paper to his mother.

SECOND OFFICER SUCCUMBS TO WOUNDS
VICTIM OF IRA "MURDER GANG"

Dublin murder, 28th September, 1920.—At about 5 p.m. in the evening of Tuesday, 28th of September, 1920, a second British officer succumbed to wounds suffered in the cold-blooded attack of Saturday morning by murderous gunmen of the I.R.A. Lieutenant Thomas Piers-Musgrave, late of the 9th Inniskilling Fusiliers, having survived several gunshot wounds and a lengthy surgery, passed peacefully without fully regaining consciousness. His body will be returned to his family for burial with military honours in Kent. Attacked in a flat they shared, Lieutenant Piers-Musgrave and Lieutenant Cameron Davidson, 5th Royal Scots, were sleeping early Saturday morning when four gunmen burst in and fired shots at them in their beds. Their cowardly assailants are still at large.

CHAPTER TWENTY-TWO

Molly

They couldn't put the poor girl on a train to Donegal, not shattered as she was by the death of Desmond or Thomas or whatever his name might have been. Confronted by the terrible reality that the man she loved, the man who'd put a baby in her, was gone forever—and was a liar from the very beginning—Molly closed up within herself, a mussel at low tide.

Peter Conway had picked her up from the wood shavings and grime, off the floor of her mother's pub, carrying her upstairs to bed. Danny witnessed the terrible thing from his perch at the top of the stairs, flying to his sister's side as she dropped and not leaving her since. Each time Eda walked by the room, she heard Danny's quiet voice through the door, reading aloud to his stricken sister or singing the songs they'd both known as children. She'd not the heart to force him back to his classes at the Christian Brothers' school, but after ten days' absence that would need to change soon.

The roiling mix of fear and humiliation had crumpled Molly like a paper sack, but she was inching toward acceptance. Getting her into a bath and washing her hair, changing her, getting some hot food into her, all these had moved Molly to the point where she could answer questions with coherent words. But the look of her still swung between dreadful despair and wild-eyed derangement. She was, Eda knew, holding on by the thinnest of threads. There was no telling what the next day or week, let alone the coming years, would bring.

The regulars in the pub tried as best they could to comfort Eda with a sense of business as usual. Those who'd witnessed Molly's collapse firsthand didn't say much, their knowing looks of pity and concern words enough. Those who'd gotten the story by hearsay shuffled their feet and mumbled snippets of what passed for kindnesses—"a terrible thing" and "such a lovely girl."

So they'd stumbled through October, the month of the rosary, but Eda hadn't ventured through the doors of St. Nicholas to join the devotions. The thought of it chilled her, kneeling among those mumbling women and old men, stupefied by the drone of the pastor's mindless canting. She smiled at the memory of her dead husband's imitation of the nasally priest while the children laughed themselves to tears, wondering whether her Molly would ever laugh with such abandon again.

It was these unsettled thoughts Peter Conway interrupted when he came through the front door of the pub and made his way to his accustomed end of the bar where Eda stood polishing glassware. She sensed him more than saw him, her subconscious imprinted with the way he swung open the door, the sound and speed of his footfalls, the telltale scent of his clothing.

Setting down a dried glass, she slipped the end of the towel into her skirt pocket as she turned toward Peter. The affection and relief at the sight of him warmed her. She smiled in welcome.

"How is Molly keeping today, Eda? Is she any better?" he asked in Irish, knowing her thoughts had been far away.

She blinked a few times, focusing to confirm it was him. Then she took a long deep breath to bring herself back and said, "No, but thanks for your asking. It's a comfort to me that there's a good man concerned for her, as her own father would've been."

Flustered by the genuineness of Eda's gratitude, he said, "Well… she's dear to me… as all your children are, you must know that." He rubbed his perspiring palms, then smiled over at Eda. She looked into his bespectacled eyes, thankful for his concern and regretful she wasn't yet able to give herself to him entirely, as she knew he wished. Perhaps soon, when things were more settled with Molly. After the baby.

Peter's face changed suddenly as he stared over her shoulder. Eda turned and watched as Molly descended the stairs, clinging to Danny's hand. Her little brother alternated between glancing at the next step and looking up with anxious concern into his sister's deathly pale face. As the patrons noticed the pair, conversations fell away one by one, the gathered men watching in reverent silence as if she were an apparition of the Virgin. None dared speak.

It was a good sign, Eda thought, noting that Molly had changed into regular clothing, and brushed and braided her hair. Eda went to the bottom of the stairs, putting on a smiling face of encouragement.

"Well, 'tis Molly Brannigan! Isn't that grand, seeing you up and about and looking yourself again!" An indistinct chorus of affirmations rippled across the gathered patrons.

Reaching the last steps, Molly released her brother's hand. Eda reached out to her daughter and laid the girl's arm into the crook of an elbow, leading her behind the bar where she might find some refuge. A few of the men nodded and spoke her name in greeting.

Her brother Francis limped toward her and said, "Good to see you up and about, Molly. You gave us all a scare."

She looked back with an unseeing expression that silenced him. She went along with her mother, not saying a word. When they reached Peter Conway, Molly lifted a hand to the man's shoulder and gave the lightest squeeze.

"Thank you." Her voice was hardly a whisper, a breeze rustling leaves. He smiled and patted her hand before she withdrew it and headed off behind the bar with her mother.

The Tippler and the Pintman stood next to Peter, behind their glasses of porter. Hearing Molly speak a little, they thought to encourage her.

"Oh, how it gladdens the heart to see our own dear Molly downstairs again," said the Tippler, who'd known her since she was a baby during the old days in New Row.

"And sorry we are, Molly, at the loss of Desmond," said the Pintman. "Struck down in the prime of his youth."

She turned to him with a strange puzzled look. Then a wan smile crossed her face.

"Will he come again, do you suppose?" The smile dimmed back to devastation as fast as it had arisen. "No, no. He's dead, isn't he?" Her hand covered her belly, hovering over the child growing there unbeknownst to all but her mother.

She turned to the shelves at the back of the bar and grabbed two bottles, then stepped over to the two men who'd offered their clumsy condolences. In her right hand, she held a green bottle of Pernod, and in her left, a bottle of dark navy rum.

"Why, here's rosemary, for remembrance," she said, pouring ounces of Pernod into the Tippler's pint. He stood gaping as the licorice scent wafted up to his nostrils. "But you'll remember Desmond well enough, and all the rounds he stood, won't you? Just as you remember my dead father?"

Turning to the Pintman, she half-filled his nearly empty glass of stout with rum. "Here are daisies, for falseness and dissembling." She slammed down the bottle next to him, in the empty space where Desmond had often stood. "I give them to you, since he's all gone and God's mercy on his soul."

The Pintman looked with painful pity across the bar and said, "Now Molly, you mustn't vex yerself so. We've all known loss. 'Tis often the way of things in this vale of tears."

Eda stood stock still, frozen by her daughter's wild words. When Molly's face twisted in anger, Eda moved toward her and slid a comforting arm round her narrow shoulders.

Flinging off her mother's arm, Molly leaned over the bar, her nose only inches from the embarrassed Pintman's, and screeched, "The way of things! They shot bullets into him while he lay abed! They took him from me with their guns and their hate!"

Peter glanced at Danny, who looked back in panic before dashing back up the stairs and hiding in the shadows at the top of the landing. Francis, roused from his own stunned silence, dropped his crutch and lurched to the bar, moving hand over hand toward his sister and mother.

"It's our brother's to blame!" Francis spit at his sister. "You know bloody well it was Sean and his gang of butchers!"

"Francis, how can you say such a thing?" said Eda.

Molly scurried out from behind the bar as her brother turned his venom on their mother.

"Stop denyin' what we all know, Mam! He's a traitor to the Crown and he's a traitor to this family! Look what he's done to his own sister! Vatican twins, my arse! Da wouldn't have stood for this and well you know it!"

Peter blocked Francis's progress. "You've had too much to drink and you'll regret such harsh words to your mother." Francis tried to get by, but Peter wouldn't give way. "I'll not have you speak that way to her. She hardly deserves it."

Francis heaved all his weight against Peter, shoulder in his chest, and both men slammed down to the floor. Peter scrambled to his feet while Francis struggled to sit up, unable to rise unassisted.

Francis shouted, "You've no claim to my mother or my family! None at all! Not even if she's letting you shag her! You're not half the man…"

The back of the mild-mannered scholar's hand cracked across Francis's face, knocking him flat to the floor again.

"Shut your mouth, lad! Shut it!" Peter hissed, bent over Francis and panting with anger. A few of the men moved to separate them as murmurs grew protesting the violence.

The boy's shrill scream silenced them. All heads snapped up toward Danny's cry in time to see Molly struggle free from her little brother's desperate clutching and throw herself down the staircase.

CHAPTER TWENTY-THREE

———◆———

Sean

Ned—
Our mutual friends would like their sons returned. Could you see to retrieving this one?

A. Pendergast

SAORTSTÁT ÉIREANN
IRISH FREE STATE

Oifig an Aire Airgeadais
(Office of the Minister for Finance)

Baile Átha Cliath
(Dublin)

<u>7th March, 1922</u>

Mister Aloysius Pendergast
111 Coolidge St.
Brookline, Massachusetts, United States

An tUasal Pendergast,

The Minister sends his warmest regards and renews his thanks for the financial support you and the Irish community in America provided to the cause of freedom. The grand result is now evident before the eyes of the entire world.

The Minister particularly asks if you might arrange for the return of Seán Ó Branagáin to his native shores at the earliest convenience. We are in great need of all our sons to secure the future of the Free State, in particular those who have demonstrated their bravery and loyalty in so marked a manner.

The Minister would consider this a great personal favour.

> Le gach dea-ghuí,
> P. Ó Conchobhair,
> Personal secretary
> (For the Minister)

"Looks like yer man Aloysius has done right well for himself," Sean shouted over the black taxi's chugging as it idled before an expansive three-story house. Sean surveyed the long wrap-around porch that ended in a round turret. "He's got himself a damn tower house."

Ned Tobin fished for change, leaning in against Sean's shoulder in the close quarters of the back seat. "One of the lace-curtain Irish. All of them moving outside the city. Power and money, money and power. My da wouldn't hear of such a thing."

"Your family's place in Southie is a right palace, compared to where I came up, Neddie boy," said Sean, slapping his hand against Ned's arm. "And good of your sister to let me stay, what with your old man bein' so… grieved and all."

Ned dropped the coins in the driver's extended palm, receiving a grunt in reply.

"He drinks a wicked amount of grief, each and every day. Best you stay clear of him until we get you on a ship."

The two passengers flipped up the door handles and stepped out onto the road, the last remnants of twilight silhouetting the peaked rooflines and leafless branches of the big elms lining the arrow-straight street. The neighborhood smelled of chilly rain and turned soil, the first signs of spring struggling against the tenacity of a New England winter.

They looked up to the Pendergast house, all the lower windows alight, likewise those halfway up the turret. Ned shifted his woolen overcoat and settled his fedora back a little on his head. Not to be outdone, Sean hitched the pea coat his sister had bought for him two years ago when he'd first come to Newfoundland, then tilted his cloth cap a little to the right.

"I trust the missus won't mind me not dressin' for dinner," said Sean, slapping Ned's arm again and raising a visible flinch from the taller American.

Ned had never gone for the kind of bluff amiability with which the Irish both sides of the Atlantic reveled. It reminded him of the laughing punches his big brother, Bobby, had dished out, leaving Ned with arms green and yellow with bruises throughout his boyhood and adolescence. They'd both gone off to the war—Ned in 1914 with the Newfoundlanders, Bobby late in the conflict after being shamed into it by the older men of the neighborhood. Ned survived the Germans' avowed desire to kill him, while Bobby, middleweight champion of the New England boxing clubs, had been laid low by an influenza virus. Now their father seemed determined to follow his eldest to the grave through the bottom of a whisky bottle, Prohibition be damned.

They clopped up the half-dozen wooden stairs and across the porch boards with their glossy paint. Light spilling over them through a pair of leaded glass sidelights, Sean pulled the bell knob.

Al Pendergast must have heard the taxi idling at the curb, appearing through the glass door before Sean had even released the knob. The door swung wide and the familiar grey hair and eyebrows set atop wide shoulders stood before them, showing the odd purse-lipped smile and angled nod that greeted every one of his acquaintances.

"Well, there you are! Get inside and get a drink into yourselves. Not sure this damp and chill will ever lift." He turned sideways, holding open the door, while Ned and Sean stepped inside. A small woman with a pinned-up pile of salt-and-pepper hair and a fashionable cobalt dress came toward them down the entry hall.

By the time Al Pendergast hung their coats and hats on two heavy brass hooks, the woman had reached the entry and motioned them inside. She smiled with the warm sincerity of a woman secure in her social position and proud of her home, then said, "It's always such a treat to see you, Ned. You leave my husband in such a fine mood with your visits."

Ned held the offered hand in his. "And it's a bigger treat for me to see your lovely face again, Mrs. Pendergast."

Her smile never wavered, well past the age of blushing at such harmless lies. After giving Ned's hand a little squeeze, she turned to the younger, smaller man.

"Do I have the pleasure of addressing Mr. Sean Brannigan of Dublin? Of whom I've heard so much?"

Sean showed a toothy grin and looked down at his scuffed shoes then back up to his hostess. "Here's hopin' they were only the good stories, ma'am." He took her hand and gave it a little tug.

"You're most welcome, Sean. I so enjoy the sound of a true Irishman in our home. It brings to mind my own dear grandfather, God rest his soul, as good and true a Donegal man as ever drew breath."

Sean brightened and said, "Why, my own mother's people are in Donegal still!"

"My grandfather missed his home terribly as he grew older. He always said Donegal was so beautiful because it was the land of the faeries," said Mrs. Pendergast, allowing herself a little wistfulness to make this young man feel welcome.

"Mam says it's where you'll find the gates to *Tír na nÓg*."

"We heard so many tales of the Land of the Young, my sisters and I, when we were small. Granddad had such a wealth of stories." Her placidness unwavering, she said, "Why don't you men have a whisky in the library, while I see the cook about our supper."

She stepped aside as Sean and Ned followed Al down the hallway, toward a set of half-opened pocket doors. Al slid them together once his guests were through, then went to a sideboard and poured three whiskies. Sean hefted the heavy lead crystal tumbler, drinking much of the contents before Al could offer his toast.

The older man chuckled and said, "What was it you said, Ned? No one will ever lose money betting on the thirst of an Irishman?"

Sean chuckled in reply, only a little embarrassed.

Al raised his glass and said, "Shall we drink to the Irish Free State, gents? And to those that made the age-old dream come true, including young Sean here?"

"Hear, hear," said Ned.

"To a free Ireland," said Sean, unsure if he was meant to drink to himself.

The three settled into seats. Aloysius sipped at his whisky and studied the two men on the couch across from him—one with the polish of a year at Boston College and an officer's commission, the other a raw and untamed lad from the Liberties, with all the easy confidence of a man who'd all his life considered the streets of Dublin his very own. They'd both done their part.

"Did you have any trouble getting away from that rumrunning schooner of your brother-in-law's, Sean? Or does he know what you're about?"

"Ach, no, he doesn't. My sister Deirdre would skin him alive if he'd let me run off—she thinks he needs my help, him bein' a kinda cripple. Not one to be trifled with, is our Deirdre. And Jack had enough trouble in the war, not gettin' himself killed and all."

Ned gave a twitch of a smile and attended to his whisky, letting Sean carry the conversation. He'd just as soon forget that first day of the Somme, when he'd taken a bullet to the shoulder. He was much the luckier for it, seeing how others suffered much worse, including his old comrade Jack Oakley.

"Ned here made an excuse for meeting us up in Kittery, where we were meant to drop the last of our load. He chatted up Jack and the others while I slipped over the side. Hid in a warehouse 'til they sailed. Ned helped them search—I heard them yelling up and down the docks for me—then let slip that he'd heard me say I'd jump ship for home first chance, what with the Treaty. We met up after the schooner sailed and he drove me to Boston."

While Sean spoke, Al rose and returned to the sideboard, fetching back the decanter. He poured another whisky for Sean, but Ned waved him off.

"Have you made arrangements for Sean's passage?" he asked Ned.

"Out on the *Celtic*, to Queenstown—or Cobh, I hear they call it now—in four days' time."

Sean sat forward, elbows on his knees, rolling the glass between his palms. "And a second class passage, if that's even to be believed. Far cry from the tramp freighter brought me the other way."

Returning the decanter, Al asked Ned, "Did you share the letter with him?"

Ned reached into his suit coat and extracted a folded sheet of paper from an inside pocket and held it out to Sean while Al settled back in his chair. Sean read over the short message, then looked up puzzled.

"Seems there are important people looking after you," Al said.

The doors parted and the lady of the house called them to the table.

CHAPTER TWENTY-FOUR

Eda

The baby didn't survive and perhaps that was for the best. Eda insisted the ambulance carry an unconscious Molly to St. Vincent's. It was near enough and the matron, Sister Mary Evangeline, would do all she could for the girl, having been so generous to the Brannigan family for ten years and more.

The doctor and the sisters had seen to Molly's injuries, setting the left arm broken cleanly in her fall, seeing to her bruises and sprains. They kept her in a bed at the end of the ward, curtained panels surrounding her while she recovered from a deep concussion. Eda had taken the matron aside and told her the sordid details of what brought her daughter to this sad condition. Sister Mary Evangeline attended the girl herself the next day when, with as little fuss and pain as could be hoped, her infant was delivered stillborn. Sometimes the Lord was merciful to broken spirits like Molly's, so different from her willful sister who'd nursed there before the war.

The Sisters of Charity kept Molly in their care longer than they would most patients, hoping to heal her anguished mind before sending her back to her mother. After five weeks, Molly reached a plateau of sorts—calm enough and no longer a danger to herself, but withdrawn and melancholic, eyes dark and sunken with the remnants of crushing grief. That was enough for Eda and she welcomed her home with sobs of relief. She'd feared her daughter would be declared a lunatic and hidden in some wretched asylum until she passed from this life, but Sister Mary Evangeline was determined to spare Eda that final loss.

Molly returned to her stool at the counter by the front door for a few hours each day. She greeted her customers with dead eyes and an unfelt smile, made their change, then returned to whatever book she'd brought down. She withdrew into her books the rest of each day and well into each night.

So the months peeled away, one after another. Letters arrived from St. John's every week—some long, others short. Always in Deirdre's hand, never Sean's. Deirdre included some newsy bits from her brother, although Eda doubted he'd asked her to do so. From all Eda knew, Sean had turned the page on Ireland, just as his married sister had done. Molly brightened a little when Eda read out the letters over breakfast, although she looked away whenever Sean was mentioned.

Eda managed to get Molly to eat enough to keep a little flesh on her bones so that the hollowness in her cheeks filled and she regained some color. She even blushed now and again, when some young patron tried his hand at chatting her up. A few asked her to walk out with them, but she looked back with such lack of comprehension they soon abandoned the effort.

Everyone—Francis included—worked hard to keep news of the escalating violence from Molly. Whenever she perched on her stool by the door, all the men knew not to argue over the tit-for-tat outrages perpetrated by the IRA and the Government forces. Every week brought more assassinations in Dublin and Cork, more ambushes on rural backroads, more bombings and shootings at police barracks across the country. The relentless brutality sapped everyone, the ambiguity of each side's claim to righteousness causing even Loyalists like Francis to begin doubting their staunchly held positions.

Peter Conway and Eda carried on their odd courtship, occasionally stepping out together for an Irish-language performance or a meal at a hotel dining room. With everything round them unsettled, they left their relationship unsettled, too.

Exhaustion with the bloodletting, coupled with the British Government's rising embarrassment as the weight of world opinion turned against them, created a begrudged opening for negotiations. After much posturing and puffing, the inevitable compromise that satisfied no one was reached and the Treaty agreed, at least for twenty-six counties. The six Protestant counties of the north would remain part of the United Kingdom, everyone blithely pretending the North Channel and Irish Sea didn't exist.

Each side gave up something dear. The Sinn Feiners offered up Ulster and their dream of an immediate republic, agreeing to remain within the Empire as an Irish Free State, whatever that might mean. This required swearing allegiance to the Crown, something that stuck deep in the craw of many rebels.

But the British gave up much more—seven hundred years' ownership of their first colony, pulling down the Union Jack from above Dublin Castle. It was obvious, even through the haze of high-minded words and pretentious posing from London, that the British had admitted defeat and would leave their dignity behind.

So Ireland was free, albeit an odd kind of freedom. The awkward relief that descended didn't last as the victorious rebels split over whether to accept the three-quarter loaf on offer or to turf out the King and continue the fight for a republic. Those who'd together endured so much turned one against the other with all the bitterness of aggrieved betrayal.

Sean arrived in April, just as the split between the pro- and anti-Treaty wings of the IRA flared into violence. By the time he'd made his way to Heuston Station in Dublin, the anti-Treaty rebels occupied the Four Courts and were at a standoff with their erstwhile comrades in the Free State's new National Army.

With no one still interested in hanging him, Sean strolled down Victoria Quay, along the river, but a pang of memory pushed him south toward the brewery and its bustling cooperage where his father had been a foreman, turning out endless barrels to be filled with porter and shipped all across the world to dull the homesickness of the men who propped up the creaking British Empire. He made his way to the heavy wooden doors, where he'd waited so many times for his father, holding tight to his mother's hand while Molly clung to the other, the bump that would soon be Danny showing beneath Mam's coat. He'd watched then with jittery excitement, examining the faces of all the men who came out by twos and threes, some hallooing. Da was always last, making sure his men had stowed their tools and tidied things for the next workday.

One of the cooperage doors was ajar and Sean stood on the pavement peering into the dim light, sniffing the warm musty air spilling onto the street. He closed his eyes and drank in the fulsome aroma of oak—white oak from America, his father said—in all its varieties of damp or dry, sawn or shaved. He looked down to the pavers and smiled at the curlicues of wood that made their way onto the street with the hundreds of coopers heading out for their pints and suppers. Some always made their way home on Da's sleeves or in his pockets.

Seven years last month, Sean thought. *Dead on that goddamned beach.*

Some hopeful springtime sunshine poked in and out of low clouds that carried the promise of soft rain. Not like the wild clouds and towering thunderheads of Newfoundland and the New England coast. They'd run into some tiny harbor ahead of big storms a dozen times during the rumrunning. He'd never been more than a serviceable deck hand. Flexing his knees a little, he pushed down against the hard pavement, thinking he'd count it a great success to never set out upon the sea again.

Cutting over to Thomas Street, Sean realized he hadn't walked the streets of Dublin without fear in the light of day for more than two years. With his senses sharpened, he reacquainted himself with the soot-stained brick houses and their bright doors, the honking and clopping, the briny smell from the fishmonger's shop and the smoky tang that trailed after a patron exiting a pub. He'd taken it all for granted, running these streets from his earliest days in search of diversion or mischief.

Found more mischief than diversion these last years.

The street widened as he approached St. Catherine's, pausing to wonder what the Protestants who worshipped there thought of the new Free State run by Catholics. These pews wouldn't be as full, soon enough. Someone had affixed a little tricolour flag to the iron-rail fence that surrounded the church. Struck by the boldness of this tiny gesture, he looked up and down the curving street and counted four more tricolours hung from buildings.

'Tis ours now. Like the one over the GPO.

It wasn't but a few minutes from St. Catherine's to the Coombe, and Sean picked up his pace as he drew nearer to home. He'd not sent word ahead, unclear what reception he'd receive from his older brother. Better not to give Francis time stewing over his wayward brother's return. He wouldn't give up his allegiances lightly, of that Sean was certain.

When he turned off Meath Street, the Coombe was as hectic as he'd remembered, all shouting and rushing. He hadn't walked ten paces when a shawlie, stooped over her cart's rough plank counter, called out his name in a shrill voice.

"Sean Brannigan, as I live and breathe!" The old woman bustled over and grabbed his free hand.

He set down the battered valise Ned Tobin's sister had given him to carry the clean shirt and few changes of underthings he'd scrounged together in Boston, all he had from his two years overseas. That and six thousand American dollars from his share of the loads of whisky and champagne they'd run down the Maine coast.

He'd never quite known why their fight was so personal to Ned, but his father was a Tipperary man so perhaps that explained it well enough. They're cantankerous to a man, the Tips. Still, there didn't seem to be much love wasted between father and son in the Tobin house, from what Sean had seen under their roof for the better part of a month. But he'd come to understand that the Irish in America were an oftentimes peculiar lot.

After news of the Treaty reached Boston and St. John's, Ned had said, "The bloody Irish can buy their own guns now," so the last rumrunning voyages he'd made down the coast fattened Sean's bankroll, no longer feeling the need to split his share with the Irish Republican Army. Ned managed to unload several dozen rifles and a couple of Maxim guns they'd not yet shipped when the Treaty was announced, selling them to some South Americans spoiling for a fight of their own. Ned split that windfall with Sean, saying it was "an end of service gratuity." Sean thought that such a delightful phrase he'd written it on a scrap of paper in his wallet so as not to forget.

"Yer ma will be o'er the moon to see ye," the old woman said, clutching Sean's hand against her drooping chest. Tears in her eyes, she gave him a gummy smile and squeezed his hand all the tighter.

Patting her leathery hand, the fingers twisted with arthritis, Sean managed to extract his own with an indulgent smile. He had no memory of her, but assumed she was one of the shawlies that drank in the snug by the back door of The Gallant. With a flicker of guilt, he realized he'd never learned her name, even after having been intimate with her urine when he'd emptied that smelly biscuit tin each morning.

"Well, that's as fine a welcome as ever a man could want," said Sean, hoping to escape before she summoned a crowd. "Now, oughtn't I be gettin' on with surprisin' my own old one?"

The woman nodded and smiled, waving Sean down the street, shouting after him, "And God bless ye, Sean Brannigan! Ye did yer part! Much as any man!"

The long brick side of his mother's place was just ahead, the gold trim on the sign across the front dirtier since last he saw it. The front door opened and two men in good suits stepped out and headed off in the direction of Trinity. One carried a cane and walked with a painful limp. The crippled man stopped and leaned a hand against the adjacent storefront, putting his weight on his good leg. His companion turned to offer an arm.

Sean saw the round glasses surrounding the familiar wide eyes.

"Peter Conway! Peter!"

After righting his friend—must be Johnny O'Fallon, Sean realized—Peter looked to the sound of his name. Sean dropped his case to the pavement and dashed past the pub, extending a hand to Peter. The quiet bookseller ignored the hand and grabbed Sean, blinking away tears and unleashing a wide grin. He squeezed Sean's shoulders and gave him a little shake.

"You're a sight for sore eyes, lad."

Sean was astonished by the look of Peter, radiating pride and affection, something he'd not seen from an older man since he'd lost his da.

"We've done it, haven't we?" Sean said.

"Aye, we have. 'Tis why I went to Mick and asked that he send for you. There's great need of you here. We've a nation to govern."

To the shock of both Sean and Johnny O'Fallon, Peter Conway wrapped his arms about the younger man and held him tight against his chest.

So only Sean could hear, he whispered, "My heart's too full for more words, son."

Pushing back to arm's length, he said, "Now, fetch your bag and get inside to your mother."

There wasn't a big crowd, since it was that awkward period near teatime when most of the drinkers were home with their families, at least until the dishes were cleared and the children sent to bed. Through the doors, Sean watched his lanky brother, crutch under his arm, in the middle of the same interchangeable crowd of old soldiers that kept him comforted or aggrieved, depending on the events of the day. He tugged the long brass handle he'd polished a hundred times.

She didn't make a sound, so Sean might have missed his sister on the stool next to the door, eyes cast down at a book. He couldn't see his mother behind the bar, her place occupied by the apprentice to whom he'd taught the pub's morning routine before going off to kill a magistrate in Tullamore.

Looking about, he saw his sister not five feet away.

"Molly?"

Once she'd overcome her confusion at his unexpected appearance, she fixed him with a dull stare. She'd been so very ill, he knew. The letters Deirdre read out to him in St. John's were clear enough, even through Mam's halting attempts to minimize Molly's deterioration after the murder of her lover. He shouldn't expect things to be the same, like when they were growing up, not after all she'd passed through. He'd been shocked when Mam wrote that Desmond was an undercover man, an English officer. But wasn't that the way with rebellions in this country, always shot through with informants and traitors, no one what they seemed?

"Molly, what's become of you?"

Her expression remained set, lifeless as a death mask.

"Mam's upstairs. I'll fetch her." With words she was like to use with any customer or stranger, she descended from her stool and shuffled up the stairs.

Sean examined the shelves of the sundries counter, avoiding his brother's notice until he'd a chance to kiss his mother. He lifted a packet of Woodbines and a box of matches from the back shelf and stood at the counter as if waiting to pay. Molly's strange reception unnerved him, even knowing of her troubles, and the excitement of his homecoming was muted by an imprecise uneasiness.

There wasn't much time to ponder this once the door at the top of the stairs flew open, knob denting the plaster wall. The hum of conversation fell into abrupt silence when Eda's voice echoed through the room.

"My boy! My dear boy!" she screamed, eyes wide with stunned excitement. Her heels clacked against the wooden treads, careening down the stairs, bouncing from a shoulder against the wall to a hip against the banister.

"*Mo bhuachaill daor féin!*" she cried, the shock of so much sudden joy toppling her into Irish. She searched the room for the familiar face. "Where's my boy?"

Sean stepped out of the shadows, pulling off his cap. The men parted like nervous sheep as Francis turned toward the door, too.

Eda flew down the remaining stairs. With arms wide, she ran to Sean, tears streaming, and embraced him with violent bliss.

"I'm so sorry for the grief I've caused," he said, burying his face in her hair, feeling her heaving with sobs against him. "I never meant to draw you into my troubles, Mam."

She held him tighter, rocking while she wept out all her relief and happiness. Everyone knew she'd given up her firstborn to a strange country on the edge of the world, sending Deirdre away to save herself after the war had left her broken. It would've been less painful for Eda Brannigan to cut off her right hand than to lose another child.

"Oh, Mam," he said, sniffing the familiar smell of her. "I'm so sorry."

She took in a long breath and shuddered as if she had fever, then took a deeper, steadier one. She released her son and stepped back, rubbing his arms with her palms, appraising the look of him after two long years away.

"Your sister's been feedin' you well enough."

Sean rubbed the back of a hand under his nose, then wiped his eyes with the palm. "Aye, she has that. And her mother-in-law's taught her to bake every kind of tart and pie. No meal's complete without a slab of one."

Eda's eyes filled again. "Is her husband a good man? And his family, have they taken to her?"

"Her Jack is as good a man as walks this world, Mam, and so dotty over her I was embarrassed for him," he said, laughing and wiping again at his cheeks. "And who wouldn't take to our Deirdre, gentle as a dove like she is?"

They laughed together, the eldest Brannigan anything but dovelike. Eda's laughter stopped when she saw Francis limping toward them.

"You should greet your brother, Sean," she said, turning him.

"Well, it looks like you might have grown a mite since you ran off in a hail o' bullets," Francis said. Sean tensed, awaiting the bitterness that was sure to follow. He looked over the surrounding faces, all smiling at the crack about Sean's enduring lack of height. When he looked back to Francis, he was smiling, too, a little awkward to be sure.

"It's good to be home, Francis." He offered his hand and Francis grasped it.

"Glad you've not taken up our sister's altogether annoyin' habit of callin' me Frank."

Sean shook his head and said, "Ach, that's just for Deirdre. None of the rest of us would ever have dared it."

The apprentice came from behind the bar and handed a pint of stout to Sean. Francis waved away the offered whisky and shifted on his crutch, clearing his throat. He looked round at the men gathered round him, gathering their reassurance.

"It's over, Sean. They've gone... the Brits... and left it to us." The weight of years of anger and accusation rendered his words halting and heavy, but he pressed on. "No matter the differences... between you and me, I mean... I've always been an Irishman first... like Da and... and our granddads before us."

"We're still a part of the Empire, Francis," Sean said, offering a little consolation for how hard this was for his brother. He glanced at the gathered veterans and saw the same painful resignation. It was obvious they'd spent long hours thrashing out the matter of the Free State and all that had happened since the Union Jack came down from Dublin Castle.

"Sure… that we are, so. But we've a nation… and we need to make … to make what we can of it," Francis shrank as he exhaled, as if someone had let the air out of him. The apprentice renewed the offer of the large whisky and Francis accepted it.

A man with a black patch over an eye and scars radiating down his cheek lifted his pint and said, "To the Irish Free State?"

Sean lifted his own glass and said, "Aye, if we can keep it."

Her face smoothed by relief at her sons' awkward but peaceful reunion, Eda called up to her youngest. "Brendan, come down and welcome your brother home."

Startled by a name he'd not heard in seven years, Sean looked to the landing at the top of the stairs and saw his younger brother sitting in his usual place against the wall. When he stood at his mother's beckoning, Sean could saw he'd grown a good four inches.

"At least my fair share of the height in this family didn't go beggin'." The men laughed, pleased to have something to lift the discomfort that had just passed.

The youngest Brannigan came across the floor and, now almost eye to eye with Sean, stuck out his hand and said, "Grand to have you home, Sean."

Grabbing the boy's hand, Sean said, "Brendan, is it? Not heard that for quite some time."

The boy looked away, reddening. His mother stepped up to rescue him.

"He told me he wanted to be Brendan again," she said. "That's when I realized what a lot of foolishness it was, me insistin' on callin' him Danny. Won't bring his father back, and my Daniel would've thought me daft."

The Tippler, well into his cups, called from the bar, "And a better man never drew breath than Daniel Brannigan!"

Sean gripped his little brother behind the neck and said, "Brendan it will be, now and forever. Since you're like to tower above me soon, I'd be wise to call you whatever you fancy, eh boy?"

Brendan smiled and flushed again, lunging from the back slaps administered by a few bystanders.

Eda looked to the counter by the door and saw Molly back in her book. "Molly, come kiss your brother. Or have you done so already?"

With studied slowness, Molly set her book on the counter and made her way to the center of the room. She draped her arms about his neck and kissed him on the cheek, pausing before pulling back long enough to whisper.

"I know what you did, Sean."

CHAPTER TWENTY-FIVE

Sean

The rickety chair complained whenever he leaned back, heels on the windowsill, not that there was much to see through the curtain of cold autumn rain slipping down the panes. Even on sunny days, the view was gloomy overlooking an interior courtyard. Eight or nine hours a day, he felt like he was in the cellar of his mother's pub. The thrill of working inside Dublin Castle had worn off within a few weeks and now he took any excuse to get out on a raid or arrest.

Although Sean was still only twenty-one, he proved old enough for the Irish Free State. With so many government bureaucrats gone, what with those who abandoned the island with the British or disqualified themselves by once picking the wrong side, the Free State couldn't be overly choosy with its staffing. Steadiness and unquestioned loyalty were at a premium and Sean had proven himself on both counts. So Mick Collins—himself made Minister of Finance at the wizened age of twenty-nine—handed him on to the commander of the Free State's new Civic Guard, the force that had taken over in January from the despised Royal Irish Constabulary.

Together with the National Army, the *Garda Síochána* was setting about suppressing their disgruntled former comrades who opposed the Treaty and were still fighting across the country. Newly minted

Superintendent Brannigan—*Ceannfort* being his more fashionable Irish title—was charged with rounding up the anti-Treaty men who'd scattered when the Four Courts fell in a blaze at the end of June, taking Peter Conway's bookstore with it. The entire Free State government was under intense pressure to maintain order, lest the British forces still remaining took it upon themselves to disprove any notion that the Irish could govern themselves. It hadn't helped when the IRA killed Mick Collins in an ambush down in Cork the month previous.

A sharp efficient knock on the heavy office door was followed by the brisk entry of *Ceannfort* Brannigan's secretary, trailed by a man in a rumpled brown suit, a dissolute cigarette clinging to the corner of his mouth.

"Sergeant… *Sáirsint* Halloran requires a signature on a detention order, *Ceannfort*," she said, standing aside to allow the disheveled officer to plop a dun folder in the middle of his superior's desk. The detective had less than a decade on Sean, but looked much older from the long months he'd spent in prisons during the fight for independence. It seemed to Sean the sergeant adhered to the Free State less from enthusiasm than exhaustion of mind, body, and spirit. That wasn't such an uncommon thing.

"Who's this for? Another one of Rory O'Connor's lads, from the Four Courts?"

"Nah, one that dodged the surrender at the Glanville Hotel," said Sergeant Halloran.

Sean opened the folder and scratched his signature across the bottom with a tortoiseshell pen. Before he absentmindedly closed the cover on the wet ink, a spotless grey sleeve reached in front of him and rolled a curved blotter across it. The secretary slid the papers away from Sean, walked to the sergeant detective, and handed him the folder while shoving him out the door. At the sound of the heavy latch, she spun on her heels with raised eyebrows and exaggerated pursed lips.

"Sweet Jaysus on a biscuit, that Halloran's a dour one, isn't he?" she said, walking behind the desk where Sean sat lighting a cigarette.

"Ach now, Maggie, he had a bad time of it from the Brits. He's a decent enough fella."

"He looks a dog's breakfast morning, noon or evening," she said, turning Sean in his chair to face her, then bending to plant a hard kiss on his mouth. She gave the front of his trousers a squeeze, smoothed her skirt, and said, "You'd think his missus wouldn't let him out on the street lookin' like that."

Sean ran a hand over her bum and gave it a pat. "At least he doesn't put on airs like you, Margaret Mulcahy."

Smoothing down her skirt and patting the side of her tightly pinned hair, she said, "We couldn't have the secretary to the *Ceannfort* creating a scandal within these august walls, could we?"

She gripped Sean's arm and tugged up his sleeve, twisting her neck to see his wristwatch. "Nearly time to bugger off. Is your flatmate still away in Limerick?"

"That he is, Miss Mulcahy," Sean said. "I suppose you'll be wantin' to drop by for a whisky and a tickle again tonight?"

"Not until you've bought me a decent supper, you randy bastard. I'll fetch my hat and coat."

Shrugging at the cigarette, he crushed it unsmoked in a tin ashtray at the edge of his desk and fetched his hat and umbrella. He glanced at the rain pelting the window and decided they'd hail a cab from the queue outside the main gates. If anyone noticed, they'd think he was doing a kindness for his underpaid secretary, giving her a lift home in the foul weather.

"Mam will be expectin' me tomorrow—I never miss a Friday supper. You'll need to find some other fella to feed you, then." Sean jerked the chain on his desk lamp and headed into the anteroom, where Maggie was pulling on a practical black coat over her sensible grey suit.

They ate round half five on Fridays, soon as Sean could get away from his work. When Eda heard him trot up the stairs and fling open the door, striding into the kitchen in a suit with a collared shirt and necktie—well, you'd have knocked her Daniel over with a feather if he were alive to see. But wasn't that just another strange thing in this new country?

She'd a nice piece of sole from the fishmonger's and had found the last of this year's blackcurrants at the greengrocer's for a tart she'd baked in the morning and fended off Brendan a half-dozen times. The boy was growing so fast she couldn't keep him filled. She'd had to increase the pub's sandwich order from the butcher with Brendan eating two or even three at one go whenever his stomach brought him rummaging beneath the bar.

Molly was at her counter with orders to shoo Francis upstairs and Brendan off his perch once Sean arrived. The apprentice would keep an eye on things while they all sat down to a fine supper.

The table set, Peter Conway came back to the kitchen where Eda was bent over the open oven checking that the whipped potatoes with which she'd sealed the fish hadn't browned too much. When she stood, Peter came beside her and slid an arm round her waist. Gentle as a man could be, he kissed her grey-streaked hair.

"I'm a sweaty mess," she said, wrapping an arm over his hand on her hip and leaning into him with a slow sigh.

He kissed her head again and whispered in Irish, "When will you ever marry me, Eithne?"

"Not long. I promise, *mo grá*."

They separated at the sound of feet trodding up the stairs and hurried to the sitting room. Sean was first through. Molly slipped in behind, with her unchanging look of distant distraction, although Eda noticed she shot looks at Sean's back. There'd been a coldness between them she couldn't understand, them having been so close before. But coldness to her brother was the least of Molly's woes and Eda was loathe to probe whatever wound might be the cause, fearing she'd set back her fragile daughter.

Francis came behind the others, one step at a time with Brendan hovering behind, extending a hand or an arm if his big brother wavered. Eda smiled at the sight of the two, Brendan now less than half a head shorter than the lanky Francis.

"Well, everyone's here. That's grand," said Eda, surprising her children each Friday as tears threatened whenever they gathered round her table. Perhaps it was only from the joy of it or maybe from the longing to see her missing daughter again. Peter promised that after they married they'd book passage to Halifax to see her sister, Nola, then on to St. John's for a good long visit with Deirdre and her husband. Sean had assured her a dozen times that Jack Oakley was as fine a man as anyone could want for her daughter, but a mother's heart needed to be certain about such things, she always said.

"Let's sit ourselves down. The fish is ready. The Brussels sprouts have just come in at the greengrocer's, so I've a lovely bunch in butter on the stove."

The only time Eda Brannigan was known to take a drink within the four walls of her public house was after supper of a Friday. She was hard pressed to keep herself away from business for long, so after the meal was finished, the family wandered down one or two at a time. Molly and Peter stayed upstairs for the washing up, both content to do so in silence.

Eda returned to her place behind the bar, dispatching her apprentice to the storeroom for restocking. She poured herself a small glass of port, with a whisky for Francis and a pint of stout for Sean. Lately she'd allowed Brendan to stand at the bar with his brothers and have one lager shandy. She lifted her glass, glowing with a satisfied smile.

"To my Brannigan men!"

They lifted their glasses in reply, beaming back at their mother. Then, his voice cracking, Brendan added, "And to Da, who we wish was here, too."

Francis leaned hard on his crutch and threw his other arm over Brendan's neck, pulling the boy's head against his shoulder. "That we do, Brendan."

Sean wrapped his arm over his older brother's and squeezed the younger between them. "A better man never walked the streets of Dublin."

Eda's towel crept to her eyes, dabbing the corners, but her smile never faltered. She seemed to her sons better able to enjoy the memories, without the stabbing pain of loss anymore, at least not so much. There was a good man in the flat above who cared for her and who'd felt no need to replace Daniel in her heart, only to make his own place there. Yes, she'd marry him soon, of that they were certain.

Business was sparse this early in the evening with all the regulars home for their suppers. They'd begin returning soon, so Eda looked up when the door opened on a familiar face.

"A mate of yours." She pointed her chin toward the door, patting the back of Sean's hand.

When Sean turned, there was Martin Gavin. He looked about the place with the pantomime swagger Sean had seen so often before, but he still had the jittery look that no amount of bluster could ever hide. The same jumpiness that convinced Sean to give him the sack before that business up in Tullamore. He'd heard not a thing of Martin since returning from America.

The door at the top of the stairs opened and Peter Conway descended, smoothing down the shirtsleeves he'd rolled to keep out of the dishwater, his suit coat over an elbow while he finished the job. After he'd come down four or five steps, Molly appeared and closed the door before coming down, too.

Sean turned to face Martin Gavin and raised a hand in welcome.

"Well, there he is now!" Martin shouted across the barroom, "*Superintendent* Sean Brannigan of the Civic Guard! As I live and breathe!" The two years that passed since last they met had been good to Martin Gavin. He looked as if he'd put on a stone or more.

As his old comrade crossed toward the bar, Sean offered a hand and Martin took it with both his, pumping like he was after pulling the shoulder from its socket. His palms were slick with perspiration, as was the broad forehead set above the ruddy round cheeks.

"Back from over the sea and a respectable man, so?" said Martin. His eyes scanned left and right along the bar while he spoke, looking away when Francis and Brendan turned to see who the new arrival might be.

"I did my days in purgatory, Martin," said Sean, "Although running liquor down to thirsty Yanks was a well-paid sort of atonement, sure."

"Haven't we heard the tales of your bootleggin' days? And the guns you sent over, too." Martin produced a handkerchief and made a show of blowing his nose, but Sean noticed he ran it up over his forehead and then worried it between his palms before shoving it back into a pocket.

"Best I could do from afar, seein' how the RUC and the Tans were keepin' a noose to hand should I return." Sean said, placing a hand on Martin's shoulder. He felt a sharp twitch at his touch.

"Mam, let's have a pint for Martin Gavin here," Sean said. "We go back all the way to the old neighbourhood, so he'll drink on my tick tonight."

Eda flipped a pint glass and slipped it under a beer pump, pulling with the long slow motion that had become second nature. "Be a grand thing if you'd put a few quid to your generosity, seein' as how your account's long as my arm." Eda set the pint before Martin Gavin and gave him a little wink.

"One of the many blessings of havin' a mother who's a publican," said Sean with a wink of his own. "To old adventures, then? *Sláinte.*"

With a nervous chuckle, Martin raised his glass and said, "Aye, to old adventures. And to the Free State, eh, Sean boy?" He said the last with a louder voice and a broad sweep of his arm.

"To the Free State," echoed Brendan and Francis, while Sean stayed silent, studying Martin. All the men at the bar took long draughts, all but Brendan who was nursing his shandy to linger with his brothers.

"And to peace at last," said Peter Conway, who'd slipped without fuss into his accustomed place at the end of the bar, standing next to Brendan. Peter had taken to hanging his hat, and in cooler weather his overcoat, off one of the brass hooks on the narrow wall that separated the end of the bar from the two snugs. Any of the regulars knew Peter was upstairs in the Brannigan flat if his coat was present and he was not, although no one dared any ribald remarks about his relations with the pub's owner. Peter's black woolen overcoat and grey hamburg hung there now.

Martin set his half-drained pint on the bar and said, "I've come lookin' for ye, Sean boy, to ask a favour. When the butcher I was apprenticin' with heard tell of my rebel work, he turfed me right out the door. With everything bein' so topsy-turvy since the Treaty, a man can have a hard time findin' an honest job."

The eyes kept up their scan of the room as he spoke. Taking Sean by the elbow, he said, "Maybe you could give me a minute or two to bend yer ear, private like, seein' as how my own situation is a little embarrassin' just now."

Martin motioned toward an empty snug, but Sean eased his elbow out of the nervous man's grip and said, "There's no one over at the tables, so we can talk free as we please there." Sean headed for the bench along the opposite wall, Martin trailing behind like a chastened pup. He set himself down and stretched out his legs, glancing up to Martin with a strained smile, waiting for him to settle himself, too.

Martin pulled a stool back a little, then stopped to fidget with his coat. When he stuck his hand into a pocket, Sean figured he was fishing for his handkerchief. The weight Martin had collected left him puffing and sweating like a brewery horse.

The dim overhead lights cast deep shadows across the floor. Of course, the pistol was black, too.

It came as a jumble to Sean, unable to piece together all he was seeing for a few long seconds. When he began to rise, Martin said, "Sit down and don't you move. I know what a cute hoor you can be." The barrel of the pistol quivered in Martin's unsteady hand.

With his back to the bar, no one else could see what the heavy-set man held. Likely a pint, most would think. Sean fixed a panicked glare on Martin's face, looking for something, anything. When the apprentice set down a wooden crate of bottles behind the bar, the clinking rattles startled Martin and he half-turned toward the sound—far enough for Brendan to see the pistol's silhouette. He jabbed Peter and pointed, the older man signaling to stay silent before reaching toward his overcoat on the hook beside him.

Sean saw what he expected to find. Sweat poured from Martin and his hand waved a foot either side of Sean's chest. He'd have been the same in Tullamore, what little consolation that was now. Fearful panicky men were still dangerous.

"Martin, what are you doin'?" he said, light as he could manage, "What are you about with that?"

The gunman licked and chewed at his lips, then said, "Thought I didn't have the nerve to shoot a man? What do you think now, Sean boy?"

He couldn't show any fear. That would only stiffen Martin's resolve. And the way to get out of this mess was to keep Martin undecided.

"It was a terrible thing, Martin. And you were lucky not to be a part of it. I still see that poor woman's blood in my dreams most nights."

"I'll bet you sleep better knowin' it brought you a fine job, turnin' on your old comrades and roundin' 'em up like pigs to the slaughterhouse."

So that was it. He'd sided with the anti-Treaty holdouts. Sean kept up his pretense of calm and said, "Martin, we've a chance to make things over, ourselves alone. You need to give it a chance, the Free State."

"You betrayed the Republic! Jayzus, Sean, you was there, right at the start. How could you swear allegiance to the bloody King after all that?"

There was movement behind Martin, but Sean wasn't about to look away. He had the wavering assassin stymied for now and wouldn't break the spell.

"'Tis a small thing, isn't it, Martin? So that we'd have our own government and all?"

Martin's flushed face turned scarlet with anger and he raised the pistol with a steadier hand.

"A small thing? You're a fuckin' traitor, Sean. Just like Collins. And you'll end here today, like that bastard did last month!"

With the realization he was about to die, everything in Sean's thoughts and vision slowed to a jerky crawl, like turning the handle on a reel at the penny arcade. He saw Martin lick his parched lips again and steady his arm a last time, knuckles whitening with the tightness of his hold on the pistol's grip.

The shot sounded just as it had in the magistrate's bedroom—strangely muffled and close. But the blood splattering hot across Sean's face and chest was different. He waited for the pain to follow.

His mother's scream pierced through it all.

He watched Martin Gavin stagger once, half his face a mass of ragged tissue, then crumple forward, crashing across the table and slamming into Sean's legs. That wasn't the pain he'd expected and it shot him to his feet as the bigger man's momentum rolled his lifeless body to the floor, still gripping tight to the pistol.

Sean panted with terror and relief as he scanned the room. His brother Francis hobbled toward him with a look of confused horror, Brendan hurrying behind. His mother stood frozen behind the bar, hands sealed over her mouth, with an awful pained look that Sean hadn't seen since the telegram had come with the news of Da's death.

Behind where Martin Gavin stood moments before, Peter Conway held a smoking pistol in his outstretched arm, not three feet from where Martin's head had been.

One of the more sober patrons inside the stunned pub responded when Sean asked someone to find a telephone box and ring up 4792 to say Superintendent Brannigan needed the duty detective with some uniformed Guards down at The Gallant Fusilier on the Coombe. Being so near the Castle, it was only a few minutes before they arrived. To Sean's relief, Detective Sergeant Halloran, cigarette dangling, shook off his usual lassitude and took matters well in hand. He posted uniforms at the front and side doors, not letting anyone enter or leave until he had some idea what had transpired.

There wasn't much to investigate. Once Sergeant Halloran had gotten a large brandy and a few cigarettes into Sean, the story turned out to be simple enough. An anti-Treaty gunman tried to assassinate a superintendent of police, whose main duty was tracking down anti-Treaty fugitives and making a good job of it. A close friend of the family killed the gunman as he was about to shoot the superintendent. No need to inquire why a Trinity tutor was carrying a pistol, these being perilous and confused times. Also best to get the body away and the mess tidied before too much was made of it all. The patrons scattered as soon as Halloran allowed them to leave. This being Dublin, they'd fan out to nearby pubs, spreading news of the shocking events at The Gallant well before closing time. In short order, an eager listener would turn out to be a man from one of the papers. Halloran would leave some Guards posted through the night, to give the family a little time at least.

The uniformed Guards wrapped Martin Gavin in an old blanket and lugged him out the back door. They hefted him into the back of a Black Maria sent to haul away the mortal remains to the morgue in the cellar of the Baggot Street Hospital. Eda's apprentice proved himself made of sterner stuff than any would have imagined, swallowing back his rising gorge while mopping the floor and scrubbing bloodstains from the crimson horsehair of the bench along the wall. All that was left after less than two hours was the persistent smell of the gunshot clung inside the pub. Peter had slid his pistol back into his overcoat pocket after Sergeant Halloran smelled the barrel and counted the remaining bullets in the cylinder.

Eda sat ashen and shaken on a stool while her sons and Peter leaned against the bar facing her. She looked up at intervals to Sean, looking as if she needed reassurance he was still breathing.

Molly was taking things better than anyone could have hoped, retreating to her stool and her book, even though no one would be coming to buy anything the rest of this sad night. The few times Eda glanced back at her daughter, she sat with the book open in her lap, her gaze fixed in the direction of her brothers yet focused miles and miles away.

Over his initial shock and elation at surviving, Sean stood pondering the evening's events. He hadn't seen Martin Gavin in over two years. It seemed the height of unlikeliness he'd happened by chance into the pub the one night he was certain to find Sean. While he stood in silence, a slow realization grew, anger and disappointment constricting this throat and threshing his thoughts.

He turned toward his older brother.

"It was you," he said, low and freighted with menace. "You made a big show of making things up with me, accepting the Treaty and all."

He shoved Francis's chest, slamming him back against the edge of the bar and said, "You told them when to find me here, didn't you? It was you, wasn't it?"

Steadying himself again, Francis said, "You're daft! Why would I do such a thing? Bring more grief upon Mam and our family?"

Sean pushed him again, then kicked his artificial limb. "Because you can't stand that you lost your leg and your father for nothing, now that we've won and pushed the English back across the water."

Stepping away from the bar and rounding on Francis, Sean said, "I'm your brother. Your own father's son. You bitter, sad bastard."

He didn't cock back. The fist came from his side, straight to Francis's jaw. Unsteady as he was, Francis went down like a sack of coal into the sawdust.

Peter Conway and Brendan went for Sean, pinning his arms back. "You don't know that to be true," Peter said. "You've no way of knowing at all."

"Six years of anger and hate doesn't vanish so easy. And now with me in the Castle, where his beloved Royal Army used to be…"

"That's enough!" Eda was on her knees, next to Francis, looking over the red welt on his cheek that would spread and darken soon enough. She shouted over her shoulder at Sean, "He's your brother... and he's a cripple, for the love of God!"

"More than his leg's crippled," Sean said. "He's resented me ever since he came back from the war, all the more since I came home." He shook loose from Peter and said over the prostrate Francis, "Just admit what you did and I'll leave you to your self-pity and your drunkenness and never return."

Eda turned on her knees with a look of horror and said, "You mustn't say such a thing! You can't—it would break my heart!"

A light touch on his shoulder intruded, and Sean turned face-to-face with Molly. She looked at him with the same cold eyes she'd shown him since his return.

"It wasn't Francis," she said, almost meekly. "I told you I know what you did, that you had Desmond killed. His boss told me, in the hospital. Just before... before he died."

It was Sean's turn at shocked denials and he said, "Molly, I was in Newfoundland when your man was shot!"

"But aren't there letters and telegrams? And weren't you sending guns and such from America? It would have been an easy thing," she said. "And did you know I was carrying his child when you had him killed?"

Sean slumped, his chest collapsing in grief. "Molly, I'm so sorry. What's happened to you? I'm so sorry," he said, eyes burning as he swallowed the knot in his throat, feeling in a rush the bitter injustice of his own false accusation of Francis.

Sean stared at his hands and muttered, "I didn't do it. It wasn't me."

She didn't believe him, he could see that. What he'd thought a vague and distant coldness these last months, he now knew was icy hatred. He heaved a sigh brimming with awful sorrow.

A hand lifted Molly's wrist from her side and Brendan stepped between her and Sean. The youngest Brannigan, the one they'd taken for granted since his father was killed, said just above a whisper to his sister, "I saw him with a friend, one night while I was wanderin' about. No one ever noticed me."

Eda regained her feet and came to her daughter, arm about her waist, so she could hear her youngest's words. Peter moved close, next to Sean.

"I followed them to a pub and waited outside. They came out later with two women and they were callin' him 'Thomas' and 'Tommy.' The friend called him 'Lieutenant.' He caught me watching and I had to run, but he didn't recognize me. I told one of Sean's Fenian mates, one that came into the pub now and again."

Molly's shoulders began to shake, but only Eda felt it. As her little brother went on, the shaking grew to heaving and she began to sob with hard gulps.

"He didn't love you, not at all. He was only tryin' to find out what Sean and the others were doin' against the British. I knew he wasn't Irish—heard his plummy English manner of speakin' when he was out with those doxies and his mate." He scratched a little in his sister's hair, like she'd done a thousand times to him, and said, "I'm awful sorry."

Eda wrapped Molly in her arms, letting her cry out this final indignity. Then she drew a long breath and looked over each of them—Brendan to Francis, Sean to Peter.

"This is the end of it," she said with vicious determination. Eda looked them over again, deep into each one, searching out all the pain and anger in the children she'd once carried within her.

"We'll have no more hidin' and deceivin', no more anger and hate. We're a family—what's left of us—and that's more important than the bloody war or the Free State. I'll have it done and over. Now, this very night."

CHAPTER TWENTY-SIX

Epilogue

Some of the regulars came by, alone or in pairs, peering through the glass panes. She'd told them each day for weeks the pub would be closed, tacked a card to the door reminding them. Still they came, needing to confirm the distressing reality that their local was shut against them for the day, and without so much as a funeral to blame. Such tender feelings didn't matter to Eda and she moved them along with the back of a hand. This was the day she'd longed for ever since the telegram had arrived from St. John's.

Francis insisted he go along with Brendan to meet the train from Cork, the one carrying Deirdre and her Jack, along with their twins. A boy and a girl, saints be praised, and what new grandmother could ask for more? Deirdre having taken so long to fall pregnant, this was a double blessing indeed.

Eda spun toward the loud clattering.

The apprentice—a new one, just started a few weeks before—struggled under a stack of plates borrowed from the parish hall, along with a pile of cutlery. There was plenty of glassware about the place, so no need to borrow more. The lad set the stack atop a long makeshift table. Peter had borrowed sawhorses from the builders up the road and knocked the hinge pins out of half the doors upstairs, laying them end to end for a serviceable enough table for the impending crowd. He'd removed the doorknobs, too, and Eda feared he'd never get them back together again, but that was a worry for another day.

Much of the bar top was covered by the groaning mass of prepared food she'd ordered in from the butcher and greengrocer, not caring to spend the day in the kitchen. Peter inspected the heaping trays and bowls, straightening a few and stepping back with a satisfied nod. He came to his wife and kissed her forehead, then her cheek.

"You'll need to remove that apron, *a chuisle*. You're the matriarch today, not the publican." He reached round her waist and pulled the bow in the apron strings. He kissed her forehead again, then walked behind the bar folding the linen.

"It appears we're the first."

The familiar English voice brought Eda rushing to the open door. A slight woman in a pale green summer frock, wide brown eyes smiling beneath a darker green cloche, stood holding the hand of a little girl desperate to hide behind her mother's leg.

"Why, Sophie dear! It's been ages since you were last here. Where's Will and your boy?"

The English woman kissed each of Eda's cheeks, then stood holding the older woman's hands. "They're paying the taxi driver. Terry must be the one to hand over the money. You know how they are at this age."

"That I do. Although mine were more inclined to nick apples than pay a cabbie what's owed." Eda bent down and said, "And this must be Lizzie."

"Yes, and she's quite shy of late," said Sophia Parsons.

"'Tis a lady's prerogative, isn't it, Lizzie?" Eda smoothed the little girl's mahogany hair, a very picture of her mother.

"There was a telegram from Deirdre when we arrived yesterday," said Sophie. "She asked that I pass on to you that Geordie King and his wife and baby are arriving with them."

"Isn't that the big fella who worked the boat with Sean? The one who saved Jack in France?"

"Yes, that's Geordie. His wife is American, from New York—a lovely woman. She helped me with Deirdre... with overcoming her... her trouble with the morphia."

Eda squeezed Sophie's hand and smiled with deepest affection. She'd met Sophie twice before, when she accompanied her husband, Will, on his regular trips to Ireland purchasing goods for Deirdre and Jack's company that hauled and sold all manner of things to the outports of Newfoundland and Labrador—all of it legal now.

"You'll be forever in my prayers, Sophie Parsons, for saving my Deirdre from that terrible curse. And I'll tell Mrs. King the same, as soon as she walks through that door."

"She'll insist you call her Lena," said Sophie.

The door opened not to Lena King, but to Sean Brannigan and his wife, Maggie, heavily pregnant but sporting a wide smile despite her obvious discomfort. Behind them followed a slender man in a blue serge suit and a boy in flannel shorts. Eda noticed a long, razor-straight scar along the lad's thigh.

"Here we are, Mam, and with a pair of Newfoundlanders in tow," said Sean, "albeit by way of London." He wrapped his mother in his arms and smacked a loud kiss on her cheek. "Mind the big woman. She's like to topple right over."

Maggie slapped Sean's back and said, "Always the gentleman is our Sean. And aren't you looking bright as a new penny, Eda? It must be because of your daughter's homecoming—you've been married long enough for that to be old hat."

Eda hugged her daughter-in-law and laid a hand on her swollen belly. "It won't be long now, so."

"Not soon enough. My ankles are big as a pig's hocks," Maggie said, then tottered off toward Peter Conway and the food at the bar.

"Welcome, Will! And this must be Master Terry himself?" The boy extended a very proper hand, which Eda shook with great ceremony. "I've heard quite a good deal about you, young man."

"My father says that you are Mrs. Oakley's mother," said Terry Parsons, solemn as any six-year-old might be meeting a strange new adult.

"That I am, although I know your Mrs. Oakley as my Deirdre," Eda winked at the boy's father, who smiled back.

Screwing up his courage, Terry said, "I'm to be forever grateful to Mrs. Oakley… to your Deirdre… because she saved me when I was hurt with a fisher's knife. Mummy says I might have died." The boy exhaled with acute relief, having rehearsed this speech throughout their crossing from England.

Eda offered her hand to Will Parsons, who took it with unalloyed pleasure.

"How wonderful to see you again, Eda. Or should I say, Mrs. Conway? Please accept my congratulations on your marriage."

"That's very kind, Will. And be sure to congratulate Mr. Conway, since I made the poor soul wait a shameful long time."

The pub swelled with conversation. Sophie and Maggie discussed pregnancies, giggling like two school girls. Sean joined Peter, the man least inclined to waste words, in observing the scene from beside the bar.

A taxi sputtered to a stop before the pub and Eda cried out, "That'll be Deirdre!" She dashed to the front windows and looked on tiptoes over the pleated half curtains that kept all but the tallest passersby from identifying who was drinking within. After one of the taxi's doors slammed, she turned with a puzzled look.

Sean darted over and said, "I near forgot, Mam. Ned Tobin and his wife and kids are up from Tipperary to see everyone, too. Last minute sort of thing."

"Then aren't we fortunate I ordered too much food," she said, scolding Sean with smiling insincerity.

Sean flung back the door and called out to the street, "Ned Tobin, get yerself inside and get a drink in ye!"

A short woman with a determined walk was first through the door, two children behind her. The younger, a girl, had the look and build of her mother. The second, a boy, looked to be ten or eleven, just starting to stretch into a ranginess that promised he'd be the tallest in the family.

She released her daughter and stuck out a hand. "You're that Sean Brannigan, then? The one that got Ned's farm burnt to the ground?" Her face spread into dimples deep as peach pits, eyes promising much future craic at Sean's expense.

"Maire Tobin, I presume?" said Sean. "And have you made a respectable man of our Ned yet?"

She scooted her children to the bench along the wall where the Parsons children were playing at circus animals, crawling along on all fours.

"Well, he was decent enough to have the same surname as my departed first husband, wasn't he?"

Sean's smile dissolved, and he said, "That was an awful business. I'm sorry to my bones for the part I played in your man's sad end."

She took his hand again, covering it in both hers. They were strong and rough as any good farm wife's. "You heed what I say, Sean Brannigan. I'll hear no more of that. My Kevin knew the risks he was takin', although he was careful to share none with me. He went off to his death as brave as any man. But wouldn't he be thrilled with the independence?"

"You've met the missus?" said Ned Tobin, stepping behind his wife. He was accompanied by a young boy, school-aged, Sean reckoned, with his father's features in less angular miniature. The boy kept behind his father's hip, looking over at the growing gaggle of children parading across the floor and crawling over the upholstered bench.

"Sean, this is my son, Édouard—over from his mother in France for the summer." Ned turned to the boy and made several signs to him. The boy tapped his extended fingers together, then pointed to Sean.

"He's pleased to meet you." Ned nodded at the boy with an indulgent smile, then signed again. Édouard dashed to the other children, jumping into the circus parade of which his stepbrother now appeared to be ringmaster.

Sean reached to draped an arm over Ned's shoulder and led him toward the bar.

"He's a handsome boy, your Edward. Is it hard not havin' him about more often?"

"Every single day he's in Paris," said Ned. "But his mother has him in a fine school for deaf children and he's smart as a whip. He'd not have that sort of opportunity in Tipperary."

Sean had learned scraps of information about Ned Tobin's star-crossed love affair with a French teacher during the last two years of the war, as well as the child that resulted from it. Why he and the boy's mother hadn't married was still a mystery to Sean but not one Ned was inclined to solve for him. Some things were best left unsaid, Sean knew better than any man.

Peter placed pints before each of them, having learned from long experience that a glass of porter would do well for most self-respecting men. Ned lifted one and offered it to Sean, then took the second for himself.

"It's a strange road brought us here," Ned said, then took a deep draught.

Sean lifted his glass in reply and drank. He licked his foamy lips and said, "A twisting and craggy road. Let's hope for easier travels from here, so."

She hadn't attracted anyone's attention, padding silently down the stairs, all of them occupied with their conversations. Molly had made her way unnoticed over to the five children. Sean smiled when he noticed her sitting on the bench with Édouard close beside to her, showing him engravings in one of the small volumes of Shakespeare she never seemed to be without. The boy looked back and forth from the book to the lovely and gentle stranger who'd appeared from nowhere beside him.

"Where's your wife, then?" said Ned. "Your sister wrote from Newfoundland of your marriage, since you're not a man known for the letters."

Sean tugged the sleeve of the woman with a thick brown braid standing a few feet behind Ned. Turning to show her pregnant front, Maggie smiled with inquiring eyebrows. Ned puzzled over her vague familiarity.

"This is my dear wife, Margaret. Maggie, this rogue of a Yank is my old partner in crime, Ned Tobin of Boston, late of Tipperary."

The quizzical expression transformed to a sly knowing look and she said, "Why Sean, have you've forgotten? Mr. Tobin and I have met before, don't you recall?"

The penny dropped for Ned. "You were his secretary? When I came to find out what Sean knew about the burning of my farm. Isn't that right?"

Maggie nodded with a self-satisfied grin. Before he could think better of it, Ned added, "Christ almighty, you were as buttoned up and dour as a nun!"

Sean coughed up some stout that went down the wrong way and said, "You Americans, do you have any kind of a way with the ladies at all?"

Ned flushed but recovered quick enough. "Then you'll recall that was the moment I learned your dear husband here was one of the outlaws who'd slept in my barn and got the place burned to the ground by the Black and Tans."

Maggie slipped an arm through Sean's, resting her wrist in the crook of his elbow. "Well, isn't he walkin' the straight and narrow now? After it became common knowledge about the Castle that yer man put a baby in me, I was given my notice. And he was promoted."

"Quick trip to the rectory and I made you an honest woman, didn't I?" Sean winked at Ned, then planted a beery kiss on his wife's cheek.

Eda fussed about the barroom, calling out to her husband for drinks and seeing that every child got a pinched cheek or tousled hair. The Parsonses joined Maire Tobin, Will sharing a few tales of her new husband, Ned, from their time together in France.

The grumbling of another taxi on the Coombe, slowing and stopping before the pub, silenced all the adults. A second automobile stopped behind the first. Sean looked over at his eager mother and nodded.

Eda shouted rather than spoke, "That'll be our Deirdre!" She rushed to the door and out onto the pavement, not caring if she made a very spectacle of herself on the street.

"Deirdre! Deirdre, *mo chroí!*"

Brendan rode up front with the driver in the first taxi and was first to step down. He heard his mother crying out and pointed her to the second vehicle. She turned as the back door of the taxi swung out and a stiff leg in trousers emerged, a slender man with brown hair emerging after it. Righting himself on the pavement, he looked over toward Eda, a fading pattern of scars down one side of his face.

He smiled but said nothing, knowing his wife needed to be first to greet her mother. He ducked his head back inside the taxi and began gathering the two small ones on the seat.

Eda hadn't noticed the other door open. It was the familiar voice, choking with happiness, that she heard first.

"Mam! Oh, Mam!"

She turned to see her daughter, wild strands of auburn flying out from under her summer hat, rounding the back of the taxi with arms opened and tears streaming.

"*Mo leanbh*, oh my child! *Mo iníon is gaire*, my dearest daughter! You're back to me… you've come back to me."

She couldn't say another word, not for long minutes while they stood locked in a tight embrace, mother and daughter. Finally loosening their arms, they stood back to examine one another, all the unwitnessed changes. A few passersby stopped to smile, nod, dab a tear along with the Brannigan women. No one would begrudge their sharing such a tender scene.

When the two had settled sufficiently, convinced they wouldn't awake from this happy dream, Eda looked over the other new arrivals. Standing nearest, she saw the man who could only be her son-in-law, blowing his nose into a white hankie. The other hand, fingers curled in a stiff clench, was clutched by a little girl staring up at Eda with wide, suspicious, green eyes. She had the same flyaway hair as her mother, albeit not as thick and three shades of red brighter. The little one knitted her brows and pouted her bottom lip, stopping Eda's heart.

"Holy Mother of God, she's the very image of you, Deirdre! I've the picture in my mind of you standin' just so."

"This sweet maid has every ounce of her mother's stubbornness," said Jack Oakley. "And left none for the dear b'y yonder, clinging to his uncle's peg leg."

Eda glanced to Francis, who was smoothing the fine brown hair of the girl's twin brother, gazing down with a fondness Eda hadn't seen in him since he was a boy himself. The little man wasn't as steady on his legs as his sister, wobbling as he gripped the wool of Francis's trousers with chubby fingers.

"I can't find words to say how pleased I am to meet you at long last, Mrs. Conway," said Jack.

He extended his good hand, but she brushed past it, clinging to his neck, hugging the breath from him. She eased away, took his face in both her strong hands, and peered into his sea-grey eyes for something she'd recognize when she found it. He didn't flinch— looking for something himself, what it was that made him love her daughter so. Whatever she was searching for, she nodded once in satisfaction, then ran her palm over the scars on his left cheek and said, "You'll be calling me Mam or I'll not let you off this pavement, Jack Oakley."

They stood together smiling, comfortable with their immediate and easy familiarity. Eda stepped back and said, "Well, and who'll be introducin' me to my own grandchildren?"

Francis bent with considerable effort, lifted his nephew, and limped over. Jack held out a finger for the boy to grab as reassurance, and said, "This is your gran, Daniel. Can you say hello?"

Francis hefted the squirming boy on his arm. "Daniel Richard Oakley. 'Tis a fine name, wouldn't you agree, Mam?"

"Oh, it's a name to conjure with, right enough," she said and gave the shoulder above her son's crutch a squeeze. The little one buried his face in his uncle's sleeve.

Jack loosed his finger from the boy's fist and motioned over to his wife. "As you might have already guessed, this little charmer is Eithne Deirdre Oakley," said Jack. "And I won't hear a word from you about her name, this being the one and only time I've stood my ground against your daughter with success."

Eda bent her knees, crouching so she could face the little girl eye-to-eye. Unlike her skittish brother, the tiny girl stood with feet apart, steady as a rock, inspecting her grandmother with solemn care.

"We call her Eddy, Mam. I hope that's all right?" said Deirdre.

"That's grand, just grand," Eda said. She kept her eyes on the little girl, letting her study the strange woman smiling across from her.

"Well then, Miss Eddy, what do you make of your old granny?"

Eddy Oakley looked over the woman with the grey-threaded hair, lines of sorrow on her brow and laughter round her eyes, then broke into a wide smile, tiny teeth showing between pink lips. She dropped her father's hand and took two lunging steps, landing with her hands on Eda's knees. With a hitching gasp, tears falling anew, Eda swept her granddaughter into her arms and buried her nose in the innocent smell of the girl's wild red hair.

She tried to pick her up as she rose, but the little one twisted and wriggled her opposition. Deirdre shrugged and laughed, taking her daughter's hand to keep her from darting away up the Coombe, headed for God knows where.

Brendan stood by the first taxi, next to a tall woman with glossy long ringlets of hair, tied back with a satin ribbon beneath a round straw hat, dandling on her hip a chubby child five or six months younger than Deirdre's twins. She was quite striking, high cheeks and dark brown eyes, the child just a shade lighter than his mother's honey-gold skin. She'd been watching the unfolding mother and daughter reunion with a placid, content smile, in no rush to interrupt a scene she'd never enjoy, her own mother dead these fifteen years.

A man was bent into the front of the cab, in conversation with the cabbie well beyond what should be required to settle the fare. The driver pointed and nodded with great animation for reasons indiscernible to anyone observing from the pavement. Finally, a large hand slapped the driver's shoulder and emerged from the cab attached to a tall and wide-shouldered man.

When little Eddy spotted the big man, she tossed away her mother's hand and ran fast as her short legs would allow straight toward him. The man bent and lifted her on his forearm with less effort than if she were a ball of cotton wool. She put her hands to his face—one on his ear, one over his mouth—and planted a tight-lipped kiss on his cheek.

"That one's a terror with the gents already, Mam," Deirdre said. "She'll turn her father's hair to grey sooner than he deserves." She encircled her mother's waist and they walked together to the first taxi.

"Mam, this is my dear friend Lena King and her sweet boy, Chester. They wouldn't hear of bein' left out of our grand adventure to Ireland, so came along for the holiday, too."

Lena extended a gloved hand to Eda, who held it in her own while she spoke in a softer voice of the things she knew she had to say to this woman.

"I've no words to give proper thanks for what you... you and Sophie...what you did for my dear girl. Seein' her clear of all that terrible... trouble with the morphia."

Lena's placid smile never faltered, and she said in her clipped New York accent, "I owe as great a thanks to you for the strength with which you raised Deirdre. She saw me through a terrible time, too, after my brother was killed on Jack's schooner. I thought I was alone in the world, but Deirdre wouldn't hear of it."

"And your boy, he's named for your brother?" said Eda.

Lena's smile widened. "He is, and it helps to have more joy than sorrow from that name now."

Eda squeezed Lena's hand for several seconds and nodded in full understanding of their mutual struggles with terrible loss, then turned to Lena's husband.

"Now, if my granddaughter could cease her flirtin' for a moment, perhaps I could welcome this big fella to my home."

Geordie carried the easy affability that comes naturally to many big men. She ran her fingers through her granddaughter's curls, and smiled up to the man holding her. "It seems the day for me to pass round all my thanks," she said. "So you're the one saved Jack and brought him to my Deirdre's hospital? Geordie King?"

"Nothing to it, Mrs. Brannigan... or Conway, isn't it?" Eda nodded. "Jackie's always had more luck than any three men deserve, so it's not likely the Germans could've done him in. And wasn't he fortunate to win your daughter, too?"

Eda placed a palm over Geordie's chest and looked up at him. Beneath the surface of amiability, it wasn't hard to discern the bone-deep tiredness of a man who'd long known physical pain. Every half a minute or so, he gave a weak cough. She'd read in Deirdre's letters of the hard time he'd had in the war—nearly killed by fever in Gallipoli, a bullet to an arm laying out with the wounded Jack, gassed in the trenches of France—all recorded in the fine lines and darkness under his eyes. She shivered a little with fear for him, then patted his chest.

"Let's get everyone inside," she said. "There's drinks and a fine supper laid. We've even a fiddler comin' later. We'll tuck the children in the beds upstairs and we old ones will have a fine *ceilidh*, like when I was a girl in Donegal."

They filed into the pub, little ones in their arms or led by the hand, the squeals of children and laughter of adults spilling out each time the door swung. Eda was the last, and she turned at the door of The Gallant Fusilier, glancing down the street as the daily bustle went on without interruption.

HISTORICAL NOTE

Coming from an Irish-American family, I grew up with a lot of apocrypha and exaggeration about Ireland and my family's connections thereto. I've read and listened haphazardly throughout my adult life to the history, poetry, stories, and songs of the country. I even took a year of Irish Gaelic while I was a graduate student at Harvard, for no other reason than it sounded interesting—and some of that study found its way into this book. However, it wasn't until setting off on this long quest to write a historical fiction trilogy with a substantial number of Irish characters and settings that I was finally forced to systematically examine a particular epoch of Ireland's past. Although the first two volumes of my *Sweet Wine of Youth* trilogy spent a fair amount of time among the Irish in Ireland, *No Hero's Welcome* is the book that I intended from the beginning to focus entirely on people and events in Ireland during the First World War and its aftermath—an era that would end with the long-sought independence for Ireland. Or most of it anyway.

Much of the book is set within The Gallant Fusilier, a typical pub of the time that was somewhat atypically owned and operated by a woman. However, as with so many other social conventions turned topsy-turvy by the Great War, there were many women who ran pubs in the absence of their husbands or brothers off to the fighting in Gallipoli and France. Some widows became sole owners after their husbands were lost in the carnage. That Eda Brannigan had the money to purchase a pub on the Coombe, a main thoroughfare cutting through the Liberties section of Dublin, is quite plausible. Her husband was a cooperage foreman in a brewery, well paid, well respected, and a member of a benevolent society—an early form of working man's cooperative insurance—into which he paid a little from each pay packet. Eda also received a death gratuity from the Government and from her husband's former employer—an unnamed large brewery on the edge of the Liberties that may (or may not) resemble a certain world-famous brewery still in operation there. The renaming of the pub was a little unusual—although the mild scandal it created among the old regulars was likely enough. Generally, a pub in Dublin was required to bear the owner's name—a regulatory requirement I nodded to when the sign maker added Eda's name to the new sign. I was just too fond of the name *The Gallant Fusilier* to abandon it over an old ordnance of the Dublin Corporation.

Setting much of the action in this book within the walls of Eda's pub also allowed me to delve into the history of pub life in Dublin. I began with a solid appreciation for the traditional importance of the pub in British and Irish life, having spent a year working as a barman at The Niblick, a pub just across from the starter's shack of the Old Course, while I was a student at the University of St. Andrews in Scotland. I was daily witness to the unique parade of long-time regulars, locals, ancient caddies, university students, and golf tourists. The physical location of The Gallant Fusilier is taken from a real pub, Shanahan's, located at the corner of Hanover Street and the Coombe in the Liberties.

Women street vendors—the shawlies—were devotees of pubs, but for respectability would limit their imbibing to the semi-private "snugs" that most Dublin pubs kept for the use of ladies or others desiring privacy. These became useful places for Republican rebels to meet, too, as in this book. The shawlies' territoriality—as well as their biscuit-tin urinal—are based in fact. Eda's firm-handed operation of the pub and her open conviviality are also well-documented characteristics of most Dublin publicans. Especially in working class neighborhoods like the Liberties, pubs were expected to sell staples in small quantities. Like Molly's, the sundries counters were near the door, again so the ladies wouldn't have to enter the drinking area of the pub.. Although fading a little in importance, pubs remain an integral part of Dublin life.

That there were so many young men with all manner of disabilities who frequented the pub is likely enough. The First World War was the first large conflict with a modern system of battlefield medical care and transportation. Taken together with new surgical techniques and an awareness of the importance of antisepsis, many horribly wounded men who would have died in earlier conflicts survived and returned home. (This aspect of the war is more integral to my first book, *None of Us the Same.*) So the cadre of vets surrounding Francis Brannigan is plausible.

As depicted in the first chapter, the Royal Dublin Fusiliers landed at Cape Helles on the 25th of April 1915, so placing Daniel and Francis Brannigan on that beach is historically correct, although in *None of Us the Same* I situated them in an unspecified new battalion of the regiment, not the 1st Battalion that made that attack. The landing was, as Daniel Brannigan observes, a bollocks—the Dubs were towed to shore against adverse tides in wooden life boats, unprotected against machine gun and artillery fire. The beach was 10 yards at its widest, providing almost no usable cover. Of the 901 Dubs who made the landing, only 375—including just one officer— were available for duty a week later.

The split in allegiances between Francis and his younger brother Sean has ample precedent. Irishmen who fought in the British Army were often stubbornly reluctant—and understandably so— to abandon allegiance to the Crown for which they'd endured the horrors of the trenches. Sean's complete rejection of allegiance to King and Empire triggered by the loss of his father in the war also has historical precedent. And the intricate web of intrigue, informants, and betrayal depicted in this book merely reflects an inevitable characteristic of Irish risings and rebellions across the centuries. After the war, the British Government in Ireland did establish a network of undercover intelligence agents, most former or serving military officers, to counteract the growing insurrection by Republican rebels.

The most famous of these groups of agents was the so-called Cairo Gang, seven of whom were killed the morning of Sunday, the 21st of November in 1920 and resulted in reprisal shootings at Croke Park that afternoon during a Gaelic football match between Dublin and Tipperary, killing 14 civilians and becoming one of the "Bloody Sundays" in Irish history. The character and story line of Desmond O'Connell/Thomas Piers-Musgrave is based in large part on the activities of the Cairo Gang, although I chose to make him a member of an unnamed undercover unit to allow more narrative freedom.

Sean Brannigan's being out with the rebels during Easter Week in 1916 isn't improbable. The rebels did use younger men and women as messengers or lookouts during the Easter Rising. I chose not to have Sean participate as an armed rebel both because of his age at the time and my desire to keep him mostly an observer of the violence. The famous Proclamation of the Irish Republic was indeed printed in Liberty Hall on Eden Quay, although the building was torn down in the 1950s and replaced by an awful modern high-rise. The distribution of the copies of the Proclamation is wholly my invention, however, and allowed me to move Sean about Dublin with the purpose to encounter Peter Conway, and to place him at the General Post Office when the Proclamation was read out by Pádraig Pearse.

Now, about Michael Collins. I generally avoid using actual historical figures as speaking characters in my books. I find it too limiting for my storytelling purposes, although I have great respect for those authors (like Hilary Mantel or Philippa Gregory) who do it very well. In this case, I needed someone to be a kind of personal mentor, even a bit of a father figure, to young Sean Brannigan as he threw himself into the life of a Republican gunman. And Collins's real story during that period was too good to discard. His open movements round Dublin and his personal direction of activities depicted in the book are historically accurate.

The double life of mild-mannered bookseller and Irish language tutor, Peter Conway, has many exemplars. That he was a Gaelic language scholar adds additional verisimilitude to his activities. After all, Pádraig Pearse, founding principal of St. Enda's, an English-Irish bilingual school for boys, was a leader of the Easter Rising and primary author of the Proclamation of the Irish Republic. Éamon de Valera, another leader of the Rising who later served as both Taoiseach and President of Ireland, was an Irish speaker and involved in the Gaelic League.

Molly Brannigan's studying for the university entrance examination was noteworthy but not impossible at that time, women having been admitted to Trinity University starting in 1904 and University College Dublin in 1908. Her and her sister's education by the Sisters of Mercy is a result of the religious order's substantial presence in Ireland at that time and the fact that I was educated by Mercy Sisters. That Sean, Francis, and Brendan Brannigan were educated by the Christian Brothers is just as likely, the order having provided education to boys from poor and working class families across Dublin, as they still do.

American readers might have found odd my use of the word "Irish" to label what most in North America call "Gaelic." However, that is both an imprecise and incorrect usage which we Yanks have fallen into. Irish is one of three Gaelic languages, the other two being Scots Gaelic and Manx, once spoken on the Isle of Man but with no living native speakers today. The language is referred to universally in Ireland as Irish. What most Americans think of as "Irish"—the Irish dialect of English—is linguistically called Hiberno-English.

Although I edited out much of the Irish language words and phrases through several rounds of revision, I kept enough to reinforce that Eda Brannigan, born and raised in Donegal, was not a Dubliner by birth and remained an outsider of sorts. Born in the second half of the 19th century, she might well have been a native Irish speaker— Donegal is still one of the Gaeltacht counties with a significant concentration of native Irish speakers. More practically, the language provided a believable nexus for the relationship between Eda and Peter Conway, with Peter a member of the Gaelic League and an Irish language tutor. In 1928, Irish was made compulsory in secondary schools and is still tested as part of the leaving certificate exams for many students. The Irish that remains in the book is, I hope, made comprehensible to readers by the surrounding text or by repetition of Irish dialogue in English. I also used the the modern style of spelling Irish words adopted in the mid-20th century.

Some readers might have recognized the Irish song Eda Brannigan sings in Chapter Six as *Mo ghile mear*. That was intentional, although

Eda gives it a different title—*Bimse buan ar buairt gach lo*. As was the convention, this title was taken from the first line of an older song by the 18th century Munster poet, Seán Clárach Mac Domhnaill, one of three old tunes from which the great 20th century Irish composer, Seán Ó Riada, cobbled together what we now know as *Mo ghile mear*. (Alas, after leading the traditional music revival in Ireland during the 1960s, Ó Riada drank himself to death in 1971, having just turned 40.) The song has been recorded at least a dozen times by various artists, perhaps most famously by Mary Black in 1984 and by Sting with The Chieftains on their wildly popular 1995 duets album, *The Long Black Veil*.

After his grandfather's farm is burned by the Auxiliaries—better known to history as the Black and Tans—Ned Tobin returns home to Boston but quickly finds in his rumrunning scheme a way to finance his revenge by supporting the Republican cause with money and weapons. This mutual interest in seeing the British out of Ireland explains his involvement with the wealthy Irish-American, Aloysius Pendergast, as well as his covert connection to Sean Brannigan, one of his rumrunning colleagues. This is not an improbable scenario, since the Irish diaspora in America long supported efforts to achieve Irish independence, from the United Irishmen rebellion of the late 18th century right through the Troubles of the second half of the 20th century. After the failure of the 1848 Young Ireland rebellion, John O'Mahony, who had participated in the '48 rising, came to America and founded the Fenian Brotherhood in 1860. This organization raised substantial funds for its sister organization in Ireland, the Irish Republican Brotherhood. The Fenian Brotherhood even attempted an ill-fated invasion of Canada in 1867, thereafter splitting into two groups in 1870, the other being the Clan na Gael. The Clan na Gael was the single largest source of finance for both the Easter Rising and the Irish War of Independence. Through the Northern Aid Committee—better known as NORAID—the Clan na Gael provided significant financial support to the Provisional IRA throughout the Troubles (1969-1998). I recall as a teenager coming up in the Chicago area in the '70s seeing fundraising jars for NORAID in Irish bars on the North Side. The Clan na Gael, which continues today, has been periodically listed as a terrorist organization by the United Kingdom Government.

ACKNOWLEDGEMENTS

No Hero's Welcome was decidedly a labor of love and I've become a semi-professional Irishman as a result. It also required assistance and support from a lot of people to make its way from my first notion of how I might finish off my *Sweet Wine of Youth* trilogy in Dublin to getting these pages between two covers.

I owe sincere thanks to the legendary Irish musician and songwriter, Brian Warfield, long a member of the much-loved Wolfe Tones, for permission to use lyrics from his strikingly poignant song, "A Soldier's Return." Brian generously allowed me to extract a verse from his song for use as an epigraph poem. The title of this book is derived from the first line of that verse.

I asked several people to read various drafts, starting as always with my editor-wife, who gave me excellent notes on two drafts and did a line edit and final proofread. Three fellow historical novelists for whom I have the utmost respect and jealousy—Wayne Turmel, M. K. Tod, and Helen Hollick—graciously read advance copies of the book and provided me cover blurbs. Mary Tod went above and beyond, surprising me with several pages of very insightful and helpful editorial notes as well. I owe my thanks again to my (then very pregnant) daughter, Lindsay Driemeyer, and my son Evan Walker for their support of all my book projects.

These very smart and well-read women generously agreed to beta read the book: Teri Collins and Mish Kara, who once again provided invaluable continuity checks with the early volumes of the trilogy, as well as their insights for this book; Pam Kanner, who provided a nuanced understanding of the characters and a sensitivity for structure and flow; Pat VanKouwenberg, who lent her hawklike editorial eye, honed over decades of teaching high school English; and Kathy Phillips, who, despite being one of the straightest-shooting beta readers imaginable, remains a beloved friend from all the way back to our university days in Scotland.

No Hero's Welcome is another novel that would never have been written but for the unflagging encouragement of my wife, Kathy Walker. As with the first two books of the Sweet Wine of Youth trilogy, there are endless reasons why this final volume book is dedicated to her.

ABOUT THE AUTHOR

JEFFREY K. WALKER is a Midwesterner, born in what was once the Glass Container Capital of the World. A retired military officer, he served in Bosnia and Afghanistan, planned the Kosovo air campaign and ran a State Department program in Baghdad. He's been shelled, rocketed and sniped by various groups, all with bad aim. He's lived in ten states and three foreign countries, managing to get degrees from Tulane, Syracuse, Georgetown and Harvard along the way. An attorney and professor, he taught legal history at Georgetown, law of war at William & Mary and criminal and international law while an assistant dean at St. John's. He's been a contributor on NPR and a speaker at federal judicial conferences. He dotes on his wife, with whom he lives in Virginia, and his children, who are spread around the United States. Jeffrey has never been beaten at Whack-a-Mole.

Connect with him:
Twitter: @JkwalkerAuthor
Instagram: @jkwalker.author
Facebook: www.facebook.com/jeffreykwalker
Website: jeffreykwalker.com

SUGGESTED FURTHER READING

Pub Life in Dublin: Much of this book takes place within a Dublin pub and much of the detail of the workings of the pub and the habits of its regulars can be attributed to Kevin C. Kearns's outstanding collection of oral history interviews collected in his book, *Dublin Pub Life & Lore: An Oral History* (Dublin: Gill Books, 1996). Additional authenticity in details was provided by the same author's *Dublin Street Life & Lore: An Oral History* (Dublin: Gill Books, 1997).

The Dublin Fusiliers and Gallipoli: My sense of the experience of the Dublin Fusiliers—particularly in those first tragic and chaotic hours on the beaches of Gallipoli—was informed to a great extent by a firsthand account, *The Pals at Suvla Bay,* by Henry Hanna, K.C. (Dublin: E. Ponsonby, 1916), written within a year of the events depicted. In addition, the Royal Dublin Fusiliers Association website at https://www.greatwar.ie/ is a treasure trove of images and details related to the regiment. For the language and songs of soldiers, I fell back on the reliably informative (and entertaining) book by Martin Pegler, *Soldiers' Songs and Slang of the Great War* (Oxford: Osprey, 2014).

Easter Rising/War of Independence/Civil War: The *Irish Times* website has an excellent timeline of the week of the Easter Rising in 1916 at <ins>https://www.irishtimes.com/culture/books/an-easter-rising-timeline-monday-april-24th-1916-1.2187749</ins>. I found myself referencing this site repeatedly while writing chapters related to those events. For a good, concise, and useful history of all the events of 1912—1927, I relied on Richard Killeen's *A Short History of the Irish Revolution: 1912 - 1927* (Dublin: Gill Books, 2007). Sean Brannigan's rebel activities in Dublin were informed by T. Ryle Dwyer's book *The Squad and the Intelligence Operations of Michael Collins* (Cork: Mercier, 2005). For the level of detail required writing the Easter Rising chapters in the early part of the book, I used Peter De Rosa's comprehensive history, *Rebels: The Irish Rising of 1916* (New York: Ballantine, 2009). Biographies of Michael Collins proved a useful resource as well, in particular Peter Hart's *Mick: The Real Michael Collins* (London: Viking, 2006).